novelists

Cynthia

Belva Plain

THE SELF-CHOSEN

OTHER BOOKS BY JEAN BAER

FOLLOW ME!

THE SINGLE GIRL GOES TO TOWN

THE SECOND WIFE

DON'T SAY YES WHEN YOU WANT TO SAY NO
(With Dr. Herbert Fensterheim)

HOW TO BE AN ASSERTIVE—NOT AGGRESSIVE—WOMAN IN LIFE, IN LOVE, AND ON THE JOB

STOP RUNNING SCARED!
(With Dr. Herbert Fensterheim)

THE SELF-CHOSEN

"Our Crowd" is Dead

Long Live Our Crowd

by JEAN BAER

ARBOR HOUSE *New York*

 Published in the United States of America by Arbor House Publishing Company and in Canada by Fitzhenry & Whiteside, Ltd.

This book is printed on acid free paper. The paper in this book meets the guidelines for permanence and durability of the Committee on Production Guidelines for Book Longevity of the Council on Library Resources.

Library of Congress Catalog Card Number: 81-66962

ISBN: 0–87795–330–9

Manufactured in the United States of America

10 9 8 7 6 5 4 3 2 1

For the two hundred fifty-four men and women who gave so freely of their time so that I could write this book.

ACKNOWLEDGEMENTS

A GREAT many people deserve thanks for making this book possible—so many that I can not list them all, and I must ask the forgiveness of those who are omitted.

First and foremost I am indebted to the two hundred fifty-four people who gave so generously of their time to brief me on their own lives, the current trends in Judaism and its future direction.

Most of my interviews lasted from two-to-three hours. Some extended over several sessions and totaled from ten to twelve hours. The notes from the interviews and research at a series of libraries fill eight file drawers.

In a few cases I obtained the interviews through friends and a far-flung network of professionals whom I have come to know in the course of my work. In over ninety percent of the cases, I wrote directly to the person I wanted to interview, telling the purpose of the book, my credentials and some of the questions I wanted to ask. I was refused by only seven people.

I am especially indebted to Ambassador Sol M. Linowitz, opera star Roberta Peters, Financial Columnist Sylvia Porter and Henry Rosovsky, Dean of the Faculty of Arts and Sciences at Harvard, who fit me into their busy schedule as if they had all the time in the world to help me.

I would like to express my appreciation to the outstanding women whose careers are documented in the two chapters on *The Women.* Cosmetics authority Adrien Arpel; Helen Galland, president and chief executive officer of Bonwit Teller; Ruth Hinerfeld, outgoing president of the League of Women Voters; Rita Hauser, senior partner at Stroock & Stroock & Lavan; G. G.

Michelson, senior vice-president for external affairs at R. H. Macy & Co.; advertising executive Shirley Polykoff; Rabbi Sally Priesand; CBS News correspondent Marlene Sanders; Thelma Schorr, president and publisher of the American Journal of Nursing Company.

Among the members of the Wall Street community who helped me enormously were Sanford I. Weill, chairman Shearson/American Express, Inc., and Stephen Schwarzman, partner at Lehman Brothers Kuhn Loeb. I would also like to thank Benjamin Buttenwieser and John Schiff of Lehman Brothers Kuhn Loeb, investment banker Robert Bernhard, securities arbitrageur Ivan Boesky, Henry Gellermann, retired partner of Bache; Alan Greenberg, chief executive officer of Bear Stearns & Company; Richard Holman, editor and publisher of the *Wall Street Transcript.*

I am deeply indebted to the many outstanding businessmen who contributed to this book: Lester Crown, president of Material Service Corporation, vice president of General Dynamics and president of Henry Crown & Company; Bram Goldsmith, chairman and chief executive officer, City National Bank, Los Angeles; Alexander Grass, president and chief executive officer, Rite Aid Corporation; Stephen Hassenfeld, president, Hasbro Industries, Inc.; Frank Lautenberg, chairman and chief executive officer, Automatic Data Processing; Henry A. Lambert, founder of Pasta & Cheese; Lewis Lehrman of the Lehrman Institute; Robert Sakowitz, president, chief executive officer and board chairman of Sakowitz, Inc.; Laurence Tisch, chairman, Loews Corporation; Elmer Winter, co-founder of Manpower Inc.

Many spoke feelingly about their lives for *The Jewish Patchwork Quilt* chapter. I would like to express my appreciation to Mrs. Irma Bloomingdale; Mrs. Elinor Guggenheimer, former commissioner of New York's department of consumer affairs; Paul Kohnstamm, president, H. Kohnstamm & Company; Betty Levin, director, Corporate Art Directions; John Loeb, Jr., ambassador to Denmark; Roy S. Neuberger; Julia Perles, senior partner, Phillips Nizer Benjamin Krim & Ballon; Josephine Stayman; Maynard Wishner, president of the American Jewish Committee and president and chief executive officer of Walter E. Heller and Company, Chicago; Milton Wolf, former ambassador to Austria.

The members of the Orthodox community were especially helpful and I would like to express my gratitude to Abby Belkin; Charles Bendheim; Mrs. A. L. Cardozo; Moses Feuerstein, Charlotte and Sidney Feuerstein, George Klein, Ira Kellner, Ludwig Jesselson, Seymour Propp, Jerry Rindner, Herbert Tenzer, Gary Schaer, and Max Stern.

Many rabbis gave generously of their time to brief me on past and current attitudes. These include Bernhard Cohn of Congregation Habonim; Ronald Sobel of Temple Emanu-El; Shlomo Riskin of Lincoln Square Synagogue; Haskel Lookstein of Kehilath Jeshurun; Leo Jung of the Jewish Center; Bernard Goldenberg of Torah Umesorah; Benjamin Kreitman, executive director of the United Synagogues of America; the late Bernard Bamberger; Stanley Schachter, vice-chancellor of the Jewish Theological Seminary; Malcolm Stern and Richard Stern—all of New York. I would also like to thank Emanuel Rackman, president of Bar-Ilan University, Israel, and Elmer Berger of American Jewish Alternatives to Zionism.

The philanthropic world was particularly helpful. I would like to express my gratitude to Mel Bloom, associate vice-chairman, UJA; Valerie Diker, vice-president of the Israeli Tennis Centers Association; Nate Freedman of the Joint Distribution Committee; Addie Guttag, who heads New York Federation's special gifts department; Sylvia Hassenfeld, a member of the executive committee of UJA and the Joint Distribution Committee; Aryeh Nesher, head of Operation Breakthrough for the UJA; Lyn Revson; Robert Smith, public relations director for the Federation of Jewish Philanthropies of New York and the UJA-Federation Campaign; Jane Sherman, chairman of the Women's Division of the Detroit UJA; Henry Taub, president of the Joint Distribution Committee; Billie Tisch, president of the Federation of Jewish Philanthropies of New York; Peggy Tishman, lay chairman of the Advance Gifts Committee of New York Federation; Marvin L. Warner, former ambassador to Switzerland; Jack Weiler of

Swig, Weiler & Arnow; and Elaine Winik, president of the UJA of Greater New York.

I would like to give special thanks to Frederick Rose, chairman, Rose Associates, Inc. who was so very helpful in the chapter *In Union There Is Strength.* And my special appreciation to Alfred Hagedorn, Jr., publisher *Real Estate Weekly,* for his help in briefing me on the New York real estate scene. I also want to thank Robert and Alan Tishman; Marvin Goldman of Detroit; Seymour Durst of The Durst Organization, and Harold Uris.

Special thanks to two "super couples" who gave so generously of their time: Dr. Helen Singer Kaplan of the New York Hospital—Cornell University Medical Center, and Charles Lazarus, founder and chief executive, Toys R Us; and Shirley Goodman of New York's Fashion Institute of Technology and her husband Himan Brown, the man who succeeded in bringing back network radio drama.

The American Jewish Committee provided much assistance. I am deeply grateful to Bert Gold, executive vice-president; Milton Himmelfarb; Irving M. Levine; Richard Maass; Burt A. Siegal; and Mort Yarmon. I would like to give special thanks to Cyma Horowitz and her staff at the AJC's Blaustein Library where I was permitted to use the extensive research facilities.

Others who helped so much include Professor Charles Liebman of Bar-Ilan University, Israel; Dr. Jacob Rader Marcus of Hebrew Union College—the Jewish Institute of Religion; Professor David Roskies of Jewish Theological Seminary; Louis Lefkowitz, former attorney general of New York and now with Phillips Nizer Benjamin Krim & Ballon; Albert Vorspan of the Union of American Hebrew Congregations; Gunther Lawrence; Sanford Solender of the Federation of Jewish Philanthropies of New York; Orin Lehman, commissioner of parks and recreation for New York State; Earl Blackwell, Dr. Albert Lyons, archivist for Mount Sinai Hospital; Adele Gutman-Nathan, Dorothy Levenson, historian/archivist for Montefiore Hospital and Medical Center; Mrs. Bennett Epstein, Mrs. Flora Straus, Mr. and Mrs. James Marshall and many, many others.

I would like to thank Barbara Levy for lending me the privately-printed *Autobiography* of Isidor Straus; and Sidney Cone, Jr. of

Greensboro, North Carolina, for giving me access to the *Cone Genealogy*.

And my very special thanks to Stephen Birmingham whom I do not know but admire very much. It was his book, *Our Crowd,* referring to the great Jewish families of New York, which made the term "Our Crowd" part of the American vocabulary.

A special note of thanks to Madeleine Conway who triggered the concept for this book in a telephone conversation, and Judy Morris, who was so helpful with library research. I would like to express my appreciation to Don Fine for bringing me to Arbor House, and to my editor Roz Siegel for her really loving concern about every word in this book.

And most of all, my appreciation to my husband for his tolerance of my 6 A.M. typing sessions and understanding of my yearning desire to write this book.

CONTENTS

FOREWORD

IT HAS been a privilege to write this book—both professionally and personally.

It is not the book I intended to write when I began. More than three years ago when I started researching, I had in mind a book about Temple Emanu-El, its glamorous one hundred thirty-seven-year history, and the prominent New Yorkers who made it great. But as I studied, observed and learned more, I became fascinated by the changes between the old "Our Crowd" Jews—with their money and German background—and today's noteworthy men and women, often self-made, and from an Eastern European background.

After many interviews and much reading, I became convinced that the moment, what is happening now, is more interesting than memories, no matter how charming these memories are. I decided to focus on today's Jewish Elite Person—the JEP.

I set four requirements: achievement, class, news value and the ability to be self-revelatory. My selections also reflect suggestions from others; almost everyone of the 254 people with whom I talked mentioned Ambassador Sol M. Linowitz as America's number one Jew.

Virtually everyone highlighted in this book is a doer. They have achieved. They are elite because of hard work and accomplishment. So elite have some become that they can afford to pick and choose among the most prestigious positions in America. Henry Rosovsky, Dean of the Faculty of Arts and Sciences at Harvard University, turned down the presidencies of Yale and Chicago. Yet Rosovsky came to this country as an immigrant at thirteen, unable to speak a word of English. Others have broken all tradition by their energy and enterprise. Financial columnist Sylvia Porter has reached the top of a man's world in direct competition with men. For years she had to use the initials S. F. Porter lest readers learn the economic authority was female.

I also searched for people with class, an extremely hard concept to define. To me, it means the essence of a person, the caliber of being. It means caring about others who are less fortunate, doing the right thing when it is difficult, acting with kindness, having a certain elegance of manner. Investment banker John Schiff is the great-grandson of Solomon Loeb, the grandson of Jacob Schiff. He comes from generations of money, breeding, social status. Henry Taub, founder of Automatic Data Processing and today president of the Joint Distribution Committee, is the son of immigrant parents. His mother's greatest dream was for him to go to college. Despite the disparity in backgrounds, both Schiff and Taub possess that elusive quality of class. The old adage says it takes four generations to make a gentleman. Taub made it in one.

In 1813, in a letter to John Adams, Thomas Jefferson wrote, "There is a natural aristocracy among men. The grounds of this are virtue and talent." I adopted Jefferson's tenets and ruled out eccentrics, however captivating, and certain businessmen who have made enormous sums of money but lacked that all important ingredient of class.

Since I have been a journalist all my adult life as was my father, I cared too for the news value of the people and events on which I reported. For that reason I eliminated a number of JEPs such as Barbra Streisand, Barbara Walters, Armand Hammer, and the late Joseph Hirshhorn because so much has already been written about them or because they had told their story in their own books.

In the case of celebrities who had spoken to the press about their profession and/or speciality, I tried to find a new angle.

I spoke with opera star Roberta Peters not about music but about her commitment to her faith. I asked Sylvia Porter, "You grew up in an era when women were supposed to be dumb. How did you get three husbands—the last when you were sixty-five years old?" She told me.

My goal was to cover new events and trends: how the son of an eminent Wall Street stockbroker, raised as a member of the German Jewish elite, has become a convert to Orthodoxy . . . how Jewish women, as well as Jewish men, have broken through the corporate curtain . . . how Jewishness has become fashionable.

I looked for people who had the ability to reveal emotion and speak frankly. I found it. CBS News correspondent Marlene Sanders, who has fought so hard for the cause of women in television, told me of her devastation over her retarded child. Sanford Weill, the Wall Street superstar, told of his lifetime shyness. Tycoon Lester Crown of the Chicago dynastic family, divulged how he had once asked his father for a raise—and failed to get it. With hesitation, I asked Shirley Goodman, who has played such an important role in New York's Fashion Institute of Technology, "Would you talk about your history of cancer?" Her answer: "Of course." This courageous woman who, after three operations for cancer, has plans for the next ten years, spoke calmly about a history of illness that would have paralyzed anyone else.

In attempting to portray who is who and what is what in the world of elite Jews today, my process has been highly selective. As I finish this book, I see that it could be written all over again under the same title with entirely different subject matter, and then a third time without repeating. There could have been chapters on the entertainment world, the Jews of Palm Beach, the Jewish elite of San Francisco, Jewish country club life—all of which figured in my original outline. There was neither time nor space for all. That is another book.

For me the book has been both a learning process and a means of personal growth. I have made many friends. Charlotte Feuerstein, of a prominent Orthodox family, lent me a fur hat so I could attend Saturday morning services and "look chic." Sylvia Porter sent me a shopping bag full of mystery books when I told her of my addiction to them. Elaine Winik, president of the UJA of Greater New York, met the train in Larchmont; her first words were "Of course, you're staying for dinner." Before even meeting me, Roy S. Neuberger invited me to come to his home and "share the Shabbos experience."

The time that these busy people, profiled here, give to their profession, their good works, their faith is extraordinary. Laurence Tisch serves as chairman of a huge conglomerate. Yet he gives one third of his time to charity and even takes a weekly Talmud lesson. Ambassador Sol Linowitz not only observes the Sabbath but when he travels abroad, he makes it a point to visit temples and synagogues. I interviewed securities arbitrageur Ivan Boesky at 7:15 A.M.; he had already been at work for an hour and after his working day would spend the evening fundraising for UJA-Federation. Roberta Peters tries not to be away from home at Yom Kippur so she can sing at the memorial service at her local temple. Builder Frederick P. Rose and his two brothers alternate in giving black tie *seders*—to which they invite the cream of WASP society.

But the most extraordinary thing about writing this book has been my own new commitment to Judaism. My parents—both Jewish—grew up in small midwestern towns where they came from the only Jewish families. Thus they had little identification with their people. After marriage they moved to the New York area, and I did get confirmed (my mother wanted me to meet "nice boys") at the local Reform temple. No one in my family was ever bar or bas mitzvahed. There was great emphasis on the "superiority" of our German background.

I started out to write this book purely as a reporter because the project fascinated me journalistically. As I attended synagogues and temples for research purposes, met noted men and women so proud of their Jewish past and tradition, learned the details of the philanthropic world and the deep faith of those who give so generously, something happened. In the process of writing this book, I became a committed Jew.

Jean Baer
February, 1982

PART ONE

THE CHANGING OF THE OLD GUARD

1

THE JUDAIZING OF AMERICA

WHO MERITS the designation Jewish Elite Person (JEP)?

Where are the great names in American Jewish history now?

What changes have taken place and are taking place in Jewish society?

Our Crowd is dying. The World of Our Fathers has been dead for sixty years. Origins don't matter anymore. Achievement does. In short, it's a new Our Crowd. However, money still serves as a base.

When Stephen Birmingham wrote *Our Crowd* in 1967, he profiled such outstanding German Jewish families as the Schiffs, Warburgs, Lewisohns, Lehmans, Goldmans, Sachses, Seligmans and Guggenheims. In large part these families have converted, intermarried, or disassociated themselves from their Jewishness.

Bruce Gimbel, son of Alva Bernheimer and retailer Bernard Gimbel, recently choked on a chicken bone and died. The *New York Times* obituary listed his clubs as the Racquet and Tennis Club of New York, the Piping Rock Club of Locust Valley, Long Island, the Stanwich Club of Greenwich, Connecticut, the Shinnecok Club of Southampton—all Gentile strongholds. The funeral was held at the Episcopal Church of the Heavenly Rest.

Comments Alan Greenberg, chief executive officer of Bear, Stearns and Company, a leading Wall Street investment banking firm, "Our Crowd is deader than a doornail. Ninety percent have disappeared and few are Jewish anymore."

Says Elinor Guggenheimer, former commissioner of New York's Department of Consumer Affairs, "Our Crowd is not 100 percent dead yet because my generation still knows the generation we knew as kids, but *it will be in another generation.*"

A few families are alive but relatively "quiet": Benjamin Buttenwieser (Lehman Brothers Kuhn Loeb), his wife Helen (by birth a Lehman) and son Lawrence; Orin Lehman, commissioner of parks and recreation for New York State; William Rosenwald, last living son of Julius; Alfred Stern, a Rosenwald descendant and president of Mount Sinai Hospital; the Loebs and Kempners of New York, the Hutzlers and Gutmans of Baltimore, the Haases and Koshlands of San Francisco and other so-called enclaves.

Says Orin Lehman, who has had two Gentile wives, "Our Crowd had been a very small closed community. The sociological change stems from the new broader social circles. Today one meets so many people at political, charitable, social affairs. Small crowds are just not possible. You might say the same for the 400."

Comments a Connecticut philanthropist, "Our Crowd is so much in the minority that it doesn't count. The members are outnumbered. They're an anachronism. There's so much more vitality in Eastern European Jews."

Remarks Robert Smith, public-relations director of the New York UJA–Federation of Jewish Philanthropies Campaign, "The old division between Eastern European and German is a thing of the past or is rapidly becoming a thing of the past. New wealth has made the change."

Just as the power of the German-Jewish aristocracy has lessened, almost disappeared completely, so has the portrait drawn by Irving Howe in *World of Our Fathers* of the Eastern European Jew as a wild-bearded, Yiddish-speaking pushcart peddler who lived in a tenement and had to go to the Educational Alliance to learn American customs. For all its wealth and power the German-Jewish elite in America dominated only in the fields of merchandising and banking ("About the only thing they had was snobbery," says one Our Crowd descendant). Within one generation the children of the Russian Jews eclipsed the Germans' intellectual achievements and within a second generation, through creativity, vitality and charm, wrested dominance from the Sephardic elite.

To illustrate, Irving Shapiro, son of Lithuanian immigrants, worked in his family's small cleaning plant in Minneapolis and used loans to go through the University of Minnesota Law School, class of 1941. He recently retired as president of E. I. Du Pont de Nemours of Wilmington, Delaware. Reportedly, he still calls his mother on Friday evening to say "Good Shabbos."

George Weissman serves as chairman and chief executive officer at Philip Morris. His father came to New York in 1891 at age seven from Central Europe via Liverpool, a name tag on his coat, and became a milliner. George Weissman majored in accounting at New York's City College, worked nights at Ohrbach's on Fourteenth Street picking up clothes that women customers dumped on the floor. After graduation he worked as a $40-a-week police reporter for the *Newark Star-Ledger,* landed publicity jobs with Samuel Goldwyn and Benjamin Sonnenberg. Among Sonnenberg's clients was Philip Morris. Within four years Weissman was working directly for Philip Morris as assistant to the president and within fifteen years occupying the president's chair. His background is quite a contrast to Joseph Cullman 3rd, his predecessor. According to Forbes, Cullman is a fourth-generation member of one of America's most influential families, descended from prosperous German-Jewish wine merchants and connected by marriage to the Lehmans, Loebs and Bloomingdales.

Fifty-eight-year-old Laurence Tisch and his younger brother Preston Robert (often called "Bobby") control Loews Corporation, a conglomerate that includes jewelry, insurance, tobacco, hotels and motion-picture theaters. In 1981 the company had revenues of $4.8 billion and assets exceeding $9.9 billion. Top executives on both coasts watch the Tisches' actions with care and some awe.

Brooklyn-born Laurence Tisch is a second-generation American. His father Al (he changed his name from Abraham to Al when he entered business) was a clothing manufacturer who also operated two small camps—Lincoln for boys and Laurel for girls, in Blairstown, New Jersey. The senior Tisch gave up the business to go into real estate and included his sons Larry and Bob in his vision. (Says Larry Tisch, "He did it for the family"). Larry Tisch, already on the road to success, had earned both a bachelor's degree from New York University and a master's from the Wharton School at the University of Pennsylvania by the time he was nineteen. Today Larry and Bobby Tisch are said to be worth between $300 and $500 million in their own right, including real estate holdings.

Larry Tisch professes, "I'm Jewish but not religious. I always had a sense of a Jewish extended family—a sense of responsibility for other Jews." He belongs to two synagogues: Reform in Manhattan, Conservative in White Plains. He gives an estimated one-third of his time to charity. His wife Wilma, whom everyone calls "Billie," serves as the first woman president of the Federation of Jewish Philanthropies of New York, a charitable group controlling 132 agencies ("For thirty-two years she's made our marriage great. If I weren't married to her, I would have had ten wives").

Both Larry and Billie Tisch felt strongly about their sons marrying within the faith. He says, "As the boys neared dating age, I told them, 'You'll never marry anyone you don't take out. Take out Jewish girls and you'll never have a problem.' " The technique worked. There is no intermarriage in the Tisch family. When three of the sons married, they chose Jewish girls. In fact, Andrew and Jimmy married the daughters of Reform rabbi Philip Hiat. Both keep kosher homes.

Larry Tisch serves as but one example of how the world of the American elite Jew has changed radically during the last thirty-five years, especially during the last ten. He made his own fortune. He did not marry up or out. His background is Eastern European. He is proud to be a Jew, concerns himself with Jewish identity and has no yearnings for assimilation. He feels that Jews can move "anyplace." He says, "A Jew can be president of the United States. That's not a problem. I just hope he's the right president."

Today the JEPs have names like Annenberg (publishing), Newhouse (publishing), Pritzker (hotels), Tishman (real estate),

Lefrak (real estate), Crown (General Dynamics), Davis (oil), Hess (oil), Petrie (stores), Block (drugs). That tight little group where all the so-called white Jews knew each other, attended dancing school together and married each other has pretty much gone. In the world of the JEPs money certainly matters but ancestors and origins do not—except to the miniscule minority of elderly Our Crowders.

Consider the roster of the Century Country Club in Purchase, New York. Century started out as the Ocean Country Club on Long Island. It was elite from the beginning, with members including such Our Crowd Jews as Joseph Cullman (grandfather of Joseph 3rd), Julius Morgenthau (brother of Henry S.), Oscar Wolff, Sam Knopf (father of publisher Alfred), Edwin and Belle Goodman (parents of Bergdorf Goodman's Andrew Goodman). Forced to move from its original site, Century tried several mosquitoey locations before it settled in Purchase.

Today it supposedly represents the cream of Jewish society. Sulzbergers (*New York Times* old money), Rosenwalds, and numerous Wall Street tycoons like Solomons, Klingensteins and Weinbergs use its golf, tennis and swimming facilities.

Yet members also include Larry and Bobby Tisch, Walter Annenberg, the multimillionaire publisher and former ambassador to Great Britain whose father Moses went to jail for income-tax evasion, and liquor czar Edgar Bronfman, grandson of a man so Orthodox that a Bessarabian rabbi accompanied him when he first immigrated to Canada. Edgar Bronfman's second marriage to WASP princess Lady Carolyn Townsend, a direct descendant of the man whose tax on the British colonies had set off the American Revolution, made headlines with its tales of scandal. According to *King of the Castle,* his third and current marriage was to an English pubkeeper's daughter.

In former days Century probably would not have admitted a single one of these four men. However, as a member of a rival country club says, "Wall Streeters who handle issues have to back them to the hilt. You can't afford to keep a Tisch out of anything."

Century serves as but one example of how Sephardic-German-Russian snobbery has lessened enormously, almost disappeared. A word of explanation: First the Sephardic Jews, who came here in the mid-1600s, tended to look down on the German Jews, who commenced arriving in the United States in the 1840s. For example, after Rosa Content, of a prerevolutionary Sephardic family, married James Seligman (German, of the then international banking house) in the mid-nineteenth century, she always referred to her in-laws as "those peddlers." Later German Jews pretty much scorned the flood tide of Eastern European Jews who began to arrive in the 1880s. When banker Jacob Schiff learned that a friend's daughter was marrying a Jew of Russian descent, he said, "She must be pregnant."

However, since World War II it makes little difference whether one's ancestors came from Toledo, Hamburg or Minsk. As eighty-one-year-old banker Benjamin Buttenwieser, member of a distinguished family, says, "What's so great about German Jews? World War II ended all that." In 1949 the American Jewish Committee, long considered by many to be an elitist group, named its first president who was not of German-Jewish descent. When Alexander Schindler, part German and part Eastern European, was installed as president of the Union of American Hebrew Congregations, he read a Yiddish poem written by his father.

NEW JEWISH HORIZONS

The JEPs have progressed in almost every corporate enterprise and industry to the highest level. Today's JEPs are not "token Jews" who receive ambassadorships to Turkey—the way President Cleveland honored Oscar Straus and President Wilson Henry Morgenthau. According to Irving M. Levine of the American Jewish Committee, "Discrimination against Jews in the corporate suite is no longer the problem it used to be though soft spots still exist in some industries."

Without denying their Jewishness, Jews have also taken places in the innermost government and social circles. When, in 1979, Stuart Eizenstat, then President Carter's assistant for domestic affairs, said to his boss, "Come for Passover *seder,*" Jimmy and

Rosalynn went. Walter Annenberg, grandson of an immigrant junk dealer, has a sprawling estate near Palm Springs, California. Richard Nixon took refuge there after Watergate. Ronald and Nancy Reagan have been guests. President Reagan liked the Annenberg style of hospitality so much that he named Leonore Annenberg chief of protocol for the State Department.

According to Webster's Third New International Dictionary, *elite* means "status . . . choice . . . superior . . . select." In former days background served as a base for eliteness. The new base is money through achievement. Background ranks a poor third. As C. P. Snow wrote, once you reach a certain financial level, people don't think of you as anything but very rich.

Says Alan ("Ace") Greenberg of Wall Street, "The elite Jews are the ones who make money. And people do not care whether they are German or Russian." Mr. Greenberg got his nickname in college by using the same kind of astuteness that has won him Wall Street success. After World War II at the University of Missouri, the male students greatly outnumbered the female. He wondered how he would ever get any dates with an "ordinary" name like Alan Greenberg. A friend suggested he take the name Ace Gainsborough. The *Gainsborough* disappeared but *Ace* took hold.

New elites have sprung up. Irving M. Levine feels that "Eliteness has changed. Money always counted. It still does. But high achievement counts more. Journalists have entered the elite. So have scientists. Nobel Prize winners have begun to play a role often in behalf of the Jewish community. Merely to be born into a good, old family isn't enough. The democratization of the Jewish Elite equals the change in the world of the Jewish Elite. There is also an elite growing out of technological genius. Jewish students come out of M.I.T. and in their twenties set up new companies on Route 128 in Boston. Because of the computerization industry, they may become "rapid elites." "

Jewish money, which used to be confined essentially to finance and retailing (Schiff, Warburg, Wertheim on Wall Street, the Macy Strauses) now stems from a variety of fields: Seventh Avenue (Schwartz, Pomerantz, Trigere), cosmetics (Estée Lauder), real estate (Lefrak, Rudin, Chanin), food processing and soft drinks (Simon), sugar (Kempner of Galveston).

Many people have the misconception that certain industries such as insurance, public utilities and banking don't permit Jews to rise from the ranks or have only a limited number of token Jews on their company rosters. Larry Tisch refutes this, saying, "Jews don't like to get into businesses where you work thirty or forty years to get to the top. Jews have stayed out of banks, insurance companies and public utilities because it takes too long to get ahead. A young fellow who wants to make his mark may not want to put years in to go up the corporate ladder."

JEPs have also entered into sports management. David A. ("Sonny") Werblin is president and chief executive officer of Madison Square Garden Corporation. Eugene Klein owns the San Diego Chargers; Irving Levin the San Diego Clippers and Samuel Schulman the Seattle Supersonics. Jews also own the Milwaukee Brewers, Kansas City Royals, San Francisco Giants, Philadelphia Eagles and Cleveland Browns. Three Levi Strauss executives own the Oakland A's.

Being a religious Jew does not impede financial success. For example, Seymour, Mordecai and Ephraim Propp, all three Orthodox Jews now in mining and securities, inherited money from their father Morris. In the early twentieth century Morris Propp bought the inventory of colored light bulbs from Eveready and sold them as Christmas-tree decorations. Says Seymour Propp proudly, "It was a pretty good idea for an Orthodox Jew."

As another instance, Frederick & Herrud is the fastest-growing company in the, of all things, pork business. The boss is Henry Dorfman, fifty-eight, a Polish Orthodox Jew who survived the Holocaust by jumping with his father off the train that carried the rest of the family to Treblinka, eventually immigrated to the United States, and bought Frederick Packing Company, a tiny pork-slaughtering business in Detroit. To Orthodox Jews, pork is *trayf*—unclean. According to *Fortune,* Dorfman's wife won't permit pork in her home. But the family sees nothing wrong with selling meat they would not eat because of their own religious scruples. As a family motto puts it: "The meat is *trayf,* the money is kosher." A reasonable and compatible distinction.

"JUDAIZING"

America has become "Judaized." This is the word sociologist Charles S. Liebman, professor at Bar-Ilan University, Israel, applied to the increasing impact of religious Jews upon the formerly mostly German-Jewish membership of the Federation of Jewish Philanthropies of New York. The same word applies to the effect JEPs have had on American life. These days it is even chic to be religious.

What is a Jew today? Definitions vary. Alan Greenberg makes three divisions: "Jews who are passing . . . Jews who don't do anything for Jews . . . Jews who do think about their Jewishness." Investment banker Robert Bernhard, a Lehman descendant, classifies Jews as "People who don't pay any attention to being Jewish . . . the old Our Crowd Jews who are still Jews . . . and the new emerging groups oriented toward Israel."

Perhaps the most cogent definition comes from Billie Tisch, who divides Jews by attitude rather than affiliation: *The positives.* They do something about their Jewishness either through contributions or activities. And they feel free enough to disagree when Jews are attacked. Her philosophy: "Being Jewish is important for me in everything I do. It's the way I approach my life. I have all kinds of friends. But in a Christian society I don't feel disadvantaged. I'm happy being a Jew."

The neutrals. They feel no involvement with the Jewish community and experience no sense of pride when another Jew achieves success. However, they do not deny their Jewishness.

The negatives. They wish to disappear, and often do, into the world of no-religion. There are even "self-hating Jews," characterized by Rabbi Isaac N. Trainin, director of Federation's Commission on Synagogue Relations as "Jews who hate their Judaism. They don't convert. They have no respect for Judaism or any religion." Some feel embarrassed when they see something very obviously Jewish like the Lubavitch Mitzvah mobiles. (These campers are run by the Lubavitch organization and park on Fifth Avenue or near the Plaza Hotel in New York. Representatives will ask male passersby, "Are you Jewish? Will you take five minutes to come in and put on *tefillin* (leather strappings worn during certain prayers)?" Men are more targeted than women, but a woman may approach a female passerby saying, "Do you light candles? Come in and let me show you the proper ritual for candlelighting.")

But for many Jews today there has been an identity swing. Instead of feeling, "I have to hurdle my Jewishness," many JEPs proclaim it. They seek a faith renewal, a reexamination of their own religious identity, have a desire to learn about Judaism. In contrast some prominent Jews used to seek involvement in the Christian community to conceal or tone down their Jewishness.

A "sha-sha" joke (the phrase means "be quiet") illustrates this tendency. Some years ago two elderly Philadelphia matrons were riding on a local streetcar. Both were thin, elegant and quite deaf. Said one to the other, "I hear you've been sick." Nodding her head, matron number two stated loudly, "Yes, I had an operation for hemorrhoids." Then she dropped her voice to a whisper and continued, "In the Jewish hospital."

One Westchester homemaker, who describes herself as "second-string Our Crowd," was brought up with virtually no religion. Her grandparents did not go to synagogue; neither did her parents and neither did she. Her family always had a Christmas tree, a practice she continued after her marriage. Eventually her boys married and always brought their wives home for Christmas. One year she found a six-pointed star on top of the tree. "That was telling me something," she says. "It was the last time we had a tree. Now we have a big Hanukkah celebration here with a menorah on the table."

Even Temple Emanu-El of New York, a stronghold of the Reform Jew, which traditionally had "Americanized" the ancient rituals, has felt the effects of Judaization. In the 1870s Emanu-El banned bar mitzvahs as "too Orthodox." In 1972 it reinstated bar mitzvahs for boys and introduced bas mitzvahs for girls. Reasons for this change included desire for roots, parental pressures, loss in membership and a widening yearning for ritual, particularly from members of Eastern European background.

Whereas the Our Crowd Jews referred to the Orthodox immigrant newcomers as "The Other People," today to be a "Dox"

(Orthodox) is in. As Milton Himmelfarb, director, Information and Research Services, the American Jewish Committee, says, "The in-between is thinning out. True Jewishness is more visible."

Says Rabbi Stanley Schachter, vice-chancellor of the Jewish Theological Seminary, "Just as there has been a total disappearance of Orthodoxy from many small Jewish communities, there has been a tremendous resurgence of Orthodoxy in larger centers."

Orthodox day schools have grown steadily, enrolling children from nonobservant homes. *Mikvets* (ritual baths for women), once the butt of uncomfortable jokes, are now appearing in the suburbs. Orthodox Jewry is increasingly organized to defend the legal rights of the religious—for example, the National Jewish Commission of Law and Public Affairs, known as C.O.L.P.A.

Consider Lincoln Square Synagogue on New York's West Side, where Rabbi Shlomo Riskin (his family named him Steven, but Riskin took Shlomo as his name when he first went to Israel in 1961; now only his mother and mother-in-law still call him Steven) sees as his mission the bridging of Orthodox Judaism to the modern world. To further this he founded two yeshiva high schools and a rabbinical school in Riverdale, (now moved to Queens) which draw students from all over the world.

Lincoln Square Synagogue is a success. It has over three thousand members, an adult-education program of over twelve hundred students, eight affiliate schools and over one thousand worshipers at four weekly Sabbath services. Riskin handles his audience somewhat like a talk-show host. He questions them concerning Jewish law, then coaches them with the answers. Occasionally he turns Bible Belt preacher (another rabbi characterized him as "Billy Sunday"), suddenly jumping up with emotion and gesturing with his hands or raising his voice to emphasize a point. He gave one sermon holding his baby daughter in his arms. Half of his Saturday worshipers are under thirty; students from Columbia, Barnard and Stern College fill the hall.

Riskin's real goal is to give Jews the opportunity to become Orthodox. It is up to them to remain observant. To the nonobservant, he says, "Try us, you'll like us." He says, "This is a teaching synagogue. People need a purpose, a meaning for their lives. They have to take part in something that's greater than the individual happens to be."

His congregation includes many Reform and Reconstructionist Jews. He calls his congregants a "whole new Orthodox breed. They're people who've made it. In the 1920s and earlier a whole wave of immigrants came. Their children were all American. The next generation is more interesting to me—a whole group of born-again Jews." (The name for the non-Orthodox who become Orthodox is *Baalei Teshuvas*—the BTs, those who return, the reborns.)

Riskin will bar mitzvah or bas mitzvah at any age. He performs father-and-son bar mitzvahs and recently he bar mitzvahed a seventy-year-old who came here from Russia at twelve.

Barbra Streisand has attended services and telephoned Riskin to get advice for her film, *Yentl,* which tells the story of a Jewish girl who disguises herself as a boy in order to study Talmud. Many see the filming of *Yentl* as part of Streisand's own concern to discover her heritage.

In the near future Riskin plans to spend six months a year in Israel, building a model community, Efrat, where he hopes five thousand families will live by 1999. With Sanford Bernstein, a JEP financier, who is a born again Jew, he is working to establish a Westchester retreat. Yet Riskin was not brought up as a religious Jew. On his father's side he has no first cousins named Riskin who are married to Jews.

There has been a theory that Reform Jews possess the most money, next in degree Conservative and then Orthodox. The Orthodox Fifth Avenue Synagogue, located on East Sixty-second Street just off Fifth Avenue on the site of the home where the late Senator Herbert Lehman, an Our Crowd Jew, grew up, tends to refute this. People call this synagogue "a private club." The JEP members include a number of millionaires representing candy, shipping, real estate, stoves, Wall Street. Before he left New York to make his home in Washington, author Herman Wouk was a member.

Why this "boom" in Orthodoxy? Says Rabbi Schachter, "The black community was the first to insist upon positive elements of the minority subculture and to demand that this be acknowledged by the black majority. Jews took an important cue from the recent black experience. One significant form of return to Jewish involvement and religious experience has been taking place for the last twelve years in a once antiestablishment framework. The primary example is the Havurah movement, which has now become establishment."

A Havurah (fellowship) is a small number of people who come together to share their Judaism in an intense, self-directed manner. It is a reaction against the impersonality of large synagogues. Often they meet on Saturday morning at a member's home and have a program of prayer and talk, followed by luncheon.

Throughout the nation Yiddish classes are booming. Many Harvard Law School students now wear *yarmulkes.* At Princeton there is a kosher eating club. Many professionals devote one noontime hour a week to Talmud study—Larry Tisch is one. Even if they often do not practice full Orthodoxy, many Jews espouse some of its traditions. For example, when the rabbinical students at Hebrew Union College of Cincinnati, which trains Reform rabbis, go out to give sermons at various area temples as part of their training for the rabbinate, many wear long beards and yarmulkes. They also keep kosher homes.

The old division between Orthodox and Reform has lessened. Lawrence Kobrin, an Orthodox lawyer, serves on the all-important Distribution Committee at Federation, which for most of its sixty-five-year history operated as a charitable base for Reform German Jews.

The story of Federation's new thrift shop on 81st Street and Third Avenue in New York City shows how wholeheartedly some modern Jews cooperate to avoid a situation that might split the Jewish community. Thrift House East began with a policy of remaining open on Saturday (the Jewish Sabbath) and Jewish holidays. Immediately the Orthodox protested. Matters came to something of a head when one of the largest contributors to UJA-Federation Campaign threatened to withdraw his contribution unless Thrift House East closed on the Sabbath. Officials instituted what Billie Tisch calls "great problem solving." She says, "Federation is now partners with Channel 13. Channel 13 has ownership on Saturday and it gets the profit on that day. It's like found money for the station—especially since the proceeds on Saturday are more than one-sixth. The professional staff works on Saturday. Our volunteers do not. Everyone is happy, including the rabbis."

MONEY MATTERS

With care and compassion the JEPs give huge amounts of money to charity—more than philanthropist Jacob Schiff ever dreamed of—and a large proportion goes to Israel. The old Our Crowd donors used to give liberally to such American organizations as the Y.M.H.A. and Educational Alliance with the aim of educating their Eastern European "coreligionists" so that their Old World ways, use of Yiddish and bad table manners would not embarrass them. (According to the late Harry Golden, "One of the chief differences between Jewish and Gentile giving is that the Jew will give the big money while he lives, the Gentile when he dies. The Jew wants to enjoy the prestige and gratitude. He also feels giving is an ingrained duty.")

The combined New York UJA-Federation Campaign (it merged campaigns in 1973) uses flair in its money-raising activities. One division is devoted to the search for "new paper millionaires" and researchers examine advertised stock offerings in every city and every prospectus issued by the Securities and Exchange Commission, always on the lookout for some name they have never read before.

Jewish philanthropy has its humorous side too. Originally the Baron de Hirsch Fund was founded to give Eastern European immigrants the opportunity to settle someplace other than New York and to become farmers. Some years ago the Baron de Hirsch Fund board had a lively debate over whether the baron, a German capitalist, would have approved of Israel. "It was a breakthrough when we started to give Israeli scholarships," says one of the trustees.

Many of today's JEPs have a different attitude toward money. They believe "quiet, old money" is just—"old." Their notion is to enjoy life. Some, like cosmetics tycoon Estée Lauder, possess numerous houses and apartments they call home at diverse times of year. Others like Charles and Valerie Diker own a large apartment (formerly the home of publisher J. David Stern) complete with art gallery. In some cases the parent corporation—the money source—pays for the family tennis court.

Not all JEP wives work. But they don't spend their days playing bridge either. They fundraise and spend money. They lunch (another "must" is the annual Spirit of Achievement luncheon of the women's division of the New York Chapter, National Women's Division, Albert Einstein College of Medicine, of Yeshiva University), buy Fendi bags, have personal shoppers. Whereas Frieda Schiff Warburg used to give tea parties for fellow Jewish women of her class group, entertain her family at Friday night dinner and live quietly out of the public eye, these new women enjoy being known to the public, and make no apologies.

One Our Crowd descendant talks about what a "terror" Frieda Warburg was. When she asked a group of women to a fundraising lunch at her home, she had "a plan." She would say she was going to pledge perhaps $500,000. In reality, she knew she would be giving rather less—perhaps $50,000. This money-raising device really worked. She shamed the guests, who were enormously pleased to be asked to her home, into giving more than they had planned. Braver individuals, knowing what was in store for them, declined the invitation.

JEPs tend to like giving buildings or sufficient money to an institution so that a building is named after them. As an eighty-sixth-birthday present to their mother, Walter Annenberg and his seven sisters gave the Annenberg Building at Mount Sinai Hospital in New York (however, the *New York Times* cast a pall on this $8-million donation for the Annenberg family by referring to the father's jail term in an article). Mount Sinai also has the Nathan Cummings Basic Sciences Building; Cummings is the retired octagenarian who used to head Consolidated Foods. At Albert Einstein College of Medicine there is the Arthur B. Belfer Educational Center for Health Sciences, the Irwin S. and Sylvia Chanin Institute for Cancer Research, Leo Forscheimer Medical Science Building, and Louis E. and Dora Rousso Center —to name a few.

It is a world of curious contradictions. The big money donations and Israeli cause loom paramount in the lives of most of the JEPs. At the same time so do more frivolous pursuits—like fashion. They do not want silk that will wear forever. They prefer budget chic and designer name chic.

Representatives of Rowes of London come to New York twice yearly. JEPs buy Rowes smocked party dresses for little girls (around $120 each) and the velvet-collared winter coats with matching hats for boys and girls ($300). These are ordered, take from six to eight weeks to arrive, and naturally the purchaser pays duty. A few save duty money by flying to London to pick up the garments in person. A socially ambitious newcomer may find that buying in the right place can serve as entree to the new elite. One thirty-eight-year-old mother explains, "I met everyone standing in line at the Carlyle to get into Rowes of London."

Art acquisitions mark the difference between old- and new-elite groups. For instance, Valerie Diker collects Louise Nevelson. Mrs. Enid A. Haupt (the *A* stands for *Annenberg*) has a collection of impressionists at her orchid-filled Park Avenue home. However, octogenarian Mrs. Richard Rothschild, daughter of the oldtime Newberger family, points to the walls of her comfortable but simple penthouse at Ninety-first and Park, saying "Our art is by our children."

New interlocking relationships have been formed. Just as non-Jews like the Cabots, Lodges, Medills and McCormicks have married each other, so have rich Jews. For instance, Roger Williams Straus (son of statesman Oscar) married Gladys (American Smelting) Guggenheim. Nathan Straus, Jr., married Helen (Goldman, Sachs) Sachs. His son R. Peter (that *R* is for *Ronald*) married Ellen Sulzberger (related to the *Times* newspaper clan) and his sister Sissie Straus married Irving (Lehman Brothers) Lehman.

The JEPs have done likewise. Nate Appleman, son of an Orthodox Oklahoma chicken killer and oilman, was a football player at the University of Pennsylvania (according to a niece, his father objected, saying, "I don't want those eleven *goyim* to jump on you"), later married Janet Greenebaum, sister of Leon Greenebaum of the Hertz Corporation. His two daughters married Jewish wealth: one married the son of financier "Dutch" Unterberg, the other married William Roberts, whose mother was from the Block Drug Company family.

Changing societal conditions have also affected Jewish marriages. Divorce plays a more prominent role in JEP lives than it did in the Our Crowd days. For example, Leonore Annenberg, niece of the late and much feared Columbia Pictures head, Harry Cohn, had two previous marriages which ended in divorce, including one to Lewis Rosentiel, the founder of Schenley Industries. According to an Annenberg family friend, while golfing at Boca Raton, the Florida resort then owned by E. Myer Schine, she met Walter Annenberg, who had been married to Veronica Dunkleman, the daughter of a wealthy Canadian manufacturer from Toronto. She divorced Rosenstiel and married the newspaper magnate.

Social trends have also had an impact on Jewish attitudes toward their own money. Says Rabbi Schachter, "For the first time Jews in America are trying to puzzle through their own relationship to the Jewish community vis-à-vis their own wealth. It used to be that Jewish wealth didn't last because of marrying out. Now second and third generations are involved in the Jewish community."

JEWS IN THE WASP WORLD

Although many JEPs have become more religious, some have broken through the WASP curtain—or even become WASPs. Says Alan Greenberg, "You find Jews everywhere who are not Jews anymore." The late Robert Moses, from a distinguished Jewish family, was buried at St. Peter's Episcopal Church in Bayshore, Long Island. Investment counselor C. Douglas Dillon had a grandfather named Sam Lapowski. Barry Goldwater, senator from Arizona, an Episcopalian, also had a Jewish grandfather. So did Caspar W. Weinberger, U.S. secretary of defense, who lists himself in official biographies as Episcopalian.

Today's Jewish elite mix socially with Gentiles as peers. "It's a cultural thing," explains Benjamin Buttenwieser of Lehman Brothers Kuhn Loeb. "Our Crowd was nouveau; they didn't mix with non-Jews except in business. I doubt if the Schiffs were ever at the Harrimans for dinner. They were admired but not accepted. The one who was accepted the most was Felix Warburg. He made no bones about being Jewish and he knew how to sail a yacht. Today in my own life half of our friends are not Jewish and one-quarter are black."

Often JEPs, who might not make it in the world of high Jewish society, do make it in the Christian world—for instance, cosmetic queen Estée Lauder, dress designer Mollie Parnis, real estator Lewis Rudin. Explains Elinor Guggenheimer, "The Jews are more snobbish. The Christians look at Jews as all alike."

David Halberstam in *The Powers That Be* points out that "Those who knew Bill Paley when he first came to New York thought he would have liked to be taken up by Our Crowd, the bastion of German-Jewish respectability, but Our Crowd was having none of it. The smell of cigars was still on his money and radio was new and flashy and perhaps vulgar. A Sulzberger would do; a Paley (who knew, after all, what the name had been before Paley?) would not. . . . Paley never ceased to be a little ambivalent about his origins, both about being Jewish and about being a Russian Jew. He was proud of his background, but as he grew older and more successful he did not necessarily want to be reminded of it. As he tried to put it aside, hang around not with just Wasps but with super-Wasps, it somehow always lurked in the background."

For years many Jews chose to enter the Christian world through marriage. For example, M. Robert Guggenheim, son of Daniel, tried to rise socially via the remarriage-go-round route. His first marriage to the Jewish Grace Bernheimer (sister of Alva, who was the mother of the recently deceased Bruce Gimbel) failed. He then converted to Catholicism to marry his second wife. At the time his father commented from his suite at the St. Regis Hotel, "I'm delighted. My son has always been a very bad Jew. I hope they'll make a good Catholic out of him." They didn't. Robert Guggenheim soon divorced his second wife to marry a third and fourth, both Protestants.

The trend continues, though in many cases the Jewish spouse remains Jewish. For example, Felicia Warburg first married Robert Sarnoff (son of RCA's Russian-Jewish David Sarnoff), then Franklin D. Roosevelt, Jr. She is now married to John B. Rogan, who owns a large cattle ranch and the Boar's Head Inn in Charlottesville, Virginia. He is Presbyterian. She says, "I'm Jewish and proud of it, but there's a difference between practicing religion and being part of the Jewish heritage and community."

Handsome, silver-haired, seventy-seven-year-old John Schiff, grandson of Jacob Schiff, has intermarried twice. His first wife was Edith Baker, an Episcopalian, and they were married by a judge. He says, "It was a compromise I made with my father-in-law and I had to promise to bring up my children as Episcopalians." Their marriage lasted for forty-one years until Edith Schiff (known as TeeTee) died in 1975. A year later Schiff became engaged to "Fifi" Fell, a childhood friend who happened to be Catholic.

Schiff worked out the religious logistics of his second wedding to his satisfaction. The event took place at his Oyster Bay home on Long Island. The entire family network from both sides witnessed the ceremony, including children, ten grandchildren, siblings including Dorothy Schiff, Schiff's sister and then publisher of the *New York Post,* and her children and grandchildren. The Reverend George B. Ford, a ninety-year-old retired Roman Catholic priest, performed the ceremony. Rabbi Ronald Sobel of Temple Emanu-El, New York, gave the blessing. Fittingly, the priest and the rabbi drove out from Manhattan together.

Many of these intermarriages seem to stem from schooling. Explains Orin Lehman, "I went to schools like Taft and Scarborough that were Christian-oriented. I also grew up in a secular democracy. I didn't look into race or religion. A mixed marriage seemed natural."

The acceptance of Jewry shows up in the matter of schools. For instance, many of the Our Crowd Jews used to stick to *unser Leute* (German for "our kind"). In New York young Our Crowd members attended the all-Jewish Dr. Sachs School for Boys (Herbert Lehman, Henry Morgenthau, Jr., Jesse Isidor Straus and Walter Lippmann were graduates) and the Dr. Sachs School for Girls, separate institutions but both located on West Fifty-ninth Street; Viola Wolff's dancing classes in Manhattan and Westchester, the Angie Jacobson holiday dances and cotillions (these were restricted to German Jews; the "whole idea was to keep the Russians out," says a sixty-year-old grandmother, recalling her youth).

Now regardless of their ancestors, Jewish elite girls go to formerly all-Gentile schools such as: Brearley, Hewitt, Nightingale. The boys attend Buckley, Allen Stevenson, Browning, Collegiate. Attending the "right schools" enables the preteens and teens to receive coveted invitations to the de Rham and Knickerbocker Greys dances formerly limited to children of the PPs (*Women's Wear Daily*'s term for the "Private People," meaning highly social WASPS).

Often these schools and classes produce a WASP merger that is unwanted by the Jewish parents. In one case, both daughters married non-Jews. One met her future husband, a Ph.D. in political science, at a St. Louis university. They both shared the desire for "a simple life." Now they make jewelry. The second daughter met her mate at a Transcendental Meditation group.

Jewish boundaries have widened. After all, Irving Berlin, son of a Lower East Side rabbi, wrote "White Christmas" and "Easter Parade." The two Friedman sisters, Abigail Van Buren and Ann Landers, are arbiters of behavior. And there are "token Gentiles." Andrew Heiskell, the WASP former chairman of the board at Time Inc. and now chairman of the board of trustees, New York Public Library, is a member of the Century Country Club. He got there through his wife, the former Marian Sulzberger Dryfoos.

Janet Misch, married to the wine authority Robert Misch and from the old-line Wolff clan (Greenbaum Wolff & Ernst has always been an elite Jewish law firm), says, "Origins don't matter anymore." Her daughter Mary first married a German Jew and then a Protestant. Her second daughter Kathy married Alan Koritzinsky "whose background is either Polish or Russian."

And sometimes origins do matter, says Robert Bernhard, a Lehman who began his Wall Street career at Lehman Brothers and then left ("They didn't want me and I didn't want them"). "Looking back, it was preordained that I'd be a partner at Lehman. It was just a question of when. I wanted corporate finance, which is what Lehman does. Being Our Crowd helped. I knew I wasn't going to be a fireman. I never doubted the area.

"Looking back on the crossroads, I think if I could have gone to someplace that was not family connected, it might have been better. When I did something right, they'd say, 'What did you expect!' When I did something wrong: 'He's an idiot—a member of the family.' I would have preferred to learn on my own."

The JEPs have done it on their own. "On their own" is the operative phase, superceding family and even money.

2

SOL M. LINOWITZ: PORTRAIT OF A JEP

As a student at Hamilton College in upstate New York in the early 1930s, Sol M. Linowitz used to read to Elihu Root. The retired statesman, who had been secretary of state under President Theodore Roosevelt, former senator from New York (1909–15), winner of the 1912 Nobel Peace Prize, was at that time a frail old man in his late eighties whose eyesight was very weak.

One day Root asked Linowitz, "What do you want to do?"

Linowitz answered, "I'm not sure. Maybe be a rabbi or perhaps a lawyer."

Root told him bluntly, "Be a lawyer. A lawyer needs twice as much religion as a rabbi."

Linowitz took Root's advice. He went to Cornell University Law School, where he led his class in 1938 and edited the *Cornell Law Quarterly.* He recalls, "I thought I was going to work in the Root firm in New York City headed by Elihu Root, Jr., but Judge Arthur Sutherland asked me to go to Rochester and go to work in his office. I was very taken with it. So I made an arrangement with the Root firm to try Rochester for a year. After a year I never wanted to change."

After wartime service with the Office of Price Administration and as a navy lieutenant, Linowitz returned to Rochester to resume his law practice and to begin, with Joseph C. Wilson, the effort that turned the Haloid Company, a modest producer of photographic supplies, into the Xerox Corporation. Linowitz served as chairman of the Executive Committee and general counsel of Xerox, later as chairman of the board. During that period company revenues soared from $10 million in 1950 to over $528 million in 1966 when President Lyndon Johnson made him ambassador to the Organization of American States. He left Xerox and served in the OAS post from 1966 to 1969. During this time he was also U.S. representative to the Inter-American Committee of the Alliance for Progress.

More recently, Linowitz, sixty-eight, a trim, elegant man with graying hair, has served as President Carter's representative (rank of ambassador) for Middle East Peace Negotiations (1979–81), chairman, Presidential Commission on World Hunger (1978–80), conegotiator (rank of ambassador) with Ellsworth Bunker of the Panama Canal Treaties (1977–78), chairman, Commission on United States–Latin American Relations (1974–76). He is now also cochairman, formerly chairman, of the National Urban Coalition.

When not serving the government, Ambassador Linowitz is senior partner in the international law firm of Coudert Brothers and has his office in a building in Washington's Farragut Square, only two blocks from the White House.

Jacqueline Kennedy Onassis once said of him, "He's quickly brilliant—and he gets on with people. He's kind." (Linowitz served as trustee of the Kennedy Center for five years.) Former law partner Edward Harris said, "He has come as far as he has and irritated nobody." People often express the same five words about him: "He is a good Jew."

What is a good Jew? In Linowitz's own words, "It means not only trying to lead a moral and decent life but to be a committed Jew—a participating Jew."

Linowitz, the oldest of four brothers, grew up in an Orthodox household in Trenton, New Jersey. His parents, Joseph and Rose Oglenskye Linowitz, were from Austro-Poland. His father had a fruit import business which suffered during the Depression. He recalls, "We lived in a mixed neighborhood that represented all cultures. On one side our neighbors were Irish, on the other side Italian. It was never ghettoized."

Even as a youth Linowitz was outstanding, a *Wunderkind* who played the violin well enough to make solo appearances from the age of thirteen.

Today Linowitz still excels in everything he does, and still carries on the traditional observances learned in boyhood. He belongs to Adas Israel, a Conservative synagogue in Washington, D.C., and says, "On Friday night we keep the Sabbath. My four daughters have flown the coop, but my wife and I go through the whole Sabbath routine. She lights the candles and we say prayers over the wine." Always active in Jewish affairs, from 1975 to 1980 he was lay head of the Jewish Theological Seminary, which trains rabbis, scholars and cantors in the Conservative branch of the faith.

Long before he became known as a brilliant businessman at Xerox or involved with public service, Linowitz moved as a Jew in the Gentile world. It started at Hamilton, where he was an extraordinary student and, as salutatorian of his class, delivered a commencement address in Latin.

Linowitz recalls, "I was one of the few Jews at Hamilton. We had to go to chapel every day and church on Sundays. At one time several of us were asked to be attendance takers at church services. I was the only Jew in my class. The college situation was curious. As a Jew, I was more observant there. The non-Jews expected it. For instance, on a holiday like Shavuoth (a harvest holiday celebrated seven weeks after Passover), I had to know why it was a holiday and to explain to my classmates why I observed it.

"There were no Jewish fraternities. I waited on table at a fraternity house and was asked to be an honorary member but I declined. I did what I wanted at Hamilton. I was on the debating team, helped edit the yearbook, was in the dramatic society, became Junior Phi Bete."

In a 1966 article in the *New York Times,* Byron Johnson, Jr., a classmate who also became a Rochester lawyer, is quoted as saying, "Everyone recognized he was one of the most astute fellows in the class, the most articulate. But he was a very humble, likable guy."

Critic Alexander Woollcott, then Hamilton's most famous

alumnus, was coaching drama at the college at the time and wanted Linowitz to go on the stage. But Linowitz stuck with the law. In his first year at Cornell University Law School (he played in the violin section of the Utica Symphony and led a dance band in Asbury Park during the summers), he met Evelyn (Toni) Zimmerman, a freshman studying bacteriology and teaching modern dance. They have now been married forty-two years.

He says proudly, "We have stayed married because she is a great person. We are very different. She was a scientist, is an artist and does sculpture and watercolors. [She also does minor repairs around the house because Linowitz considers himself ham-handed.] She has great serenity and tranquility. She always travels with me."

All four Linowitz daughters studied Hebrew. Jan and Ronni are unmarried. June and Anne are married (Mrs. Kenneth Mozersky, Mrs. Gabriel Gerstenblith). His two grandchildren go to Sunday school and Hebrew school.

ON HOW JEWS HAVE CHANGED. "There has been a vast change. The things we used to think of as barriers are no longer there. For example, when I was starting out in law, there were many firms that did not take Jews. When I was job hunting in New York, I knew there were certain firms not to talk to. Now I don't know a single law firm that does not take Jews. Similar changes have occurred in every area.

"There are more Jewish senators, more Jewish congressmen —the same in politics as in the broader society. There is less looking for the Jewish 'seat' but more asking who is the right man for the job. It is a healthy phenomenon. We have made massive strides and are continuing to do so. Imagine a Jew having been head of Du Pont and a Jewish dean at Harvard turning down the presidency of Yale."

But there is still room for change.

ON OPENING DOORS. Linowitz admits he has tried and is trying to do this for fellow Jews. "In Rochester I was asked to join the University Club, which had a policy of not taking Jews. I told them I would not join unless that policy was changed. I held out until they agreed. Then I joined along with other Jews."

Today Linowitz is on the board of directors of Time Inc., Pan

American World Airways Inc., Mutual Life Insurance Company of New York and, until he resigned, he was also on the board of the Marine Midland Bank. He says he hopes he is opening doors for others.

ON NAME CHANGING: "Way back when I was starting as a lawyer, I thought of changing my name. Others advised me to do it. But I didn't. By then I was what I was." (However, his three brothers did change their name to Linowes.)

ON RABBIS: "I decided law was the place for me, but I never lost my interest in the rabbinate. A number of rabbis have become my friends. When I travel abroad, I go to synagogue and temples. A few years ago I went to synagogue in Iran. The combination of Hebrew and Moorish influence there was fascinating—to enter the temple you had to take off your shoes."

ON REMAINING JEWISH PROBLEMS: 'Success has created problems for Jews. We fought hard to open fraternities and sororities. We encouraged and pressed for social intermingling between Jews and non-Jews. We succeeded, but that same social intermingling led inevitably to mixed marriage. We succeeded —and therefore created new problems. If the restrictions had remained, we would probably not have had so much intermarriage."

ON TRENDS: "I see kids with *yarmulkes,* the growth in Orthodox services, young people seeking more religious observance. It is not surprising when you see all the different cults. Young people today are groping. Organized religion has failed to reach these young kids. The Havurot give them a sense of belonging. They want to participate without too much ornamentation. They feel, as someone said, 'We used to have wooden chalices and golden priests, now we have golden chalices and wooden priests.'

"These young people resist show. To be effective, religion has to touch something deep within them. They will not be satisfied with cursory observance. Religion has to touch them through emotions."

ON BEING A JEW TODAY: "The American Jew is more relaxed about himself and about being recognized as a Jew. Today you can be a Jew and be a central part of the American system. There is no dichotomy. Jews, Protestants, Catholics—they are all Americans. I have found the more I respect myself, the more respect I get from others. The more I acknowledge being an observant Jew, the more respect I get. People honor commitment."

Today Linowitz holds honorary doctorate degrees (L.L.D. and L.H.D.) from thirty-three colleges and universities. He is a fellow of the American Academy of Arts and Sciences and the Royal Society of Arts. He sits on ten boards.

Twice he turned down a cabinet post and he has also refused to enter politics: "I can't see myself running for elective office and saying vote for me over someone else. That would bother me."

ON OUR CROWD: "All that has died. You do not see or hear 'Where is he or she from?' anymore. The situation among Jews has changed. You don't know where people originally came from—Germany, Poland, Russia or anywhere else. You judge on the present merits, achievements, kind of person he or she is."

A Depression child of immigrant parents, Linowitz has made it completely on his own. After his brilliant success in law and at Xerox, he went into a second career in public service. Moving in a world of men and women at the top, he openly avows his Jewishness. He practices his faith. A very special human being, he exemplifies the quintessential JEP.

3

FROM THE *JEWISH MAYFLOWER* TO THE AMERICAN MAINSTREAM

AMERICAN JEWISH history divides into four periods: Sephardic, German, East European and American. The first Jew of record was not allowed to remain in America. He was Salomon Franco, who came from Amsterdam to Puritan Boston in 1649 —twenty-nine years after the *Mayflower*—with a consignment of goods from a Jewish merchant in Amsterdam to Major General Edward Gibbons of the Boston militia. There seems to have been some question about who was responsible for paying Franco, and, while the argument went on, the ship which brought Franco sailed away and the Puritan city fathers were left with a Jew on their hands—the first that any of them had seen. "But a live son of Israel they could not absorb," said Rabbi Malcolm Stern in a talk on "Assimilation of American Jews." They voted to keep him at public expense up to ten weeks with the proviso that he depart by the next available ship.

In 1654 some twenty-three Jewish refugees from Recife, Brazil, arrived on the *St. Charles,* often called the *Jewish Mayflower.* Actually, the band's journey had begun thousands of miles away and years before in fifteenth-century Spain and Portugal. According to Stephen Birmingham in *Our Crowd,* there, after the violence of the Inquisition, the Catholic monarchs had ordered all Jews to adopt Christianity or depart the Iberian Peninsula. Those who would not convert had fled and scattered—to Italy, Turkey, Hamburg and various Baltic ports. Many had been drawn to the tolerant atmosphere of the Netherlands, and when the Dutch conquered Recife in 1630 and urged settlers to go there and form colonies, many Jews had migrated to South America, where they enjoyed a few years of peace. But in 1654 Recife had been reconquered by the Portuguese and Brazil no longer served as a haven for Jews. Once again, they fled.

The great Sephardic families of New York, many of them descended from the *St. Charles*'s arrivals, include the Hendrickses, Cardozos, Baruchs, Lazaruses, Nathans, Solises, Lopezes, Lindos and the Seixases. In Manhattan, the Sephardic families and Shearith Israel, their synagogue, had special status. Many of their band had fought on the side of the colonies in the Revolutionary War as well as helped finance, provision and outfit the armies.

But the flow of Sephardic Jews soon stopped. Says historian Dr. Jacob Rader Marcus, "By 1720 the Sephardics were a minority. The Sephardic Jews stopped coming to the United States because they had a chance to make money in Europe. Few came after 1720."

By 1840 the Sephardic age had begun to wane as German Jews began to trickle in. Says Gary Schaer, director of the American Sephardi Federation, "Only four of the old Spanish synagogues are left—one mother and three daughters. Shearith Israel is the mother and it is 70 percent Ashkenazic (German and Eastern European). One daughter in Charleston is now Reform. One daughter in Philadelphia is 99 percent Ashkenazic, and then there is the famous daughter in Newport, Rhode Island—the Touro Synagogue."

After 1840 German Jews tended to shape the destinies of American Jewry. Many came to America to avoid army conscription or because of the replacement factor—German laws forbade Jewish marriages until a married person in the community died. In the United States people started to refer to the "Nathan-type Jew" (Sephardic) and the "Seligman-type Jew" (German).

The "forty-eighters" were an extraordinary group of German immigrants with talent, imagination and vigor that included Rabbi Benjamin Szold, father of Henrietta—the outstanding woman who founded Hadassah; Rabbi Adolph Huebsch, whose son Benjamin eventually headed Viking Press; Joseph Goldmark, whose daughters married Dr. Felix Adler and Supreme Court Justice Louis Brandeis; Mayer Lehman, founder of the great cotton and banking firm and father of Herbert and Irving. Other German Jews who came in that period and whose names have become part of the American legend include Adam Gimbel, peddler, merchant and founder of a department-store dynasty; Meyer Guggenheim, merchant and mining magnate; Adolph Lewisohn, copper-mine magnate and philanthropist; Henry Morgenthau, lawyer, financier and diplomat; Samuel Rosenwald, merchant and father of Julius, who established a great humanitarian foundation.

Another group was the Jewish "forty-niners" who came not only from Germany but from all over Europe. Attracted by the discovery of gold in California, they were among the founding fathers of San Francisco. A few came across country on wagon trains. The majority, from Germany, England, France, opted for the somewhat easier route across the fever-infested Isthmus of Panama known as the "Panama Shortcut." Most chose to be merchants rather than miners. One story from the period theorizes that the prosperity of a mining town could be measured by the number of Jewish shopkeepers it held. The prospectors wore a tough overall made from blue canvas called "denim" with a heavily stitched pocket—the forerunner of Levi's blue jeans. The pants were made by Levi Strauss of San Francisco, who came to that city in 1850 at the age of twenty. Other Jewish "argonauts" (named for Jason's hardy band of adventurers who sought their own golden fleece) included Fleishhackers, Koshlands, Newmans, Verdiers, Gerstle and Sloss.

According to Irena Narell, writing in *Hadassah* magazine, "The fact that Jews played a key role in the creation of the economic base of frontier society gave them entree to that society. All of California's upper strata was a product of the gold rush and complete social acceptance of Jews was due to their arrival with other immigrants." The Jewish migration to San Francisco, unlike migration to other areas, was concurrent with the founding of San Francisco as an American city.

Many German Jews during this period also settled in Baltimore, since this city was the principal port of the Hamburg-American Line in the United States. Some went further south. According to the late Harry Golden in *The Southern Landsman,* "The Cones of Greensboro, North Carolina are the only Jewish family in the South to have achieved 'Our Crowd' status along with the Schiffs, Warburgs, Guggenheims and Speyers of New York. And they made it all in textiles." Not only did the descendants of Herman Cone (he had been Kahn) found what is today an eighty-seven-year-old firm known as Cone Mills, but their local philanthropies are legendary.

The old Our Crowd German Jews kept their ties to the fatherland. In their first years in America, these Jews turned to German groups, German theater, halls and concerts, education, societies. Jacob Wertheim's children (third-generation American) had a German governess. Banker Joseph Seligman's early letters to his wife were always in his native tongue. Jacob Schiff, who was always preaching the doctrine of Americanization, invariably wrote in German to Sir Ernest Cassel (Cassel was a millionaire German Jew, a good friend of Edward VII and knighted by the queen in 1899).

Because of cultural roots, sentiment and relatives still living there, banker Abraham Kuhn and scholar James Loeb retired to Germany. Jacob Schiff took frequent vacations there, and it was in Frankfurt that daughter Frieda Schiff met Felix Warburg, her husband-to-be. Germany was also a source of wives. Nathan Straus, when there on business, married Lina Guthers, in Mannheim, in 1879. Joseph Seligman went to Munich and married his first cousin, Babet Steinhardt, in 1848.

If they could afford it, German families often obtained a German education. Jefferson Seligman, son of James, graduated from Columbia in 1878 and then studied medicine in Germany, although he later joined the New York banking firm. Jules and Leopold Bache both went to school in Frankfurt and Brussels. Morris Loeb, a chemist, was educated at Harvard, Berlin, Heidelberg and Leipzig.

Dr. Sigfried Wachsmann, the medical director of the Montefiore Home and Hospital for Chronic Diseases, revisited Germany to make sure the buildings reflected the latest thought in hospital planning.

Today few households have German tutors or governesses and not one passenger boat plies between the United States and Germany. Perhaps the biggest change in the Old Guard manifests itself in the use of language. As recently as the late thirties Our Crowd households tended to punctuate their conversations with such German words as *endlich* ("at last," especially when a spinster finally married) and *umbeschrien, unberufen* ("knock on wood"). Now even German Jews as well as some Gentiles use Yiddish expressions, such as *schmaltz* and *schnook;* they are part of the American language.

Toward the end of the nineteenth century the age of the Eastern European Jew began with a mass immigration of Jews from Eastern Europe. According to scholar Max Dimont, by 1918 there were over 2.5 million Russian Jews in the United States—ten times the number of German Jews.

In their eagerness to contrast their own modern and westernized ways with the "uncouth" Russian Jews, the German Jews called the Eastern European Jews "Asiatics," while describing themselves as "members of the Hebrew persuasion" or "Israelites." Often, when referring to the Russians, they used the expression "our coreligionists" in order to emphasize that their relationship with the Russians was solely religious and did not involve cultural, social or intellectual affinities. According to historian Moses Rischin in *The Promised City,* "Germans, embarrassed by Russian business competition, dismissed their rivals, whose names often ended with 'ki' as 'kikes.' " One descendant born into Our Crowd, recalls that in her college days her father would say chidingly, "You're not popular. You are just popular with kikes."

With a kind of ugly poetic justice, the new depreciation was soon thereafter applied by American non-Jews to all Jews.

At the root of the Germans concern was the fear that the settling of the Russians in large urban ghettos, especially the Lower East Side of New York City, and the resulting social problems would engender an anti-Semitic backlash that would engulf the Germans and destroy the social acceptibility they had secured from non-Jewish Americans. To the newly arrived Eastern European Jews, the German Jews supplied money, material goods, and educational facilities—not only for humanitarian reasons but to accelerate their Americanization.

The Eastern European Jews had talent, energy, push. From their ranks came Irving Berlin (born Baline, son of Rabbi Baline of the Lower East Side), George and Ira Gershwin, a galaxy of movie moguls such as the late Samuel Goldwyn (born Goldfish). In addition to New York, they settled in such urban centers as Boston, Cleveland, Pittsburgh, Chicago. They became cigar makers, pants pressers, buttonhole stitchers, proprietors of candy shops, tailor shops, "mom-and-pop" stores, peddlers who worked hard and saved their pennies. They believed in the American dream.

They became an elite intellectual group that crowded into night schools, read Marx and Schopenhauer and fostered a unique generation of Jews. As soon as the forces that had held them down in Russia were removed, abilities that had been inhibited for centuries seemed to explode in the heady freedom of America. While many of the immigrant parents remained garment workers and shopkeepers, they sent their children to school with the admonition: "Learn. Make something of yourself." And these children became doctors, lawyers, college professors, artists and more.

Full of charm and vitality, they frequently married the children of German Jewish gentry. To some Our Crowders this was as undesirable as marriage between Jew and Gentile. Despite their Orthodox *shtetl* background, some Russian Jewish sons even became Reform rabbis, studying for the rabbinate at Hebrew Union College in Cincinnati, which had such a large German-speaking population that it was virtually bilingual, and where they frequently married the daughters of old-line German families. "Today the students at Hebrew Union College do not marry local girls," asserts historian Dr. Jacob Rader Marcus. "They come with wives."

Milton Himmelfarb, director, information and research services, American Jewish Committee, says, "Just as it had with the German Jews, the Americanization factor dominated the Russian Jews. For example, the second-generation Orthodox Jews wanted its Judaism to look very American. So they turned Conservative and dressed their rabbis in ministerial robes. It was important that their English be very good. The Jewish Theological Seminary had a professor of elocution."

In 1921 the first immigrant-quota law was passed, a law that was to restrict Jewish immigration and to serve as a forerunner for similar and more drastic acts. And with it began the age of the American Jew. The quota laws, which in effect cut off Jewish immigration to these shores, meant that within a generation most Jews in the United States would be native-born. Cultural and social leveling, intermarriage and fusion were inevitable. The "Spanish," the "German," the "Russian" Jews were diminished as entities. On the rise were "Americans," Jews with little knowledge of their European origins and heritage and with a growing disregard for traditional ethnic differences—in short what historian Jacob Rader Marcus calls a *"homo novus,* the American Jew," who viewed himself no longer by his origin but by his common American heritage.

The result: today elite Jewry includes such second- and third-generation Jews as Saul Bellow, winner of the 1976 Nobel Prize for literature, who grew up in the Montreal ghetto; economist Milton Friedman, winner of the 1976 Nobel Prize in economics and a descendant of Eastern European Jews; and Barry Goldwater of Polish-Jewish background on his father's side, even though he himself is a Protestant. (One of the jests among Jews during the 1964 campaign was that they always knew the first Jew to run for president would be an Episcopalian.)

WHY DID OUR CROWD DIE?

Quite simply, many of the old Our Crowd Jews simply faded away.

In the late 1950s Sara Straus Hess, daughter of Isidor Straus, gave a party in her Park Avenue apartment. Its purpose: a reunion of the Straus clan, some of whom had not spoken to each other for years. The Strauses (known as the "single s" Strauses as distinguished from the numerous "double s" Strausses like the Levi Strausses) were all descended from Lazarus Straus, who came to this country from the Rhenish Palatinate in 1852, started a crockery and glass business and prospered. Lazarus and his eldest son Isidor inaugurated the crockery and glassware department at R. H. Macy & Company in 1874. Both prospered. Subsequently, Isidor and his brother Nathan bought Macy's. They made large profits and then joined some friends in the dry-goods business by way of Abraham & Straus in Brooklyn. Lazarus's third son, Oscar, was the only one of the three brothers to receive a higher education. He had been class poet at Columbia College, graduated from Columbia Law School, stayed with law for a while, switched to crockery, and then moved into diplomacy, serving twice as ambassador to Turkey and then in Theodore Roosevelt's cabinet as secretary of commerce and labor (he was the first Jew to serve in the cabinet).

In 1912 the *Titanic* foundered and Isidor and his wife of forty years went down with it. According to the appendix of his privately printed *Autobiography,* Isidor had written a letter to be opened after his death which directed his three sons, Jesse, Percy and Herbert: "Look to his [Nathan's] reproves or his approvals as you would look to mine. . . . Cultivate between yourselves frankness and cordiality. . . . Never let any differences, should they arise, rancour in your breasts. . . . I would consider my life's work a failure if ever there would arise any serious difference between you."

But things did not quite work out as Isidor wanted. His three sons frequently found themselves at odds with Uncle Nathan. Isidor and Nathan had owned everything half and half. However, according to *The Merchant Princes,* Nathan realized that his sons were younger and less experienced than his nephews and unlikely to catch up to them in store management positions. Isidor Straus's sons offered to buy him out and for some $7 million, which included his nephews' interest in A & S and the family crockery business; Nathan Straus pulled out. Herbert, Jesse and Percy Straus were left to run Macy's, which they did with enormous success.

The night of Sara Straus Hess's party, some seventy-five Strauses showed up. The Macy contingent—including the writer Barbara Levy (she is a great-granddaughter of Isidor and her name is pronounced as in collecting a tax), her uncle Jack Straus, then chairman and chief executive officer of Macy's, and cousin Kenneth Straus—came late. Macy's was in the middle of a strike, and this was one of the nights the store did not close until nine o'clock. Nathan II and Nathan III were on hand for the event, as was Roger, Jr., publisher grandson of Oscar I, and his wife Dolly. Each guest received a small, black, calf-bound book *The Autobiography of Isidor Straus.* As each guest arrived, he or she was given a name tag for identification purposes. Few of the invitees knew each other. Many second and third cousins had to be introduced.

In large part, the descendants of Oscar and Nathan had stayed Jewish. Conversely, many descendants of Isidor had turned Episcopalian, often converted by the late, famous Reverend Arthur Lee Kinsolving.

The Strauses typify what has happened to many outstanding Our Crowd families. They possess dignity, breeding, talent—the qualities that come from four generations of money and accomplishment. They are "quiet"; they prefer that their names do not appear in the newspapers. Most of the grandchildren and great-grandchildren of the original Isidor-Nathan-Oscar triumvirate have left the retailing field for public relations, communications, publishing, education, social work. Only two Strauses still work at Macy's. Kenneth Straus, great-grandson of Isidor, is chairman, R. H. Macy Corporate Buying; and Elizabeth Levy, Barbara Levy's niece and great-great-granddaughter of Isidor, recently began a stint on Macy's training squad. Those who have remained in the Jewish faith are not leaders in the Jewish community, although Oscar Straus II, grandson of the original Oscar, serves on the board of New York's Temple Emanu-El.

What caused the diminuation of influence of Our Crowd Jews?

Rabbi Malcolm Stern, the noted genealogist and author of *Americans of Jewish Descent,* which includes only those Americans descended from Jews who arrived in the United States before

1840, puts it succinctly, "The most prominent German Jews became so non-Jewish. There was no place to go but get out."

LEAVING THE FAITH

They became non-Jewish in various ways and to various degrees. Some just simplified their names. Gutfreunds became Goodfriends, as later Russian Jewish Berkowitzes became Berkleys. According to Leon Harris in *The Merchant Princes,* the Brandensteins, a pioneer San Francisco family in the tea and coffee business, became Branstens. Some said they had "circumcised their name."

Others converted or intermarried. Comments Rabbi Stern, "They did it to achieve a certain upward mobility—to be socially accepted in America in an era when it counted."

August Schonberg pioneered in the process. The son of a poor merchant, he was born in 1816 in the Rhenish Palatinate in western Germany. Possessed of an extraordinarily keen mind, he somehow managed to get his foot in the door of the Frankfurt Rothschilds, who reassigned him to Havana. There he heard about the New York panic of 1837 and decided it would offer scope for his money-making talents. He took a ship for New York and, during the voyage, two changes took place. He changed his name to Belmont (the French equivalent of Schonberg, meaning "beautiful mountain"). He also became a Gentile.

Many second- and third-generation Our Crowd members preferred intermarriage to marriage with a person of Eastern European descent. Dorothy Schiff, until late 1976 publisher of the *New York Post,* is a granddaughter of Jacob Schiff, daughter of Morti and Adele Schiff, and sister of investment banker John Schiff. In her family their Jewish origin (Jacob was very observant even though he was a pillar at the Reform Temple Emanu-El) was referred to as "the background."

The family did go through some motions. At Norwood, the family home, a Long Island estate, a rabbi conducted a bar mitzvahish ceremony for Dorothy and John. In her biography,

Men, Money and Magic, she calls this her "confirmation."

In the same book Dorothy Schiff reveals that after appropriate instruction she was "confirmed" again by Herbert Shipman, rector of the Church of the Heavenly Rest. Shortly afterward she married her first husband, socialite Richard B. W. Hall, and the officiating cleric was the Right Reverend Shipman, who had become Episcopal suffragen bishop of New York. Later, after divorcing Hall, she was introduced to George Backer, a fringe intimate of the Algonquin group, by Herbert Bayard Swope. Backer's father was a Polish Jewish immigrant and his mother a Russian one. When Dorothy introduced her new beau to her mother, Adele Schiff said, "My God, what is this? It looks like what I have been avoiding for years." In preparation for marriage to Backer, Dorothy decided to abandon her conversion to Christianity. She sent for Rabbi Jonah Wise of Central Synagogue, who told her not to worry about it. She was still a Jew.

Dorothy Schiff has married four times. Theodore O. Thackrey (non-Jewish) was number three and Rudolph G. Sonnenborn (Jewish) number four.

One of Dorothy Schiff's childhood friends, Marie Norton, also married out of Judaism and into upper-class society. Marie's parents had been Sheridan Norton, a prominent, non-Jewish New Yorker with money, and Beulah Einstein. Marie had had a Jewish grandfather but been brought up Catholic. She married into the top strata of WASP society. Her first husband was Cornelius ("Sonny") Vanderbilt Whitney, whom she divorced, and her second was statesman Averell Harriman.

In *The Merchant Princes* Donald Blun Straus recalls, "Jewishness was like sex. It was absolutely taboo as a subject for discussion with either of my parents. By example rather than word they raised the three of us to be anti-Semitic. One did not go to a Jewish school or club or summer resort. As a matter of duty and tradition only, one might serve as the director of a Jewish charity, but the goal was to be on the boards of directors of non-Jewish charities, museums and businesses. It was just as clearly preferable to meet and take out Christian girls, and, of course, we all married Christians."

Many assimilationists simply wanted to be Gentiles. Columnist Walter Lippmann, himself a product of the "gilded ghetto" world of Dr. Sachs School for Boys and Temple Emanu-El, called the Jews "conspicuous." He avoided the perils of "conspicuousness" by immersing himself through his two Gentile marriages, his social life, his professional contacts into the dominant white Protestant society.

Henry Morgenthau was another kind of assimilationist. As his granddaughter, historian Barbara Tuchman, wrote in *Commentary* (May 1977), "His Zion was here. What he wanted was what most immigrants wanted at a time when liberty glowed on the western horizon: Americanization. This meant to him . . . Americanization as a Jew with the same opportunities to prove himself and the same treatment by society as anyone else. . . . Assimilation, for him, did not mean to cross over to Christianity. It meant to be accepted in Bar Harbor as a Jew. . . . He wanted to be a Jew and an American on the same level as the best."

Born in Mannheim, Germany, in 1856, Henry Morgenthau came to the United States with his parents in 1865, learned English, graduated from public high school at fourteen, entered City College for a career in law but was forced to leave before the end of his first year to help support the family by working as an office boy for $4 a week. After clerking in a law office for four years while teaching in an adult night school for $15 a week, he put himself through Columbia Law School and was admitted to the bar at the age of twenty-one. With two friends, he formed a law firm in 1879 where the average age of the partners was twenty-six.

Morgenthau made a fortune in real estate, donated a large sum of money to Woodrow Wilson's campaign for the presidency and was rewarded with the minor ambassadorship to Turkey.

In the same *Commentary* article, Mrs. Tuchman writes, "This intense faith in equal opportunity for the Jew in America and the fear of being thought to have another loyalty made him and others like him resist so strongly the movement for a separate Jewish state. Prior to Hitler and the ultimate disillusion, he believed the future of the Jew as a free person was here and that it was threatened by the demand for a separate statehood."

Although his view of Judaism lead to an anti-Zionistic stance, Henry Morgenthau never attempted to play down his Jewish identity or remain passive in regard to his people. On the contrary, he emphasized his ties to his religion throughout his life, serving as founder, trustee and officer of the Federation of Jewish Philanthropies, the American Jewish Committee, B'nai Brith, Mount Sinai Hospital in New York and many other Jewish organizations. But always there was that longing for complete Americanization. In his seventies he established his summer home in the WASP stronghold of Bar Harbor, Maine.

His children did not leave the faith. It was Morgenthau's son Henry, Jr., who, on leaving Roosevelt's cabinet (he had been secretary of the Treasury), assumed the chairmanship of the United Jewish Appeal from 1947 to 1950 and raised the funds critical for the survival of Israel in the endangered first years of statehood. His grandson Robert Morgenthau is attorney general of New York and a member of Temple Emanu-El. Their Jewish and American identities had and have merged.

Some Our Crowd Jews were apparently more bored with their group than disaffected or opposed. They became progressively less Jewish to escape from the essential sameness of their social set, the stress on finance, the German roots and the Jewish background. Recalls writer Jill Capron, daughter of the late newspaper publisher, J. David Stern, "My mother wanted to get away from Our Crowd. She wanted a more interesting life." Recalling her own youth, Mrs. Capron says, "The Our Crowd in Philadelphia all married each other and settled in Elkins Park or Jenkintown. When they died, they married each other's widow." Mrs. Capron recalls that as a young woman she spent one summer acting at the Cleveland Playhouse. Somehow the Our Crowd Jews of Shaker Heights heard she was in town and deluged her with dinner invitations, attempting to draw her back into the fold. The same sort of Our Crowd networks existed in Pittsburgh and St. Louis as well.

By the end of World War II, the terms *Spanish, German* and *Russian Jews* had essentially lost their old social impact. Though such terms are still used, relatively few today take such national origins seriously. Some German Jews still consider themselves the social elite of American Judaism. Yet intellectual accomplishment has tended to pass to the children and grandchildren of Russian Jewish immigrants.

Occasionally one still finds traces of snobbery. Some Spanish and Portuguese write *Samekh tet* after their name. These are the Hebrew letters that signify "Sephardic pure," meaning they can trace their roots to Spain. The Moroccans from Casablanca look down on the Moroccans from Fez—and vice versa. At a recent party an importer said proudly to his dinner partner, "We Syrian Jews are the German Jews of the Arab world."

Two couples recently had dinner together. The hosts were Lynn and Norman—she a fourth-generation Midwestern German Jew; he a second-generation Polish musicologist. (Her first marriage had been to an Our Crowd Wall Streeter, but she divorced him.) The guest couple consisted of Jan, another fourth-generation German Jew, and her psychologist husband of Hungarian descent. The talk turned to a revival of *Fiddler on the Roof,* and both women declared, "I won't go. It's too Jewish. I didn't come from a background like that." The musicologist looked at his wife and guest with pity: "I'm sorry for the two of you. You're culturally deprived."

Such a perception is a marked change from the 1930s when the coowner of Camp Accomac, a camp in Hillside, Maine, for Our Crowd daughters, agonized over admitting two sisters, saying, "Such lovely girls, but they are Russians."

THE NEW "JEWISH" JEWS

The effect of the Holocaust, creation of the State of Israel, the search for roots and its cognate—a meaning for living, the shift to more basic values have for many made the old German-Jewish attitudes seem rather snobbish, foolish and outdated. Today Jews tend to feel a deeper commitment to their Jewishness. Some of the old Our Crowd Jews have turned more Jewish. Even vocabularies have changed. One no longer hears those two familiar words of the pre–World War II era: *assimilation* and *nouveaux.* Assimilation has tended to go out of style, and nouveaux

Jews are what they are. In fact, the most *nouveaux* are those who have affirmed or reaffirmed their Jewishness. The enormous popularity of novelists such as Cynthia Freeman and Belva Plain, as well as the works of Elie Wiesel, can at least in part attest to this.

According to Barbara Tuchman, writing in *Commentary,* "The German experience of annihilation was the experience that turned assimilationists into supporters of statehood, anti-Zionists into reluctant pro-Zionists. Nor was it Hitler alone who accomplished the change but the reaction of the Western democracies—the lack of protest, the elaborate do-nothing international conferences, the pious evasions, the passive connivance in which Hitler read his cue, the avoidance of rescue, the American refusal to loosen immigration quotas when death camps were the alternative, the refusal of even temporary shelter, the turning back of refugee ships filled with those rescued by Jewish efforts . . .

"The accumulation of these things slowly brought to light what had long lurked in the shadows of ancient memory: a bitter recognition that a Gentile world—with all due respect to notable and memorable exceptions—would fundamentally have felt relieved by the Final Solution. That the Jewish 'establishment' came to believe this about the Gentiles can not be documented because it was the great unmentionable, too painful to acknowledge, but basically this is what shattered the faith of the assimilationists and brought out the funds for the support of Israel."

The statehood of Israel has indeed made Jewishness not only acceptable but fashionable. (An influential member of the Federation of Jewish Philanthropies of New York recently said with undisguised scorn, "Margaret Kempner and Benjamin Buttenwieser are still talking about assimilation!"). Says feisty Jack D. Weiler, a real estate tycoon, "Israel has made Jews proud. Jews aren't known as cowards anymore. People have respect for Israel's accomplishments and what it stands for. Because of Israel, Jews can hold their heads higher. They can be proud to be a Jew. In thirty-three years they have built a whole nation."

In *The Jews of America* Max Dimont writes, "The birth of Israel solved all problems for all sects. One no longer had to make up one's mind: history had made the choice. The Reform discovered, as Brandeis had assured them, that there was no conflict of dual loyalty—one could be American and pro-Israel. The Orthodox discovered, as their own rabbis assured them, that no conflict of dogma was involved—one could have the state of Israel first and the Messiah later. Only two groups were left out in the cold—the extreme right wing Orthodox still denying the legitimacy of Israel, and the extreme right wing Reform, still proclaiming that Judaism was only a religion." (The term *right wing* has no political overtones; it is used to signify an extreme degree of religion.)

The fate of the American Council for Judaism, an organization dedicated to fighting Zionism and composed mainly of German Jewish men and women, illustrates the change in attitude. The ACJ was born in 1943 after discussions held in the summer and fall of 1942 among a number of rabbis, including Louis Wolsey of Temple Rodeph Shalom, Philadelphia (he was dubbed "Cardinal Wolsey" by Zionists), Samuel Goldenson of Temple Emanu-El, New York, and Irving Reichert of Temple Emanu-El, San Francisco. They enlisted the aid of lay people, and the philanthropist Lessing Rosenwald, who had been chairman of the board of Sears, Roebuck and Company, became its president and agreed to underwrite the expenses of the group. Rabbi Elmer Berger (termed by a fellow rabbi as "wildly anti-Zionist; nobody was enough of a Reform Jew to suit him") became the ACJ's executive vice-president, a post he would hold until the 1967 Israeli-Arab War.

The ACJ flourished even during the Holocaust, issuing broadsides, answering statements and making many of its own. Many prominent German Jews belonged, including Henry Loeb, an investment banker and the late Richard K. Korn, the conductor. The ACJ took the position that Judaism is a religion and not a nationality. Many members also feared Zionism more than anti-Semitism. The latter, they felt, could be overcome with the help of Gentile allies. A Jewish state, however, would be an ever-present wedge between the Jew and Gentile. The Jew would now be seen as the member of a national minority group and what if the policy of the Jewish nation clashed with that of the United

States? Would a century of Jewish-American achievement be wiped out?

By the early 1950s the ACJ had greatly lessened in influence, with founder member Malcolm Stern admitting, "I recognized the council for what it had become, an apologetic group of Jews uncomfortable in their Judaism. The achievements of Israel were giving the rest of us growing *nachas*—gratification and pride."

It took the 1967 Arab-Israeli Six-Day War to deliver the *coup de grace* to the council in terms of further effectiveness. At that time, as thousands of American Jews became so caught up with the cause of the Israelis that they flooded the United Jewish Appeal Israeli Emergency Fund with contributions that totaled more than $20 million, Rabbi Berger gave an interview to Albin Krebs of the *New York Times*. The *Times* article on July 16, 1967 stated that in the view of ACJ members, the American emotional reaction amounted to "hysteria."

The *Times* article also mentioned names of ACJ members, including Stanley Marcus, president of Neiman-Marcus, Henry Loeb of the brokerage concern Loeb Rhoades and Company, Walter N. Rothschild, president of Abraham & Straus; Donald F. Klopfer, vice-president of Random House, Inc.; John Mosler, chairman of the Mosler Safe Company and president of the Urban League of Greater New York; and Joseph H. Loucheim, deputy commissioner in charge of the State Department of Social Welfare's New York City Division. According to a formerly active ACJ member, those named were outraged, and the council lost their support.

Berger went on to write a book, *Memories of an Anti-Zionist Jew,* and to found the group American Jewish Alternatives to Judaism. The council still exists but is no longer a force. Some former council members have become active in the rapidly growing American Reform Zionist Association. ARZA, according to Rabbi Stern, has become a political factor in the World Zionist Organization, speaking out for the "non-Orthodox elements in Israel."

Still, old attitudes die long and hard. In 1973 the Federation of Jewish Philanthropies of New York sponsored a dinner honoring William Rosenwald (a Zionist) of the Sears Roebuck family on his seventieth birthday. His brother Lessing, the ACJ founder, was to make the presentation. Lessing didn't come down from his hotel room until the fundraising for Israel was finished.

A CHANGE IN IDEOLOGY

As well as a new awareness of Jewish heritage, the shift in values among present-day elite Jews shows up in a lessening of plumage and the spending of leisure time.

In 1914 when eighteen-year-old Gladys Guggenheim married twenty-two-year old Roger Williams Straus in the Grand Ballroom of the St. Regis, the young couple took their vows under a canopy of white roses and smilax, sustained by eight columns of silver. The idea: that no one should forget the metal that paved the way for this moment.

Elinor Guggenheimer recalls that in her youth there would be huge balls at the Ritz-Carlton followed at 11:30 P.M. by an act from a Broadway show. Today's young JEP set goes to discos or the movies. Felix Warburg's Fifth Avenue home has become part of the Jewish Museum.

The late Wilfred May, editor of *The Commercial and Financial Chronicle,* who died in 1969, a man of slight build and bookish appearance who suffered from Parkinson's disease, used to give an annual Easter luncheon in the Persian Room of New York's Plaza Hotel. May liked having important people as guests, men and women in the news. A female friend, Marge Wels handled the yearly seating of some two hundred well-known guests. Says Mrs. Wels, a well-known decorator married to a third-generation German Jewish lawyer, "Today nobody would want to go to something like that luncheon. Young people are into different things. They would find it a pest."

As a further sign of change, the Persian Room at the Plaza has been converted into a series of shops. Money-making practicality has, it seems, replaced elegance.

The matter of dancing classes reflects another change in the Jewish social world. According to Enid Goldsmith, ninety-three, of Scarsdale, New York, the late Viola Wolff started her dancing classes in 1932, in the middle of the Depression, when husband Walter Wolff's woolen business was doing badly. A friend suggested, "You love to dance. Why not have a school? Use my playhouse." The school expanded from the Tarrytown playhouse until classes were held in a variety of locations in Westchester and Manhattan. "When Viola started, everyone knew everyone else. Those friends told others. She never did any advertising," recalls Mrs. Goldsmith. For several decades attendance at Viola Wolff's was a social must for the sons and daughters of the members of Our Crowd.

Her son Bob Roland of Naples, Florida, remembers, "She made many romances. She was a matchmaker by nature."

Today the attitude is different. Comments a Connecticut homemaker, "I went to Viola Wolff's. My sons went to dancing school at Greenwich Country Day and were so bored they climbed out the window."

For all her success and popularity, when Viola Wolff died in 1980, at ninety-two, there was not even a mention in the *New York Times.*

The change in values also shows up in country-club membership rosters. Many Our Crowd children do not choose the country-club way of life. They have other things to do on Sunday rather than play golf. When the sons of members do not join, outsiders become eligible, and thus Century Country Club, long a haven for Our Crowd Jews, has space for newcomers Messrs. Annenberg, Tisch and Bronfman.

The possession of enormous wealth with the accompanying lust for privacy and even secrecy about one's affairs has helped contribute to the relative obscurity of Our Crowd descendants. Some retired young to the peace of a vast estate. Other Our Crowd descendants clip coupons, sit on charitable boards and, more often than not, do not work in highly visible nine-to-five positions.

Edward M. M. Warburg (those *M'*s stand for *Mortimer Morris*), the only living son of Felix Warburg, banker and philanthropist, is, according to a Geoffrey Hellman article in the *New Yorker,* a "book art-collecting-Warburg." He was in his early thirties when he listed himself in the decennial yearbook of his Harvard class ('30) as "Art patron and philanthropist." In later years he listed himself as "Executive and social service." Warburg has raised millions for Jewish causes but he has never had to work for a living.

SONS AND SONS-IN-LAW

The Our Crowders with strong sons survive. Most others are expiring peacefully. In the case of the Ochs-Wise-Sulzberger dynasty a strong daughter has power. Adolph Ochs grew up in Cincinnati. One night he went visiting at the home of the famous Reform rabbi Isaac Mayer Wise. There he met daughter Iphigene (called "Effie"), married her, and, in 1891 purchased the *New York Times.* At eighty-eight, their daughter Iphigene, named after her mother, is thus Wise's granddaughter, Ochs's only daughter and heir, the widow of former *Times* publisher Arthur Hays Sulzberger, and mother of current *Times* publisher Arthur Ochs Sulzberger, known as "Punch." Reportedly, four of her thirteen grandchildren work at the paper.

In *Iphigene: Memoirs of Iphigene Ochs Sulzberger of The New York Times Family,* she describes what happened when her ailing husband Arthur had become chairman of the board and son-in-law Orville Dryfoos, who had taken over as publisher, died on May 23, 1963, of a heart attack following a 114-day strike. She and Arthur had to decide who would take over as publisher. They ruled out Amory Bradford, *Times* general manager, who had shown himself during the strike to be "an arrogant man who didn't get along well with people." For three weeks they considered the alternatives and then, "wanting to keep the *Times* a family enterprise if possible," they named their son "Punch" as the new publisher. Predictably, Bradford resigned.

As noted, Oscar Straus served American long and well. So did his son Roger Williams Straus, a founder of the National Conference of Christians and Jews and chancellor of the New York State Board of Regents. His son Roger, Jr., heads Farrar, Straus & Giroux, a book-publishing firm. After apprenticing in his father's firm, Roger III joined Times Books and is therefore in competition with Farrar, Straus & Giroux.

A few of the remaining Our Crowders possess the same spirit that enabled their ancestors to become leading entrepreneurs. In November, 1979, Walter A. Haas, Jr., sixty-five, chairman of Levi Strauss & Company and great-grandnephew of the gold-rush outfitter Levi Strauss, together with son Walter J. and son-in-law Roy Eisenhardt, bought the Oakland A's baseball team for $12.7 million.

However not all Jewish elite have been fortunate with their sons. The original Meyer Guggenheim, founder of the smelting clan, had seven. When these sons started to beget female off-spring instead of male, the Guggenheim family sinew commenced to fade. In other cases, lack of sons signified a breakdown of family business continuity. Today there are no Wertheims at Wertheim & Company; Klingensteins head the firm. Banker Maurice Wertheim, who died in 1950, had three daughters—Josephine, Anne and Barbara (Tuchman)—and no sons. Says one of the present partners, "If Barbara Tuchman had wanted to be a merchant banker, she could have been."

In other instances the story has a rather sadder ending. Walter Annenberg's son, slated to command the family publishing empire, committed suicide, but now his daughter Wallis works at the *TV Guide,* Los Angeles, headquarters of Triangle Publications, Inc. and many feel she is destined for command.

SIMILARITIES BETWEEN OUR CROWD AND THE JEPS

Present-day JEPs tend to want the same inbred continuity that meant success for the Our Crowd founding fathers. They too achieve it with the help of sons and sons-in-law. At Swig, Weiler and Arnow Management Company, a real estate concern, Jack D. Weiler, chairman, says "My son-in-law Bob Arnow is the best thing that ever happened to me. He runs the show." In 1974, Robert Arnow was named president of the realty company, which includes such extensive holdings as the Fairmont Hotels in San Francisco and Dallas and 1411 Broadway, New York. Weiler's son, Alan Weiler, a lawyer, shares a mammoth corner office with his father in the Grace Building at the corner of Forty-second Street and Avenue of the Americas, New York City, and performs all the legal work for the firm and family. Says the senior Weiler proudly, "He's known as the best real estate lawyer in the city."

Recognized internationally for his philanthropy, Jack Weiler came to the United States from Russia at five and a half and grew up in the Bronx. While he had only one year at City College, he recently received the degree of doctor of philosophy *honoris causa* from Bar-Ilan University, Ramat Gan, Israel. The only successful member of eleven children, he makes it a rule that only his immediate family works for him. He feels strongly about family participation: "You don't want to build an empire and have it deteriorate. You want your own family involved in the ownership. The whole idea is to have it go on and on. At the same time it's important to teach your children and grandchildren how to give to the proper causes, not lead a selfish life and to spread their wealth. My son and son-in-law are doing exactly that. That's the highlight of anything I can teach."

The Swig in Swig, Weiler and Arnow stands for Benjamin Harrison Swig, who died in 1980 at eighty-six, a self-made man whose father had emigrated from Lithuania at fourteen and started as a peddler. The Swig-Weiler partnership was based on a handshake and endured without an argument for fifty years until Swig's death. Today his son Richard serves as president of the Fairmont Hotel Company and the Weiler and Swig families reportedly still split all profits.

At Amerada Hess, the ruggedly independent and publicity-shy Leon Hess, son of a Lithuanian immigrant, serves as chairman of the board and chief executive officer of this major oil company. His son John, a vice-president and director of the company, holds the title "coordinator of planning and control," and according to *Business Week,* "is apparently being groomed for better things." A nephew, Nathan K. Trynin, is senior vice-president for international exploration and production. Hess's octogenarian father-in-law, David Wilentz, also sits on the board. Wilentz, a native of Lithuania, had been attorney general of New Jersey in 1936 when the Lindbergh kidnapping trial was held and he personally prosecuted Richard Bruno Hauptmann.

The founding father of the famous Pritzker family, Nicholas J. Pritzker, migrated to Chicago from Kiev in 1880 at the age of nine. His son A. N. (A for Abraham) is now the "Papa Bear" of the clan; son Jay controls hundreds of companies and is chairman of the Hyatt Corporation and Hyatt International. Jay Pritzker's son Tom is president of the Hyatt Corporation and another son John is general manager of Hyatt Lincolnwood.

Loews Corporation serves as another example of current JEP dynastic management. Laurence, chairman, and his brother Preston Robert, president, work closely together. Laurence Tisch's oldest son Andrew is president of the Bulova Watch Company, which is owned by Loews. James, third of the four sons, also works for the company.

THE WORK FACTOR

Our Crowd forebears made news through speeches, predictions, activities, financial acumen, successful deals. Above all, they were workers. The late Otto H. Kahn, a senior partner at Kuhn Loeb & Company, was known to work an eighteen-hour day and almost always went to his office on Saturday. On one such Saturday he usurped some of his partners' offices and held five simultaneous meetings, ranging from a discussion of railroad bonds to a talk with a Metropolitan Opera soprano about her contract. Kahn darted from one office to another until he had settled everything to his satisfaction.

"In one day," wrote columnist Lincoln Schuster, "Otto Kahn can lay three cornerstones, endow a new opera house, attend *Chauve-Souris,* the Ziegfeld Follies and the Theatre Guild, occupy his box at the Diamond Horseshoe, preside at banquets of the Art League and the Authors Club, welcome a dozen visiting virtuosi at the pier, address a music-week meeting in the Bronx, reorganize two defunct railroads, float an international loan and issue a formal ukase against the excess profits tax, all without impairing the inimitable twirl of his silver white mustache."

Franklin P. Adams distilled Kahn's life into a couplet:

The sun it never shone upon
A busier man than Otto Kahn

Like Otto Kahn, many of today's JEPs are also workaholics. A circle is being completed; a new invigoration is taking place.

Alan Greenberg, chief executive officer, Bear, Stearns & Company, a mild-mannered, balding man who sits in the trading room in shirt sleeves, works, plays (he is a national bridge champion), fundraises (UJA and the American Jewish Committee) and gives major contributions to the University of Oklahoma in memory of his mother.

Greenberg started as a clerk at Bear, Stearns & Company. Instead of going out for lunch, he used that time to visit the trading room. One day a senior member of the firm asked him, "What do you do?" Greenberg answered, "I work in back." The man countered, "Would you like to work here?" Given his chance, Greenberg quickly rose in the firm.

In 1978, the Fourth of July holiday fell on a Tuesday and many Wall Streeters, feeling business would be slow on Monday, took a four-day holiday. Not Greenberg. He went to the office, where he conceived an idea for Resorts International, involving the exchange of common stock for Warrants. He recalls, "I called Resorts International and found out that because of an SEC problem, it had to be done that day. By 6:30 P.M. we had completed the proposal. It was lucky that someone had also come in that Monday at Resorts International. We got a good fee. If you figure it on the basis of hourly work, it was ridiculous." When the announcement of the Warranty exchange appeared in the newspapers, there was the sentence, "The undersigned acted as financial advisor to Resorts International, Inc. BEAR, STEARNS & CO., Members of the New York Stock Exchange, Inc."

Ivan F. Boesky, the energetic forty-five-year-old securities arbitrageur who heads Ivan F. Boesky Corporation, sleeps about four hours a night. He leaves his suburban home at 5:00 A.M., arrives at his desk at 1 State Street Plaza in lower Manhattan about an hour later. The light is still faint on the Hudson River. A lone security guard is the only other person there.

"From 6:00 to 9:00 A.M. I have a lot of appointments," says the slim, graying Boesky. "At 9:00 I get focused on the securities world, following hundreds of securities in which we have an interest. I do not eat lunch. I have appointments with merchant bankers. I have appointments in midtown, and these may go on until evening. I am highly scheduled." (A member of a rival firm once told the *Wall Street Journal,* "Boesky may be the only man who could get a *Fortune* 500 chairman out of the bathroom to talk at seven o'clock in the morning.")

In addition to work, Boesky gives an enormous amount of time to philanthropy; he started this at fourteen when he was "head of the young Jewish community in Detroit."

The son of a "self-made upper-middle-class Detroit businessman who came from Russia at twelve and was in business for himself at sixteen," Boesky attended Cranbrook ("That's our Exeter"), then the University of Michigan, first became a lawyer, then switched to accounting and eventually entered the Wall Street world of finance. In 1975 he formed his own company and has been extraordinarily successful in the complex world of securities arbitrage. His belief: "Anyone with talent has the ability to succeed if he is willing to work." The articulate Boesky adds, "The feeling of achievement comes from confidence. Mastery comes from hard work."

Connections have always signified power. Our Crowd Jews had them. Enterprising JEPs have them too.

It was a Jew who enabled Mrs. Lincoln, widow of the assassinated president, to receive a pension. When the Civil War began on April 16, 1861, with the firing on Fort Sumter, the most prominent German-American of Jewish birth was August Belmont, the agent of the Rothschilds. When the war ended, Joseph Seligman, after founding an international banking firm, had taken first place. His was a true Horatio Alger success story —the German boy who rose from peddler to figure of national importance who is remembered in the name of two American towns, one in Arizona, the other in Missouri.

Seligman was an early member of the Republican Party, where he became so prominent that for many years he was elected a vice-president of the Union League Club, together with Peter Cooper and William Cullen Bryant. He was among those who urged Lincoln to name Ulysses Grant to the high command. As president, Grant had the Seligmans appointed the fiscal agents of the State and Navy departments, offices they held through numerous Republican administrations. Grant offered Joseph Seligman the secretaryship of the Treasury.

The eight Seligman brothers were active in Jewish affairs. Henry Seligman had served as president of Temple Emanu-El in San Francisco. In later years brother James was president of Temple Emanu-El in New York, and brother Isaac, a foremost member of London's chief synagogue. Joseph was a founder of the Hebrew Orphan Asylum. He supported Dr. Felix Adler and became the first president of the Society for Ethical Culture, but remained proud of his religion, from which he was unwilling to become disassociated. There is the anecdote of his caustic reply to his brother William, when that head of the French branch of the banking firm suggested that the family, having arrived socially as well as financially, should change its Jewish name. "An excellent idea," replied Joseph, "but we might as well keep our initial letter, and for you I suggest the name Shlemiel."

Seligman's influence in government was greater than Mary Lincoln's. Lincoln's widow was so disliked by the American public that Charles Sumner had been unable to persuade his fellow senators to vote her a pension. With her youngest son she had left the country.

Henry Seligman, head of the German branch of the banking firm, found her in an old ramshackle house in Frankfurt, in seemingly impoverished circumstances. Thereupon he wrote a long and eloquent letter to three of his senatorial friends. "Why had you dear sir," he told Carl Schurz, general in the Civil War, senator from Missouri and later minister to Spain, "seen her as I have done last New Year living in a small street in the third floor in 2 dirty rooms with hardly if any furniture, all alone, grieved and nearly heartbroken, you would have said with me:

'Can it be possible that the wife of our great man lives in such a way, & is our Nation not indebted to him who gave up his life for the sake of freedom?' "

In July, 1870, after the Seligman letters, a yearly pension of $3,000 was approved by Congress.

It's not so different today. No one would suggest that Leon Hess made a poor choice of a father-in-law in David T. Wilentz, for many years a powerful New Jersey Democrat. Having Wilentz as a company insider could not help but bring Hess closer to the sources of power. According to a report in *Fortune* (January 1970), Hess had the help of New Jersey's then Democratic Governor Richard J. Hughes when he decided to build his Virgin Islands refinery, and another active supporter was Ralph M. Paiewonsky, then the Democratic governor of the islands. He had the support of Governor Paiewonsky and the New Jersey Democrats in Congress in his successful bid to obtain an oil-import allocation for the Virgin Islands refinery, and the bid was also ardently backed by Congressman Michael Kirwan, the Ohio Democrat who headed the House Interior Appropriations Subcommittee, and Congressman Wayne Aspinall, the Colorado Democrat, chairman of the Interior Committee.

Another instance of the importance of the connection factor: the late Nat Holman, who for many years served as basketball coach at City College, also ran a summer camp, Scatico, in Elizaville, New York. One of the campers then was Marvin Davis, now the three-hundred-pound millionaire oil executive who recently took over Twentieth Century-Fox ("He was a sort of schleppy kid; when we chose teams, nobody wanted him," recalls a fellow bunkmate, now a Wall Street figure). It was Ira Harris, a virtuoso of the merger field, with Salomon Brothers, Chicago, who salvaged the Twentieth Century-Fox deal with Davis when observers believed it had collapsed. Both he and Davis were vacationing in Palm Beach. Harris was once a waiter at Camp Scatico.

New elite Jews make parties just as the remnants of Our Crowd still do. But for many the tone is more explicitly Jewish.

It is this Jewish identity that marks a major difference between old guard and new.

Every year Jack Weiler goes to enormous expense and effort to construct a "Sukkah in the Sky" on the roof of Manhattan's fifty-story Grace Building to celebrate Sukkoth. (Sukkoth is the Feast of the Booths, a fall harvest festival which commemorates the pioneer days of the Jewish people when they lived in tents during their exodus from Egypt before entering the promised land. *Sukkah* means "booth" and is built in a certain traditional way.)

Weiler's temporary structure, which he claims is "the highest Sukkah in the world," has the traditional thatched roof and wooden sides. To build it, Weiler breaks through brick and even installs portable toilets. The Sukkah can accommodate 100 sitting down. Each day for a week, Weiler plays host at a dairy-food buffet luncheon for members of such organizations as the United Jewish Appeal, New York Board of Rabbis, Joint Distribution Committee, Israel Bonds. The organizations change yearly. Guests range from the Israeli ambassador to politicians to hundreds of youngsters from local yeshivas.

Peggy Tishman represents the attitude of many when she comments, "The Sukkah is marvelous. If Jack forgets to invite me, I call up and invite myself."

Says Weiler, "We started having this annual Sukkoth celebration seven years ago when the building was finished. Since then many others have copied us. For many guests it is the first time they have ever seen a Sukkah. When the late Arthur Levitt, the city comptroller, came, he said, 'This is the closest I have ever been to God!' "

Jews in America have indeed come a long way.

4

BREAKING THROUGH THE BUSINESS BARRIERS

"PEOPLE USED to think of Jews as pushy. Now they call us motivated."

So says fifty-eight-year-old Frank Lautenberg, chairman and chief executive officer of Automatic Data Processing, a firm with 1981 revenues of over $558 million and whose worth has been estimated at $900 million.

The difference between the words *pushy* and *motivated* is significant. It means that Jews, often from lower-middle-class backgrounds, have broken through the WASP corporate curtain and are currently changing their image from maverick and entrepreneur to team player.

Lautenberg sees "the coming of the Jew in corporate life as a postwar phenomenon. It became respectable to hire Jews in the corporate hierarchy. These Jews had gone to business school. They had portable skills. They did not have to be a doctor, lawyer, jeweler. Suddenly there was an inclination to accept the Jew, a recognition that Jews had talent—that they could be as valuable in corporate business as in their own business. Jews were given the opportunity. That is when Jews began to change."

Were Jews "given the opportunity" or did they use their own talent, drive and instinct for survival to create that opportunity? How did "My son the doctor" become "My son the corporate president"? Do Jews still have to create their own business to become "first-class citizens" in the executive suite? How do Gentiles feel about Jews in the corporate hierarchy?

SOME PSYCHOLOGICAL ATTITUDES

Most people seem to think that the history of executive-suite bias goes back to the anti-Semitism of medieval Europe and to discrimination in the guilds. However, executive-suite discrimination in the United States is relatively new. Jews figured prominently in the commerce of colonial America. Haym Salomon, who had come from Poland, worked closely with William Morris and the Continental Congress as a broker and helped raise a particularly large sum for the revolution. For his services he was given the official title "Broker to the Office of Finance."

Even as recently as the Civil War, prejudice in the boardroom hardly existed. As free America prospered, Jews prospered too. They founded many of the mercantile stores (Straus, Kaufmann, Rich), were among the first cotton brokers (Lehman) and investment bankers (Kuhn, Loeb).

As America changed from an agricultural to an industrial nation during the latter half of the nineteenth century, Jews again played a key role in founding new industries and financing others. But, as the economy prospered, a change took place which affected Jewish and Christian entrepreneurs alike. To underwrite expansion, captains of industry had to acquire additional capital. The financial institutions from which they borrowed—chiefly the big Anglo-Saxon-controlled banks of Boston and New York—demanded a share of the operation of the business, including the right to install their own representatives in the corporate hierarchy.

Up to the last decades of the nineteenth century or the beginning of the twentieth, most corporations had been operated by individual founders or their families. Now responsible positions were more and more filled by professional managers, representing financial institutions. And these professionals, bank nominated, tended to be Anglo-Saxon Protestants, the type bankers knew best. They were "people like us" who "spoke our language," "safe" people who had come from the "right" families, gone to the "right" schools, belonged to the "right" clubs and attended the "right" churches.

Somewhere along the way a series of myths became ensconced in the corporate mentality: (1) that Jews were too impatient for the long grind of corporate advancement—a tenet that someone as astute as conglomerate head Laurence Tisch still avows. Management could always prove this by the dearth of applications. (2) Jews entered Jewish rather than Christian businesses because they were "clannish" and "preferred their own kind." (3) The Jews wanted to be entrepreneurs rather than employees.

Aware of the barriers in heavy industry, shipping, banking and insurance, Jews turned elsewhere. They established and guided the American movie industry and helped found advertising.

In 1936 when anti-Jewish restrictionism was at its peak, *Fortune* magazine made a survey of Jews' impact on American economic life and named clothing manufacture, tobacco buying and the scrap-metal trade as essentially Jewish businesses. *Fortune* also found substantial Jewish participation in meat packing, distilling, textile converting, boot and shoe production and upholstered furniture manufacturing. In addition, Jews have been prominent in wholesaling as well as more recently in new industries such as plastics, air conditioning, electronics and frozen foods.

In the last thirty-five years, boardroom mentality has changed. Gentiles have realized that Jews can work in the corporate structure. Says Henry Taub, founder of Automatic Date Processing, "To compete, a corporation must draw on the best talent and people. If it does not, the business will not achieve its full potential." Companies have acknowledged that if they do not hire Jews, they are overlooking a pool of professional talent.

There were always corporations that recognized the merits of outstanding individuals. The late Sidney J. Weinberg, partner in Goldman, Sachs & Company, one of Wall Street's leading investment houses, never went beyond the eighth grade and started at Goldman, Sachs as a janitor. Yet his financial wizardry won him the title "Mr. Wall Street." At one point he was on thirty-five boards of directors, including the Ford Motor Company, often thought of as an anti-Semitic company. When he died in 1968 at seventy-seven, he was still on the Ford board.

Jewish attitudes have also changed. "American Jews now wish to work for American corporations and wish to compete," claims forty-three-year-old businessman Lewis Lehrman, grandson of an immigrant peddler. "Anti-Semitism never excluded them. Now Jewish children are educated in professional schools and are recruited by banks and companies." (Lehrman, who, according to *Forbes* of June 8, 1981, has been a "mentor" to David Stockman, Reagan's director of the budget, divides his time between the Lehrman Corporation, the family money-management firm, and the Lehrman Institute, a think tank, and is currently trying to enter politics.)

So has Jewish behavior changed in the eyes of others. Alluding to the hero of the 1941 Budd Schulberg novel, Taub comments, "You do not see too many what makes Sammy run around anymore."

For their part Jews have recognized that while going to Groton, Harvard and Harvard Business School proves helpful in getting into a big-league, primarily WASP company, it is not necessary. One can be a Jewish lawyer from a poor background and make it to the top echelon of the executive suite. Irving Shapiro, whose rise to the top of Du Pont reads like a New World sequel to *Fiddler on the Roof,* serves as the prime model for every ambitious MBA.

The Shapiro Saga

Irving Shapiro's father, an impoverished immigrant from Lithuania, worked as a pants presser in a dry cleaning shop in Minneapolis. At home there was hardly enough food or heat and young Irving wore shoes with soles of cardboard. He suffered intensely from asthma and allergies. Father Sam Shapiro, who fled from a harsh life in Lithuania, was determined his eldest son should become a lawyer. Although Shapiro leaned toward becoming an accountant, he bowed to his father's wishes, took a prelaw course across town at the University of Minnesota, then went on to law school (class of '41) and graduated fourth in his class. Poker helped pay for his education.

Unable to pass his army physical examination because of his asthma history, he spent the war as a lawyer with the Office of Price Administration in Washington, D.C. Later he moved to the Criminal Division of the Justice Department, where he earned a reputation as a superb writer of briefs. In 1951 he was offered a legal job at Du Pont and Shapiro moved his family to Wilmington. He soon became heavily involved in the government antitrust suit charging Du Pont and many members of the Du Pont family with conspiring to control General Motors. When the Supreme Court overturned Du Pont's victory at Chicago, and ordered the company to divest itself not only of General Motors but of its monopolistic holdings all down the line, Irving Shapiro was the lawyer who drew up the plan the Court eventually accepted. It was said to have been so carefully and brilliantly constructed that it saved the Du Pont family nearly a billion dollars in stock it might otherwise have had to sell. Shapiro also won enormous respect for his counsel on such difficult decisions as the abandonment of Corfam and on his negotiation of the merger of Christiana Securities Company into Du Pont.

Most of Shapiro's friends think his ultimate ambition was to become Du Pont's general counsel. But in December, 1973, he was elected chairman and chief executive officer of E. I. Du Pont de Nemours & Company, at the time the twenty-third largest industrial enterprise in the world and possessor of one of the most famous and patrician names in American business. The son of a poor Jewish shopkeeper had moved to the top of the most family-dominated of the nation's major corporations, becoming the second chairman in history who was not related to the Du Pont family.

At the time many businessmen said, "Some of the Du Ponts must have turned over in their graves when Shapiro took charge." His son Stuart stated, "It was an absolute bombshell. A Jew does not become chairman of Du Pont."

But to others it was not such a surprise. Shapiro himself said, "It's the American system that has paid off. The opportunity was there and my family said 'Get an education.' There is plenty of benefit in the way the system operates if we use it the way it is supposed to be used." Shapiro retired in April, 1981, to begin a new career as an attorney with the New York law firm of Skadden, Arps, Slate, Meagher & Flom in its branch office in Wilmington. He continues as director and chairman of Du Pont's Finance Committee.

Breaking Through

The corporate success of Irving Shapiro did not just happen. Frank Greenberg did not inherit his post as head of Burlington Industries nor Ross Barzelay his as vice chairman of General Foods nor Irwin Lerner his as president/chief executive officer of Hoffmann-La Roche Inc. nor Stanley Gewirtz his as vice-president of employee communications for Pan American World Airways (airlines are traditionally non-Jewish firms). These events were foreshadowed by a series of successful businessmen who paved the way.

They found room at the top, overcoming anti-Semitism in the process. Consider Jacob M. Kaplan, at ninety still erect and articulate, the son of an Orthodox rabbi from a rabbinical family that had lived for several generations in Riyalistok, Russia. Kaplan was born on a farm outside of Lowell, Massachusetts, on December 23, 1891, and started selling newspapers at the age of five. He sold more papers than any boy in the five-to-ten-year-old age group. On rare occasions he treated himself to a cupcake for two cents. This made him feel like a spendthrift and he would wonder if the time would ever come when he would no longer experience such remorse. At home the family talked Yiddish and not English. Kaplan was twelve and in the eighth grade when his mother died (his father, a Talmudic scholar, had died when he was nine) and Kaplan quit school. Eventually, with the help of his half-brother from his mother's earlier marriage, Kaplan went into the molasses business, where he remained for twenty years, living in Cuba, Santo Domingo, Mexico, the Philippines and Java—all sugar-producing areas.

When a world cartel paid his asking price, a handsome one,

for not competing in the field, Kaplan sold his company. After some months of business inactivity, he went to Chautauqua, New York, on a social visit, rented an old Ford car and toured the area, where the grape-growing farmers were in desperate straits because they were unable to compete with the "table-grape" producers of California. Kaplan assumed the direction of a small bankrupt group of grape growers who were unable to sell their grape juice. Believing that grape juice could be merchandised at a price not higher than Coca-Cola, he bought their whole operation in 1933.

Kaplan persevered, increasing grape juice and jelly sales, and selling to A & P, Kroger, Safeway and others under their labels. After seven or eight years he bought the Welch Company, which had belonged to the Welch family for three generations but was experiencing hard times. Kaplan rebuilt the Welch Company and inaugurated a policy which made business history.

He gathered together all of the two thousand grape growers in seven states and, through tremendous perserverance, "that New York Jew" organized them into a single cooperative, the National Grape Growers Co-Op Association. After a few years the growers, at first skeptical, pooled their grape production. They began to see many benefits and became almost single-crop growers because Kaplan encouraged and financed grape growing and guaranteed excellent services and prices. Eventually they came to Kaplan to say they feared an unknown owner in the event that something might happen to Kaplan.

That's when Kaplan made it possible for that Co-Op group of owners to buy the company for $25 million, all to be paid over the ensuing years by setting aside 10 percent of sales, which was actually Welch's profit at the time. It worked out that in less than ten years, the $25-million purchase price was accumulated. During that time the growers learned to work with the processing and marketing executives of Welch trained by Kaplan. At that point Kaplan turned over the presidency to a leader of the cooperative and moved out. Never during his presidency did he draw either salary or expenses for his tireless and ingenious services.

The whole saga did not come easily. It took Kaplan more than ten years to build the company and establish steady profitability and assured growth. During his ownership, seven plants in seven states were modernized and enlarged in the states of New York, Ohio, Pennsylvania, Michigan, Missouri, Arkansas and Washington. Kaplan initiated the cooperative as an ideal for these working farmers to democratically enjoy all the benefits of their united efforts.

Kaplan never sought to hide his religious origins, but they never stood in the way of his success. He constantly heard statements like "Here's a Jew from New York who's going to hook your guys. I don't know how he's going to do it because he's too smart. He's got a lot of fellows down in New York to figure it out." But he figured everything out himself, and it was the growers who benefited.

The Welch business has continued to grow steadily over the years and is now known and accepted nationally as the producer of fine grape products. Kaplan established the J. M. Kaplan Fund, which has given away about $30 million. His daughter Joan K. Davidson is now president.

They became as entrepreneurial as the Gentiles had before them. Explains Lewis Lehrman, "People talk about Jewish entrepreneurs. The entrepreneurial tradition is not an ethnic or class phenomenon. Newcomers are always entrepreneurs. Jewish immigrants were just latecomers to America. Most came around 1900. The most entrepreneurial business of the middle nineteenth century was that of a Scotch Presbyterian, Cyrus McCormick, who sold his reaper to humble farmers.

"America was built by entrepreneurs—people like John D. Rockefeller, E. H. Harriman, banker James Stillman. The first chain food store was built by Huntington Hartford. There were chains like Kresge and Woolworth. They succeeded because they had a good idea. That is the American way. It had nothing to do with race, creed or class."

Within this century three Jewish entrepreneurs stand out.

A Russian-born Jew, David Sarnoff, who grew up on the Lower East Side without a word of English when he arrived, was the pioneer in the great electronics industry with his Radio Corporation of America.

William Paley, who at eighty-one is still chairman of the board of CBS, took a few failing radio stations and shaped them into a giant communications empire. He was a child of immigrants, but not poor. In his autobiography, *As It Happened,* he explains that his family, who came from Russia in the late nineteenth century "was among the fortunate ones with a stake to invest in the new world." Bill Paley started out in his father Sam's cigar business. So in 1928 when through family friends and in-laws the chance came along to buy into a fledgling radio network called CBS, Sam Paley encouraged his son to get in on it and put up some $400,000 of the family money. Bill Paley was then twenty-seven years old. For fifty-four years he has been the supreme figure of modern merchandising, first in radio, then in television. He made the American home the focal point of the American marketplace, selling not just the American dream but an endless series of material products through whose purchase that dream might be realized.

Paley jumped aboard an existing merry-go-round. Inventor Edwin Herbert Land (born a Jew, bar mitzvahed, but according to relatives now not a practicing Jew) created a new free enterprise. An inventor (he holds an estimated 524 patents), Land was originally bankrolled by old-line money of W. Averell Harriman, James P. Warburg and Lewis Strauss. He developed a plastic sheet he called Polaroid that cut glare without distorting the light passing through it. He found a small but ready market in sunglasses, and made optical devices during World War II. Toward the end of the war, Land was in New Mexico with his family when three-year-old Jennifer asked why she could not see the pictures of herself that Land had just snapped. He thought about it, then took a long solitary walk around Santa Fe. When he returned he had worked out in his head the idea of an instant camera.

In 1980 Land stepped down as chief executive officer of Polaroid Corporation while remaining chairman and consultant for basic research (his stock is said to be worth around $80 million). Land has received some thirty or so medals and awards. He is a recipient of the National Medal of Science and the Presidential Medal of Freedom. An admiring executive at Kodak has said,

"Someday Edwin Land will be ranked with Thomas Edison, Alexander Graham Bell—and George Eastman."

There was a change in the business psyche that said service businesses had become part of the national scene. A service business fills a vacuum. The man who owns it usually has a good chance of having the field to himself for a while before competition starts. Nowhere does the "fill-a-vacuum" tenet show up more clearly than in the cases of four post–World War II Jewish businesses which, in each instance, started with an idea and subsequently *spawned whole new industries.*

The late Leon C. Greenebaum started at Metropolitan Distributors as a maintenance man in the garage of the trucking concern which was founded by his father with a horse and wagon. A year later he was promoted to dispatcher and later spent a year learning the office routine. Eventually he became president, in the process expanding Metropolitan into one of the largest truck-leasing concerns in the United States. He joined the Hertz Corporation as a director when it acquired Metropolitan, later becoming president. RCA took on Hertz in 1967 and Greenebaum became a director.

Greenbaum had an innovative business philosophy. He was convinced that Americans were gradually changing their thinking from the concept of ownership to rental or lease—not only of motor vehicles but of other kinds of equipment and merchandise such as boats, works of art, hospital devices. He once said, "Renting and leasing save a lot of the headaches that go with ownership, and after all, this is the age of convenience." The Hertz Rent-All Corporation, formed during the latter part of 1960, entered the field of party-supply rental, as well as hospital equipment and other merchandise. But, of course, Hertz's main business was the renting and leasing of cars and trucks.

Today one can rent everything from cars at airports to paintings from galleries—much as a result of Greenebaum's original concept.

At an early age Alfred S. Bloomingdale, son of Hiram and grandson of Lyman Bloomingdale, wanted none of the family business. "My ambition," he once said, "was to make as much money on my own as my family left me." After attending Brown, where he "majored in football," he ran a shipyard in Rye, and worked three years (despite his ambition) at Bloomingdale's. He spent the next ten years producing some twenty shows. He had inherited his father's love for the theater but success did not come easily. There is the often-told, perhaps apocryphal story of how Bloomingdale brought playwright George Kaufman to see a show he had backed that was having trouble out of town. After seeing a performance, Kaufman's advice to Bloomingdale was "Close the show and keep the store open nights."

Bloomingdale made more of a mark in a different kind of entertainment industry. He founded a credit-card company on the West Coast in 1950, later met with the Diners Club founders Frank McNamara and Ralph E. Schneider, and after two meetings the two systems were merged. Bloomingdale revolutionized the restaurant, hotel and night-club business as well as auto rentals, service stations, gift shops. Following the success of Diners, American Express, Hilton and many others issued the magic cards. Today Diners has approximately 4 million members worldwide and is issued in sixty currencies. The company has more than 450,000 hotels, motels, airlines, restaurants, stores and other participating establishments in its rank. Bloomingdale is no longer active.

Another concept that was to grow into an enormous industry was founded on the need for manpower. Elmer Winter, the self-made businessman from Milwaukee and a pioneer in the temporary office-help field, and his brother-in-law founded Manpower, Inc., in 1948. In 1954 it went public. In 1976 it was sold for $28 million to Parker Pen. Winter is also a lawyer, author of nine books, a prize-winning artist and the founder of Youthpower, a free job service for youths which operated for eight years.

His own family circumstances were "modest." His father owned a men's retail store where Winter always had a summer job. Forebears on his father's side were from Prague and on his mother's from Hungary. Winter was the youngest of three children. Older brother Jack is now a successful manufacturer of women's pants. ("He started with a warehouse in the basement of my father's store.") During the Depression, Winter washed dishes to get through the University of Wisconsin.

Winter had a law practice with his brother-in-law Aaron Scheinfeld. In 1948 an emergency struck their law office. Half the secretarial staff was out sick just when an important brief had to be prepared for the Supreme Court. And when an informal survey later convinced them of a widespread need for temporary office help for many kinds of situations, they set up Manpower Inc. Winter dropped law in 1953 to build Manpower Inc. full time.

Winter recalls, "We were widely copied. There were a large number of regional companies plus hundreds of small local companies. It wasn't a difficult business to get into. With modest capital you were in business. People who worked for us then went into their own business. There were thousands of offices with hundreds of people who had originally worked for us. Today some 5 million people work for temporary-help offices in the United States."

At Manpower, Winter always liked to serve as "family" to his branch managers. In one case, when one of his female branch managers, planning to be married, phoned him in tears to say she had no close relatives to attend her wedding, Winter hopped on a plane for Buffalo and proudly gave the bride away.

At seventy, Winter is hardly retired. He is a consultant to Parker Pen. He is currently working on Operation 4000, a project designed to find jobs for minority youth, is involved in the economic development of Israel. Winter works with local industry to penetrate the Gentile executive suite. He says, "We work with local insurance and utilities companies to get them to open the doors to Jews. There are a number of companies where the job has just not been done. On the other hand, the head of a local gas company told me, 'We'd hire a Jew in management, but Jews just don't think we are exciting.' "

He advises young people to get into service areas—as he did. Inaugurate a private mail corporation that can get mail across town in one day or a shredder service where companies deposit locked bags of mail. He notes that futurists, in this case Alvin Toffler in *The Third Wave,* feel that people in the years ahead will work out of their homes rather than offices. This will create needs for repair services, take-out deliveries. He says, "The great part of being an entrepreneur is that people will buy new ideas." He adds, "I like to take tough jobs. If someone else can do the job well, let me take one where there is trouble."

Winter has three *W*s that he feels every business person should use as guides.

- *Why?* Why are we doing this in this way. Is there another way? Ask "Why?" constantly.
- *What if?* What if something happens tomorrow—like a big law suit—that could affect the company. If you are running the company, this forces you to think ahead.
- *When?* When do you do the work that needs to be done? Constantly force yourself to adopt certain timetables. Otherwise there is a tremendous drift.

Yet another major industry started by a Jew is computer services. Thirty years ago the computing services did not exist. In 1980 computing services was a $14-billion industry. Predictions show that computing services as an industry will overtake computer manufacturing in size sometime during the middle of this decade.

Automatic Data Processing (then called Automatic Payroll, Inc) was founded by Henry Taub, son of a Polish immigrant, in 1949 for the express purpose of doing payrolls for companies at a realistic cost. When Frank Lautenberg joined the company as a part-time employee in 1952, it processed payrolls for twelve clients and had an annual revenue of about $35,000. Last year, revenues exceeded $550 million and there were over one hundred thousand clients, including many *Fortune* 500 firms. From a single storefront in Paterson, New Jersey, ADP now operates in over two hundred locations in the United States, the United Kingdom, Western Europe and Brazil.

Lautenberg represents a true JEP success story. Son of Eastern European immigrants, he grew up living above the neighborhood mom-and-pop store and sharing a bedroom with his sister. He recalls how, when he was ten, his father took him to the Paterson, New Jersey, mill where he worked. The manual machinery made an almost unbelievably loud noise. The rank smell of oil permeated the steamy air. "Do you hear that noise," asked his father. Cowed by the oppressive atmosphere, Frank nodded. His father took him by the hand, looked him in the eyes and said, "Do you see how dark and awful it is in here? *Never let yourself be put in a position where you have to work like this!*"

Lautenberg entered the computing business by accident. After graduating from Columbia Business School ("My uncle paid for my education—Uncle Sam"), he went to work for Prudential Insurance Company in the sales training program in Paterson. His office was in the same building as Taub's and the two men became friends. Fascinated by Taub's payroll project, Lautenberg went to work with him as a part-time salesman, and became full time in 1954.

He recalls, "The service included picking up the raw payroll data from the client, bringing it to our processing center and returning the finished payroll to the customer with checks ready for signature. The cost for the service in those early days was $25 for a 100-employee payroll. It would have taken the firm two days a week to process the same payroll. Henry and I only aspired to 'earn a living' one day from payroll service. We had no money, no capital. I used to go to work at 8:30 A.M., get home at 1:00. I had my first child in 1957. I used to see her at the 2:00-A.M. feeding. I never took a weekend off. If someone had suggested a $900-million company, it would have seemed as absurd as the idea that someday men would walk on the moon.

"When we started, there were six computers in the world. Now there are over 2 million. ADP did not computerize until 1961 when we brought in our first IBM 1401—twelve years after the founding of the company. We went public that same year. Anyone willing to gamble could have bought 100 shares of ADP for $300 at the time of our first underwriting. Today that investment would be worth $100,000 with dividends amounting to over $1,300 a year."

What began as a single-product company now provides dozens of services to diverse industries: banking and thrift institutions, auto dealers, brokerage firms, governments, manufacturers and wholesalers. In the space of thirty-three years ADP has moved from a single Underwood accounting machine to a processing environment in which almost half of ADP's nonpayroll revenues derive from teleprocessing based service. Today ADP pays almost 6 percent of the work force of America through its facilities. Its board includes such luminaries as Laurence Tisch and Alan Greenspan.

Says Lautenberg, "Most people believe we live in a highly industrialized nation. Actually, our manufacturing work force was surpassed by our information work force twenty-five years ago. Between 1960 and 1979, the total number of white-collar workers grew almost 72 percent while the total work force grew only 45 percent. Of the 30 million new jobs created since 1960, about seven out of ten were white collar. All these workers—about half the labor force—are concerned with *information* in one form or another. In the broadest sense these 50 million workers constitute the marketplace which ADP and others in the industry serve."

Lautenberg has a strong sense of humor. He tells the story of how in 1965 his ADP holdings became worth $1 million. He called his mother, a career woman in retailing, and told her his good news. Her terse comment: "Frank, just tell me how much money you *save* every week."

With ingenuity and hard work Lautenberg, Greenebaum, Bloomingdale and Winters created industries. The same innovative process continues.

A few years ago, Henry A. Lambert, a gourmet and amateur chef who traveled a lot in his real estate job, realized that fresh pasta was available in commercial areas—North Beach in San Francisco, Melrose in Los Angeles—but not in residential neighborhoods. Also one could purchase the pasta but not the sauce to go with it. So, in 1976 Lambert opened Pasta & Cheese at Seventy-ninth Street and Third Avenue, New York.

He recalls, "We needed the cheese to get a lease. Most people thought pasta was pizza. I was so ignorant I had to ask a girl I was dating at the time to take a bag of assorted cheeses around to a delicatessen and ask which ones they were. She said she had been given them for Christmas. We bought a pasta machine, had attractive salespeople and made our own pâté with a recipe we got from the chef at Le Lavandou."

Now there are seven Pasta & Cheese stores plus the Pasta & Cheese Café at Bergdorf Goodman. The products are sold in supermarkets like Daitch and King's as well as at Zabar's and Macy's. The business has annual sales in excess of $5 million. This is a part-time activity for the highly motivated Lambert, who holds down the full-time position of president of the Reliance Development Company for the Reliance Group and spends three days a week traveling. When in his home base of New York, he goes to Pasta & Cheese at 7:00 A.M. for an hour, arrives at his office for an 8:30-A.M. meeting, spends the day there, then goes back to Pasta & Cheese at night. His rule: "Get in earlier and leave later."

He credits the success of the pasta shops to his love of cooking and the fact that he had been connected with a large business, explaining, "This kind of shop was usually a ma-and-pa operation."

This identification and satisfaction of consumer needs often creates a new family dynasty. Block Drug Company was founded by Jewish immigrant Alexander Block, who started a drugstore on Brooklyn's Fulton Street in 1907, turned wholesaler by 1915 and by 1925 was in the drug-manufacturing business. Today son Leonard is chairman of the board and chief executive officer of this Jersey City-based company.

In 1958 Alexander Grass, now fifty-five, a lawyer, saw the profit in the discount drug business, and founded Rite Aid Corporation of Harrisburg, Pennsylvania, with a single discount drugstore. Now there are 967 and Rite Aid is the third largest chain in the United States with over $1 billion sales a year. Grass is president and chief executive officer.

Grass was born in Scranton, the grandson of an immigrant peddler. His father was coowner of Grass-Grossinger Hats and Caps, a small manufacturing firm. Grossinger was a relative of the resort family. His father died when Grass was nine; his mother moved the family to Miami. As a child, Grass worked in two drugstores and later went through the University of Florida law school on the G.I. Bill.

Exemplifying the precept of hard work, Grass says "To get ahead you do not have to go to the right tie school. But you do have to have drive." He recalls a discussion he had with three other students in 1947. They asked themselves the question, "If somebody offered you a job on graduation for $10,000 a year, would you accept?" The other three said yes, but Grass answered, "I want more money than that."

He came to Harrisburg in 1950 as a young Revenue Department tax lawyer and in 1952 joined Louis Lehrman and Son (founded by Lewis Lehrman's grandfather) as a wholesale food salesman (Grass's former wife is a Lehrman). He learned the business, added a nonfood line of toys and health and beauty products and decided to try a retail store. He says, "We developed gradually. That is what is good about the food and drug business. You open and operate one store at a time. For a steel plant, to begin you need all the facilities."

Grass has remarried but still runs the family business, has "retained a decent relationship" with his first wife and a close relationship with former brother-in-law Lewis Lehrman. Three of Grass's children work at Rite Aid, and a new drug dynasty is in the making.

They penetrated industries once closed to Jews, like banking. Jews did not always rise through the ranks. In some instances, they just took over. Says Bram Goldsmith, fifty-nine-year-old chairman and chief executive officer, City National Bank, Los Angeles, whose parents were of Russian-Polish origin, "I penetrated by coming in from the top. Our bank was put together at Hillcrest Country Club" (the elite Los Angeles club whose members include actor George Burns, comic Milton Berle and even non-Jewish Frank Sinatra).

"It was formed as an independent bank. After years in other industries (liquor, lumber, real estate), I felt it was time for a career change and new challenge. I had been an outside director of the bank for twelve years before becoming chairman. When I go to banking conventions, the only heads of Jewish banks are Sterling in New York and one in Florida. But today there are senior Jewish officers. Jews are recognized for senior positions.

Of 15,000 banks in the U.S., we are 135th."

Goldsmith notes that "Today the Jew is recognized as a dynamic, bright person who can work in the system and be a leader. He is no longer thought of as a maverick. But Jews themselves want industries that are dynamic: finance, energy, information, electronics, pay TV." However, banking still has some closed doors for Jews. As recently as 1979, Dr. Steven Slavin, a professor of economics at Union College, Cranford, New Jersey, did a survey of job offers by New York banks to Jewish M.B.A. graduates of NYU and Columbia. Morgan Guaranty and Irving Trust did not offer a single job to any Jewish applicant surveyed.

They became actively Jewish and found it made Gentiles respect them more. Few of today's leaders try to hide their Jewishness. Instead they are active in the Jewish community. Irving M. Levine of the American Jewish Committee has said, "You can be avowedly Jewish now and get away with it. The ethnic identity movement has had an impact on all classes."

Lautenberg, Grass and Goldsmith played major roles in the national United Jewish Appeal. Winter served as president of the American Jewish Committee.

Lautenberg exemplifies today's big-business chief executive who is actively Jewish. In addition to his work for the UJA presidency, he has raised funds for Hebrew University in Jerusalem, where he founded a cancer-research center. Yet, as a child he admits he was "ashamed to be Jewish." As a seventeen-year-old, trying to get a job as an office boy, he denied his Jewishness. He went to school on Yom Kippur. He thought of changing his name to F. Raleigh Lautenberg (*Raleigh* is really his middle name). He married a Jewish girl whom he met skiing ("Jewish girls did not ski then") and his mother was "amazed." Many years later, at forty, Lautenberg met a Reform rabbi whom he liked and joined a temple. At forty-three, he made his first contribution to the UJA, and, at forty-five, first visited Israel. Since then he has been making up for lost time.

He says, "I have a tremendous sense of pride in being Jewish. Look at the race for ethnic identification. We Jews have carried it. Through man's horrors we have survived. It comes from a sharpened survival instinct that forced us to be better, to strive harder."

Executive Suite Action Against Discrimination

Men like Shapiro and Lautenberg have broken through business barriers. However, even with these and other notable exceptions, evidence suggests that probably a majority of large U.S. enterprises practice executive-suite discrimination or tolerate it, either wittingly or unwittingly. It is not a matter of money. In terms of income Jews are on a par with Episcopalians and Presbyterians. What troubles Jews about any executive-suite discrimination is that it implies judgment of group inferiority and disregards individual merit.

Studies have shown that executive-suite discrimination begins with the recruitment of college graduates, is continued in corporate personnel and promotion practices and even extends into social clubs and social activities where executives mingle with potential executive candidates. That "old-school-tie network" still functions. Old attitudes and habits die hard.

Says Alexander Grass, "You do not find Jews in the city clubs. Look at the board of directors of the Chamber of Commerce, of social and fraternal organizations. It is an obstacle that can be overcome, but not easily."

Adds Bram Goldsmith, "The *Los Angeles Times* referred to it as 'five o'clock shadow.' There are few occasions where Jews and Gentiles mix in the evening. We are accepted and work well together, but the social area has not been meaningfully penetrated."

Mistakes occur because of misleading ideas on both sides. Jews still sometimes mistakenly assume that a particular industry is closed to them and decide not to train for it—with the result that companies perfectly willing to hire Jews may not be able to find any qualified candidates. For their part, corporations often labor under the delusion that centuries of persecution and isolation have made Jews "hypersensitive" and "overly aggressive" and left them well qualified for trade but without the loyalty necessary for big business.

Moreover, both sides frequently succumb to what has been termed the "Einstein syndrome"—the notion that all or most Jews have a special gift or liking for mathematics, research, science and the creative arts and that none is interested in the field of corporate management. One steel executive said, "Why would creative people like the Jews want to go into a dull business like steel?" The Einstein syndrome has often been used as a rationale for placing Jews in nonviable "staff" positions (legal and accounting) in a corporation rather than in "line" jobs (production and sales) that lead to executive positions. Sometimes Jewish employees are kept out of sight in deference to the actual or supposed preferences of others, who, it is thought, might take umbrage at seeing a Jew in a position of leadership.

To fight discrimination against Jews in American corporations, in 1955 the American Jewish Committee set up an Executive Suite Committee that sponsors task forces in many communities.

Today the New York Regional Task Force on Executive Suite has an advisory board, consisting of five non-Jews and a Jew. Chairperson is William M. Ellinghaus, president, American Telephone and Telegraph; and other members include Ross Barzelay, vice-chairman, General Foods (the lone Jew); Henry A. Correa, president, ACF Industries; Coy Ecklund, president, The Equitable Life Insurance Society of the United States; J. Peter Grace, president, W. R. Grace; John W. Hannon, Jr., president, Bankers Trust; and Charles F. Luce, chairman of the board, Consolidated Edison.

Ellinghaus has said, "In the face of intense competition from other industrial nations, it is essential that we make full use of the best brains and the finest talent to help overcome the many economic problems that confront us. For this reason—as well as the reasons of basic quality—we can no longer tolerate the exclusion of any person from management and executive positions in the corporate structure for reasons having nothing to do with ability."

AJC task forces in communities throughout the nation are making it their goal to see that companies: (1) examine themselves thoroughly to find out whether a problem of discrimination exists; (2) instruct personnel departments to carry out the equal-opportunity policy with the same emphasis as other company policies; (3) communicate their nondiscrimination policies to executive recruiters; (4) promote or transfer minority-group members where they will be visible to present and potential employees.

Are the barriers going down? The answer: an emphatic yes.

In a letter to Ellinghaus, a top executive at Arthur Young, Executive Resource Consultants, reported that the firm is developing "a special executive retrieval file to assist its clients with equal employment opportunities and affirmative action. A major section of the file is devoted to Jewish professionals and executives. In each executive search which we conduct in the future, the first source of candidates to be considered will be these affirmative action files, which can be sorted by functional experience and by compensation level."

Says Lewis Lehrman, "There is no area of American life not open to Jewish leadership. However, to be a chief executive officer requires a lifetime of commitment. When Jews will give thirty years to banking or oil, they will emerge as heads of corporations in these fields."

Yet with all the progress in the corporate enterprise, the nagging worry about anti-Semitism in the boardroom persists. Sometimes it exists. Says Rabbi Stanley Schachter of Jewish Theological Seminary, "Anti-Semitism is always there under the surface, a preoccupation in the minds of lay leadership."

On other occasions, with sensitivities developed by years of persecution, Jews imagine it. Recently the AJC heard that in Wall Street the word *conglomerate* was anti-Semitic code for Jews like Meshulam Riklis, the head of the Rapid-American Corporation, who has been called everything from "cocky" to "pushy." After checking, the AJC found no truth in the rumor. It was just another case of "Jewish apprehension."

In addition to the changing corporate attitude, two factors play an important role in relation to the Jewish rise in the boardroom. One is talent and the recognition of it. Not only does the Gentile Ellinghaus chair a committee to help Jews enter and rise within the corporate structure, but in September, 1980, Morris Tanenbaum was elected vice-president of American Telephone and Telegraph. (In the thirties and forties, along with Du Pont, AT&T was considered by many to be an anti-Semitic firm. Jews knew better than to apply.) Tanenbaum, who comes from Huntington, West Virginia, and got his doctorate in physical chemistry, had previously been the first Jewish president of New Jersey Bell Telephone Company, an AT&T subsidiary. There are rumors from authoritative sources and insiders, that Tanenbaum may be the next president of AT&T. It could be another Shapiro saga.

The second factor: a free and mobile society. Unlike many of their parents who grew up with the fear of pogroms, despots and death camps, today's JEPs grew up in the American democratic society, where they had the chance to achieve a higher education and make their way in a free nation.

Henry Taub, son of a Polish father and Lithuanian mother, was a poor boy. For Henry to obtain the college education they lacked became a parental dream. At sixteen, Taub, accompanied by his mother, took the train from Paterson, New Jersey, to Manhattan, the subway to NYU to register. While Taub filled out the forms, his mother sat in Washington Square Park. When he came out of the school building, she cried and told him, "This is the happiest day of my life."

Today, at fifty-four, Taub, the creator of Auromatic Data Processing, serves on its board, is part owner of the New Jersey Nets basketball team, and gives 50 percent of his time to charity. With intense feeling, he says, "In America, the streets are not paved with gold but with opportunity."

5

THE JEWISH PATCHWORK QUILT

YOUNG OR old, rich or poor, famous or unknown, the members of America's Jewish community display a range of attitudes toward their faith. Some worship in large temples, some in small *shuls.* Others do not pray at all. Just as assorted materials sewn together form a patchwork quilt, diverse religious practices and feelings comprise the body of American Jewry. They are united in a common sense of identity, the recognition that "I am a Jew."

Many Our Crowd Jews, who were rarely overtly Jewish, still retain their sense of Jewish identity. Others, of Eastern European descent, have held fast to the strong sense of religious commitment possessed by their parents and grandparents. Still others, reared without any sense of religious identification, have become born-again Jews, completely altering their life-style in the process.

Many of the Our Crowd Jews, their ranks thinned by age and intermarriage, continue to work for the Jewish organizations that had always been a tradition in their group. Mrs. David Klau, eighty-four, of New York, is an active philanthropist, serving on the boards of Hebrew Union College, Montefiore Hospital and Medical Center, the Scholarship Fund at Hunter College, Fun for Sunshine Nurseries. Of her religion, she says, "I never wanted to change. All my friends are Jewish."

But age affects active participation in the Jewish community. Mrs. Herbert Bloch, eighty-eight, is the third generation of her family and her great grandchild Jane will be the sixth generation attending Isaac M. Wise Temple where her ancestors were founding fathers and presidents of the board. "Most of my good friends are gone or incapacitated," says Mrs. Bloch. "Most of my associations are with my children's friends and with people throughout the community of different interests and ages—but still younger than I am." Mrs. Lewis Bloomingdale of Scarsdale, New York, echoes the refrain, "Most of my friends have passed on."

Mrs. Lewis Bloomingdale

At ninety-four (she was born on February 2, just one month before the Blizzard of 1888), Mrs. Bloomingdale wears a beige shirt, sleeveless tan sweater, a beige and green kilt, brogues, and exclaims, "I'm in good health." She lives in a modern house ("I moved to Scarsdale in 1916 when there was one house by the station, a business building, a drugstore and a butcher"). All her life she has had a Jewish identity in an upper-class way.

She was born Irma Asiel (*el* means "God" in Hebrew). Her father's firm was Asiel & Company on Wall Street and her nephew Bill is still head of the company. Mrs. Bloomingdale had the typical Our Crowd Jewish education of her day. She attended Dr. Sachs' School for Girls, studied Italian, French, and German from kindergarten on.

She met her husband-to-be, Lewis Morgan Bloomingdale, in Elberon, New Jersey, the "Jewish Newport" of its day. Lewis, the son of Joseph (a president of Cooper Union) worked on Wall Street. His father had been in the hoop-skirt business and suddenly hoops went out of fashion. So Joseph and his brother Lyman (there was a third brother, Emanuel) established a notions store at Fifty-sixth Street and Third Avenue in Manhattan—on the very site which today houses the offices of the American Jewish Committee. Eventually Joseph retired, and the Bloomingdale Brothers store moved to its present Fifty-ninth Street location in 1885. The store is now owned by Federated Department Stores, but the property still belongs to the family.

At twenty-one, Irma Asiel was married to Lewis Bloomingdale and eventually they bought property they called "Elm Ridge Farm" at the north end of New Rochelle. But Mr. Bloomingdale died in 1939 and Elm Ridge Farm was sold in 1977. Today there are seventy-two houses on the thirty-two-acre site. Memories are painful. Mrs. Bloomingdale refuses to drive by her former home.

Irma Bloomingdale has spent her entire life raising her five children (three daughters, two sons) and working for charity. She says, "When we first started, we were very satisfied with a $5 or $10 gift. I had to put my foot in the door or occasionally they would slam it in my face." A friend fondly recalls that Mrs. Bloomingdale was always a good fundraiser.

She is an original member of the Scarsdale Women's Club and still takes French lessons there on Monday mornings, but she and Irving Grinberg are the only founder members left of the Reform Jewish Community Center of White Plains.

Except for her modern home, Mrs. Bloomingdale's life-style has hardly changed. She still spends her summers at Knollwood, a six-family club on Lower Saranac Lake in the Adirondacks, an isolated, elite "enclave." Her father, Elias Asiel, and George Blumenthal, a foreign exchange banker, were among the six families who founded Knollwood in 1900. All the wooden houses are the same. There are common tennis courts as well as a boathouse with a second story, containing a piano, record player, pool table. Knollwood was formerly run with a common dining room, but during the Depression this facility was dropped.

Other elite families still summer there: Mrs. David Hays Sulzberger (sister-in-law of the late Arthur Hays Sulzberger), Mrs. John Frank, Kenneth Bijur, Mrs. Madeline Gimbel, Ulrich Schweitzer, Mr. and Mrs. James Marshall. The Marshall house was built by Louis Marshall, father of James ("Jimmy") and known as a great constitutional lawyer. An observant Jew, Louis Marshall used to conduct his own religious services there. Baseball is still the Sunday-afternoon activity. Says Mrs. Bloomingdale, "I bat, but someone has to run for me."

Mrs. Bloomingdale, winner of many awards for her Jewish charitable work, still works for the Federation of Jewish Philanthropies and American Red Cross. However, she says simply,

"The office lost my big list of donors. Now I just contact people I know."

Paul Kohnstamm

Paul Kohnstamm serves as another example of the Our Crowd Jew who has stayed actively Jewish. He is president of H. Kohnstamm & Company, a chemical company established by his forebears in 1848. Now in its second century, the company is believed to be the oldest privately owned American chemical and color manufacturer.

Kohnstamm, an articulate graying man in his late fifties, notes, "There was no reason to leave Judaism. It is the rock of our salvation, as the prayer book says. Intermarriage hurts. It is a centuries-old religion. Why leave it?

"My parents' generation was interested in Jewish matters but not ostentatious Jewishness. They were not closet Jews but were reluctant to be too open about their Jewishness. They helped with checkbooks and worked on committees but did not participate in parades or picketing. They stayed behind the scenes. If Henry Morgenthau (secretary of the Treasury under President Franklin D. Roosevelt), had been more open about his Jewishness, he would have accomplished more for the Jews. But that was not the style then. They did not want to be aggressive Jews."

Kohnstamm, who is president of the Hospital for Joint Diseases, and his wife Maisie (she is descended from Guggenheims and the Cincinnati Loebs, the original founders of the Kuhn Loeb banking house) have six children. He notes the generational difference: "My children's generation is more aggressive about Jewishness. They are more determined. They do not hang back as much as their grandparents did."

Kohnstamm has lived in Poundridge, New York, since 1945. All six children were confirmed—either at the Beth-El Temple in Chappaqua or Sinai Temple in North Stamford, Connecticut. With pride he points out that "Today there is a mix of new and old traditions." His oldest son recently married a Minneapolis girl in a traditional wedding. There was a *chuppah* (marriage canopy). The couple broke the glass. But prior to the ceremony, the guests played baseball and tennis.

Ambassador Milton Wolf

Many of the New Crowd with Eastern European backgrounds also have retained a strong sense of Jewish identity. Milton Wolf, fifty-eight, a prominent community leader in Cleveland, Ohio, served as ambassador to Austria from 1977 to 1980. American Jews were not always welcome in Vienna. According to an item in the *New York Times,* the Austrian government rejected President Grover Cleveland's designee as ambassador to Vienna in 1885 because he had a Jewish wife. An adamant President Cleveland refused to nominate someone else, and, for some time, the Austrian capital was without an official United States envoy.

Wolf, a tall, elegant, silver-haired man, dressed in ambassadorial-type blue suit, white shirt and staid red and blue tie, knows the right wines and restaurants and orders with flair. But despite his sophistication, his sense of Jewishness comes first. "I could live in a city that did not have an orchestra or ballet," he says, "but not one that did not have a synagogue."

Wolf was raised in an Orthodox home, keeps a kosher home; his wife lights the candles on Friday nights. Both parents were immigrants. His father came to the United States about 1912 at age fourteen, his mother, as a baby. Somehow his father found his way to Cleveland, where "the established Jews took care of newcomers." They arranged for the young immigrant to work in the local police department. The senior Wolf became a detective, "The only Jewish detective in Cleveland," and remained one until his death in 1961.

Milton Wolf admits to growing up in modest circumstances, but notes, "I did not consider myself poor. There was always a *pushka* (box) for the poor in the kitchen. If you had two pennies, you dropped them in. As a young man I was aware that there were greater needs than my own."

Wolf worked his way through Ohio State ("At the time the tuition was something like $12 a quarter"). He waited on tables, sold shoes and worked until 2:00 or 3:00 A.M. as a teletype operator for the Associated Press.

World War II interrupted his college career but he eventually received his B.A. at Ohio State, later a B.S. in civil engineering at Case Institute of Technology. And he married Roslyn Zehman, daughter of a local builder, and went into business with his father-in-law.

"I went into construction big," he recalls, "but I always went to school. The university was always holy for me. While I was building apartments and shopping centers, I used to take two courses a semester. I missed every other class, but I graduated Case summa cum laude. I even went to medical school for a while, later got an M.A. in economics and did three years of doctorate work in economics. My four kids are all scholars."

Wolf became a wealthy man. He also became known as a fundraiser for Jewish causes ("When I raise money, the easiest to get it from are those who earn it. The difficult are those who inherit it"). He divides his life into four areas of commitment: business, education, family, the Jewish community.

His exposure to the political world came when working on the senate campaigns of Howard Metzenbaum (Jewish), now senator from Ohio, and John Glenn, senior senator from Ohio. Carter aides approached him for support when Carter was running for president in 1976. At first he refused, then accepted with the condition that he would not help "until the local federation drive is over." In May, 1976, Carter came to Wolf's home. Wolf points out, "The chemistry was good—good with his people: Hamilton Jordan, Robert Lipshutz, Stuart Eizenstat. They had trust in me." Wolf served on Carter's Advisory Committee, later won the post of ambassador to Austria.

Notes Wolf, "In my case my appointment came as a surprise. Carter did not appoint many campaign people to political spots. I was anxious to go to Austria. My people had come from Austria-Hungary. My father was born one hundred miles from Vienna in what was once part of the Austrian-Hungarian Empire, became Czechoslovakia after World War I and Russian after World War II."

After winning the post, he experienced "not one angstrom unit of anti-Semitism while in Austria." In Vienna, Wolf attended the Seitenstetengasse, the oldest synagogue in Vienna. He comments, "The synagogue has a new life. Many old Jewish Viennese went back, but also many Eastern Europeans have moved to Vienna. In fact some Jewish organizations such as the Joint Distribution Committee, HIAS and the Jewish Agency have headquarters in Vienna."

Wolf hosted the Salt II Summit Conference in Vienna in 1979 (Carter and Brezhnev) and was decorated by the government of Austria with "Great Gold Medal of Honor with Sash," Austria's highest decoration, marking the first time it was ever given to an ambassador in office.

Wolf's commitment to his faith is as strong as his commitment to America ("In America a person can take his life and make it worthwhile"). His temple is Conservative ("the right sort of ritual"). His wife was president of Park Synagogue Sisterhood in Cleveland, as her mother was before her. Wolf's mother, eighty-one, has been president of the Sisterhood of Taylor Road Synagogue, the largest Orthodox synagogue in Cleveland. The family has an annual family *seder* with one hundred guests. He also notes with pride, "My children would not think of not fasting on Yom Kippur. They are all American kids, but they are so happy they are Jewish."

All four children—a son Leslie and three daughters—show the effects of the Americanization process on Judaism. The three daughters—Caryn, Nancy, Sherri—attended the Hathaway Brown private school in Cleveland and Ivy League colleges. Caryn, the oldest, had been May Queen at Hathaway Brown. Now married, she still keeps a kosher home. While Wolf was in Austria, Sherri attended Phillips-Andover. At this elegant eastern prep school, she would not eat anything that was not kosher.

Today, Wolf is a trustee of the Library of Congress, Jewish Community Federation of Cleveland and the Mount Sinai Medical Center, Case Western Reserve University, among others. He is a member of the Council on Foreign Relations; American Economic Association; Resources Committee, Case Western Reserve School of Medicine. He is also Distinguished Professorial Lecturer in Economics at Case Western Reserve University.

He says, "No generation has a choice in the problems it inherits but does have a choice in how it faces up to the problems." He faces them as a Jew.

Maynard Wishner

"Jewish life has changed," says Maynard Wishner, president of the American Jewish Committee, another JEP of Eastern European ancestry committed to his people.

Now president and chief executive officer of Walter E. Heller & Company, Chicago, the principal commercial financing and factoring operating subsidiary of Walter E. Heller International Corporation, Wishner was born in Chicago in 1923, the son of Polish and Russian immigrants. His parents met in a sweatshop. His father was a knitter, his mother a finisher. "They organized a union that resulted in a union at the shop," he recalls. "My mother shut off the power. My father was the leader of the knitters. They married. He knitted. She sewed. They sold to stores and had a retail outlet in the storefront. Both worked all the time. I knew I would go to school. I felt well off."

Wishner's parents were deeply committed to "Jewishness and devoted to the Yiddish language." (His mother still addresses him as "Maishele"). Young Wishner studied Yiddish at a Workmen's Circle *(Arbeiter Ring)* school in Chicago where dancer Pearl Lang was a classmate. The Workmen's Circle was created by a handful of Jewish immigrants in 1892 who wanted to set up a society that would bring together workers of Socialist persuasion while also providing them with essential benefits—sick care, burial service—which the traditional *landmanshaften* (associations of people coming from the same place) offered. It became a national body in 1900 and is still in existence, with programs that teach Jewish and Yiddish culture.

Taking the streetcar to his Yiddish class, Wishner would hide his books under his jacket: "The books represented a sense of danger." He had already been called a "dirty Jew" in public school (his mother assured him "You are the cleanest boy").

Wishner attended the University of Chicago, acted in a resident Yiddish theater after school ("We set box-office records with a Yiddish version of *Anna Lucasta*"), went into the army and obtained his law degree from the University of Chicago Law School in 1947.

After serving as staff counsel, executive director of the Mayor's Commission on Human Relations in the City of Chicago, and chief city prosecutor he started his own law firm, joining Walter E. Heller as vice-president in 1963.

Wishner dismisses the whole German Jewish prejudice against Eastern Europeans as "a thing of the past." He recalls that as a youth, he had no knowledge of this bias. His first awareness came when as president of the University of Chicago's Hillel chapter, he was invited to a meeting to be held in Chicago's Standard Club, an elite downtown club organized in 1869 by German Jews. "I did not know what it was," he recalls. "It was my first contact with the downtown establishment.

"I got to know them, and, as my stereotype broke down, developed respect for them. At first I thought those were the rich Jews. They didn't understand anything. I found out they were committed and hardworking. Today Hamilton Loeb is a good friend and serves on the Heller board. Someone called Hammy, 'You blue blood.' Hammy answered, 'My great-grandfather was a Jewish peddler.' "

Yiddish is still an important part of Wishner's life. He is known as the "Yiddish-speaking president" of the American Jewish Committee, often considered an elitist organization. However, he is not the first AJC president to speak Yiddish.

Since Yiddish was considered by many Our Crowders "déclassé," in 1902 Louis Marshall, an AJC president of German-Jewish descent, set up the *Yidishe Velt* (Jewish World), a Yiddish newspaper designed "to be everything that existing Yiddish newspapers are not, namely, clean, wholesome, religious in tone, the advocate of all that makes good citizenship, and so far as politics are concerned absolutely independent."

In establishing this newspaper Marshall had the help of a phalanx of German Jewish millionaires: Schiff, Warburg, Guggenheim, Lewisohn, Seligman, Lehman, Bloomingdale and others. Marshall even learned Yiddish himself in order to direct his staff more effectively, but the paper was subjected to ridicule from the Orthodox *Tageblatt* and the radical *Forward* and it failed. As Irving Howe writes in *World of Our Fathers,* "Uptown was uptown, downtown, downtown, and it would take another half-century in the warmth of affluence before the twain could meet."

Wishner avows his mastery of the Yiddish language has been of enormous help to him as head of the American Jewish Committee. During a trip to South America, one of the leaders of the Buenos Aires community asked, *"Habla español?"* Wishner gestured no. The man pressed on, "Yiddish one should not trouble to ask?"

Wishner responded, "We can talk in Yiddish." He recalls, "They nearly fell off their chairs."

"I made it with the help of my mother and father," credits Wishner. "They gave me an education and the whole basis of how I view the world. They were successful in passing on to me the precious treasure of knowing who and what I am—the richness of being a Jew and the blessing of being Jewish in America."

Julia Perles

"I feel very Jewish, very committed. I identify deeply. I belong. But going to temple is not my idea of being Jewish. Temple is organized, and I get turned off by any kind of organized religion. To me religion is a private thing between me and the good Lord. When I hear Jewish music or go to a bar mitzvah, I feel very Jewish. But I do not identify with the ritual."

So says Julia Perles, now a senior partner at the prestigious law firm of Phillips Nizer Benjamin Krim & Ballon. She represents another kind of Jew—one who is committed without being observant. Perles has fought her way up the legal ladder. In the process she encountered two kinds of prejudice—sexual and religious.

At sixty-eight, her name appears frequently in the newspapers because of the often sensational matrimonial cases she handles. She refuses to name clients but will admit, "When I go to Lincoln Center, I look at the names of people on the board and many have been a client of mine at one time or another." She is active in the New York County Lawyers Association, has headed the Divorce Law & Procedure Committee of the Family Law Section of the American Bar Committee, is known to peers as "the best."

It was not always this way.

"I think of myself as a late bloomer," says Perles. "Until ten years after law school I never felt like a lawyer. I spent ten years in a law firm where I was kicked around for being female.

"I got married late—at thirty-seven.

"I left home late. I lived with my parents until I was thirty-four years old."

Perles is the oldest of four—two younger brothers and a sister, now deceased. Both parents were Russian-born. Her father sent for his mother and four sisters. Finally, he went abroad to escort his father to the United States. He accompanied the senior Perles to Ellis Island, where officials discovered he had trachoma and refused him permission to enter. "We never saw him again," sorrowfully recalls granddaughter Perles. "He literally got lost."

Julia Perles grew up in Brooklyn, where her father was first a dancing teacher and then a caterer with a real estate business on the side.

"At twelve or thirteen I decided to become a lawyer," she remembers. "Why, I don't know. As I got older I thought maybe it was to be as different from my mother as I could be."

After graduation from tuition-free Brooklyn College, Perles went on to Brooklyn Law School ("There were six or eight women in the graduating class of five hundred"). For the first three years of her legal career she "bounded" from one job to another. ("I was not happy—small offices, routine work.")

She spent 1942 to 1952 at Schwartz & Frolich. This was a "first-generation" firm; the members' parents were Eastern European immigrants and had lived on Delancey Street. "With this firm I was tutored like a rich kid. I was needed."

During this period Perles experienced much prejudice because of her sex but none because of her Jewishness. "My only fight was to be accepted as a lawyer because I was a woman," she claims. "The problem was not with clients but with other lawyers."

Then Perles received an offer from a famous firm—let us call it MSW. The firm's officers were second-, third-, even fourth-generation assimilated Jews who had gone to prep schools, Ivy League colleges, and then on to Harvard and Columbia law schools. Many were active in the Ethical Culture Society. Perles's strong Jewish identification and immigrant roots presented quite a contrast.

"At first I did not notice any prejudice," she says. "I was not conscious of it. Then, as my career progressed, and I was given more important work, I realized younger people were being promoted over my head. Five became partners. I was not promoted.

"I was always on the outside. I did not belong to their clubs, social circles. Their friends were not my friends. I was not at the weddings of their children or their parties, with the exception of one senior partner who was friendly to me and one or two juniors. The others respected me as a lawyer. They did not want me as a friend.

"I pushed for a partnership. I went to the head of the firm and told him, 'I think I am too Jewish for you. I went to Brooklyn College, to Brooklyn Law School.' I saw a look come into his face. Then I began to realize.

"The German-Jewish bigotry was a subtle, amorphous thing, but it was there."

Through a stratagem Perles finally obtained the MSW partnership she craved so much. She decided to try for an appointment as a judge in Family Court. MSW heard about it and asked, "Do you want to be a judge?"

She told them, "I do not want to be a judge. I want to be a partner."

Bitterness in her tone, she adds, "It took me twelve years to get that partnership. It was my Jewishness that kept me from getting it.

"In the legal world of New York today there is no German-Jewish snobbery," she notes.

While she encountered social problems at MSW, she did find

a specialty: matrimonial law. Says Perles, a statuesque woman with enormous vitality, "I think specialization in any field is just as much thrust upon one as chosen."

She was given a complaint in a divorce case to read "just to see if it was in order." The husband had gone to Mexico and obtained an invalid divorce, then remarried and had a child. The ex-wife wanted this marriage declared void and the baby illegitimate.

The senior partner insisted she handle the case.

Comments Perles, "The ex-wife was a horror. But I represented her. I hated her all the way through. This was my first matrimonial case. It was my first lesson in objectivity.

In 1970 a partner at Phillips Nizer approached her: "We need someone to head up matrimonial." She kept sending people over but no one satisfied them. One day, during a chance street encounter, another Nizer partner asked, "Are you happy where you are?" She told him, "I'm not unhappy and I am very expensive." He suggested lunch. She recalls, "Until that moment it never occurred to me that I would not live out my days at MSW." In her mind Perles set two goals: a guarantee of a certain amount of money—$10,000 more than at MSW—and a partnership. She received the terms she wanted.

Perles made this move when she was fifty-six years old—an age when many men and women are thinking about retirement or have already retired. Laughingly, she says, "Who changes a career at fifty-six? I was finally independent."

Commenting on new attitudes, she says, "Nizer is a different world. You are accepted for what you are. Today MSW operates in a different way. It is now run by people who are not as conscious of different kinds of Jews as the past partners were."

Always Perles stresses her commitment to her faith: "Being Jewish is part of my life. Anything that affects any Jews anywhere affects me. That is how I feel about being Jewish."

Throughout the length and breadth of the nation Jews are making a public mark. Jewish identity is no longer a problem; in fact, some find it an asset.

Says Orin Lehman, commissioner of parks and recreation for New York State, "Jews have more positions in government today. When Herbert Lehman was a senator, it was unusual."

At this writing, the mayor of New York is Jewish. So is the borough president of Manhattan. Says Louis Lefkowitz, former attorney general of New York, first Jew to be elected president of the National Association of Attorney Generals, and now with Phillips Nizer Benjamin Krim & Ballon, "There is no such thing as the Jewish seat. Some Jews say 'I will vote only for a Jew.' But only a small amount. Most vote for quality. I don't want to hear that Jewish-seat business."

Jews in public life work for both Jewish and non-Jewish causes. Although retaining their Jewish identity, they may expend their energies primarily on public-service activities that are more "American" than "Jewish."

Elinor Guggenheimer

Gray haired, small boned and sharp minded, at sixty-nine Elinor Guggenheimer does not believe in dawdling. She has been a moving force in day-care, child-development and welfare programs in New York and a trustee of dozens of philanthropic organizations such as the Federation of Jewish Philanthropies.

From 1974 to 1978 she served as commissioner of New York's Department of Consumer Affairs. More recently she wrote the book and lyrics for the off-Broadway *Potholes.* Yet, like others who grew up in the so-called gilded ghetto of Manhattan of the late twenties and early thirties, she was not programed to be a doer in the public eye. She gives full credit for this to her mother-in-law, the indomitable Minnie Guggenheimer of Stadium Concerts fame.

Daughter of financier Nathan Coleman (he was the uncle of Alvin Coleman, a past Temple Emanu-El president), Guggenheimer did all the Our Crowd "right things." She was confirmed at Temple Emanu-El, attended the Edith Shelby dances (Shelby organized society parties and holiday dances for the Jewish elite; she was the forerunner of dance doyennes Angie Jacobson and

Viola Wolff). It was at a Christmas ball at the Ritz-Carlton that Elinor Coleman met Randolph Guggenheimer, her husband-to-be.

Guggenheimer's grandfather was the first Randolph Guggenheimer, who arrived on the New York scene from Lynchburg, Virginia, at seventeen and worked as a clerk in a woolen-goods house to put himself through New York University's law school. He became a specialist in real estate law. As commissioner of the common schools for nine years, he introduced the German language into the basic school system and at his death the flags on all New York City schools were flown at half-mast. He also served as acting mayor of New York from 1897 to 1901 in the absence of Mayor Van Wyck.

Guggenheimer married Eliza Katzenberg, a tiny dynamo of a woman, and their son Charles married Minnie Shafer. Minnie yearned to rival her awesome mother-in-law with some accomplishments of her own. This she achieved with the establishment of the outdoor Stadium Concerts, held at Lewisohn Stadium in New York City.

At eighteen, Elinor Coleman became engaged to Randolph Guggenheimer II and transferred from Vassar to Barnard. She says, "I married him for his Packard Phaeton car." The bridal attendants from the *New York Times* account of the wedding reads like a Who's Who of Our Crowd with names like Fox, Ehrich, Forsch, Hochstader, Bijur, Schafer (Straus kin), Liebman, Rothschild, Untermyer, Weissberg. The marriage has lasted for fifty years.

Elinor Guggenheimer has been an exception to many of the Our Crowd German Jews who—like the Storrs and the Guggenheims—married away. Her sons are Jewish. Her grandsons are Jewish. But they are not active. Years ago she tried to have a *seder* ("I thought it would be wonderful"). There was a fight: "My family took it as a joke. I bought all the books. I still have them."

Her own Jewish identification is strong: "The people who stayed Jewish were the more secure. They had the more stable marriages."

But many of her activities have nothing to do with being

Jewish. Of them all—radio spots, the outstanding TV show "Straight Talk," work for the Civil Service Commission—she preferred her work on the City Planning Commission. She notes with pride, "That was my most satisfying experience. I could dream and see results. There are parts of New York that I put there. An expanded block at Lincoln Center resulted from work I did on the planning commission. Breezy Point—the whole federal park—along the shorefront in the Rockaways—I started the action that led to that."

Supposedly retired, Elinor Guggenheimer has turned to a new career. As she puts it, "The closet lyricist has come out of the closet." The musical comedy *Potholes* was a revue about New York's urban plight and in it she took potshots at some of the outstanding problems—garbage on the sidewalks, pickpockets on the subways and, of course, potholes. She says, "I never had so much fun in my life. I have always loved writing lyrics.

John L. Loeb, Jr.

In some cases prominent Jews help call the attention of America to their age-old heritage.

The Daughters of the American Revolution has long been known for its conservatism, exclusivity, even bigotry. In 1939 the D.A.R. canceled a concert in its Constitution Hall, Washington, D.C., by world-famous black opera singer Marian Anderson. Eleanor Roosevelt intervened and switched the concert to the Lincoln Memorial, where thousands of people heard Anderson sing. So it seemed like a grand coup when on December 10, 1980, the D.A.R. sponsored an exhibition, "The Jewish Community in Early America—1654–1830" at the D.A.R. Museum in the nation's capital.

Formally dressed members and guests, including at least ten ambassadors and Lady Bird Johnson, gazed up at the balcony where a group of "generals," the D.A.R. officers, stood along with former President Gerald R. Ford, Postmaster General William Bolger, and John Langeloth Loeb, Jr., the man who originated the idea for the exhibition.

Loeb, an investment broker, financial supporter of Ronald

Reagan, member of his foreign-affairs task force and currently ambassador to Denmark, suggested the show, helped finance it and gave a dinner after the opening. Says the tall, dark, aristocratic Loeb, "Everyone seemed fascinated that the D.A.R. would honor the Jewish community in America."

Loeb, a member of the Sons of the American Revolution, is the son of Frances (Lehman) Loeb and John L. Loeb, the investment banker. The exhibition came about as a result of Loeb Jr.'s desire to pay tribute to his Sephardic southern grandmother. In honor of the bicentennial, the Loeb family had made a contribution to expand the museum space at Fraunces Tavern, the New York City landmark where George Washington said good-bye to his troops after the revolution. The addition they funded is known as the Adeline Moses Loeb gallery.

First an exhibition, "The Jewish Community in America, 1654–1800," was held at Fraunces Tavern. Loeb Jr. wanted the exhibition to travel to Washington, but a number of places, including the Smithsonian Institution, showed no interest. Loeb called the D.A.R. curator, Jean Federico, who went to see the exhibition, then sold the idea to the D.A.R. and expanded the years covered by thirty. Loeb contributed twenty-four large-size photo panels, showing paintings, prints, documents and decorative arts relating to the life of early Jewish settlers. The D.A.R. exhibition also included paintings of Jewish patrons and patriots by such artists as Gilbert Stuart and Thomas Sully, silver (some of the best work of famed colonial silversmith Myer Myers), jewelry, furniture, manuscripts and pottery.

The D.A.R. had never before shown a loan exhibition in its museum, hardly publicized the fact that it had a museum and certainly never honored the Jews.

Loeb adored his grandmother, a member of the D.A.R., who died in 1953. Adeline Moses Loeb was born in Sheffield, Alabama. Her father, Captain Alfred Huger Moses, who fought for the Confederacy, founded Sheffield, Alabama, immediately following the Civil War. Captain Moses's brother Mordecai Moses was a three-term mayor of Montgomery, Alabama. Mayor Mordecai Moses's home in Montgomery has recently been placed on the National Historic Register.

In the financial panic of 1893, the family of Adeline Moses lost all its money and moved from Alabama to St. Louis, where they took boarders ("My great-grandfather ran the boarding house; lots of people did in those days," says Loeb). Adeline Moses fell in love with Carl Moses Loeb, a boarder visiting St. Louis as representative of a German metals firm. Her family thought "they could go no lower," claims Loeb with a smile. "Not only was she marrying a German but an immigrant." That immigrant became a wealthy and influential American Jew.

At the D.A.R. opening, former President Ford lauded the Jews: "Jews fought and died during the American Revolution and in every war since then . . . Jews have won Congressional Medals of Honor in time of war and Nobel Prizes in times of peace in every area of endeavor: art, philosophy, science, medicine. . . . I am optimistic that this exhibition, 'The Jewish Community in Early America—1654–1830,' signals a new era in our nation. It will be an era which upholds, honors and reveres the great principles and ideals which were the roots of our history and our national life. These principles and ideals, properly understood, unite all the people of our nation of whatever religion or race. It is a unity founded upon diversity and respect for the religious views and customs of our people."

With deep feeling, Loeb comments, "There is so much misunderstanding between Christians and Jews. It is helpful to show the Christian community how much of a part Jews played in the founding of our country. Christians today think of Jews in terms of Israel. This exhibition reminds them how long Jews have been here. It should help remind the world that the Jews did many of the same things as Protestants—and in some cases earlier."

Very much the product of Hotchkiss and Harvard, Loeb has been accused by some of denying his Jewishness. His response to this charge: "If I did that, I would not be having an exhibition and talking to audiences at temples." Although his life-style is not aggressively Jewish, he is a member of Temple Emanu-El, New York, and Century Country Club and did make possible the stunning exhibition, now touring under the auspices of the American Jewish Historical Society.

Because of Loeb's feat, the D.A.R. acquired a new more liberal image. Everyone was happy, including a young girl who wrote to Mrs. Richard Denny Shelby, president general, National Society Daughters of the American Revolution: "Dear Madame President. I want to thank you for what you did for the Jews. Please send your picture and autograph. I am nine and go to Hebrew School."

Josephine Stayman

Some JEPs have followed the lead of the Our Crowd Jews and become less overtly Jewish. Josephine Stayman's family changed their name, became financially successful and moved away—almost completely—from their Eastern European origins. Her story typifies what has happened to many JEPs.

Friends call Mrs. Sam Stayman "Tubby" because she was once fat. Her husband is the legendary grand-master bridge player, creator of the Stayman bidding convention. The Staymans are members of the Harmonie Club, (New York City's elite club originally composed only of German Jews), live on Park Avenue, have a second home in Palm Beach. "Tubby" Stayman grew up as an Orthodox Jew in Tulsa, Oklahoma.

Her grandfather Herman Appleman came from Lithuania; her grandmother was from the same *shtetl* (little village). The Applemans moved successively from Duluth, Minnesota, to Parkersburg, West Virginia, where they became involved in the oil business, then to Kansas City, Missouri, and finally to Tulsa. Her father was Abraham Jacob Lewis: "They called him 'Jeb' and his family name had been Oschinsky. He was one of thirteen children and had gone to C.C.N.Y."

She recalls, "After my parents' marriage, he took her to New York. My father worked for Oschinsky and Valentine, a shirt company. The Valentines were related to the Tishmans. Then my mother's father convinced him to move to Oklahoma and my father went into business with him. They called it Central Petroleum. My grandfather was not just in the oil business. He had been a chicken killer. When he died, he had his own coop.

"It was very ghettoized in Tulsa. To the Christian community the Jews were freaks. My father was president of the synagogue. He had to arrange for *minyans.* To get the necessary ten men, we had to fetch them to the synagogue and bring them home for breakfast. I had years of Hebrew school while the Christian girls went horseback riding. I used to lie, saying, 'My mother wants me at home.'

"There was one time at grade school when my father made a fuss. I was very small, so I was going to be the baby in the manger in the Christmas play. He would not let me do it. He did not allow us to sing Christmas carols. I felt strange—again, like a freak. At high schools, there were sororities and fraternities. My sorority was Iota Tau, a Jewish sorority. All the Christian sororities met in a beautiful area at the high school and the Jews had to meet in the Trophy Room. Even there we were ghettoized. My friend Happy explained it to me, 'We'll no longer be going to the same events. My country club is restricted from having Jewish guests.' We would nod hello in the hall.

"Twelve months a year my two sisters and I would go on Saturday morning to the synagogue. In summer we would walk five miles there and walk home and then play tennis. In fall after the service, we would walk to see the Tulsa Oilers play. In winter we would walk to synagogue and then go to my father's office for sandwiches—no hamburgers; I lived on egg salad and grilled cheese—and then we would go to the movies. We would have bought tickets the day before (Orthodox Jews cannot use money on Saturdays). Then we would wait until dark and drive home. Eventually a Reform temple was built in Tulsa; it became *the* temple.

"We were not allowed to go to a coed school. All three of us went to Goucher College. At Goucher I was not accepted by the Jews. I was a hayseed. I did not even have a good academic background. I had had five years of Oklahoma history. I felt out of step. The other girls were better equipped, better looking, better groomed.

"At eighteen, my father told me, 'Make your own decision about religion.' I gave up synagogue.

"I married my first husband, Rennold Wacht, to get away from my parents. I loved a dentist, but my stepmother [her mother had died] said, 'Dentists are just people who don't get into medical school.' Wacht was just out of the army and at Yale. His father was in real estate and he went into it. My parents were delighted; his grandfather was I. Miller of the shoe industry. We married and had three children. We were divorced in 1960, the same year my father died of cancer.

"A year and a half after the divorce, I met Sam on a blind date. He is fifteen years older than I. At first the age difference bothered me. I thought he is not the kind of man who will play football with my son."

But the Staymans have been happy. "Sam still competes at bridge tournaments. He goes to three nationals. The Stayman Convention is world famous. Bridge is his hobby, an avocation. He won the world championship four times. When I met him, I did not play, but now we love to play together."

The Staymans belong to Central Synagogue, a Reform temple. Originally from Worcester, Massachusetts, Stayman, the son of a Russian Jewish immigrant, went to Dartmouth, the Tuck School of Business, started his business career at Macy's. His mother was religious; his father rebelled and founded the Unitarian Church in Westport.

Still involved in Jewish philanthropic causes, twice a year Mrs. Stayman organizes fundraisers in the bridge world for UJA-Federation of Jewish Philanthropies. She says, "Because of my Orthodox roots there are certain things I insist upon. My children married in the faith, but are not active templegoers. But the sense of Judaism permeates family thinking. The kids always come home for the Jewish holidays.

Betty Levin

While some Jews have moved away from ritual, others move toward it.

Betty Levin, born Loeb, is a typical Our Crowd Jew. (She is a cousin of John Loeb, Jr.) Levin went to Brearley and Wells College and right after graduation married a man she met at fourteen in Viola Wolff's Sunday afternoon "alumni classes."

She had four children and in 1975 became a reentry woman with her own firm, Corporate Art Directions (art consultant to corporations). In addition, Betty Levin, now forty-two, who had been brought up with little religion and a history of Christmas trees instead of Hanukkah candles, recently became a born-again Jew.

"I had perhaps been to one Yom Kippur service in my life," she explains. "But I started to listen to the people I respected. There was a recurring theme: One should not be too complacent. I thought it was time that I learned what being Jewish was and that my kids learned too."

She arranged for a Hebrew teacher, John Lifshutz, to come to the house and teach her children the history of Judaism. He came once a week, for a year, but her older son, Henry, now nineteen, wanted to be bar mitzvahed. She was able to persuade Temple Emanu-El to allow him to be bar mitzvahed there even though he had not completed their course of study. But for Henry, learning about his roots was an earnest matter. Even after his "coming-of-age" ceremony, he and a group of friends kept on with their studies, holding their last session in an Israeli bar in Greenwich Village.

But religion for her children was not enough. Levin wanted her own involvement. Before founding her business, she had been active in charitable organizations. Now she decided to organize a Business and Professional Women's division for the New York Federation of Jewish Philanthropies. Four years ago she and a friend, Cynthia Colin (sister of New York Congressman William Green), founded the group which now includes teachers, psychiatrists, writers, art directors, stockbrokers and lawyers.

She now belongs to two temples—Emanu-El and Central Synagogue—and is planning a bar mitzvah for her second son.

She says, "I think there is a big trend back to Judaism. My generation of parents today are more involved in Jewish affairs. The children are involved because their parents are. You are not kidding anyone when you become 'assimilated.' You cannot hide from being Jewish. Like everyone else, I am looking for something to hold on to. The Jews are terriffic. When Federation started, the members were Warburgs and people like that. Now there are lots of wealthy Jews and they cut across every social strata."

Roy S. Neuberger

"I was never bar mitzvahed," says Roy S. Neuberger, another Jew who has also discovered his Jewishness. "There was nothing Jewish about my family. They never celebrated a single Jewish holiday. The family religion was Ethical Culture. My mother had gone to school there and so did I—from nursery through high school. We celebrated the American Christian holidays."

Eight years ago Roy S. Neuberger, son of the well-known stockbroker and art collector Roy R. Neuberger and Marie Salant Neuberger, became an Orthodox Jew.

How did this come about?

Neuberger, now thirty-nine, spent five years at the University of Michigan, where he acquired a B.A., M.A. and a wife Linda (from a Reform assimilated family; her father owns the furniture-store chain Maurice Villency Inc.). Neuberger went on to spend a year at Oxford, work for August Heckscher in New York, and then bought a newspaper, the *Cornwall Local* in Cornwall, New York.

One night the Neubergers just happened to hear Rebbetzin Esther Jungreis, the tiny, intense Orthodox Jewish revivalist from Long Island, speak at the Conservative temple in nearby Newburgh. Many people call Jungreis "the Jewish Billy Graham." Her Hungarian accent and blonde hair make her look and sound a bit like Zsa Zsa Gabor. In 1973 she founded a Jewish revivalist movement called "Hineni," ("Here I am"—the words Abraham spoke when God called him) that now has thousands of followers. According to *Time* magazine, "her sole mission is to lure, cajole, or otherwise summon secularized Jews back to their faith." She also has a weekly talk show for the new Jewish National Television hookup which goes to seventy-two cable outlets. She calls those who ignore their heritage "Jewish amnesiacs."

After hearing Rebbetzin Jungreis speak and attending her

Torah learning classes, the Neubergers completely changed their life-style. Jungreis and many follower families live in North Woodmere, New York. The Neubergers moved there too. "We wanted to be with people who live it," Neuberger explains simply. "We had so much to learn."

Neuberger sold the *Cornwall Local* and worked for the *Long Island Press* until it went out of business. He now serves as principal at an elementary yeshiva in Brooklyn.

He is also the father of five. Married for eighteen years, he had only two children when he moved to North Woodmere. He explains, "Very honestly, before we made the switch we felt this was not a world where we wanted to have children. We were going to have a small family. Because of our work with Rebbetzin Jungreis, we got a sense of hope, a feeling of purpose to life."

How do his assimilated parents feel about his new mode of living? He pauses before answering: "That is always the number-one question. They thought we would get over it. At one time I had their prejudices. I thought Orthodoxy was something from the Stone Age. But since we changed, I go out of my way to make sure my parental relationship is good. The Rebbetzin encouraged me. The Commandment says, 'Honor thy father and thy mother.' "

When the Neubergers visit his parents at their Fifth Avenue apartment, they bring their own food for dinner or "They give us something simple like cottage cheese and fruit on paper plates." Sometimes both generations go to a kosher restaurant —Moshe Peking or La Difference at the Roosevelt Hotel, which is "both chic and Glatt kosher."

Neuberger's friends are not restricted to the Orthodox world. "That is what most impressed us when we first heard the Rebbetzin," he comments. "She believes that all Jews are links in a chain. She wants to unite the Jewish community, not let them disappear in silence. Now we try to educate others."

What does Neuberger get from Orthodoxy that he did not receive as a nonpracticing Jew? His firm answer: "A way of living. Until we heard the Rebbetzin speak, we were really like a ship drifting without direction. We lived a life of darkness. Young people are suffering. They are looking for something.

This is why the cults are flourishing. They are looking for something in which to believe. You ask am I happier now. It is as if I never ate and now can eat. Or as if I could not breathe and now can. I am alive. Before I was not."

Rita Hauser, senior partner at the prestigious law firm Stroock & Stroock & Lavan, New York, served as U.S. Representative to the U.N. Commission on Human Rights from 1969 to 1972 and was a member of the U.S. Delegation to the 24th U.N. General Assembly.

President Jimmy Carter; Milton Wolf, ambassador to Austria; Soviet interpreter Victor Souhodrev; Soviet President Leonid Brezhnev at Salt II Summit in Vienna, 1979. Wolf is the well-known Cleveland philanthropist and fund-raiser. *Credit: Wally McNamee–Newsweek*

Shown here on a construction site, Frederick P. Rose serves as chairman of Rose Associates, Inc., a family real estate business based in New York. *Credit: Gordon Vaughan*

Shirley Goodman, who has held every job at New York's Fashion Institute of Technology from acting president down, is one of the most honored women in the fashion industry. *Credit: Martha Holmes*

Sanford Weill, chairman of the board and chief executive officer of Shearson/American Express and chairman of the executive committee of the American Express Company, with former President Gerald Ford who serves on both boards. *Credit: Skip Hine*

Millionaire businessman Lewis Lehrman takes time off from the Lehrman Institute to bicycle in Central Park with his wife and five children. *Credit: Bob Skilmann III*

Betty Levin, director of Corporate Art Directions recently became a born-again Jew. She helped organize the Business and Professional Women's Division for the Federation of Jewish Philanthropies of New York.

Rabbi Sally Priesand, ordained in 1972, is the first woman rabbi in the U.S. She is now the rabbi at Monmouth Reform Temple, Tinton Falls, New Jersey.

As senior vice-president for external affairs at R.H. Macy & Company, Inc., G.G. Michelson represents the company in relationships with the community, handles programs in philanthropy and deals with shareholders.

PART TWO

WHO'S WHO

6

THE WALL STREET SUPERSTARS

On June 29, 1981, the shareholders of Shearson Loeb Rhoades Inc., Wall Street's second largest brokerage house, gathered for a specially called meeting at the World Trade Center in downtown Manhattan. The purpose: to give their blessing to the merging of the company with American Express, the international credit-card giant, in a stock trade valued at more than $900 million. Not only did they approve the merger, but they gave a standing ovation to Sanford I. Weill, forty-eight, Shearson chairman and chief executive officer. An emotional man, he cried. So did his wife Joan. Weill had come a long way from the unsure young man who once stated, "I was not looking to be the man out front."

Seven weeks later, on August 17, 1981, Stephen Schwarzman, thirty-four, sat in his unpretentious office on the forty-fourth floor at Lehman Brothers Kuhn Loeb, the prestigious investment house. His two phones rang constantly; a series of calls from partners and competitors about a mysterious $500-million sale; a potential client setting up a luncheon meeting; a Wall Street arbitrageur making a late afternoon date for a meeting at the Harvard Club. In talking on the Speakerphone, Schwarzman used the Wall Street jargon in vogue "among the younger guys in the merger business": "print that ticket" (get the deal done), "max fee," "min fee," "play Lone Ranger" (lots of risk), "do some intelligence," "mercy killing" (get it over with). Four days later the meaning of "$500 million" became clear. Pan American World Airways had sold Intercontinental Hotels Corporation, its most profitable division, to Grand Metropolitan Hotels, the British conglomerate, for $500 million. Representing the sellers, the dynamic Stephen Schwarzman had spent this summer Sunday working out the deal.

These two JEPs stand out among the superstars taking over Wall Street today. Due to changes in the securities business and old age, the elegant old guard has virtually disappeared. The name of the game is young. According to blue-eyed Schwarzman, "A superstar is bright, hardworking, driven, competent, rational, orderly, professional. He is a member of an elite, but a far different elite from that of former days. It is an educated achievement elite. Most members have been to Harvard Business School or a good Ivy League school. Background does not matter anymore. We care about talent."

Benjamin Buttenwieser, eighty-one, with Kuhn Loeb since 1917 and the only firm member to make the White House "enemies" list under President Nixon, typifies the Old Guard. An advisory director, he sits at a leather-topped desk in a large room with seven other desks (states a senior partner, "The younger people were not trained to work in one room; they want their own offices"). "I was not born with a silver spoon in my mouth. It was platinum studded with diamonds," says the courtly and highly articulate Buttenwieser. "The gang does not mean anything anymore. It is a new crowd."

Buttenwieser, who walks the eighty blocks or so from his apartment on Fifty-second Street and the East River to his office in downtown Manhattan, sums up one major Wall Street change succinctly, "There is less importance attached to family background now than there was in the past. If you have ability, character, conscientiousness and are willing to work hard, you can rise on Wall Street now without family connections."

He cites a poem:

> The heights by great men reached and kept
> Were not attained by sudden flight,
> But they, while their companions slept,
> Were toiling upward in the night.

Weill and Schwarzman come from far different backgrounds than the aristocratic Buttenwieser. Brooklyn-born Weill's parents were Orthodox Polish immigrants who kept a kosher home. Schwarzman comes from a Conservative background, a mix of Russian (father) and German-Austrian (mother). Schwarzman's father has a dry-goods store. "He is an underachiever," comments Schwarzman frankly, "but he is happy."

Weill and Schwarzman also have different personalities. Weill exudes a conditioned confidence, achieved by a series of small steps and quantum leaps. Both his admirers and detractors claim he has "elbowed" his way to the top. On the other hand, Schwarzman says about himself, "I was always president of the class or something." He was made a partner just six years after his graduation from Harvard Business School. Weill is already a superstar. Schwarzman is getting there.

Wall Street was not always so open.

A FINANCIAL MARRIAGE

In the late nineteenth and early twentieth century Wall Street was peopled with many Our Crowd Jews with partnerships descending only to sons and sons-in-law. Famous names included Hallgarten, Stralem, Neustadt, Heidelbach, Seligman, Loeb, Kuhn, Schiff, Warburg, Goldman, Sachs, Lehman, Bache.

According to its history *Investment Banking through Four Generations,* it was not until Kuhn Loeb was forty-four years old in 1911 that it first admitted a partner who was not one of the immediate family. According to its centennial history *Lehman Brothers 1850–1950,* Lehman Brothers did not have a nonrelative as partner until 1924. And many a man—particularly at Kuhn Loeb—got to the top by marrying the boss's daughter.

Today at Lehman Brothers Kuhn Loeb (insiders always pronounce it "coon") there is no one named Lehman, Kuhn or Loeb.

Honorary chairman John Schiff, seventy-seven, great-grandson of Solomon Loeb and grandson of Jacob Schiff, has a corner office uptown on Madison Avenue where formerly active partners make their headquarters but possesses limited power. ("I was terrified of Grandfather Schiff," the silver-haired septuagenarian admits, "but I did not realize how important he was until I went to his funeral.") His son David T. (that is for Tevele, a collateral forebear who sold the family house in Frankfurt am Main to the first really rich Rothschild and moved to England, where he became chief rabbi of London's Great Synagogue in the 1800s) goes to work every day, and, according to another partner, occupies himself "a great deal with philanthropy."

Philip Isles, great-grandson of Philip Lehman, is a partner. His father, Philip Ickleheimer, changed the family surname to Isles.

In December of 1977, Lehman Brothers, founded in 1850, and Kuhn Loeb and Company, founded in 1867, merged, marking the consolidation of two of the most widely known and oldest investment houses on Wall Street. Newspapers throughout the nation headlined "The Merger Wave Envelopes Our Crowd" and "Our Crowd Less One."

Today the two people in command at Lehman Brothers Kuhn Loeb are Peter Peterson, chairman and president, who is the son of Greek immigrants, Gentile and former secretary of commerce and international trade expert for the Nixon administration; and Lewis Glucksman, managing director, who, without connections or lineage but with brains and moneymaking abilities, made his way to the top rungs of Wall Street.

The story of what has happened at this internationally known firm illustrates two points: (1) the American melting pot still exists. (2) It used to be family and friends. Today it is who you are and what you do—an attitude that has made possible the emergence of superstars Weill and Schwarzman.

THE WAY IT WAS

Both Lehman Brothers and Kuhn Loeb had their origins far from Wall Street.

Lehman was founded by three brothers—Henry, Emanuel and Mayer—who emigrated to Montgomery, Alabama, from

Bavaria to establish a cotton-brokerage business in 1850. Because frequent trips to New York were necessary to convert the promissory notes they received in payment for cotton into cash, Mayer and Emanuel (Henry had died of yellow fever) opened an office in New York in 1858.

As late as 1900 Lehman was still considered essentially a commodity brokerage house. But when the second generation of Lehmans began to run the firm, they moved vigorously into corporate financing—and made their mark by handling companies in such industries as retailing, textiles and apparel that other investment brokers would not touch.

Later in the twentieth century, the family produced a United States senator and New York governor (Herbert), a distinguished judge (Irving) and a noted art collector who headed the firm for many years (Robert). Arthur L. Goodhart, a nephew of Herbert, became the first American chairman of the faculty of jurisprudence at Oxford. He received the grade of knight commander of the Order of the British Empire in 1948 and would have been entitled to the designation *Sir* had he not been a U.S. citizen.

Robert Lehman, the third generation of his family to run the firm, was the first to welcome nonfamily members. He attracted a heterogeneous cast of entrepreneurs, like the late socialite polo player Thomas Hitchcock, Jr. According to Marilyn Bender in *At the Top,* "For though Lehman was a sportsman who kept polo ponies and racing stables and was a towering patron of the arts, as a Jew he was denied entree to some of the clubs where Wall Street and the corporate establishments transact their business in social settings."

At Kuhn Loeb the family ties remained stronger. The concern was established as a dry-goods business in Cincinnati, then the third largest city in the United States with such a large German-speaking population that it was virtually bilingual, by two German-born brothers-in-law, Abraham Kuhn and Solomon Loeb. In 1867 Kuhn and Loeb opened Kuhn, Loeb & Company, a private banking house in New York with a capital reputed to have been $500,000 (Loeb's second wife had insisted they leave Cincinnati, which she hated). Kuhn returned to Germany. Early partners were Abraham Wolff and Louis Heinsheimer; from 1869 through 1911 the firm had no partners who were not related to Mr. Loeb or Mr. Wolff.

Then the marriages started. German-born Jacob Schiff, who became well known, at least by reputation, in all the wealthy households, married Therese Loeb, Solomon's daughter from his first marriage. Schiff became an American citizen in 1870, a Kuhn Loeb partner in 1875, the owner of a large house on Fifth Avenue and the head of Kuhn Loeb in 1886.

The Warburgs also obtained key positions at Kuhn Loeb through marriage. Felix married Jacob Schiff's daughter Frieda. Paul, like Felix born in Hamburg, married Solomon Loeb's daughter Nina from wife number two and thus became his brother Felix's uncle. He also became a founder of the Federal Reserve system.

According to Benjamin Buttenwieser, who knew both the old and new regimes, "Jacob Schiff was the boss. Then came Otto Kahn, the patron of the arts (he married Adelaide Wolff, daughter of partner Abraham Wolff); Mortimer Schiff, son of Jacob, and Felix Warburg." (Buttenwieser was there when Kahn died of a heart attack in a private dining room at the firm's offices, then at 52 William Street, and announced the news to the press in a brief typewritten statement).

Jerome Hanauer was the first partner who was not one of the immediate family. He had started at Kuhn Loeb as an office boy. Years before, his father Moses Hanauer had gone bankrupt. At the time, Moses Hanauer had been on the board of an elite New York hospital along with Jacob Schiff. At a board meeting Schiff stated he would not be in a room with someone who "could not honor his debts," and exited. Shortly afterward Moses Hanauer committed suicide.

Later Schiff, perhaps motivated by a sense of guilt, hired Moses's son Jerome as an office boy for the investment house. Hanauer, who had attended the College of the City of New York for one year, went through nearly all the departments of the banking house before he became a partner. Eventually his daughter Alice married Lewis Strauss (pronounced Straws), a partner at Kuhn Loeb, who was to become atomic energy commissioner and a highly controversial figure in the Robert Oppenheimer hearings.

While the Loeb sons-in-law built the business, the Loeb sons left it. Morris became a famous chemist. James established the Loeb Classical Library, moved to a small town in Germany near Munich. The Schiff family remains with Kuhn Loeb to the present day.

When the linkup of Lehman Brothers Kuhn Loeb took place in December, 1977, newspapers described it as a merger. And their reversible billing in the new firm—known as Lehman Brothers Kuhn Loeb in the United States and Kuhn Loeb Lehman Brothers in other countries (the flip-flop was due to Kuhn Loeb's first-class banking business overseas)—tended to reinforce that impression. Most people thought that these two grand old Wall Street firms were joining forces on an equal footing.

Within the investment community the impression was very different. One veteran deal maker said at the time, "It was a buy-out, with Lehman having first option on the Kuhn Loeb people."

One partner says now, "This was not a merger. It was an acquisition. The Lehman partners were more productive. The Kuhn Loeb people were gentlemen. They had so much money they did not have to work. Robert Lehman had hired hungry guys who wanted to work. They were more energetic. Most of Kuhn Loeb people are gone now. They could not keep up the pace."

Along with Goldman Sachs and Lazard Frères, Lehman Brothers Kuhn Loeb is considered one of the leading Jewish investment houses. However, its members include such people as George W. Ball, who was under secretary of state in both the Kennedy and Johnson administrations, and James R. Schlesinger, a former head of the Central Intelligence Agency and the Defense and Energy Departments.

Lehman Brothers Kuhn Loeb is a private corporation. The eighty or so managing directors (as a "kindness" the firm keeps some veterans on who "do little and have no money in the firm") call themselves partners. Each has invested his own money. As a private corporation, Lehman Brothers Kuhn Loeb does not have to disclose its specific-earnings figures. However, according to a story in the *Wall Street Journal,* in the year ending September 30, 1981, Lehman Brothers Kuhn Loeb earnings set a record and that "pre-tax profit rose almost twenty percent to $118 million from the year-earlier pre-tax net of about $100 million."

With headquarters in a fifty-one story tower at 55 Water Street, Lehman Brothers Kuhn Loeb retains its elegance and some aristocratic ways. Liveried butlers walk around carrying dainty china trays with an individual cup of coffee or tea. There are perks: There is a private partners dining room with antique mahogany furniture plus several other executive dining rooms. Free cigars are available. Partners also have a health club on the forty-third floor equipped with a gymnasium and sauna.

In the reception area on the way to the swank dining rooms hang the dignified ancestral portraits of Mayer and Emanuel Lehman, Jacob Schiff, Solomon Loeb, Abraham Kuhn, Felix Warburg, Arthur Lehman, Robert Lehman, Otto Kahn.

Yet in the financial community, the past hardly matters anymore. Says savvy Stephen Schwarzman, "Wall Street is no longer a gentleman's business. It is a pretend gentleman's business."

AS IT IS

In layman's language there have been many changes in Wall Street.

The familial aspect is dying. Says investment banker Robert Bernhard, who is of Lehman descent, "We used to come into this business through nepotism. Today nepotism has gone by the boards. You have to be a professional—and it is not easy."

Henry Gellermann, retired partner of Bache, echoes this tenet with, "You no longer can enter the Big League in Wall Street because you belong. For example, Jules Bache owned Bache. Harold was his nephew. He took it for granted he would take over. This does not happen now."

There have been fewer partnerships. Says Gellermann, "Formerly the Street was composed of partnerships. They were a close-knit family of men, linked socially as well as in business. Now inbred continuity is on the way out. The Street is far more open to outside brains and capital than ever before."

A major reason for the shift to publicly held firms rather than private partnerships is economic. Since partners' profits are taxed as high as 70 percent, after-tax profits for reinvestment accumulate very slowly. Therefore when a partner dies—and the estate has to be bought out—the surviving partners have to find new money or cut back the partnership's activities to offset the amount of money leaving the firm. Comments Benjamin Buttenwieser, "If the partnership has $100 million of capital and one partner has $25 million and he dies, the firm has to pay off. The capital has to be great."

The merger wave has transformed the financial community. Just as Shearson Loeb Rhoades stockholders eagerly tendered their shares to American Express, Salomon Brothers sold out to the Phibro Corporation (a $26-billion-a-year commodity giant) and the Dillon family sold its controlling interest to San Francisco's Bechtel family.

"Some ten or twelve years ago Saul Steinberg was going to make a takeover offer for the Chemical Bank," comments Richard Holman, editor and publisher of the *Wall Street Transcript.* "It was unheard of that someone try to take over a firm now listed on the New York Stock Exchange and a bank to boot. Now takeovers happen every day. A guy can come out of the woodwork and take over a company."

The attitude is tough. "In the old days they lived in a fool's paradise," recalls Buttenwieser. "They would not poach on each others' preserves. The attitude was if Central is a Morgan client, do not muscle in. Now they all compete. It's good. The whole emphasis has changed from *caveat emptor* to *caveat vendor.*"

According to a series of interviews with Wall Street men at the top, several Jewish superstars stand out. John Gutfreund ("German but not old German," says the chief executive officer at another investment banking firm), the managing partner of Salomon Brothers, which recently merged with Phibro, is one. Another: Felix Rohatyn of Lazard Frères. Known as Felix the

Fixer, he orchestrated New York City's recovery from the edge of bankruptcy and is considered by many a natural for the next secretary of the Treasury under a Democratic presidency. Still another superstar: Leon Levy, a City College graduate, who helped turn Oppenheimer & Company into a major force. But two names keep recurring: Sandy Weill as a Wall Street *wunderkind* and Stephen Schwarzman as a young man destined to reach the very top.

Sandy Weill

Sandy Weill has become one of Wall Street's most viable personalities. Along the way he has gained a reputation for a temper, ruthlessness and a penchant for running a one-man show. He is tough and oriented toward the bottom line, yet fair in his personal interactions, willing to listen to others and to change his mind. At the time of this writing, insiders wonder how Weill, the self-made entrepreneur from Brooklyn, will be able to work with James Robinson III, the financial prodigy from an old-line Georgia banking family who heads American Express. Weill himself, however, seems imperturbed.

Not long ago when David Rockefeller flew in his private helicopter to Cornell Business School to speak at a forum Weill was slated to address at another time, Weill asked if he could tag along to see how it was done. Rockefeller happily obliged. "I thought, only in America," recalls Weill, "would Sandy Weill, a kid from Brooklyn, end up hitching a ride with David Rockefeller."

Unlike many of Wall Street's Horatio Alger stories, Weill's was not characterized from the start by a burning desire to take charge of his own business.

"I am always running scared," says Weill of himself. But no longer. "He has changed," comments his attractive and adoring wife, the former Joan Mosher. "He is much more self-confident. He used to go up to people and say, 'Hello, I am Sandy Weill.' He has stopped doing it. Now people come up to him. He is basically a shy person. He has become much more outgoing. We have worked on him. He is educatable. He likes to learn."

Today Weill, who smokes eight cigars on some days, two packs of cigarettes on others, has a seven-room apartment in New York and a thirteen-room house on nine acres in Greenwich, Connecticut—equipped with a sauna, wine cellar, pool and tennis court (in his young days Weill was a Junior Davis Cup player). In his youth he went to Hebrew school and was bar mitzvahed; today he belongs to two temples: Emanu-El in New York and Emanuel in Great Neck.

Weill started with few affluent trappings. His mother had been a bookkeeper. His father went into his father-in-law's dress business.

Weill learned to adapt early to whatever fate tossed his way. When he was eleven years old, his middle-class family moved to Florida for a few years. Upon their return to Brooklyn after the war, he was sent to the Peekskill Military Academy because there was no room for him in his grandparents' crowded apartment. He found he liked military school. "It taught me discipline," he says. "I was supposed to go for one year. Instead I went for four."

Weill started as an engineering major at Cornell University, but, after a few difficult courses, switched to business. His approach to engineering had been more imaginative than scientific. In a physics course, unable to figure out the trajectory line of a missile that was shot into a particular orbit, Weill wrote "My missile never got into orbit."

The transition from Weill's early days to becoming chairman of the board and chief executive officer of Shearson/American Express and chairman of the executive committee of American Express Company is the story of one man's success on Wall Street over a period when others have found such success hard to win.

The story begins in 1955 when the newly married Weill was in New York City looking for a temporary job. His life was in a state of confusion. Earlier in the year, in the closing months of his senior year at Cornell, he had been planning after graduation to serve as an air force officer and then join his father in business. But his father left his mother, and the family turmoil caused Weill to miss his midterm examinations. "On graduation day, I found out I was not getting my diploma," he says.

In the previous year he had met Joan Mosher. His aunt recognized her father, a publicist for bandleader Kay Kyser, from Hebrew school in Brooklyn and arranged a blind date. He went to her house to look her over ("I did not want to take out a girl I had not seen. We stayed up talking until 3:00 A.M. and we have been talking ever since"). Joan Weill says it was 5:00 A.M. She was born in Brooklyn "around the corner from Sandy" and is of Austrian and Russian descent.

In his search for a temporary job, Weill walked into a Bache office on Forty-second Street and thought it looked very exciting, so he decided to go to work for a brokerage firm. He was turned down by Merrill Lynch and Harris Upham but got a job at Bear, Stearns & Company as a runner for $150 a month. In his first year he received six raises and was earning $250 a month.

After taking the job, Weill finally got his degree from Cornell. And he decided not to go into the air force. "Bear Stearns saw that I had a college degree," he says, "while all the other runners were on Social Security, so they decided to train me to be a salesman."

Thus, by happenstance, did Weill embark on what was to become a career and an obsession. His wife comments, "I am a first wife. I do not have another woman to follow. I have a firm." It did not take Weill long to progress from sales to management. In 1960, he and three partners founded the securities firm of Carter, Berlind, Potoma & Weill. It was capitalized at $250,000, $30,000 of which was Weill's.

He explains how he acquired his share of the capital: "When I got married, my in-laws were willing to spend $5,000 on the wedding. Instead we had a small wedding for $1,500, and they gave me the remaining $3,500. I invested it. The first year I had one winner and twenty-four losers. Early in the game I made a lot of typical mistakes. I learned a lot. I learned to listen to tips. You can do well if you pay attention. I was lucky that first year. I learned what *not* to do.

"I had about $2,000 left, and in four years—by 1960—we had accumulated $31,000. We put $30,000 into the business, and saved $1,000 for emergencies. We put the house money into the business." To save that amount Sandy and Joan had lived in a series of Long Island apartments while other couples their age had bought houses.

By 1970, the concern was known as Cogan, Berlind, Weill & Levitt Inc. And in September, 1970, it acquired twenty-eight branch offices of the shaky Hayden Stone Inc., selling in the process $7 million of its stock to certain Hayden Stone holders at twice book value. In 1973, Sandy was named chairman and chief executive of Hayden Stone. The following year saw the acquisition of Shearson, Hammil & Company. And then came the announcement that Shearson Hayden Stone would absorb Loeb Rhoades Hornblower—with Sanford Weill as chairman and chief executive officer. It was heady stuff. Weill's firm had absorbed the company, headed by John Loeb, one of Wall Street's elder Our Crowd statesman.

His success permanently infected Weill with the growth bug and merger after merger ensued. Some did not work out—for instance, the Kuhn Loeb affair. In 1977, talks were well along when Kuhn Loeb decided that Lehman Brothers was a more appropriate merger partner than Shearson. Many people feel that the deal fell through because the aristocratic German Jews who dominated Kuhn Loeb at the time preferred their own kind. They did not think Brooklyn was good enough for them—and Weill knew it.

Angry at the time, Weill now has the confidence of success. "So it did not happen," he shrugs. "Kuhn Loeb felt better off with Lehman Brothers. In retrospect, it left us free to acquire Loeb Rhoades."

In less than ten years Sandy Weill has brought his company from $50 million to $1 billion. When it merged with American Express, Shearson was in the security industry's second-place spot, just behind giant Merrill Lynch Pierce Fenner and Smith Inc.

Weill has two adjoining offices. One is filled with beautiful antiques, including an enormous English hunt table which he uses as a desk. The second is a sitting room which he uses when two meetings go on simultaneously. He used this to talk privately with Joan about the American Express merger.

"I called her up and told her to come down," he recalls. "I asked her, 'Should we do it?' We spent an hour and a half talking with Jim Robinson in the next room. She told me, 'I think it will work out well,' so I went ahead."

From the beginning Sandy and Joan Weill have worked together: for themselves, their two children, their financial success. "We started with nothing," he says lovingly. "I always brought the business home. We would discuss people, possible mergers. She has not worked for money, but she has worked for me."

Joan explains what he means: "I do a lot of entertaining. I know a lot of people in the firm well. I travel with him. I hostess at conventions. I enjoy people. My study and work in psychology is helpful" (Joan minored in psychology at Brooklyn College and has spent several years as a Bellevue Hospital volunteer).

Many critics have commented on Weill's insecurities, the fact that he surrounds himself with currying employees, his quick temper, his need "to be accepted and loved," his competitiveness.

Weill is the first to admit he has hang-ups. "I am driven to be an achiever," he says, showing an engaging vulnerability. "I am demanding of myself and others. For a long time I had a tremendous drive to be accepted. By whom? By whoever was on the acceptance committee. About a year before the Loeb Rhoades merger, I first felt a sense of security about myself. I do not think I have to prove myself anymore.

"Until 1973 I loved to be a second-guesser. I felt I could not be wrong. I finally convinced myself that I had enough background that I could stand up and be counted. I grew to the point where I could take the responsibility for being wrong—that enabled me to take the credit for being right.

"My drive now is to build the greatest financial-services company in the world—to continue that creativity. Today the consolidation of the financial industry is driven by the ability to deliver a cost-effective product so that the consumer can get a financial reward for saving. The secret to success in the future is the ability to deal with the consumer directly. The consumer is more sophisticated. The money-market funds have proven that the smaller saver has found out he can get more than 5 percent.

"I do not put up with nonsense. I am interested in getting down to basics. I guess I am called aggressive because I am aggressive. Our company's rate of growth is aggressive. During the past ten years we have been one of the top-ten growth companies in the country. Socially I am not aggressive. I used to be very shy.

"I have not had a year that I did not enjoy more than the year before. It is not just one experience. It is cumulative. You draw from all your experiences and use them to make the next one better."

Wife Joan describes Weill as a "pragmatic dreamer." She says, "I remember years ago Sandy and a neighbor used to plan the deck they would build. He did it. About one of the mergers, his lawyer said, 'It is just impossible.' Sandy responded, 'That is the way I want it.' "

The informal Weill, whose office door is always open to employees, frankly admits he is consumed with business. "My wife claims I am intense," he says. "I spend a lot of time thinking about what we should be doing. I really can't wait to get up in the morning and read the papers and think about what kind of day we are going to have. I truly enjoy what I do."

The trappings of success are felt. Weill and family recently left Sunningdale Country Club for Century, the most prestigious Jewish country club in the metropolitan New York area.

Stephen Schwarzman

To Stephen Schwarzman, a thirty-four-year-old partner at Lehman Brothers Kuhn Loeb who has earned the reputation as their "merger maker," Sandy Weill is a middle-aged man.

In addition to the sale of Pan American World Airways hotel division, Schwarzman has played an instrumental role in the Bendix Corporation's winning bid for the Warner & Swasey Company, R.C.A.'s $1.35-billion acquisition of C.I.T. Financial, and the Beatrice Foods Company's $488-million acquisition of Tropicana Products Inc., and most recently the $348 million sale of Chrysler Defense Inc. to General Dynamics Corporation.

Schwarzman has always had a strong drive to succeed. He was an athlete in track—100, 220, 440 yard—and never on a losing team. He once finished running a cross-country course even after he tripped and broke his wrist. He admits, "My competitive spirit was so strong that while in training I used to vomit every day."

Raised in Philadelphia, the eldest son (he has twin brothers three years younger) of a middle-class family, he attended public school, lived in a split-level house and was very much the product of a stable home ("My parents never raised their voices to us kids or each other").

At Yale, where he majored in "culture and behavior," Schwarzman had a motorcycle. "I traveled with another guy," he recalls. "I always wanted to be ahead. I need other people. I do not care who is running against me. I want to be the best. Without the other person, it is no fun. I need to satisfy the desire to win."

At Yale, where he was a member of the exclusive Skull and Bones Society ("I must have been the fifth Jew in its history"), he turned his college thesis into a business enterprise by paying people to respond to a survey and then hiring others to keypunch the results—all financed by the school. He also organized a Yale ballet series and arranged a survey that helped abolish parietal hours.

After college he took a year to find himself. He worked for Donaldson, Lufkin, Jenrette Securities Corporation ("Bill Donaldson had gone to Yale—he saw himself in me"), went into the army for six months ("I had been with so many intellectuals; I wanted to be with real people again"), realized he would be "incompetent" in Wall Street without training ("I had never even taken an economics course") and went to Harvard Business School for two years. He was recruited on campus in 1972 and joined Lehman Brothers for $17,000. He claims, "I have had only one job," noting that he was one of the few Jews to be offered a job by Morgan Stanley. Schwarzman's success at Lehman Brothers and later Lehman Brothers Kuhn Loeb was such that he became a partner in 1978.

There is an up-from-the-ranks procedure at the firm. Schwarzman explains it. "You start in general corporate finance. Lehman has historic relationships with companies. I work on R.C.A. and Bendix. Most of the companies were here before I got here and will be here after I go. You start at the bottom doing support work for a guy four or five years older than you. When he becomes a partner, you become him. I became a partner when my clients started merging. I'm a natural. I like gamesmanship, competition, glamor, being with top people. I have the ability to relate to older people and figure out what is on their mind."

Schwarzman also feels his knack for telling the truth has helped him move to the top at a very young age. In one instance, the prospective buyer for Macmillan appeared to him too small. Although he was representing Macmillan and wanted to sell, he took him aside, saying, "Today you are a rich guy. You may get the money to buy now, but if you handle it wrong, you will be in trouble. This is free advice. Buy a company you can handle."

"Hey, you are supposed to be selling the company," commented the surprised businessman, who was at least fifteen years older than Schwarzman, who was thirty at the time.

Schwarzman repeated his free counsel, "Don't do it." The man did not.

Mergers are tricky. In some cases the top members of the company may be against spending money on an acquisition because they want the money for their own operations. "The financial advisor must have a sense of integrity," says Schwarzman. "Some deals should not get done—not because you do not like the guys, but because the deal is not right."

In one case, Schwarzman was working with a company head who wanted to merge, but Schwarzman was not sure that the acquisition of the desired company was a wise move. On a Sunday the head of the company came to his house and told him, "You are the only one holding out. Do the deal. Tell the chairman tomorrow."

The next day Schwarzman did talk to the chairman. However, he told him that buying this particular savings and loan company, which at the time was making $100 million net profit, was a risk. The chairman did not buy. Today the company is losing $40 million after taxes.

Schwarzman is very frank about his success: "My things always work. I care. My blend of talents is right for this business."

On a $500-million deal, the fee can run from ¼ percent to 1 percent. Says Schwarzman, "If I have done the job, I believe I deserve the largest fee possible." He estimates that in the last two years he has made between $20 million and $25 million for Lehman Brothers Kuhn Loeb.

He explains that the directors Peterson and Glucksman decide on the disbursements at the end of the year. "I get disproportionate cash to my interest in the firm. It is an incentive for younger people to get paid more than older people who have more stock in the company. The firm gets the money from a merger. Each partner has a percentage interest. Our cash percentage is based on performance. Our retained earnings is based on the percentage in the firm." In Schwartzman's second year as partner he received one of the highest cash bonuses in the firm.

Schwarzman's first break in the merger area came in 1977. He was in Chicago conducting research for a merger between UOP Inc. and the Signal Companies, being handled by a senior partner at Lehman. Late one Friday afternoon, a call was relayed to him from Kenneth Barnebey, president of Tropicana, asking him if he would fly down to Florida that night. The company wanted him to address a 9:00 A.M. board meeting the next morning to evaluate a proposal by Beatrice Foods to acquire Tropicana.

Mr. Barnebey had met Schwarzman only once and Schwarzman was not yet a Lehman partner. After he received Tropicana's call, Schwarzman phoned several Lehman partners to insure that there were no conflicts in taking on the assignment. Because of snowstorms in Chicago, it was nearly 4:00 A.M. before he landed in Florida. He first saw the detailed merger proposal at 8:00 A.M., an hour before he was to make a presentation to the directors. Sixty minutes later, after some quick consultations with Lehman partners in New York, Schwarzman presented his recommendations and fielded questions for two hours. By 5:00 that afternoon, a merger agreement had been drafted and signed.

Says Schwarzman, "Trends change and you change with the trends. People wonder if there is anything left to merge. In the next cycle we may take them apart."

He analyzes his own work: "I have a high level of excitement over everything I do. I try to press the limits of everything achievable. I do most transactions more thoroughly than they need to be done."

The self-confessed workaholic lives with his wife and two young children in a spacious Park Avenue cooperative and has a weekend house in the Hamptons. His suits are custom-made, and he almost always takes taxis rather than subways. He regards luxuries as part of the reward for working hard.

He feels "I am like a doctor who is on call all the time—like a psychiatrist who cannot cancel an appointment. It is a young man's game. You have got to be crazy to do what I do. I am constantly responding to crisis. I desperately want to succeed."

Schwarzman claims he does not know where he wants to go. "Perhaps politics," he says candidly, "but not for some time. You have to know yourself to do that. I am in no rush. When I am ready for it, it will come to me."

During the Reagan campaign for the presidency, a friend was having a birthday party in Detroit for Congressman Jack Kemp during the Republican convention. Schwarzman was invited but preferred not to go. "I am seduced by power," he admits. "I want people to be impressed by me. If I went to the party, I would meet someone who would want me to do something in Washington. Then, against my wishes, I would probably end up with some government position." Schwarzman refused the invitation, thus avoiding a possible problem. "I did not want to turn myself on in that situation and find myself caught up in it. I have a good sense of timing. You can get ahead of yourself and be self-destructive. You have to know when to slow down."

"He is a remarkable young man," Peter Peterson, chairman of Lehman Brothers Kuhn Loeb, told the *New York Times.* "He plays a really important role in spite of his age. Normally chief executives are reticent working with someone that age, but he is being sought out by major clients."

It is the Wall Street wizards who are a cross between the ancient matchmaker and the modern financial expert. It is the investment bankers with the right clients and contacts who do the big business, who know what deals can be put together and whom to call in when a deal starts to gel. One thing that separates the junior bankers from the big players is the size of their contacts. And Schwarzman's circle grows daily from lunches, meetings, Hampton weekends.

Does family matter any more, as a stepping stone to success?

Schwarzman is very happily married to the former Ellen Philips, whom he met while at Harvard Business School. "She graded my papers," he says with a twinkle. "I wanted to marry someone who would fit in where I was going." On her mother's side, Ellen is from the venerable Our Crowd Frank family of Cincinnati.

As for Weill, he believes in nepotism. "Not in the old-fashioned way—not in the old way son and cousin have an automatic way to the top," he says. "But a company makes a mistake in preventing a relative from coming to work. You should not shut them out, but you should not grant them special favors." Weill's son Marc, twenty-five, works in the money-management division at Shearson/American Express.

Plus ça change, plus c'est la même chose.

7

THE WOMEN—TRADITION AND TRANSITION

In 1866, at the age of nineteen, Annie Nathan told her father that she had just passed the examinations into the Collegiate Course for Women at Columbia College. Drawing her to him, Mr. Nathan said with finality, "You will never be married. Men hate intelligent women."

The immediate goal of a college education became more important than acquiring a husband. In her autobiography, *It's Been Fun,* Annie Nathan Meyer tells that upon hearing her father's pronouncement, she sorrowfully recited to herself some popular verses of the time:

> "Where are you going, my pretty maid?"
> "I'm going to lecture, sir," she said.
>
> "May I come with you, my pretty maid?"
> "You don't understand it, sir," she said.
>
> "What is the subject, my pretty maid?"
> "The final extinction of man," she said.
>
> "Then you won't marry me, my pretty maid?"
> "Superior girls never marry, sir," she said.

Annie spent her whole life refuting her father's mid-Victorian theories. Within a year she married Dr. Alfred Meyer, who fascinated her with his playing of Chopin's Prelude in C Minor at a piano club on West Fifty-fifth Street in Manhattan. She spent two years studying at home because only men were allowed in Columbia College. Then at twenty-two, overcoming tremendous opposition, this sheltered girl founded Barnard College, the first women's college in New York. At the time the only institution for women within several hours of New York City was the Harvard Annex, a forerunner of Radcliffe, but even that did not offer a degree.

An active lecturer, she served as trustee of Barnard College, wrote many plays and books about women in business. She lived to hear her husband again play Chopin at their golden-wedding-anniversary celebration and died in 1951 at the age of eighty-four. Yet, looking at the *New York Times Index* for that year, one finds Annie, who revolted at the canons of her age and who always wrote under the name Annie Nathan Meyer, listed as "Meyer (Mrs.) Alfred."

Annie Nathan Meyer exemplifies one of many Jewish women who have risen to the top in America, and the troubles she encountered were a result of her sex, not her religion.

Do Jewish working women today encounter special problems that other women or Jewish men do not have? If and when they do, the difficulties often stem from centuries of cultural conditioning.

In the December, 1897, issue of the *Ladies' Home Journal,* Dr. Gustav Gottheil, rabbi of Temple Emanu-El, New York, wrote, "The case of the Jewess is different. Her sphere is the home, and has been so from the beginning—at all events from the day, some two thousand years ago, that the last chapter was added to the Biblical Book of Proverbs."

Described in Proverbs 31:10–31, the ideal woman rises early and works late. She spins and weaves and labors in the field. She provides for her family and cares for the poor. She supervises the household, so that her husband will have time to sit among the elders of the land.

In short, tradition decrees that the role of the ideal Jewish woman is that of wife and mother. For his part, the husband's role is that of breadwinner, student or community leader. According to Rabbi Haskel Lookstein of Kehilath Jeshurun Synagogue, New York, the Jewish woman has "equality of value, but not of function. She has separate but equal identity." This cultural tradition of thousands of years has become so ingrained in Jewish women that it is difficult to break.

"Today's Jewish woman is more conflicted," recently said the late Dr. Edrita Fried of New York's Postgraduate Center for Mental Health. "She wants badly to work, but the message stay-at-home-and-take-care-of-your-husband is strongly there. It is a symbiotic condition. The non-Jewish woman does not have the conflict to the same degree."

Thelma Schorr, president and publisher of the American Journal of Nursing Company, sums it up succinctly, "Jewish men do not feel that they have to come home and make dinner." But even successful Jewish women continually deal with the problem of guilt. Consider Rita Hauser, a senior partner at the prestigious law firm Stroock & Stroock & Lavan, New York, who was a candidate for the first woman appointee to the Supreme Court. "Jewish women have the same problems as Jewish men in the business world," she explains. "The difficulty is in reconciling differences within the home. Non-Jewish women are more loose. I feel an enormous sense of guilt—not with my husband but with my kids.

"Jewish women are raised in the culture of the responsibility of the home. I would come home after being away for six to eight weeks at a time because of my international practice. The first thing I would say is 'Did you have enough for dinner?' I still do it. I walk in the door and ask, 'Did you have dessert?' "

Mrs. Hauser, who served as U.S. representative to the United Nations Commission on Human Rights from 1969 to 1972 and was a member of the U.S. delegation to the Twenty-fourth General Assembly, has been asked to run for office many times. "I could not do it when the kids were younger," she says. "How could I manage it and young kids? I put the stability of marriage above all else. I knew if I would be away and available on demand by the public, something would give."

The Brooklyn-born daughter of immigrant parents confesses, "I am in my forties. People in their twenties are different. I want to be best. There is the drive to be superwoman. I have to do everything well or I get a great sense of guilt. I am not home enough. I do not give enough dinner parties. My husband (Gustave Hauser, chairman and chief executive officer, Warner Amex Cable Communications, Inc.) is very proud of me. The problems are all inside me."

Yet despite this strong sense of guilt, inherited ideology, the double standard, stereotyped roles, mother's verbal legacies from another day and age, Jewish women have always made it in the proverbial man's world in many ways. This escape from tradition was not a sudden break.

WHO WAS WHO AMONG JEWISH WOMEN

Jewish women found success within a religious framework.

Rebecca Gratz (1781–1869), the first woman of importance in American Jewish history, enjoyed a national reputation among Jews, and possibly even among the Gentiles. She came from a well-to-do Sephardic family; her brothers were active in a number of Philadelphia's best-known cultural institutions. She presided over a kosher house and she was consistently devout. Each day began and ended with a prayer. Some of America's best-known writers and politicians were her friends—for instance, Washington Irving and presidential contender Henry Clay.

She served as a prototype for those competent middle-class Jewish women who were to adorn the American Jewish community in the last decades of the century before they were ultimately pushed aside by male professionals. In her twenty-first year she became the secretary for the "Female Association for the Relief of Women and Children in Reduced Circumstances." She was a founder of the Philadelphia Orphan Society in 1815. In 1838 she founded the Hebrew Sunday School Society, borrowing this idea of a Sunday school from the Protestants.

Though rich and beautiful, it is said she remained a spinster because she was in love with a Gentile whom she refused to marry because of her faith. Rumor has it she served as a model for Rebecca in Sir Walter Scott's *Ivanhoe.* Washington Irving, a friend of both, told Scott of Rebecca's love for a Christian, of her beauty, pride and religious devotion. When Scott finished his novel in 1819, he sent a copy to Irving and wrote him, "How do you like your Rebecca? Does the Rebecca I have pictured compare well with the pattern given?"

Emma Lazarus (1849–1887) also came from a wealthy old Sephardic family that reached back to the eighteenth century. She was concerned about the Russian refugees who waited fearfully at Ward's Island for asylum on these shores and was also sympathetic to the new Jewish Palestinian nationalism. She was the first in America to suggest the importance of industrial training for Jews, and she helped create the Hebrew Technical Institute of New York. In 1883 she wrote "The New Colossus," a sonnet which was engraved twenty years later on a plaque at the base of the Statue of Liberty. The single sheet of paper upon which Emma Lazarus wrote her poem is preserved in the American Jewish Historical Society:

> Give me your tired, your poor,
> Your huddled masses yearning to breathe free
> The wretched refuse of your teeming shore.
> Send these, the homeless, tempest-tossed to me,
> I lift my lamp beside the golden door!

A native American, Henrietta Szold (1860–1945), eldest daughter of the Reform Baltimore rabbi Benjamin Szold, was one of the original founders of Hadassah. Just as Rebecca Gratz had helped to found the first Jewish Sunday school in America, Henrietta founded the first night school in America for immigrant adults. In 1893 she became the literary secretary for the Jewish Publication Society and functioned as the society's editor until 1916. It was during this period that she prepared for publication the multivolume editions of the *American Jewish Yearbook,* Heinrich Gräetz's *History of the Jews* and Louis Ginzberg's *Legends of the Jews.*

(According to Joan Dash in *Summoned to Jerusalem,* Henrietta Szold was madly in love with the erudite Ginzberg, a professor at the Jewish Theological Seminary and some fourteen years her junior. Completely unaware of her passion, he married a much younger woman.)

Szold moved to New York in 1903; in 1912 she and a group of friends, members of a study circle, founded the organization out of which Hadassah soon emerged. The group's goals: to further Judaism in this country and to aid the Jews of the Holy Land. These American Jews called their new society Hadassah, the Hebrew name of the legendary Persian heroine Queen Esther, whose exploits are recounted in the Bible. Henrietta Szold presided over Hadassah from 1912 to 1926 and saw it become the largest of all the Zionist groups and the largest women's organization in the world. In 1981 its roster listed over 374,022 women.

The labors of Szold and her associates were extensions of the social work carried on by Jewish women in the United States. Hannah Greenebaum Solomon (1858–1942) was a member of the Chicago Greenebaum clan, people of means and influence, important in the cultural and musical circles of the larger community. In 1904, she served as an interpreter for Susan B. Anthony when both were delegates to the Berlin International Council of Women. Later she was a founder of the National Council of Jewish Women, which subsequently worked for slum clearance, low-cost housing, better public schools, child-labor laws, juvenile courts, mother's pensions, uniform marriage and divorce laws, civil-service reforms, public-health measures, legislative remedies for social ills and international peace. Later they were concerned with golden-age clubs, "meals on wheels" for the impoverished elderly and raised large sums to further education in the State of Israel.

They pioneered in helping-hand areas.

One of America's most respected social reformers was Lillian Wald (1867–1940), a public-health nurse who left the security of her German-Jewish middle-class environment and, beginning in 1893, cast her lot with the underprivileged on Manhattan's Lower East Side. With the financial help of Jacob H. Schiff, she founded the Henry Street Settlement in 1895 in order to help the slum dwellers cope with their problems.

In less than two decades, she and her associates had established a visiting service manned by some ninety-two nurses who made over two hundred thousand calls a year in Manhattan. Because of her, the New York City Board of Health introduced public-school nursing. Most important, she served to bridge the gap between "uptown" Jewish women and the downtown ghetto; by bringing the former downtown to help the latter she made it possible for two dissimilar social classes to relate to each other.

They turned their traditional interests in Kirche, Küche, Kinder into moneymaking ventures.

In 1900, a group of Milwaukee Jewish women established a neighborhood house, which they named "The Settlement," the first charitable institution of its type in the city. As an adjunct, they established a cooking school and, to expedite their work, in 1901, published a manual titled *The Way to a Man's Heart, Under the Auspices of "The Settlement."* The compilers of the fifty-cent cookbook were Mrs. Simon Kander and Mrs. Henry Schoenfeld. Increasing sales and new revised editions generated enough revenue to fund the local "Settlement House," provide scholarships for students and finance a nursery school.

After a few printings, Mrs. Kander became the sole editor. In early editions the cookbook served as an important medium of acculturation. Because many of the readers were immigrant Jews who kept kosher, in early editions pork was taboo. Directions remained simple: for washing dishes, an early edition states, "Have a pan half filled with hot water. If dishes are very dirty or greasy, add a little washing soda or ammonia." At this point the *Settlement Cook Book* has gone through forty editions and is still selling well.

Some started social services and then shifted into business and politics. Consider Belle Lindner Israels Moskowitz (1877–1933) who began her career at the Educational Alliance, a Jewish settlement house on the Lower East Side of New York, helping Eastern European immigrants to become adjusted to a new way of life. Later she became advisor on social and economic projects to Governor Alfred E. Smith, who served eight terms in Albany (1919–1921, 1923–1929) and "wielded more power than any other woman in the United States." When he won the nomination for the presidency in 1928, she came nearer than any woman ever had before to being the maker of a president. She died in 1933 when Smith was in Albany for the inauguration of Governor Herbert Lehman. Smith's comment on being told the news: "She had the greatest brain of anyone I ever knew."

They also starred in areas requiring artistic talent.

Tiny, talented fashion designer Hattie Carnegie (1886–1956) came here as Henrietta Kanengeiser to join her immigrant father on the Lower East Side. Starting as a teenage messenger girl at Macy's with a wardrobe of three blouses and one skirt, Hattie eventually presided over an $8-million fashion empire, including the manufacture of dresses, jewelry, millinery and a retail store for dresses on East Forty-ninth Street.

Jewish women have long been outstanding in the performing and fine arts. Adah Isaacs Menken (1835–1868) achieved recognition as an actress. In a Victorian age her sensationalism made her famous. In the title role of *Mazeppa,* she wore flesh-colored tights. Alma Gluck, a Rumanian immigrant (1834–1938) made her debut at the Metropolitan Opera House in 1909. Her son, Efrem Zimbalist, Jr., became a noted actor. Her daughter Marcia Davenport wrote a fictionalized account of her mother's life, *Of Lena Geyer.* But Alma converted to Christianity.

Penina Moïse (1797–1880), the child of French refugees who had fled from Haiti to Charleston after the slave insurrection of the 1790s, was probably the first American Jew to publish a volume of poetry. Her volume, *Fancy's Sketch Book,* was published in 1833. Like Rebecca Gratz, she turned down the man she loved because he was not Jewish. This woman, who was blind for twenty-five years, left beautiful hymns as her legacy to future generations. These hymns show both her religious beliefs and innermost yearnings.

Halleluja! May our race
Heirs of promise and of grace,
Enter Heav'n beyond Life's goal,
Blessed Canaan of the soul!

By the 1970s Jewish women had been known as writers and authors for about a century. Edna Ferber (1887–1968) and Fannie Hurst (1889–1968) were two native Midwesterners who found their niche in the writing of popular fiction. Ferber, who never married, won a Pulitzer Prize. Hurst, from a prominent St. Louis German-Jewish family, married a Russian-born Jewish musician, Jacques Danielson. They lived in two separate apartments at the Hotel des Artistes, New York.

Laura Keane Zametkin Hobson (b. 1900) wrote *Gentleman's Agreement,* a novel portraying the experiences of a Gentile journalist who pretended to be a Jew in order to study anti-Semitism. The novel sold more than 2 million copies and, when translated to film, won the Academy Award for the best motion picture of 1947. Proud of her heritage, she attended a party and heard a guest blandly inform the group that some of his best friends were Jews. Mrs. Hobson responded, "So are mine; my mother and father." Her father, Michael Zametkin, had been an editor of the *Jewish Daily Forward;* her mother had run for assemblywoman on the Socialist ticket.

More recently Jewish women have starred in the women's movement since its inception. Betty Friedan (born Naomi Goldstein in Peoria, 1921) triggered the current women's revolution with her 1963 book *The Feminine Mystique,* in which she argued that women had to be free as men in every way. Frieden helped found both the National Organization for Women (1966) and the Women's National Political Caucus (1971).

Karen Lipshultz DeCrow, who served as president of N.O.W., and Muriel Fox, executive vice-president of Carl Byoir & Associates, a major public-relations firm, exemplify other successful

Jewish feminists. Fox not only joined N.O.W. but persuaded her husband, Dr. Shepard Aronson, an internist, to become a member. Dr. Aronson became the first board chairman of N.O.W. When people asked him why he got involved, he would say, "I want my wife to make more money."

Gloria Steinem, founder and editor of *Ms.,* is a byword for the women's movement all over the world. Few realize she comes by her interests honestly. Her Polish-born grandmother, the suffragist Pauline Perlmutter Steinem (Mrs. Joseph), spent most of her life in Toledo, Ohio, where she served as president of many groups, including the Ohio Woman's Suffrage Association and Toledo's Hebrew Associated Charities. In a public statement, Pauline Steinem once said, "How do we know what women can do, when we have never yet allowed them to try? No man knows what woman would do, if she were free to develop the powers latent within her, nor does she herself know as yet."

But Jewish women are finding out. Eight of the twenty-five most influential women listed by the *World Almanac* for 1981 are Jewish.

To consolidate their success, scores of top executive women have formed groups with the objective of what they call "networking," in essence, organizing networks of successful women in various professions. The groups are business- rather than feminist-oriented and many are frankly elitist. The major New York City group is called Women's Forum Inc. Its 140-member roster includes the most successful women executives in Manhattan, ranging from company directors to authors and even a college president. Of this group at least 22 percent are Jewish.

Historian Dr. Jacob Rader Marcus has spoken about the "homo novus" who views himself no longer by origin but by his American heritage. But Dr. Marcus also feels there is a "femina nova," often from Eastern European ancestry, and that "Jewish women are more determined to get ahead." In his outstanding book *The American Jewish Woman: A Documentary History* he writes, "Because Jews as a group have always been frowned upon, their tacit regulation to secondary status has only served to incite them to prove themselves, and when opportunity opened doors for them, the Jewish women rushed in."

BREAKING THROUGH

Like Jewish males before them, contemporary Jewish women have penetrated the barriers of religious bias and boardroom prejudice. But they have had to cope with the additional problems of their sex, feelings of insecurity in a man's world and the self-conditioned image of Marjorie Morningstar (the Herman Wouk heroine who in the end chose the professional husband and the big house in Westchester).

Dr. Marcus claims that "Today's Jewish woman—married or unmarried—is hell bent on a career. That means she has to make adjustments in the home."

Some make compromises out of choice. "We agreed to stay in New York City because both my husband and I could maximize our careers," admits lawyer Rita Houser. "In 1969 when President Nixon wanted me in the White House, I did not go. I did not want to separate. I could not say to my husband, 'You find something else to do.' Compromise proved best for both of us."

Others show the effect of social conditioning. In 1977 Rosalyn Sussman Yalow became the second woman ever to win the Nobel Prize in medicine for her development of radioimmunoassay (RIA). The younger child of lower-middle-class parents (both first-generation Americans, they did not go beyond grade school), Yalow was born in the South Bronx, married the son of a rabbi from upstate New York and reportedly keeps a kosher house to please her husband.

She told the *New York Times* that running a house is a woman's responsibility. "The thing I get irritated about is the feeling that because you want to work, your husband has to take on half the household responsibilities, or you make contracts about the amount of time each of you takes care of the children. Well, this isn't for me. I think if a husband feels like doing things, it's fine, but I think that running a house is the wife's responsibility."

Yet, despite their familial and self-inflicted conditioning, Jewish women have risen to the top.

8

THE WOMEN—AT THE TOP

How HAVE Jewish women achieved their current status in American business and cultural life?

What problems—expected or unexpected—did they meet on the way?

Here is how nine leading women JEPs achieved success. Each overcame a different problem in a different way. All triumphed completely on their own without family money or connections. Each shares three qualities in common: drive, physical energy, willingness to work. Seven are currently married. The husbands not only respect their wives' work but encourage it. They are all successful too—some more so.

JEWISH WOMEN HAVE MADE THEIR WAY IN INDUSTRIES ONCE DOMINATED BY JEWISH MEN—ADVERTISING AND COMMUNICATIONS.

Shirley Polykoff

A member of the Advertising Hall of Fame, Brooklyn-born Shirley Polykoff, who coined the headline "Does She . . . Or Doesn't She?" for Clairol, was the middle daughter of Russian immigrants ("I was supposed to be a boy named Leo") who needed a *fardeener* (money-maker) to make it in America. At the end of her first year in high school, her parents suggested she "fardeen" a little during the coming summer vacation.

Through an ad in the *New York Times,* Miss Polykoff applied for a job as a file clerk and listed her experience as none and religion as Jewish. She did not get the job. In the ladies room the girl who did asked her name. "Shirley Polykoff," she said, and was told, "They never hire Jews at these places." On her next interview at the "So and So Underwriters" she said her name was Shirley Miller and landed the job. She kept getting raises until the time came for her to return to high school. When Miss Polykoff confessed the lies about her religion to her father, he cried. She heard her mother say, "Ah, that anti-Semitism. It is the curse of the Jews." "Not of the Jews," he answered, "on the Jews."

Miss Polykoff went on to a meteoric career as an advertising copywriter, where she was often "the only woman among twenty men." As a teenager she worked as a secretary for *Harper's Bazaar.* By 1929 she was earning $85 a week as a copywriter for a woman's specialty shop and her ads began to show the Polykoff pizazz ("Look like you're going to the races when you're only racing to the grocer"). In the thirties she produced retail-fashion ads and in the forties she worked for an agency that handled six different shoe accounts.

Yet attitudes were surely different then. On the side, Miss Polykoff wrote a story for a major magazine about a career woman who stopped working in order to raise her child and then realized she longed desperately to return to her job. The heroine decided that the possible loss of the child's affection to "nana" was the price she might have to pay. The editors forced Miss Polykoff to change the ending so that the heroine remained "plain Mrs. William B. Carstairs, housewife."

In the fifties Miss Polykoff dreamed up "Chock Full O'Nuts is that heavenly coffee," and then came the alliance with Foote Cone and Belding advertising agency and eventually the Clairol account, for which she penned "Does she . . . Or doesn't she?" the line that launched a thousand quips, made hair coloring respectable and raised Clairol's advertising budget from $400,000 to $33 million a year.

Polykoff herself started lightening her hair at fifteen, which went undetected until she went to a Passover dinner at the home of her fiancé George Halperin, a lawyer whose father was an Orthodox rabbi. Halperin's mother asked him that most humiliating of questions: "Zee paint dos huer? Odder zee paint dos nicht?" (Freely translated this means "Does she paint her hair or doesn't she paint her hair?")

She followed the "Does she . . . Or doesn't she?" line with "Hair color so natural only her hairdresser knows for sure." She wrote headlines out of her insecurities and dissatisfactions: "How long has it been since your husband brought you flowers?" . . . "What would your husband do if suddenly you looked ten years younger?" . . . She wondered, "Is it true that blondes have more fun?" She begged, "If I have only one life, let me live it as a blonde." She ordered, "Hate that gray? Wash it away."

Shirley Polykoff became a "fardeener" to make any parent proud. Always surrounded by men, she served as senior vice-president and the first woman on the board of directors of Foote Cone and Belding. However, she admits that "Girls would not work for me because I was a woman" and that "I was considered for president of Foote Cone, but they said I did not have the head for financing." In 1967 she was named Advertising Woman of the Year by the Advertising Women of New York and eventually opened her own advertising agency. She named it after herself, Shirley Polykoff Advertising.

Shirley Polykoff rose to the top of her field in an unliberated world, but she had her own insecurities about success. She deliberately kept her salary down to $25,000 a year rather than earn more money than her husband did. When he died in 1961 of cancer, the ad agency doubled her salary and a few years later doubled it again. By the time she retired from Foote Cone in 1973, she was earning more than $100,000 a year.

She used two names: Shirley Polykoff at the office and Polly Halperin at home. "I wanted a good marriage and in those days if you were called by your maiden name, it was a humiliating thing for the husband," she confesses. "Some people would think my working meant he was not a success. But you have to put what I did in the context of the times. The most important thing was not to make him feel he was inferior—which he wasn't."

She went into her own advertising business with $1—but she came with clients. To be a success on one's own, she feels, "You have to have a brilliant mind or put it in with labor. Knock on doors. Make sure you have financial backing. You have to keep on excelling."

Miss Polykoff is tapering off now even though she is still working on some Clairol. On March 26, 1981, she became the first living woman and third of her sex to be inducted into the Hall of Fame of the American Advertising Federation. She still preaches the doctrine, "Do not give up the advantage of being a girl. If you look pretty, you are much more influential."

It is women like Shirley Polykoff who paved the way for Sherry Lansing, daughter of Margo Heimann, a Jewish woman who fled to the United States from Nazi Germany. Lansing, a thirty-seven-year-old ex-model, math teacher and actress, is president of Twentieth Century-Fox. She is the first woman production boss at a major studio in the history of Hollywood. Like advertising, the movie world has always been dominated by Jewish men.

Marlene Sanders

Marlene Sanders, a CBS News correspondent, specializes in documentaries. For CBS Reports she was correspondent and cowriter of "What Shall We Do about Mother," a recent Emmy Award winner. The sex barriers she has broken in broadcast journalism link her name with Pauline Frederick (non-Jewish) and Barbara Walters (Jewish). Before joining CBS, she was vice-president and director of television documentaries at ABC News. This post, to which she was appointed in 1976, was the highest executive office then held by a woman in any network news division. At ABC she was the first woman to anchor a network evening newscast as a substitute in 1964, and a Saturday evening show on a three-month assignment in 1971.

In her twenty-five years in broadcasting, Sanders has won more than twenty-five awards. Yet with all her success, she feels, "Women in broadcasting have come a long way—but not far enough. Today, if you are a woman in news, you will find that entry jobs, once closed, are now open. Most of the time it is generally possible to be promoted a notch or two. But the higher you want to go, the more discrimination you will face, and if you do air work, in the kind of assignments you will get.

"The fact is, the news business is still a Boy's Club and women are not members. Women still are not considered entirely equal. Even worse, women are generally not considered: We are outsiders still! In this clubby business, we do not go out to lunch with the boys or play (usually) in their tennis or poker games; that helps keep us outsiders. People are sized up in these informal situations, confidences are exchanged and decisions are made there."

How did she get to the top? She claims, "I did not graduate from college. I was self-made. I had a lot of drive. I was serious. Being pretty did not hurt."

Growing up in the Cleveland area, she attended Shaker Heights High School, where she compensated for lack of funds in a moneyed area by excelling in both academic and extracurricular activities. "I was an achiever," she recalls. "The trouble is, I did not stop. When I became gung ho in all directions, my mother said, 'Now, dear, remember, boys don't like girls who are too smart.' I knew then that the traditional role was not going to be enough for me."

Upon graduating from high school in 1948, she spent a year at Ohio State studying speech, earned enough money to study one summer at the Sorbonne, tried to get a job acting. "At twenty I was floundering," she remembers. "It took me a while to get on the right course. I had odd jobs—teaching, swimming, working for typing services. In one year I got twenty-three W2 forms. Until I got my first TV job, I was confused and at sea."

While working as an assistant to the producer at a summer theater in Matunuck, Rhode Island, in 1955, Sanders met Mike Wallace, the broadcast journalist. He was responsible for getting her her first television position in the fall of 1955 as a production assistant on his newscast, which was just starting on WABD-TV (later WNEW-TV) in New York City. Marlene Sanders was responsible for scheduling guests for the hard-hitting

"Night Beat." Later she became a coproducer with John Wingate in the role Mike Wallace had created.

During her first ten years in broadcasting, she was a writer and producer at WNEW-TV in New York, assistant news director of WNEW radio and a producer at Westinghouse Broadcasting Company. At each of those places she was the only woman in her category of work. In those days the newsrooms and the studios did not employ women in any capacity except as secretaries or an occasional production assistant. There were no women writers, producers or broadcasters ("Being the only woman on the premises is a distinction of a sort but a lonely one").

In 1964 Marlene Sanders joined ABC News as the network's second woman correspondent. *Variety* headlined, "Second News Hen Hired by ABC." When the other correspondent, Lisa Howard, left ABC, Marlene Sanders replaced her on the daily news program "News with the Woman's Touch," a five-minute newscast. Soon she had the chance to set an important precedent for women: Ron Cochran, anchorman of the fifteen-minute nightly news, lost his voice and Sanders was asked to replace him.

In 1966 she went to Vietnam—the first woman in broadcasting to do so. She covered many events as a correspondent for ABC, ranging from the assassination of Robert Kennedy to the Democratic and Republican conventions. She scored another breakthrough for women in television when in April, 1971, she was chosen to substitute for the regular anchorman on ABC's late Saturday evening news show. For three months she replaced Sam Donaldson, who was on a temporary assignment in Vietnam (no other woman had done an evening job on the television network!).

"It is a male business," she states. "Men run it. Some women have gone far compared to what it was when it started. There are a few women in top management, but there are a lot in the middle. We had a women's group at ABC. We made headway. The management became aware. At NBC the women met unbending resistance and had to go to court. That lawsuit dragged on for many years but the network ultimately lost. When the ABC women's group started, there was one woman vice-president—in personnel. I was the first one in news."

She has not encountered anti-Semitism. A noticeably attractive woman with blue eyes and strawberry blonde hair, Marlene Sanders feels, "People do not know I am Jewish. Also, I live in New York, where Jewishness is not a handicap." Stresses Marlene, "TV wants newscasters and anchorpersons to have the all-American nonspecific look—not an ethnic look.

"It is the woman problem that overshadows everything else," she says with feeling. For her, there were difficulties in assignments. She would be asked to interview the wives of candidates. Marlene Sanders is very much a sports fan, but when Joe Namath was very much in the news, the assignment editor did not send her; he sent a man who hated sports.

She states simply, "You need good luck. People like you or they do not like you. I had a setback. When I was a correspondent, one producer would not use me. I had no assignments. I got myself into documentaries and became a producer. *I got away from him.*"

She theorizes that the best bosses in news are married to full-time dedicated career women. The man with a traditional wife has a hard time "realizing we are more like them in some ways than we are like their wives, with the same ambitions, interests and goals as our male colleagues."

Miss Sanders has yardsticks for judging women's advancement in network news. Are there women vice-presidents? Do women make policy or execute it? Can they hire and fire? Next, how many women are there? Do they anchor any of the main news broadcasts? Are women highly visible in the big jobs, the major news magazines or nightly newscasts?

She offers two basic rules: (1) "Find out who is in a position of power. The right people have to be aware of you." (2) "Speak up when a man, younger, with less experience, comes into the department and gets paid far more than a woman for the same work or is promoted over qualified woman producers.

"We are late entries in the business world," she stresses. "We have to figure out a way to keep the pressure on. There is a great deal to do. Until women are in top management positions in large numbers, we will never have our fair share of the jobs. This may take years. How long will depend probably on the progress women make in our overall society. Until many more women occupy positions of authority in industry and government, it is unlikely that women will seem as authoritative and fully competent in this business of broadcast news. We must continue to keep on the pressure and not allow ourselves to drift back into the invisibility of the past."

In 1958 Sanders married Jerome Toobin (there had been a brief early marriage and divorce), who is the director of news and public affairs at WNET-TV, New York. "My husband says the more I make the better it is for him," she claims. "He reads those women's articles on women not making more money than their husbands and says, 'I think they're out of their mind.' My working was never a problem in the marriage. It was one of the things Jerry found attractive about me."

But Marlene Sanders has had other problems, principally the one faced by all working mothers: coping. When Jeff, her older boy, was young, she "was very well organized and had good help." She planned the meals for the week on Sunday night and posted them on a board along with a list of specific tasks (Monday—the laundry and shopping). She never had to say "Did you?"

When she met Toobin, he was running The Symphony of the Air. It collapsed. She recalls, "It was a disaster. We had put up some of the money. I had cosigned a loan."

At thirty-six, she had her second child, a retarded boy. "It was devastating," she states simply. "I went through a period of self-blame because I had waited so long. Jeff had been born when I was twenty-nine. This was before amniocentesis (a test that can tell if a child is going to be a mongoloid before it is born). I was so depressed. After two weeks I went back to work. The experience had a humbling effect. It made me realize that some things are just not under one's control. It took me a year to understand this. He was in the hospital for a while after birth. I had a chance to research. The authorities said, 'The difference you can make is so slight. It is too much of a handful.' The whole placement process took years. We tried several places. Jerry was terrific. He took a lot of the burden off me. I could not deal with the child for a year. Now I deal with it—I see him, keep in touch with the people who care for him, buy his clothes, but I do not react emotionally."

In contrast, the experience with her older son Jeff, a Harvard senior who spent last summer editing the *Crimson,* has been extraordinarily rewarding. With pride Marlene Sanders says, "When Jeff learned of his admission to Harvard, he thanked us. He realized how we had contributed to this by the kind of atmosphere in our home."

LIKE JEWISH MEN, JEWISH WOMEN HAVE BECOME ENTREPRENEURS.

Jewish women have been particularly successful in the beauty business. When Polish-born Helena Rubinstein died at ninety-four, in 1965, she had a cosmetics empire with total assets of $17.5 million with factories, salons and laboratories in fourteen countries.

Adrien Arpel

A new cosmetics queen is forty-year-old Adrien Arpel, granddaughter of Russian immigrants, who serves as president of the multimillion-dollar cosmetics company that bears her name. Adrien Arpel launched her career at the age of seventeen when she opened her first cosmetics shop in Englewood, New Jersey, with $400 in babysitting money. By the time she was eighteen, her label was in salons all over the country. In 1969 Adrien Arpel joined forces with Seligman & Latz, a major operator of beauty salons and jewelry departments in stores and now has four hundred and fifty boutiques and skin-care clinics in the United States and eleven foreign countries.

The dynamic and articulate Adrien Arpel feels that Jewish men have a harder time in business than Jewish women. "The Jewish women I know are successful and good-looking and pulled together," she says. "Jewish men are not as attractive. Look how many Jewish women have their noses fixed (as she did). They are diet careful. They have to be. My sister and I call their big rears and thighs 'the curse of Kiev.' Jewish women take better care of themselves than Jewish men. Look at middle-aged Jewish women and you will find they are thinner and better groomed than their male peers."

This concept is borne out by Lillian Roberts, a noted personnel counselor, who claims, "Being Jewish or non-Jewish does not matter; the attractive person will get the job."

Adrien Arpel is her own best example. "I was forty in July. I wear my hair with bangs on my forehead not simply because I think the style is becoming to me, but because it covers what is not good," she says, shaking a mane of reddish brown hair. "And after you are thirty, it's not at all good. You have to camouflage. My bangs cover my forehead, which is lined." She lifts her bangs to reveal the beginnings of expression lines. "I'm also very gray," she remarks. "Although some gray can be beautiful, a yellowy gray is not pretty. I cover mine with henna."

Adrien Arpel's twenty-one-year marriage to Ron Newman has been an experience of change and growth for both. Brought up with typical conditioning (her mother told her "Get married—I will give you a set of glasses"; her father never thought she "could do anything"), Adrien Arpel reveals she was always competitive. "It was an intense desire to be a success, to be it all," she says. "You cannot learn that burning desire. I was born with it.

"My husband originally was a male chauvinist pig. It would have pleased him to have me stay home, decorate the house and have kids." When Arpel married Newman, she sold her first business, became pregnant and modeled for a line of dresses during her pregnancy. She recalls, "There was a song at the time 'Is That All There Is?' That was the way I felt. When my husband saw how important the business was to me, he did a complete reversal. He had been a stockbroker. We ended up in business together. He ran the financial end. I ran the creative. We were not competitive. He taught me the financial part of the company, and then he left to go into his own hair-treatment business. I wish he were still here."

Adrien Arpel credits her competitiveness to being a member of the "chosen people." She says, "Jewish people have always had to fight for everything. In the past we were always second-class citizens. We could not own real estate, so we became the best merchants ever. We are always proving ourselves. Being Jewish has always been an asset. Being a woman in business has always been a problem. Everyone thinks because you are a woman, you are stupid."

Recently Adrien Arpel attended a meeting where the nine others present were men. They spoke to her in baby talk. "Let me explain the accounting procedures to you" . . . "Do you understand this statement?" they said to this woman who has written two best sellers and run her own enormously profitable business since her teens. The men knew she had to leave the meeting early to catch a plane and kept pointing to their watches. Finally, one man—looking at Miss Arpel—asked, "What time is it?" Adrien Arpel could stand it no longer. She responded, "The big hand is on twelve and the little hand is on ten."

Like Adrien Arpel, glamorous Diane von Furstenberg (she was born Halfin; Furstenberg is the name of her divorced non-Jewish husband) also has a multimillion-dollar fragrance and fashion empire. According to *New York* magazine (May 4, 1981) Diane, who started her career after marriage, has recently discovered her Jewishness. In her New Milford, Connecticut, farmhouse, she keeps a picture of generations of her Belgian Jewish family. At a recent B'nai B'rith luncheon where she was presented with a Woman of Achievement award, she told five hundred Jewish women, "Everyone knows about Diane von Furstenberg's drive and ambition. Maybe it's because two years before I was born, my mother was in Auschwitz."

LIKE JEWISH MEN, JEWISH WOMEN HAVE BECOME SUCCESSFUL IN THE CORPORATE SYSTEM.

G. G. Michelson accomplished this feat without ever being called "aggressive" or "bitch."

G. G. Michelson

As senior vice-president for external affairs at R. H. Macy & Company, Inc., G. G. Michelson represents the company in relationships with the community, handles programs in philanthropy, has some dealings with shareholders. The job represents a first for the company; she is defining it herself.

Michelson (her first name is Gertrude but an old beau used the *G. G.* initials and they stuck; they create a minor problem—mail comes addressed to Mr. Michelson) spends half her time at Macy's. With the encouragement of Macy management she spends the other half sitting on boards. These include Goodyear Tire and Rubber Company, Harper & Row Publishers Inc., Quaker Oats Company, Chubb Corporation, General Electric Company, Stanley Works, Inc. (A Macy's public-relations executive says, "She is wonderful. She is our star").

According to an article, "The Women Who Serve on Boards," in the spring, 1981, edition of *Business and Society Review,* "The old boys are making room for the new girls." Author Leonard H. Orr points out that in 1969 only 46 women served on the boards of the nation's top 1,300 corporations and many of these women were related to company principals. The recent 1980 totals show 324 women occupying 464 positions on the boards of 387 companies. G. G. Michelson is right up there along with such non-Jewish female luminaries as Anne Armstrong, former ambassador to Great Britain, and Juanita Kreps, former secretary of commerce.

Michelson is a graduate of Pennsylvania State University and recipient of an LL.B. from Columbia Law School in 1947 (fellow classmates included the now controversial Roy Cohn and Howard Squadron, chairman of the Conference of Presidents of Major Jewish Organizations). One day the head of the placement committee said to her, "What about yourself?" Mrs. Michelson told him she preferred to go into industry rather than practice law. As a result, the placement head suggested, "Talk to the Macy's people. They have good trainees."

Shortly afterward Mrs. Michelson started on Macy's Executive

Training Squad (Most trainees go into merchandising; management had the "understanding" with Mrs. Michelson that she would go in a different direction). She became assistant to the labor relations manager in 1948. Serving successively in management positions, she became vice-president for employee personnel in 1963 and senior vice-president for labor and consumer relations in 1970, and, in 1972 assumed the responsibility of senior vice-president for personnel, labor and consumer relations. In November, 1980, she was elected senior vice-president for external affairs.

The dark, slim executive expresses tremendous interest in the future of today's young women. She counsels: (1) Credentials matter. Get the best education you can. She believes in a liberal-arts education along with some accounting. The idea: to show you are a person of "substance." (2) Have direction but not be hidebound in a five-year plan. (3) Achieve a balance. People who get the furthest are those who understand other people, the arts, cities and the environment. (4) More women need to get into engineering. That's the last unconquered search field.

In her extraordinary career Mrs. Michelson has not encountered anti-Semitism. Like Marlene Sanders, people are inclined to think she is not Jewish (she is a non-New Yorker who grew up in upstate New York). However, feeling that it is important to "be counted," Mrs. Michelson has always gone out of her way to be identified as Jewish. At Penn State, she pledged A. E. Phi, a Jewish sorority. At Macy's, she has always taken off the Jewish holidays.

She has not experienced problems in the corporate boardrooms because of her sex. She points out that showing up at board meetings does not represent the important work of directors. The important function comes when the board member receives an emergency phone call from the chief executive officer of the company and has the resourcefulness to solve the problem.

Mrs. Michelson does a great deal of *pro bono* work—for example, she is a member of the New York State Financial Control Board. She is also a trustee of Columbia University, and a trustee of the International Council for Business Opportunity—to name a few.

While in law school, she met and married Horace Michelson, a fellow student. They have one married daughter. She gives Michelson full credit for her success. When she was pregnant with her first child (one daughter died in a tragic accident), she was ready to submit her resignation. Macy's wanted her to take a leave and return. Her husband told her, "Consider it. You may not like staying home." He knew more about her than she did about herself.

Helen Galland

Helen Galland, the diminutive merchant princess who serves as president and chief executive officer of Bonwit Teller, a thirteen-store specialty chain, is one of a select group. Only a "fistful" of women are chief executive officers or presidents of major fashion-oriented retail organizations in the United States—and two of these are in family-owned businesses.

Miss Galland was born in Brooklyn and raised in Washington Heights, New York. Both parents were immigrants (her father from Russia, her mother from Austria). She speaks frankly about her upbringing: "My father was in the auction business—it was a hard living. I worked because I had to. I had two jobs in college." Every Wednesday and Saturday afternoon she sold over a counter at Lord & Taylor. Three nights a week she had a second job writing mail orders at the now defunct Best & Company. It was while she was at Lord & Taylor that Galland discovered that retailing was her life's career. "I liked it and I did it well. All that gave me a sense of security."

Helen Galland has been married twice. Her first husband, a lawyer, died. She is now married to handbag manufacturer Fred Loewus. Between them they have five children; three are hers.

She has spent most of her working life at Bonwit's. She joined as buyer of better millinery in 1950, eventually rose to become a merchandise manager for accessories and general merchandise manager and then a senior vice-president, leaving in 1975 to become president of Wamsutta Trucraft. Then Allied Stores bought Bonwit's from its parent company Genesco and Helen Galland returned to Bonwit's as senior vice-president, becoming president in 1980.

Everyone marvels at her. Roz Gersten Jacobs, a college classmate, who also started at Lord & Taylor with her and now is a merchandising consultant, told the *New York Times,* "She got where she did thoroughly on merit, without walking over people, by paying attention to the job at hand. She has kept her friends from the past and when she has a dinner party you meet a mixture of college friends and current achievers."

Helen Galland's very happy second marriage came about through a college friend Janice, who, on a visit to her dentist, told him Helen had lost her husband. At her next dental session, Janice came with Helen's daughter Judy and remarked, "Look at Judy; that is just what Helen looks like." Next time, the dentist asked Janice, "Did you see that man who just left? He's a widower. He would be nice for your friend Helen." A blind date followed ("His credentials were good"); so did marriage.

There have been many highlights in Helen Galland's career. "Getting this job as president was a pinnacle," she says. There were also creative merchandising successes along the way. Years ago, when she was Bonwit's millinery buyer, one June—a time when "nobody bought hats or wore them"—Galland decided she was going to promote wigs. "Then wigs were barely at the hairdressers," she recalls. "I could not locate a manufacturer. I looked everywhere. I had to find a doll-wig manufacturer. The final results were wonderful. We ran an ad and customers fought to buy those Bonwit Teller wigs. In the middle of July, there were women on line to buy those wigs."

She feels the quality that enables a woman to rise to the top is "persistence—sticking to it and not giving up." She says, "A woman cannot be a shrinking violet and achieve success. The trick is to keep your charm through it all. A tough broad is never well received—either in the business or social world. If a woman has charm, it becomes part of getting ahead. You charm people to do things your way. You coerce people in a charming way."

She cites the example of Bonwit's current redecoration of its

Oak Brook store near Chicago. This was scheduled to be a two-year project to be carried out by Allied's construction people. "I looked at the blueprints," she explains. When the decision was made to have no escalators, Helen asked, "In that case, why must we wait two years? Can't you do it in one year?" "No," they said. Then she turned on her charm: "If you put your mind to it, between May and December you can make the store look beautiful." She says proudly, "No man would have said that, but we are getting the job done in 1982." She adds a warning: "You must be sincere. You cannot be cloying."

At one point her father told her, "I am so proud of you. You did it on your own."

"That is just not true," says Helen Galland. "There was always someone who believed in me. Nobody gets there all by themselves."

Now she tries to aid young women starting out who want a career at the top. "I counsel," she says. "I put them on to someone else who can help. You owe back." Some of her counsel: "Meet as many people as you can. Contacts are important. You never know from where the next step up will come. Of course, do well at what you are doing. Be involved with outside projects. Give a little of yourself. If you do, you get back a lot."

Helen Galland "gives" a lot. She was president of The Fashion Group from 1979–81; is vice-president and member of Board of Directors, City of Hope Hospital and Research Center; member Board of Directors, National Home Fashions League, member, Advisory Board Laboratory Institute of Merchandising —to name just a few. She has received many awards and sits on many boards.

That is how she landed her present job. She did not know Allied Stores president Thomas Macioce through business dealings. "He saw me on various daises," she explains. "He asked me to come back to Bonwit's and then promoted me to president."

She feels there have been changes in the working world for women. She has helped make them. When she was very young and going from Lord & Taylor to Bonwit's as millinery buyer, the buyer at Lord & Taylor told her, "You must make good or you are going to spoil it for every young woman who comes after you."

Helen Galland feels strongly, "More and more women are taking their place in the upper echelons of business. If these women make their mark, it will open the door for other women to follow."

JEWISH WOMEN HAVE BECOME SUCCESSFUL IN A NON-JEWISH BUT NONSEXIST WORLD.

Thelma Schorr

Dynamic Thelma Schorr serves as president and publisher of the American Journal of Nursing Company. She recalls a troubled childhood in New Haven, Connecticut: "Because my mother was sick, we were always in debt to doctors and hospitals. This may have influenced my going into nursing. I received a partial scholarship to Radcliffe but could not take it. Where could I have gotten the rest of the money? Back then New Haven was stratified. At the top of the triangle were the C-minus Yale boys who joined DEKE and Sigma Chi. The presidents of heavy industry—all those gunmaking companies like Remington—came next. We lived in the Jewish ghetto and rated about number seven in the hierarchy. *I knew there had to be something better than that.*"

Eager to live in New York, Thelma Schorr attended the Bellevue School of Nursing, which later merged with Hunter ("There were two Jews in my class; I was one of them") and later got her B.A. from Columbia. In 1950 she started as an editorial assistant at the *American Journal of Nursing* magazine (she was the only Jew there). Her father sold food wholesale to institutions like the Jewish Home for the Aged and, at the time, a nurse there told him, "Do not let her go there. They are anti-Semitic."

Now, from the vantage point of success and three decades with the same company, she analyzes, "Being Jewish did not hinder me. It could have if I had not been proud of it. People respect the fact that you are observant."

Thelma Schorr and her husband Norman, a public-relations executive, maintain a religious home. The three daughters bring their friends home for the Sabbath ceremony ("If they are not Jewish, we explain the customs"). At Passover, the Schorrs hold two *seders* ("People fight to come"). They also often give a dinner to mark the breaking of the fast after Yom Kippur. Norman Schorr serves as president of the Society for Advancement of Judaism, a Reconstructionist synagogue founded by 101-year-old Rabbi Mordecai M. Kaplan in 1922.

The Schorr daughters carry on the familial religious traditions. When middle daughter Margie spent a semester at Oxford under the auspices of the Experiment in International Living, she gave a *seder.* Of the twenty young people in the group, only five were Jewish. All twenty came.

In her travels Mrs. Schorr hears the word *Jewing* (meaning bargaining) often and has also encountered anti-Semitism "not on the coast but in states like Utah." She was once the keynote speaker at an event given by the state nursing association of a northwestern state. The president asked her, "Why do you live in New York? Isn't it full of Jews?" Mrs. Schorr says, "Sometimes I don't answer something like that, but this was so blatant that I spoke up. I said, 'It doesn't bother me. I am one myself.' "

At times her religion and her job gave been in conflict. One year a board meeting was scheduled for Rosh Hashanah. Mrs. Schorr send an associate to represent her ("I was not even on the board then; I was just going as the editor to observe"). Embarrassed by her absence, at the next meeting the board members apologized.

She too emphasizes that on the whole the businesswoman has problems because of her sex rather than her Jewishness. "I think basically a woman is still a second-class citizen," she states firmly. "In the Orthodox prayer book there is a statement, 'Thank you for not making me a woman.' It's in Hebrew. Probably men do not know what they are saying."

Mrs. Schorr has developed two basic solutions to the problems that stem from being a working mother: paid help and handling things in shifts. "Jewish women do not mind housekeepers; I was raised to know I would have a maid," she says. She stresses that daily help enabled her to be a better mother: "When my kids were small I made a rule. I would leave my office at 5:00. The time between 5:30 P.M. and 7:30 P.M. belonged to my kids. They said that other mothers did not have child time. They were too busy making dinner. I did not have to cook. I had a housekeeper. My kids approved."

Thelma Schorr reiterates the necessity of continually shifting priorities: "The day of the month that the complete editorial was due, work took priority. If one of the kids was sick, that took priority. If the editorial was due and a kid was sick, I would stay home by the child's bed, writing by her side with a secretary coming to type the pages as fast as I did them. Sometimes I felt so guilty. I walked around saying, 'I have a need for identity' until Betty Friedan said it for me.

"There have been so many Mother's Days when I was not home. I have been away on the kids' birthdays. I could try to do something special—like sending a birthday telegram to the school. If you are a working mother, you have less time. You have to make it count more."

Her daughters, one a college student and the other two out in the working world, feel that "because of me they have to be success oriented. They are—and sometimes they resent it."

Norman Schorr has enormous respect for his wife's career and creativity. In the spring of 1980, Thelma Schorr, then editor of the *American Journal of Nursing,* was in Kansas City on a work trip when she received a call from San Francisco. It was the chairman of the board, telling her she had just been promoted to the presidency. She, in turn, telephoned her husband in New York. When his secretary answered, she bubbled, "Tell him the president is calling." And Norman Schorr told her lovingly, "It is so wonderful to be so proud of someone."

JEWISH WOMEN HAVE BECOME SUCCESSFUL IN THE JEWISH WORLD DESPITE SEXISM.

Sally Priesand

On June 3, 1972, Sally J. Priesand, then twenty-five, was ordained at the Isaac M. Wise Temple in Cincinnati, becoming the first woman rabbi in the United States, and, it is believed, the second in the history of Judaism. Her sole known predecessor, Regina Jonas, finished her theological studies at the Berlin Academy for the Science of Judaism in the mid-1930s. Her thesis subject: "Can a Woman Become a Rabbi?" The faculty accepted the dissertation, but the professor of Talmud, the licensing authority, refused to ordain her. A rabbi in Offenbach did ordain her and she practiced until 1940, primarily in old-age homes. The Nazis sent her to Theresienstadt concentration camp, where she died.

When Priesand graduated, Rabbi Alfred Gottschalk, president of Hebrew Union College–Jewish Institute of Religion, told the audience of twelve hundred relatives and friends, "It attests to the principles of Reform Judaism long espoused—of the quality of women in the congregation of the Lord." One by one the candidates (Priesand and thirty-five males) went to the altar, where Rabbi Gottschalk presented each with the certificate of ordination. When Priesand was called, her fellow graduates rose and gave her a standing ovation. She cried.

Rabbi Priesand was born in and grew up in Cleveland, Ohio. At first, the Priesands lived on the East Side, where Sally Priesand attended a Conservative synagogue. When Priesand was in the eighth grade, her family moved west to Fairview Park. There was only one Jewish congregation in the area: the Reform Beth Israel. Recalls Rabbi Priesand, "It was a change. When I saw a woman reading from the Torah, I was shocked."

At sixteen, Sally Priesand decided she wanted to become a rabbi. "I do not remember why," she muses. "I had wanted to become a teacher. You want to teach what interests you. With me first it was English, French, math, then Judaism. My parents gave me a tremendous amount of support. I never doubted I would accomplish it."

When she entered Hebrew Union College–Jewish Institute of Religion, she did not think much about being a pioneer. "No one there took me seriously," she says. "They thought I was studying to marry a rabbi rather than be one." Someone told a young rabbi she dated, "Marry her and get rid of her."

After four years at the university, she was able to skip the first year of rabbinical training. Suddenly she was a second-year student. She remembers that people said, "Oh, is she still here?" She felt competitive: "I felt I had to do better than my classmates so that my academic ability would not be questioned. It helped to know that I had the support of Dr. Nelson Glueck [the late president of HUC-JIR, who died in 1971]. He told his wife that there were still three things he wanted to do in life—one was ordain me."

At the end of the eight-year training Sally Priesand had the problem of finding a job. She became assistant rabbi at the Stephen Wise Free Synagogue in New York. She comments, "I was among the last to get a job but got the best."

Priesand served as assistant rabbi from 1972 to 1977, as associate from 1977 to 1979. Then she resigned. She explains the circumstances, "Rabbi Edward E. Klein, the senior rabbi, had a stroke. He was in the hospital. The responsibility for the congregation fell on me. I did a competent job. He came back. It is difficult to go back to being an associate when you have been running the show. He announced he would stay five more years (in actuality, he did not). I did not want to wait so long, so I resigned. I wanted some commitment. I would have stayed if someone had said, 'After five years we will let you have the senior-rabbi spot.'

"By then I had had a lot of experience. I did not think I would have trouble finding a congregation. I was wrong. I am a woman, and congregations just are not prepared for women rabbis. I was interested only in a solo or senior position. I was eligible. My classmates already had such positions."

For months Sally Priesand could not even get an interview, much less a job. The Central Conference of American Rabbis submitted her name to twenty locations, but only three congregations with a vacant rabbinical post granted her an interview. During this depressing period she worked part-time at Temple Beth El in Elizabeth, New Jersey, and served as a part-time chaplain at Lenox Hill Hospital, New York.

Finally, as a result of an interview at Monmouth Reform Temple, Tinton Falls, New Jersey, "everything clicked." She took the job in the spring of 1981. "This is the first time a woman has a full congregation of two hundred families," she explains. "It is a step forward for me and women." Now Reform congregations must sign a statement that they will not discriminate in age or sex in hiring a rabbi.

But Rabbi Priesand feels that room exists for change and growth. For example, few women teach at HUC-JIR. If they do, they teach something like speech. Wonders Rabbi Priesand, "Why don't they choose women who have shown excellence in school and train them? That is what they do with men."

She estimates that there are now fifty women rabbis in the United States who have won their degrees from HUC-JIR or the Reconstructionist Rabbinical College, Philadelphia. The Conservative and Orthodox groups do not allow women rabbis.

In 1972 Sally Priesand received its Man of the Year award from Temple Israel, Columbus, Ohio. Remembering, she says, "It provoked a chuckle. But now my own consciousness has been roused. I might not accept it today."

JEWISH WOMEN HAVE SUCCEEDED IN CREATING A NEW FEMALE POLITICAL FORCE.

Ruth Hinerfeld

"Our members reflect many women over eighteen in the United States," claims savvy Ruth Hinerfeld, now completing her second term as of this writing as president of the 115,000-member League of Women Voters. "The change is not in the league but in the women of this country. We symbolize what is happening to women generally. The women's movement has made women a mainstream in the work force. Half work."

A major change in the sixty-two-year-old league came about in 1974 when it amended the bylaws so that men could belong. Now it has four thousand male members, including Hinerfeld's husband, Norman Hinerfeld, chairman, executive committee, Kayser-Roth Corporation, apparel manufacturers based in New York, and her younger son Joshua, a junior at Vassar College, her own alma mater. (Even with its new roster of male members, the organization has not changed its name. "The members do not want to give it up," explains Hinerfeld.)

She grew up in Milton, Massachusetts, where her Russian-born father, Morris Gordon, a liquor distributor, bred racing pigeons as a hobby. After a public-school education that included the Girl Scouts and volunteer activities leading to a course of social-science study at Vassar, she knew she did not want a traditional outcome to her training. "The traditional thing was to go to school and get a master's in social work or a Ph.D.," she recalls. "I decided to do something different." So she entered the Harvard-Radcliffe program in business administration to give herself a year to think about where she would like to go. It was in the years before the Harvard Business School took women, and this one-year program was the system's way to try to assuage the interest of women in this field. At the time she felt she was a failure because she was not engaged by the time she graduated from college. She comments, "That is one area where there has been a great improvement in women's status. Girls today do not feel they have to marry right out of school."

Yet, she was to marry soon after. She met Norman Hinerfeld, then in his last year at Harvard Business School, married him on Christmas Day, 1952, and embarked on a stint as an army wife.

"When I first married, I was doing dilettante things," she explains. "I painted, potted, started doing volunteer work. I was looking for something." So twenty-eight years ago she joined the league. "The league has changed my life," she says. "It set me on the track. It gave me my career."

It was Ruth Hinerfeld who introduced the 1980 Reagan-Carter TV presidential debates on domestic and world issues sponsored by the league's Education Fund (the league had also sponsored the Carter-Ford debates in 1976). She has held many posts in the league at the local and state level, including the important one of voters service chairman in Los Angeles (sign of the times; now the national board uses the word *chair*). "There was so much mail after the 1980 debates," she recalls. "Some said they were wonderful; some said terrible. The debates were the most fulfilling thing of my league career because they were challenging, taxing and demanding. The league had a lot on the line in bringing about the debates. From 1960 to 1976 there were no presidential debates. We wanted people to recognize that a debate is part of the presidential process, and we wanted to bring it about in a way in which we retained dignity and autonomy in presenting it.

"We did emerge with the league's reputation for nonpartisanship intact. And we achieved the goal of bringing about an event which would educate the voting public on candidates and issues. Some 120 million Americans and 100 million foreign viewers watched the Cleveland Carter-Reagan debate."

Ruth Hinerfeld earns no salary but does receive travel and hotel expenses. She comments, "I do not need a job in terms of self-worth. I define the job in terms of satisfaction—*that is the attitude a volunteer has to have.* I was predisposed to volunteerism. Vassar girls were supposed to marry and go out in the community. It was expected you would not waste your education."

The league was founded on February 14, 1920, six months before the Nineteenth Amendment—votes for women—was finally written into the Constitution after a seventy-two-year struggle spearheaded by the National American Woman Suffrage Association. Leagues are organized at the local, state, regional and national levels. They exist in all fifty states. The league's purposes include the encouragement of registering and voting; providing solid nonpartisan information on candidates and ballot issues at election times and on issues of public concern, such as social welfare and equal opportunity, at all times; helping shape legislation at every government level to meet the public needs and strengthening citizen participation in the political process.

The image of the league itself has changed from quaint earnestness to mainstream force. Mrs. Hinerfeld explains it: "The role of women has changed and social condescension to us has changed. We are also more professional in the way we do things and more effective in our action."

Ruth Hinerfeld was the league's first vice-president in charge of legislative activities immediately preceding her election as president in 1978. During 1972–76 she chaired the league's International Relations Committee, of which she had been a member since 1969. She was also the league's United Nations observer from 1969 to 1972.

In 1975, former President Ford appointed her to the White House Advisory Committee for Trade Negotiations, to which she was reappointed in 1978 by President Carter. From 1975 to 1978 she served as secretary of the United Nations Association of the United States of America, a private organization which provides education on United Nations issues and promotes greater public involvement in that organization. She continues to be a member of the Board of Governors and Board of Directors of the UNA-USA. In addition, she helped form the National Business Council for the ERA.

"Volunteerism did not go away; it was discredited," muses the slim, blue-eyed dynamo. "Now, volunteerism has a whole new look. People have gotten tired of hearing volunteerism given a bad name. The volunteer is back in fashion and she has a new status."

Mrs. Hinerfeld defines her own personality: "In some ways I am an obsessive-compulsive type A. I like things ordered and neat. I like to feel things are in control. I am competitive in that I have to do the best job I can. I seem to need a pressure to operate. Yet I procrastinate. I am not one to do it three weeks ahead. When there is no more time left, I sit down and do the task. If I have a speech to give, I will do a lot of reading. My husband will tease me, 'You are procrastinating.' "

What will Ruth Hinerfeld do when she becomes league president emeritus in May, 1982? She says simply, "I want to do something where all those years in public service can be applied."

JEWISH WOMEN HAVE SUCCEEDED BECAUSE OF SHEER TALENT.

Roberta Peters

"From the age of thirteen, I have been tied up with my career. My teacher and mother were constantly telling me how wonderful I was. I was wrapped up in myself. It is a miracle that I have a home and kids."

So says opera star Roberta Peters, fifty-one, who recently celebrated her thirtieth anniversary with the Metropolitan Opera, is married to Bertram Fields, a real estate executive, and has two sons, Paul, twenty-four, and Bruce, twenty-two. Diva Peters was the first American-born artist to receive the Soviet Union's Bolshoi Medal for outstanding artists. She has sung for every U.S. president from Kennedy to Reagan. In 1980 she appeared in China—the first American singer invited to the People's Republic since diplomatic relations with the United States were resumed. She staged four recitals and three master classes in twelve days and sang a Chinese song especially learned for her visit.

Tiny-waisted Peters, a petite woman of five feet two inches, 119 pounds, who vows, "I will never be a 250-pound dumpling," lives in a Tudor-style house in Scarsdale, New York. It is large, comfortable and has its own tennis court. It could also belong to any middle-management executive. A grand piano stands in the corner of the living room. Cabinets, holding her music, flank the couch in the sunroom. Needlepoint pillows abound. She made them.

In terms of success and life-style, Peters has come a long way. She grew up in a sixth-floor walk-up in the Bronx. Her father was a shoe salesman, her mother a hat trimmer ("I love hats," she says).

Both her parents were born in the United States, but her maternal grandmother, who lived with them, came from Austro-Poland at nine. Her parents kept a kosher home and "Grandma took me to the *shul* on the corner. It was an unadorned room with the women upstairs and the men downstairs."

Pointing out "My mother loved me to sing," young Roberta Peterman (her real name), became a regular on radio's Horn & Hardart "Kiddies' Hour." At the time her grandfather was the first maître d' at Grossinger's. Her mother wanted to know, "Should she bother with my career?" so one weekend when opera star Jan Peerce was singing at the resort hotel, her grandfather asked him, "Can you hear my granddaughter sing?" Tenor Peerce agreed and an appointment was arranged at his coach's studio. Upon hearing her, Peerce agreed she had a voice, but must be careful. "He did not want me to be a child prodigy," she recalls.

At thirteen she started studying voice with William Herman, coach for numerous opera stars, who suggested she shorten her name to Peters. After the seventh grade she left school. The principal of PS 64 in the Bronx let her walk out with a letter from the vocal teacher which promised that her education would be taken care of and that she would be concentrating on languages, dance, music, piano. She remembers that subsequently "The Music and Art High School rejected me because of the written test. That was the turning point."

With just a trace of wistfulness, she comments, "There were no proms for me. No kids my own age. My teacher was always there. We would go to the Met together. And then I would go home to the Bronx. I was never afraid to go on the subway alone."

Two months before her actual debut at the Metropolitan Opera as Zerlina in *Don Giovanni,* twenty-year-old Roberta Peters had auditioned for Rudolph Bing, the Met's general manager, and was signed for her debut as Queen of the Night in Mozart's *The Magic Flute* in 1951. She had recently been discovered by impresario Sol Hurok, who had heard her sing at her teacher's studio. It was Hurok who arranged her audition with Bing.

But luck was with her. On November 17, 1950, when a lead fell ill five hours before the performance of *Don Giovanni,* Bing asked Peters to sing Zerlina. "I knew the part," recalls Peters, who was hastily coached and clad in borrowed costumes, "but

I had never sung before with an orchestra." At the finale the bravas and four curtain calls proclaimed that a star was born. Bing has said of her, "That's the Cinderella story. Roberta could sing. She was also very attractive. That didn't hurt."

Peters has said that if things had happened differently she probably would have had to struggle just as do most aspiring young singers.

She does not stress the loneliness, the grueling seven years of study, the problems her parents had in financing that musical education, the long months of exercises and scales, practice and more practice before actual operatic roles could be tackled, the physical training to strengthen her diaphragm. When she made her Cinderella-like debut at the Met, she had never sung on any stage before nor had a rehearsal with an orchestra. The Met was gambling on a completely unknown singer with an all-star cast before a sold-out house. But the management knew she had been meticulously schooled. Roberta Peters was ready.

After that fairy-tale beginning, Peters went on to sing the roles of most of the famed coloratura heroines of grand opera such as *Lucia di Lammermoor,* Gilda in *Rigoletto,* Rosina in *Il Barbiere di Siviglia,* and many others.

Peters reveals she still suffers from stage fright: "I always get nervous before I go on. But once I start singing and concentrating on the song, it goes away. We are not machines, you know. We feel one way one day and another way the next. Some times are worse than others—opening nights, doing an opera for the first time. The first note could be a croak."

Peters is one of a handful of Jewish opera stars. These include the late Alma Gluck, a Rumanian immigrant who as noted, converted to Christianity, and Richard Tucker; today's Jan Peerce, Robert Merrill (to whom Peters was once married for "about a minute") and Regina Resnik.

Peters and Merrill, who met when they sang a duet in *The Barber of Seville,* fell in love, married before 1,000 guests, then separated two months after the wedding. Friends now, they perform together about once a year.

During a 1953 guest performance with the Cincinnati Symphony, Peters caught the fancy of Bertram Fields, a Brooklyn

College graduate who was then a bachelor hotel executive. "The conductor was living at Bert's Alms Hotel," she recalls. "Bert tried to get an invitation to the cast party." He got the invitation but there was no room at Peters's table. Later he gave a party for her after a concert at the Brooklyn Academy of Music. Again, no seat at her table. He did drive her home—with mother, father, grandmother in the car. Then he plighted his courtship in a letter. Peters replied that she had no time for social life. However, she included her telephone number in the note. They were married by Rabbi Julius Mark of Temple Emanu-El, New York, in his study and have stayed married for twenty-seven years.

Of her husband, Peters says, "He is his own man. He knows who he is. He is never thrown if someone says Mr. Peters. He is very supportive of me. Without a supportive husband, I could not have been wife, mother, opera star. I am not your average housewife, but my husband does not mind. He travels with me when he can.

"I was lucky that Bert was as settled as he was. He is nine years older. He had learned to bend a bit. He did not outwardly show much affection. I am so outgoing. It could have been a problem. I would think, 'What is the matter with me? What did I do?' He has learned what I need. I have helped him to loosen up."

She notes that singers get very emotionally involved with their teachers: "My teacher did not want me to marry. He fought against my marriage to Merrill. After that broke up I was back on the pedestal. He fought against my marriage to Bert. He even tried to get my mother on his side. It was real Svengali-Trilby."

She adds frankly, "I have been lucky. It has been a combination of fortunate circumstances. That first marriage could have wrecked everything."

Her two sons are her pride. Paul is studying business and economics at the graduate school of American University. At Colby, Bruce studies Russian and economics (he spent his junior year in Leningrad as part of the Colby College program).

Of his mother, Paul has said, "The older I get, the more in awe of her I become." There was one occasion when both sons experienced filial nervousness about their mother's work. Peters was scheduled to sing at Scarsdale High School when both Paul and Bruce were students. The boys felt their mother might not suit the taste of their rock-oriented classmates. Peters remembers, "They were so worried. They told me, 'If they throw spitballs or walk out, don't let it throw you.' I was so nervous, but I got a standing ovation."

Did she feel guilty as a working mother with a tremendous schedule of out-of-town concerts? "Oh, such guilt," she replies. "Every other month I was changing nurses. Once my mother called—the nurse was hitting the child. I was very guilty. When the boys were four and six we were lucky to get Marie Gagnon as their nurse. She disciplined them but with loads of love. She is still with us today, but as housekeeper and 'major general.' Luckily, the boys never had any major crisis. I overdid it with presents, and, when I was home, I spent a lot of time with them. They went to Europe with us every year. They spent two summers with us in Salzburg—it was the first time they saw a cow. It has not been easy. I am happy I did not turn them off altogether. Once in a while they come to hear the old lady sing."

She notes, "I was an only child. I am glad I had boys. Girls are more difficult. Teenage girls can be a temporary problem. There can be jealousy and other problems if the mother is not around. My husband bridged the gap. He helped them understand what I was doing. In my house Bert is the disciplinarian. He felt the boys wanted to be disciplined."

For Peters her Jewish religion "means everything." The Fieldses belong to Westchester Reform Temple in Scarsdale, and when she is in town, they always attend Friday-night services. On Yom Kippur she fasts all day and then sings two numbers—the Twenty-third Psalm and "They Are at Peace" on an empty stomach.

She says, "This means a great deal to me. I have to do it. I experience a feeling of exultation. Rabbi Stern [Jack Stern, Jr., rabbi at Westchester Reform], says they fill up the temple for me. I try never to be away for Yom Kippur."

Once Peters was away for the holiday. In Los Angeles filming an episode for TV's "Medical Center" series, she attended services at a local temple. The rabbi announced to the congregation, "We have an actress with us." Eyes glowing, she says, "I was so excited. Imagine being called an *actress!*"

Peters opens her home for many UJA-Federation meetings, has spoken for many causes and received many awards from Jewish organizations (such as the Scopus award from Hebrew University). She is active in Israel Bonds, is a life member of the board of the Cystic Fibrosis Foundation and devotes much of her time to fundraising. "A friend of mine's child has cystic fibrosis," she explains. "I try to visit youngsters who suffer from it in the hospitals wherever I am." She is also on the board of directors of the Metropolitan Opera and Carnegie Hall.

She feels her most emotional professional experience was singing in the Negev Desert in 1967. It was May, and she was singing with the Israel Philharmonic. She recalls, "The musicians knew there would be the Six-Day War. We did not. The war started. They were evacuating Americans. I got a call: would I stay and sing for the troops. It was a scary time. I could not even send a telegram to the kids. On a Saturday late in May, we were at the guest house of the Philharmonic in Ramat Gan and then an Israel pilot took us to the plane. I asked the pilot, 'Where are we going?' He answered, 'If you get any closer to Egypt, you will be speaking Egyptian.' "

So on a balmy evening with a makeshift platform and an accordian substituting for a piano, Roberta Peters sang for three thousand Israeli airmen and women. "I sang for an hour," she recalls, "arias, lighter things, Jewish songs. We got down on the sand and did Jewish songs together. There was no feeling of danger. The Israelis were so calm. It was not that way in 1973."

Asked the most emotional experience in her personal life, she responds without hesitation: "My sons' bar mitzvahs. My older boy was bar-mitzvahed in May and we had the reception outside at home. My second son was bar-mitzvahed in December. My mother was trying to stay alive to attend. But she could not make the trip to Scarsdale. She died two days later."

Peters admits to certain embarrassing operatic experiences. On one occasion, singing in *Così fan tutte,* she went blank and forgot to sing her recitative, which led to the next aria of Eleanor Steber. Steber had to sing both parts. Peters skipped to the wings and "There was Mr. Bing. He said, 'What are you doing here?' "

Another minor stage disaster took place when she lost her wig when playing in Noel Coward's *Bittersweet* in summer theater. She laughs as she remembers, "The tenor turned to embrace me after a duet and the wig went whish and there I was with a stocking on my head. The audience gasped and then the tenor started laughing and I did too. The audience joined in." Peters calmly put the wig back on and continued.

Another incident: she was doing Mozart's *The Marriage of Figaro.* She remembers, "I had a duet with Cherubino coming up, and I was supposed to let her in through the door. But the door jammed." So there she was pulling with all her might, the set undulating wildly. "Cherubino finally had the presence of mind to jump through the window."

Peters is both irresistibly appealing and remarkably unpretentious. She states that she and her husband are most friendly with the three couples from the neighborhood who came to the hospital when she had her first child. These include a radiologist with a wife who is active in many charities, a lawyer and a businessman whose wives write. She explains, "It is not the opera world. There are few opera people who socialize together. It is not like being in a play where you are thrown together every night. In opera you give six or eight performances—and then you are off."

Her favorite roles? She says, "The roles I am doing at the moment." In recent years the Peters repertoire has expanded to include Mimi in *La Bohème* and Violetta in *La Traviata.* Recently she told the *New York Times* that there are parts she once did that she would no longer attempt—such as the difficult coloratura role of the Queen of the Night in *The Magic Flute.* "It's a little high," she explained. But Peters shows no signs of slowing down. In 1981 she performed fifty-two concerts in forty states along with her opera engagements in New York and elsewhere plus many TV talk-show engagements.

She names Mozart as her favorite composer. Like many opera stars, she hates to hear her own records ("I always think I could do that better"). She admits she is not very neat but likes to clean up ("Lucy, the cook, prepares the dinner but I love to do the dishes").

She speaks candidly about herself. "I feel I am neurotic. I am up and down and seldom on an even keel. I have to work. I will always sing. Someday the Met will be over for me. But there is so much music to learn. I cannot do anything but sing. It is part of me. I do it for myself. Learning something new I get a new high."

Will she teach? "Only if I find the person to give the opportunity to that Jan Peerce gave me. Teaching is a great art. I would take it very seriously. You take a life in your hands."

She emphasizes that her suburban household is a liberated one. "It sure has to be liberated if I am out all the time. We do our own thing. We are a very caring family. My sons call a lot, and they call when I ask them to do it."

And always along with career, home, husband, children, there is the strong commitment to Judaism.

Strongly against intermarriage, she comments, "I would be unhappy if the boys married out of their religion. If the girl converted, it might be all right. But it is a basic gut reaction: *I want them to marry Jewish girls.* If they do not, I will not disown them. I would try to make the girl welcome. They have dated non-Jews and the girls have spent the weekend here.

"I am Jewish down to my toes, my soul. I have always felt that having a Jewish soul has colored my life in the very best sense. I sing better, have an aliveness. There is a certain beauty to being Jewish that sustains me. When I go to temple, I always talk to the Eternal Light."

9

IN UNION THERE IS STRENGTH

MOST PEOPLE picture the children of the rich drifting away from the family companies that made their fortune. They envision them as using family funds for dilettantism, a career in politics or frivolous pursuits such as sports-car racing.

In fact, there are cases of what Richard Maass, former president of the American Jewish Committee, calls "downward mobility." The grandfather made a fortune. The son chose the professional way of life as a clinical psychologist and maintains an intellectually creative home. But his three children show little aptitude for the family business—or any business. One works in the back office as a clerk; the other two live on the income from the trust funds left by Grandma.

However, even in these days of professional managers and conglomerate ownership, there are still some heirs who continue to mind the businesses that their forebears built. And there are others who are creating new dynasties. (According to *Webster's Third New International Dictionary,* a dynasty is "a family that establishes and maintains dominance in a particular field or endeavor for generations.")

For both Jews and Gentiles, the key determinants of success seem to be the availability, talent and willingness of sons to work in the family business, the new trend to daughter participation and, as in the days of the Our Crowd men in Wall Street, the competent and ambitious son-in-law.

THE DYNASTIC BASICS

The family business offers the opportunity to start at the bottom and probably get to the top. "Jews tend to go into the family business if there is a family business for them to go into," claims sixty-two-year-old Marvin Goldman, vice-president of Grant-Southern Iron and Metal Company, Detroit. "Where else will you get a good job for $20,000 to $25,000 to start?"

Just before the turn of the century, Goldman's Russian immigrant grandfather started the junk business in Detroit. His father inherited it and carried it on for some sixty years. "I never thought of another business," proudly says Goldman, who, with his brother Irving, has worked in it for some forty years as it changed from Riverside Scrap Iron and Metal to Southern Iron and Metal to Grant-Southern Iron and Metal Company, from a little yard by the Detroit River to a thirty-two-acre site, from five employees to eighty.

While Marvin Goldman never thought of another career, his sons did. Two became doctors. But third son Robert, twenty-eight, is learning the privately held family business, which processes scraps from industry—like pieces that fall off the hood of a car—changing them into something usable for resmelting by foundries and steel mills.

Similarly, septuagenarian John Schiff, honorary chairman, Lehman Brothers Kuhn Loeb, whose family has been with the Kuhn Loeb part of the investment firm for four generations and whose son David makes a fifth, notes, "My second son Peter, who is sixteen years younger than David, was at Chemical Bank, is now at Warburg Pincus (a New York financial firm involved with venture capital). He wanted to do something different from his brother."

While retailing and real estate are known to be Jewish family businesses, few people today think of the rabbinate as an inherited family business. Yet it is. Traditionally, in Europe, there were long dynastic lines of famous rabbis. Here, some American sons seem to defect. Dr. Samuel Adler served as the second rabbi at Temple Emanu-El, New York, from 1857 to 1874. His son Felix Adler studied abroad for the rabbinate (Emanu-El is said to have paid for the schooling), then turned down Emanu-El's pulpit and went on to found the Society For Ethical Culture. Dr. Gustav Gottheil was the fourth Emanu-El rabbi (from 1873 to 1899) and the first to speak in English rather than German. His son Richard Gottheil became a noted Oriental scholar. He also founded Zeta Beta Tau as a Zionist fraternity in the days when relatively few elite Jews espoused the Zionist cause. It has been said that the Greek letters originally signified the characters of a Zionistic phrase, "Through justice Zion shall be redeemed" (Zion B'mishpet Tipodeh—Isaiah 1:29).

In *The Merchant Princes,* author Leon Harris writes about the time that Edgar Kaufmann sold Kaufmann's of Pittsburgh to the May Company chain in 1946. He notes, "His reasons were many, but his son's unwillingness to work at the store was one. In the third and fourth generations of these merchant families, the sons (to the mixed anger and pride of their fathers) frequently refused to come into the store or otherwise soil their hands in the marts of trade. They preferred often to join professions that poverty and prejudice had closed to their fathers and grandfathers, and when they became attorneys or physicians or professors, their performance could not readily be compared to that of a father or grandfather."

But some sons do elect the family business. On October 12, 1981, the *New York Times* reported that Robert D. Haas, a thirty-nine-year-old great-great-grandnephew of the founder, had been named chief operating officer of Levi Strauss & Company, the nation's biggest apparel manufacturer.

At the Newhouse chain of newspapers, magazines, publishing house and cable-TV systems, there are some twenty in-house Newhouses. Before his death in 1979, Samuel Irving Newhouse (known as S. I.), the son of a poor immigrant, amassed a huge chain of newspapers ranging from the *Newark Star-Ledger* to the *Pascagoula* (Miss.) *Press.* Today, his sons Samuel Irving Newhouse and Donald Newhouse run the business. Two uncles and a cousin of Samuel Jr. each oversee half a dozen or so newspapers. Samuel Irving Newhouse III, twenty-nine, is general manager of the *Jersey Journal.* The Newhouse family maintains a strict adherence to the methods of the founding father (cost consciousness and a laissez-faire attitude on the part of family members toward editorial content). "It worked for him and it's working for us," Samuel Newhouse, Jr., has said.

To succeed in the family business, the heir must be both willing and able. In 1946, Joseph Lauder, a New Yorker who had had his ups and downs in several small businesses from textiles to luncheonettes, formed a partnership with his wife Estée to market a few preparations developed by her uncle John Michael Schatz, a cosmetics chemist, and went into business with a group of four products. These few products have grown into a Lauder line of more than one thousand products, from a single New York account to hundreds of fine department stores, boutiques and perfumeries in nearly all the developed nations of the world. The company has also gained recognition as an industry trendsetter. In addition Estée Lauder has ascended the social ladder of Palm Beach and Saint-Jean-Cap-Ferrat, had a friendship with the late Duchess of Windsor and is known as a hostess to the rich and famous.

It is very much a family business. In January, 1973, Leonard Lauder, the elder son, replaced his mother as president of Estée Lauder Inc., still a privately held company. She took the title of chairman of the board, formerly held by her husband Joseph, who became executive chairman of the board. They still have the same titles. Younger son Ronald is executive vice-president.

Both sons worked in the business during their student years at the Bronx High School of Science, a New York public school for very bright students. Leonard Lauder used to make deliveries in the afternoon and weekends when he was not attending classes. Later, younger brother Ronald helped his father make creams.

Today both Leonard Lauder's wife Evelyn and Ronald's wife Jo Carole play active roles in the company.

Leonard Lauder attended the Wharton School at the University of Pennsylvania, the Columbia Graduate School of Business and served with the U.S. Navy. He joined Estée Lauder Inc. officially in 1958 and his whole business career has been with the family.

In his official company biography, he explains, "Actually, I had worked for the company from its inception in 1946—afternoons after school, weekends, vacations. For four years I was the billing clerk. I kept all the store records. And I've been involved in every aspect of the business—product development, packaging, marketing, public relations. I predate nearly everybody who's here now."

The older Lauders have always shown enormous confidence in their steady older son, who is an enormously personable man. According to Marylin Bender in *At the Top,* when he was sixteen and just graduating from high school, they planned to take a vacation and leave him in charge of the factory. But he came down with chicken pox, so they could not go.

And Leonard Lauder treats his parents with great respect. In business discussions he uses the impersonal reference and calls his mother "Mrs. Lauder"—and sometimes "my boss."

But a family business can spur both psychological and practical problems.

Fifty-five-year-old Brooklyn-born Sy Syms, who serves in simultaneous roles as president of Syms Clothing, a women's, men's and children's discount apparel chain, and as the president of Sulka & Company, a better men's wear retailer-wholesaler, has six children. Four work in the family business. According to *Women's Wear Daily,* Marcy, thirty, shares responsibility with him. Stephen, twenty-eight, is Sym's buyer of dress shirts, neckties, shoes and leather products. Robert, twenty-six, is buyer of outerwear, raincoats and slacks and an extensive traveler in the Orient for imports, and Richard, twenty-four, serves as manager of the store in Westchester County.

Syms has said, "I never can disassociate myself from the fact that I am working with my children. I always know that they are both family and employees. It is much more difficult for them than for me. But all of us are gregarious and when we have difficulties, we are able to talk them out. I once fired one of my sons on a Friday—I forget why—but he came back on Monday and was rehired. I try to teach my children not to worry about someone else in the organization being envious of them. These persons, not us, have to live with the envy. My sons and daughters would not be in their particular jobs unless they were good at them. I strongly feel they will grow even better as time goes on."

The Hasbro toy company illustrates some of the splits, twists, turns and traumas experienced by some dynastic lines.

Stephen Hassenfeld, forty, and his brother Alan, thirty-three, run Hasbro Industries Inc., a toy manufacturing firm in Pawtucket, Rhode Island. They represent the third generation in the family business, which was started in Providence as Hassenfeld Brothers Company by Henry and Hillel Hassenfeld, who had immigrated to the United States from Poland. They began by selling textile remnants, using leftover fabrics to cover the pencil boxes made by the company whose eight employees were all family members.

Then the second generation took over. Merrill and Harold Hassenfeld, sons of Henry, went to work for the company the day after their respective college graduations. It was Merrill's idea to go into the toy business to fill slack periods in demand for school supplies. In 1946 Merrill and Harold bought the Empire Pencil Company in Tennessee. That was the beginning of the separation of toys and pencils. Each was run rather autonomously.

Then came the third generation. Merrill Hassenfeld said to sons Stephen and Alan, "As your father, sure I would like to have you in the business, but I have friends in their forties and fifties who hate what they do. I don't want this to happen to you. Don't do me any favors unless you really want it."

Stephen always wanted it ("I loved the environment"). Early in his senior year at Johns Hopkins University, he decided he was just "wasting time," so he quit school to work for Hasbro. After a ten-year apprenticeship he succeeded Merrill (now deceased) as president in May, 1974. Alan did not want to join the business, but changed his mind in his junior year at the University of Pennsylvania. Now he is executive vice-president and handles all international operations, sourcing and manufacturing in the Orient.

Some years ago both Stephen and Alan expressed the possibility that an outsider someday might head Hasbro. "The next president of Hasbro could very well be a non-Hassenfeld," Stephen told the *Wall Street Journal* in 1975. Alan said at the time, "I'm not sure if another Hassenfeld as president would be the right thing. Maybe it should be someone outside the family."

This feeling may have stemmed from the internecine warfare that had developed in the family. "My dad ran the toy side. Harold ran the pencil side," recalls Stephen Hassenfeld. "A certain amount of friction developed. One side would say 'We are not in his inventory.' The other side would say "Why spend so much on TV?" When Merrill Hassenfeld died in 1979, brother Harold refused to acknowledge Stephen as chief executive of Hasbro Industries. Commented *Forbes* recently, "Everyone knew that Hasbro was being torn apart by the two feuding branches of the Hassenfeld family which together owned 75 percent of the stock. . . . The atmosphere was hardly conducive to a turnaround." In September, 1980, Harold Hassenfeld tendered his Hasbro shares for shares in the Empire Pencil Corporation.

"The first discussion of separation took place in 1974 between my uncle and my dad," says Stephen Hassenfeld, a slim, warm executive with a head of curly black hair and a teddy-bear manner. "We have completed what my father wanted."

Now there are no business problems. Since the business split, both companies have enjoyed a record year. With a smile, Stephen Hassenfeld, a caring, committed man who serves on many boards, reveals his three wishes for the future: "To build this into an even more exciting business. (People say to stress security, but I know people with security who are unhappy. . .); To build up the family's commitment to the community even more. (My grandfather and father felt the responsibility to give it back.) . . . To have my own family."

Neither Stephen nor Alan is married. They share a house in Bristol, Rhode Island.

Stephen Hassenfeld analyzes his bachelorhood: "I probably met the right girls in my early and mid-twenties, but I was busy proving things. Business was my mistress. You get into a pattern. Providence is not the easiest place to meet people. My brother and I do more socializing in Boston and New York. At thirty-three, I used to wish all those matchmakers would get off my back. As I have gotten older, I do not view it as nagging."

Meanwhile, the two brothers are known as "the best catches in Rhode Island."

In some families the daughters and sons-in-law carry on the tradition.

It has been noted (chap. 3) how proud builder Jack Weiler is of son-in-law Robert Arnow, president of Swig, Weiler, & Arnow. The daughter of Lawrence Wien, noted lawyer famous for his "syndicate deals," married Peter Malkin, a Harvard Law School graduate. The name of the firm is Wien, Lane & Malkin.

In 1911 Ben Kahn came to the United States from Russia, where he had a lumber business in Berezino. In 1920 he started Ben Kahn Furs, which became known as chief supplier of furs to moviemakers and stage productions. Ernest Graf, president of Ben Kahn Furs, married Kahn's daughter Rhoda. They have a son Edward and a daughter Julie, all part of the company today. Kahn customers include Elizabeth Taylor, Barbra Streisand, Jennifer Jones. Graf has said proudly, "We are the oldest American fur manufacturer still in business."

In the nineteenth century two daughters of the famous abolitionist rabbi David Einhorn married men who went on to become famous rabbis—Kaufmann Kohler and Emil Hirsch. In this century, as just one example, Bernhard Cohn, rabbi at Congregation Habonim, New York, is married to the former Miriam Hahn, daughter of the late Rabbi Hugo Hahn, Habonim's first rabbi. Another example: the two daughters of Rabbi Joshua Haberman of Washington Hebrew Congregation, Washington, D.C., have each married rabbis. A new rabbinical dynasty is forming.

THE MEN WHO CONTROL NEW YORK

Certain Jewish dynasties have been so influential that they have made an enormous impact on American life. Ever since Peter Minuit bought Manhattan Island in 1626, New York has been the city of landlords. The fundamental source of wealth and power has been the development of the skyline.

Today the great majority of the New York landlords are Jewish. They have family names such as Uris, Durst, Tishman, Rudin, Lefrak, Fisher, Rose. In some cases, like the father-son team of Jack Resnick and his son Burton Resnick of Jack Resnick & Sons, their influence represents a half-century of personal achievement. In other instances, the heirs to real estate fortunes have inherited it from grandfathers, even great-grandfathers.

Why so many Jews in real estate? Explains Seymour Durst, "Real estate development has a great deal of gambling to it, and this fits in with the Jewish nature. The garment business used to be like that. But every season was a new business. One season you would be rich, the next season wiped out."

He makes the point: "The immigrants were selected people. They had economic and religious problems in the places from which they came. The ones who came to America had courage, confidence, a competitive spirit. They came in the steerage, feeling they could make it. They were at the top of the place they came from. That is why they made it."

The Dursts

The Durst Organization was founded in 1915 by Joseph Durst, who came from Austria (the part that became Polish) at twenty in 1902. He had no money, could not speak English and had had no education in his homeland. He started in the store of a relative, worked a twenty-hour day and began his own textile business. Eventually he became an officer of the Capital National Bank and founded The Durst Organization in 1915 to oversee the few Manhattan tenements he had managed at the turn of the century.

The three Durst scions joined the firm and are still with it (as boys, they had worked there during summers and Christmas vacations). Seymour Durst handles land assemblage, leasing and financing. He assembled the eighty-five parcels of land for Manhattan Plaza; it took fifteen years. Roy Durst heads the management division. David Durst handles construction and design (he has also achieved a reputation as a sculptor). Seymour Durst's two sons—Robert and Douglas—work for the privately held corporation, as does David Durst's son Jonathan and his sister's son Peter Askin.

Seymour Durst is a student of the New York real estate scene. He maintains a narrow four-story brownstone on East Forty-eighth Street as a library and museum crammed with out-of-print books.

Harold Uris

Harold Uris, seventy-six, a quiet man dressed immaculately in a dark blue suit, claims, "At dinner my father was always talking real estate. The real estate world was our table talk. As a child of eight or nine, I would go down to his office at Twenty-sixth Street and Eleventh Avenue. I would follow him around to buildings. Then everyone worked on Saturday morning. Later I got right off the sleeper from Ithaca after my graduation from Cornell and went to his office. It was six in the morning. I never thought of going in any other business."

Harris Uris, father of Percy and Harold Uris, came to the United States from Russia in 1892 and started an ornamental-iron business (he built fire escapes). After graduating from Columbia Business School, Percy Uris saw there was more money in building than there was in iron.

Between World War II and 1971 the Uris Buildings Corporation put up over 13 million square feet of office space in Manhattan—more than all the office space built in Boston or Philadelphia during that time. They are credited with having a profound effect on shaping the Park Avenue skyline above Forty-fifth Street.

However, Percy Uris died in 1971. Comments Harold Uris, "My brother was the financial genius. He ran the show, but I was the builder. He never made a decision without consulting me and neither of us ever raised our voice to the other." Two years later Harold Uris sold his stock in the Uris Buildings Corporation to the National Kinney Corporation. Today he owns only two buildings—the former Ritz-Carlton Building at 380 Madison and 300 Park Avenue.

For Uris the problem was, as the saying goes in these families, he "daughtered out." The daughters got divorced. One former son-in-law is a doctor. But two had been in the business and one was Harold Uris's financial advisor. He recalls, "After the divorce I could not tell him my business. If I had sons would they be in the business? Sure they would if I could make them."

Now Harold Uris gives most of his time to philanthropy. He recently gave $10 million to the Metropolitan Museum of Art for the creation and endowment of the Ruth and Harold D. Uris Center for Education. He is giving $3 million to redo the library at Cornell University.

Are there any challenges left? Says Uris, "I am too old to go into anything speculative. I sit around a lot. I give half of my working time to charities. I look back on my whole career with pride. Did you ever sail in from Europe and see that skyline? It is the most gorgeous thing in the world."

The Tishman Saga

"All dads love to put their sons in the business—it is a continuation of their efforts. If a son is no good, the business will not go to a third generation. By a third he will have to sell. I put my son-in-law in."

So says Robert Tishman, sixty-six, a genial, kindly man. He and his son-in-law Jerry Speyer are general partners at Tishman Speyer Properties with offices located at the Tishman Building at 666 Fifth Avenue, New York. Across the hall is the separate headquarters of the Tishman Management and Leasing Corporation, headed by brother Alan Tishman, sixty-four. On still another floor is Tishman Construction and Research, headed by cousin John Tishman.

On their mother's side Robert and Alan Tishman come from a Lithuanian background. Their grandfather was Russian. Both men are now considered old money on the New York social scene. Alan Tishman went to Dartmouth College. Robert Tishman attended Cornell University. Both have highly educated and articulate wives and are active in Jewish affairs.

Their grandfather Julius came from Minsk. "He was an individual entrepreneur," recalls Robert Tishman. Tishman Realty was started in 1898 when Julius Tishman, a clothing manufacturer from Newburgh, New York, discovered there was money to be made developing tenement buildings on New York's Lower East Side. His five sons, including David (father of Robert and Alan), Alexander, Louis, Paul and Norman, all went into the family business. The company developed into a big firm known for its luxury apartments.

"My father never left the business," proudly states Robert Tishman. "Half the buildings on Park Avenue were built by us. I was programed to go into the business." Alan Tishman was also programed for the real estate business. He says, "It's normal to go into your father's business. At one time I thought air conditioning was a big field, but my parents wanted me in the family business."

In 1928 the Tishman Realty and Construction went public ("My father was sold a bill of goods by a Wall Street house," says Alan Tishman). David Tishman, who had been active in the business for twenty years, became its president. After decades of trying to boost the price of the stock, the Tishmans gave up in 1978 and liquidated the business. Most of the property was sold to Equitable Life Insurance; the construction business went to Rockefeller Center, which bought the company's name and logo.

Comments Robert Tishman, "The company should not have gone public. My father did it at the peak of good times and got chicken feed for it. Then things got bad."

Says Alan Tishman, "A real estate company should not go public. We found out the hard way."

Asked what he considers his biggest success, Robert Tishman replies succinctly, "The fact that I survived the family business and with what was left of the family was able to put together the portfolio the family has. You have no idea of how different it is working for yourself than in a public company. It is more relaxing. You do not have the same sense of responsibility you have when working for stockholders. It is more relaxing to use your own money. It is rewarding to create a successful venture in a pioneering effort."

Robert and Phyllis Tishman have two daughters. One is married to a doctor. Lynne is married to Speyer. Comments his father-in-law, "I talked him into coming here in 1966. I told him, 'I will give you great opportunities.' Eventually the opportunity came with the liquidation of the company and we set up Tishman Speyer Properties."

The same opportunity came to Alan Tishman who retained 90 percent of the real estate personnel and its regional offices upon liquidation of the public company. His only son David was killed in an accident during his senior year in college. He has two married daughters. Asked about who will take over his business, he says wistfully, "I have no sons to go into the business but maybe grandsons."

Frederick P. Rose

Asked to name the classiest of the New York real estate community, the members respond almost unanimously "Rose Associates." The Rose line came to the United States in 1870 from Miszrich, a small town in Poland. They had emigrated earlier from "somewhere in Germany." A number of families with the same name are related.

Frederick Phineas Rose (that Phineas comes from his Hebrew name Sholom Pincus) heads Rose Associates and is in charge of design and construction and matters related to New York City properties. Younger brother Daniel Rose takes charge of joint ventures (with other partners) and out-of-town properties. Still younger brother Elihu, who has a doctorate in military and political history, oversees residential renting and leasing, tenant relations and building maintenance, general administration and personnel.

Frederick Rose's great-grandfather came to the United States with his grandfather just after the latter had been bar mitzvahed. His late father Samuel was born in 1889 and Uncle David, ninety, who is still active at Rose Associates, was born in 1891. After World War I, father Samuel entered a fur-tanning business which was successful from the very beginning. Through a brother-in-law, Uncle David Rose had entree to the construction business. By the late twenties, Samuel and David were already established as apartment house builders and owned some one thousand apartment houses in the Bronx and Manhattan and was one of the few building firms that continued to build in the Depression.

"I was told to enter the family business, but I did not have to be told," recalls Frederick Rose. "At six, or even earlier, I had gone on the steam shovel with my father and my uncle. The only question was, 'Do you want to be an architect or an engineer?' I chose engineering because I cannot draw. The name and pseudo-Gothic buildings drew me to Yale. I was so sure I would get in that I never applied anywhere else."

During World War II, Frederick Rose was in the Seabees. When he was on Guam, his Uncle David wrote him about plans for the first postwar building on East Seventy-ninth Street. "I could not wait to come home to get started," he remembers. "I got off the boat on Friday and was on the job by Monday A.M."

Rose Associates is very much a family business. Frederick Rose has three sons and a daughter. The daughter is an epidemiologist. Oldest son Jonathan is with the business and was recently written up in *New York* magazine for the condominium lofts in his newly restored American Thread Company Building in TriBeCa which is equipped with a computer terminal hooked up to a data bank; this in addition to cable TV for stock-market use.

Says Frederick Rose, "There were times at Yale when I had second thoughts about going in the family business. I got A's in the humanities, mediocre grades as an engineer. I should have taken more humanities and gotten a graduate degree in engineering. I did not encourage any of my three sons or my daughter to do anything other than what they wanted. I did not want them to feel obligated or repelled because they could not express their own individuality.

"Jonathan spent a few years at Berkeley as an environmental planner, then got his M.S. at Penn and entered the family business. He heads the rehabilitation department. Dan's boy David spent two years as urban consultant to Senator Moynihan. He recently joined the firm."

Rose points out that, "The real estate business is really the last home of the entrepreneur. It is difficult to go public, provides great satisfaction, has the advantage of large profits and unlimited opportunity or expansion."

He adds, "The father-son connection derives from real estate, not religion. You have Jewish father-son businesses like the Resnicks and Dursts. But you also have the Trumps—Donald Trump is Fred's son—and the De Matteises and Trammell Crow."

Refusing to give figures, Rose notes, "We do very well." Rose Associates Inc., a privately held firm, does everything but the single family house. They own a wide variety of buildings but also act as representatives, consultants and building managers for others, both buildings and institutions. They manage Roosevelt Island, Waterside East, Wingate, Vendôme. They built the Sheffield on West Fifty-seventh Street near Columbus Circle and 280 Park Avenue, the Keystone Building in Boston, and are developing Pentagon City, a 116-acre tract in Arlington, Virginia, that is situated directly across from the Pentagon on Interstate 95.

"We build our buildings to own them rather than sell them," states Rose. "A builder is beholden to no one except the financing agent (a bank or investment house). We are the surrogate for the eventual occupant of the building.

"The analogy I use are the movie moguls. We are the producer. The architect is the screenwriter. The renting agents are the distributors. The actor is for hire; he may get a piece of the entrepreneurial pot. Large fortunes are not made in brokerage. They are made and lost on the entrepreneurial level. Young M.B.A.s coming out of Harvard and Yale want to be developers. The money and the power are there."

Rose proudly claims, "There are no bodies buried here. The three of us have never had a major dispute. We each have our own area of authority." This contrasts with certain other families in the real estate business. For example, one prominent developer used to be married to another developer's sister. The two men were in business together. The developer "dumped" the sister. The couple divorced. Now the two developers do not speak. The feud is such that the ex-brothers-in-law are rarely mentioned in the same press story.

The Roses not only work but celebrate together. In 1922, father Samuel Rose, brother David and four sisters began the custom of giving a black-tie *seder.* "He wanted the black-tie *seder* to separate the sacred from the profane," explains Frederick Rose. "Then the family got so big that we split into separate groups. Now my two brothers and I rotate every year." Last year it was Frederick Rose's turn to be *seder* host. Among the guests were Robert Oxnam, president of the Asia Society, and Mr. and Mrs. William Macomber, Jr. (he is president of the Metropolitan Museum of Art). "I wanted them to see what a *seder* was like," states Rose simply.

(The Tishmans also celebrate at family parties. At one point Paul Tishman, the uncle of Robert and Alan, hosted a cocktail party for his many nephews, nieces and their children. "Our children did not know each other," recalls Alan Tishman with a smile. "We needed name tags, but did not have them.")

In the Rose family brothers Frederick, Daniel, Elihu are noted for their charitable contributions and are committed to their Jewish religion. Frederick Rose belongs to Westchester Reform Temple in Scarsdale (as does opera star Roberta Peters). Elihu Rose serves on the board of Central Synagogue in New York and Daniel Rose attends Manhattan's Temple Israel. Daniel Rose has been president of the National Jewish Welfare Board. Frederick Rose has been president of the Federation of Jewish Philanthropies of New York. He has also been president of the Scarsdale Board of Education, served on the board of the Metropolitan Museum of Art, Consolidated Edison (see chap. 14).

He gives half his time to charity. "I am overloaded," he admits. But time pressure does not stop him.

He stresses, "We do not have fights. Maybe it is dumb luck. There is only one prep school for ourselves and our sons (Horace Mann) and one college (Yale). We are all equally interested in UJA-Federation. There is no dispute. There is consensus. We feel free to add our individual interests. I feel blessed by my family. My brothers feel the same way."

Rose's son Jonathan felt deprived without a middle name, so

he adopted his father's. Now he calls himself Jonathan F. P. Rose (for Frederick Phineas).

Like many of the elite in this book, Frederick Rose has a very happy marriage. He met his wife in 1947 when he was going skiing with a friend. It rained and the friend said, "Let's stop off in Poughkeepsie." There he met Sandra Priest, who was a freshman at Vassar. He says fondly, "I fell in love right away, and I have been in love ever since." They married in 1948, and subsequently Sandra Rose got her degree at Manhattanville, her graduate degree at the College of New Rochelle. She is now a reading consultant and teacher.

For Frederick Rose, a graying, compassionate man with instinctive courtesy, to be elite means having character, a record of accomplishment, honesty, civil involvement. He notes, "There are those people at the other end who have just made a lot of money." He adds, "The heart is more than money."

A CHICAGO DYNASTY

Some of the JEPs in the financial community love reading about themselves. Others abhor publicity. A clan that falls within this latter category is the Crown dynasty of Chicago—a family that epitomizes the American progress process. The Crowns have been extraordinarily successful in business. They also possess a strong sense of commitment to family, community, and their faith.

Colonel Henry Crown (the rank he held as a procurement officer in World War II), eighty-five, the son of a penniless Latvian immigrant, has parlayed his family's sand, gravel, lime and coal business into an immense range of interests. He is best known for his triumphant fight in 1970 to regain control of General Dynamics Corporation.

In *Who's Who* Lester Crown's name comes shortly after that of his father Henry Crown, chairman of the board, Henry Crown & Company, one of the most successful men in the nation who never finished high school. The year Henry Crown was born, a fire burned out the family business and home on Ashland Avenue, a block north of Milwaukee Avenue. Henry Crown's father Arie, a weaver of men's suspenders, had branched out into the match business with disastrous results.

From that inauspicious beginning has emerged a huge business of diversified companies, railroads, shipping, hotels, banking, agribusiness, real estate.

Lester Crown

Son Lester Crown, a genial, thoughtful man of fifty-seven, who is president of Material Service Corporation, vice-president of General Dynamics and president, Henry Crown & Company, speaks frankly about the pluses and minuses of going into the family business: "I always wanted to go into the family business. It afforded a tremendous opportunity to learn from people I respected. I could start two steps up the ladder. The opportunity was there. It would have been foolish not to take it. We've offered our sons [there are three] the same opportunity to come into the family business, but it is certainly not mandatory that they do so.

"Like my boys, I worked in the business from the time I was twelve years old. I did labor work in the quarries and building material yards. I was paid the going wage. My boys have done the same thing. One son worked as a deckhand on a barge. The others got jobs for themselves."

Working in the family business is not always easy. In 1943 Lester Crown was working on the construction of a naval base at Great Lakes and Glenview. It was a distribution yard of sand and gravel. He received $22.50 a week and $5 extra for working on Sundays. He worked a sixteen-hour day. His friends were getting $1.02 an hour with no responsibility. Crown asked his father for more money. He recalls, "My father turned me down."

Lester Crown makes the point that "When you have nepotism, you naturally can have some problems. If there is not ability or motivation, the business suffers. If the head of a company is within the family, he has got to be better than a person from the outside would be. He is looked at more critically. He should be better. It is tough on him—doubly tough."

Crown's oldest son Steve (actually Arie Steven; Arie was his great-grandfather's name) worked in numerous plants and quarries as a boy. Crown recalls that Steve, now thirty, told him, "I want the opportunity to fail. If I do something wrong here, I have the feeling someone will make it right for me. I want the opportunity to find out what I can do on my own."

Lester Crown found a solution that would give son Steve an opportunity to make it on his own in California. "At the time we took over an operation that had been run into the ground," he remembers. "I told Steve, 'Take this over.' A year and a half ago he did. It is not as yet a proven success but Steve has done a tremendous job of developing a reliable product at a satisfactory and predictable cost." The business is Uniqey, a security system for hotels. Instead of a key, the hotel guest uses a plastic card like a credit card to unlock the room door. Each guest gets a new card, so there is no security problem as there is with lost keys.

According to Crown, tempers can run high in family-owned businesses. "With the family, you do not hold your temper," he explains. "Discussions can be hotter. On occasion I would want to do something, but my father would not agree. He was the boss, so we did not do it. We happen to be fortunate. My father has very little of ego. He lets you do it your way and make your own mistakes."

Lester Crown, a graduate of a public school (Evanston Township High School, where he was one of three Jews out of about thirty-five hundred pupils), Northwestern University and Harvard Business School, is married to the former Renee Schine, daughter of the late J. Myer Schine, real estate, hotel, theater and broadcasting operator. Crown met his wife-to-be at Boca Raton Hotel, Florida, when her father still owned it. He comments, "Renee's judgment is better than anyone I know. She grew up in a business environment. She would be the best executive I know."

Admitting that he "is a workaholic like my father," the tall, blue-eyed Crown claims he learned through his family environment. He states, "My mother and father showed by example. They lived ethically and morally and received mutual benefits.

If you have the business opportunity along with that kind of conditioning, you are far ahead."

Like Frederick Rose, Lester Crown is active in Jewish life. He says, "I am concerned with the perpetuation of Judaism. There cannot be perpetuation without strong Jewish commitment by the next generation. The acceptance of the next generation into non-Jewish life endangers the perpetuation of Judaism." He admits that some of his children are more committed than others and that "This worries me."

He belongs to the North Shore Congregation in Glencoe, serves as chairman of the Board of Overseers of the Jewish Theological Seminary, has been an officer at Michael Reese Hospital and is an officer of the Jewish United Fund. He is on several boards of directors, including that of the New York Yankees ("Baseball and sports in general have sex appeal"). His wife has been very active in Jewish affairs and serves as chairman, Women's Board of the Lyric Opera of Chicago and member of the board of Channel 11. She also serves on the national board of the Multiple Sclerosis Foundation and is a member of the board and executive committee, Syracuse University.

Lester Crown, who has been called "patriarch in training," comments on German Jews in Chicago: "The German-Jewish snobbery is pretty well past. It just does not exist. The whole leadership situation has changed. The German Jews had resources and leadership. As time passed, new leaders emerged. There has been a dramatic change." He is a member of the Standard Club, once the province of Chicago German Jews.

He expresses concern about anti-Semitism: "In many ways today's Jews are the victim of their own success in integration. Jews have been accepted in all areas—like the Chicago Club. But anti-Semitism is under the surface throughout the world. It comes to the surface when things go wrong."

His brother Robert died in a car crash in 1969. His brother John did not join the family firm. He is a judge in circuit court, Cook County.

Lester Crown always returns to the subject of the family business. He stresses, "The right environment plus the right person accelerates development. There have been problems, but we have been able to get over most of them. You can affect what kids do, but basically it comes from within them. All the boys can come here. It will be their decision." He adds, "I have always talked business with the kids. I did not turn the switch off when I left the office."

These days anything can be a Jewish family business. Recently, a seventeen-year-old high school senior Robert Milton (assumed name) visited a friend who lived in Cambridge and became fascinated by the beautiful buildings at Harvard. Robert came from a family where his grandfather had been a well-known columnist. His uncle is a best-selling novelist who makes news with his many marriages and popular books. Both parents are editors at top publishing houses. Upon returning home from his Cambridge weekend, Bob, who had planned to attend a state college, had a new goal: to go to Harvard. For that he would need money. He asked his mother, "Ma, how do you write a book?" For him, writing was the family business.

10

THE NEW ORTHODOX

For the last five years Abby Belkin, a well-known newswoman, has served as confidential writer and researcher for the governor of the state of New York.

As president of Philipp Brothers Chemicals, Inc., Charles Bendheim directs a far-flung empire of plants and warehouses.

Dr. Sidney Feuerstein, clinical professor of otolaryngology at Mount Sinai School of Medicine, New York, recently served as president of the American Academy of Facial Plastic and Reconstructive Surgery.

These three leading professionals differ in age, sex and occupation, but they have one thing in common. They are committed Orthodox Jews. As such, they believe in and practice integration without assimilation. While leading successful lives in the secular world, they follow the same laws and rituals that observant Jews have practiced for thousands of years.

Last year Abby Belkin, widow of the late Dr. Samuel Belkin, formerly president of Yeshiva University, attended the annual awards dinner of the Newswomen's Club of New York, which was held on a Friday night in the Grand Ballroom of the Hotel Biltmore. In order to do so, that night she slept in the hotel suite which the organization had rented for the affair. The next day she walked forty-two blocks to her home. Orthodox Jews do not ride on the Sabbath (a twenty-six-hour period from just before sundown on Friday to just after sundown on Saturday).

Non-Jews like to work for Charles Bendheim. In the dark days of winter when Sabbath commences around 4:30 P.M., Bendheim closes his office at 2:30 P.M. The Gentile employees leave with the Jews. They also get every Jewish holiday off.

Orthodox Jews are supposed to spend the Sabbath quietly. They do not work. The only justification for breaking Sabbath rules is to save life. Dr. Feuerstein may perform an emergency operation on Saturday, but while he rides to the hospital, he walks home.

WHAT IS AN ORTHODOX JEW?

Although the stereotype of the Orthodox Jew as an Eastern European with a white beard and black gabardine suit or a woman with a shorn head who wears a *sheitl* ("wig") still persists to some extent, the Orthodox Jew most Americans meet cuts a very different figure. The man wears a business suit, is clean shaven, the woman fashionably dressed. Many possess a college degree and belong to the same socioeconomic class (middle and upper-middle) as their non-Orthodox and Gentile peers.

Says real estate tycoon Jack Weiler, "My father had a beard. I never took him to school with me. He was not welcome. The Irish threw stones at him. Now kids have beards."

Today, lacking the visible ethnic associations that some American Jews were trying to forget, the Orthodox have emerged as an important social and economic force. Says Rabbi Emanuel Rackman, former rabbi of the Fifth Avenue Synagogue, New York, who is now president of Bar-Ilan University, Israel, "The Orthodox have become articulate."

One reason for Orthodox emergence and acceptance is money. Says an official of the American Jewish Committee, "There has been a change. The Orthodox Jew brings big money into the community. Orthodox Jewish philanthropy is as moneyed as old German wealth. There is a new base for Orthodox renaissance in the contemporary mold. There is an Orthodox-based Jewish renaissance."

In an age of increasing secularism, Orthodoxy thrives with a new vitality. Says one teacher, "We do not talk about belief. We live it."

The acceptance of ethnicity these days makes it easier. Now there is so much tolerance for difference that one is no longer considered odd for adhering to particular dietary restrictions or wearing a *kippah* (the Hebrew word for "skullcap"). Where once Jews tried to blend into the Gentile world, they now feel free to express their difference.

Says sociologist Charles Liebman, professor of sociology at Bar-Ilan University, "Until ten or fifteen years ago non-Orthodox middle-class people would not know any Orthodox people except those of their parent's generation. They certainly would not know any professional people. The tolerance level of Jewish life has risen. For instance, people at the Federation of Jewish Philanthropies in New York used to be intolerant of observing Jewish dietary laws. Today all Federation affairs are kosher. Also these days the Orthodox find it easier to assert themselves publicly and they do."

The attitude of Reform Jews has also changed. Many of the Reform German Jews used to look down on the Orthodox. At one major elite Jewish law firm, a former partner deliberately designated Saturday payday so that he would not have any Orthodox lawyers in the firm. Now several members wear *yarmulkes* and they certainly do not work Saturdays unless they wish to.

The Orthodox world has two divisions, each with subgroups. One is modern Orthodox. This is the Orthodox Jew, who is anxious to be worldly and accepted in the non-Orthodox world. Failing to see any incompatibility between strict Jewish law and modern Orthodoxy, his goal is to enjoy the good things of the secular world and yet remain faithful to his religion. He wants the best part of the Jewish world and the best part of Western society.

In New York the modern Orthodox worship at such synagogues as the Fifth Avenue Synagogue, Jewish Center, Kehilath Jeshurun and Lincoln Square Synagogue.

The second major group consists of the neotraditionalists or "right-wingers" who hew a harder line religiously. Says Professor Liebman, "I think there are two ways of defining the religious right in Jewish circles. First, Jews on the religious right interpret Jewish law more rigidly and prohibitively than Jews on the religious left. Secondly, they are less tolerant of deviations from Jewish law than are those on the left. These neotraditional Orthodox recognize the incompatibility of living in the modern world and leading a strictly observant life."

The Orthodox have customs that appear strange. They pay homage to God in the morning, after lunch, at dusk and before each meal. A man tries to say his morning prayers in the synagogue. He wears a *tallit* ("prayer shawl"), a *yarmulke* or *kippah* (again, "skullcap") and *tefillin* ("phylacteries"—small, black-leather cubes containing biblical verses on parchment that boys over thirteen and men are required to don each morning, except on Sabbath and fesitvals.)

Many laws exist concerning sex. After her period a woman is not allowed to have sex for seven days, and before having it she goes to the *mikveh* for a ritual bath.

Although women are excused from daily prayer, they do carry the chief responsibility of maintaining *kashrut,* the dietary-laws system. Forbidden foods include any seafood without fins or scales such as swordfish or shellfish, any predatory animal. The housewife must not mix dairy foods with meat foods, although eggs, fish, fruit and vegetables may be used with either.

It is the housewife who ushers in the Sabbath. After filling the Kiddush ("sanctification") cups with wine, she lights two candles and says prayers over two loaves of *challah* ("twisted bread"). At this moment, usually eighteen minutes before sundown on Friday, the Sabbath formally begins. From then on, until an hour after sunset on Saturday, there is total rest. One does not exchange money, lock a door, flick an electric switch, drive or even shave. During this time the Orthodox Jew may only eat, pray, talk, walk, visit with friends.

Because of the rules, the Orthodox Jew tries to live within walking distance of his synagogue. Charlotte and Sidney Feuerstein knew they wanted to attend the Fifth Avenue Synagogue on East Sixty-second Street, New York, so they bought an apartment just a few blocks away. It is on the second floor, so they do not have the problem of ringing for the elevator on Saturday.

Some observant Jews find certain jobs call for "manipulation" of the system. Ari Goldman, a reporter specializing in transportation for the metropolitan desk of the *New York Times,* works a Sunday-through-Thursday week. He says, "It took me a while to get the seniority to get Friday and Saturday as my days off. I had to do things like exchanging days." However, when Goldman was covering the state legislature last year, and the legislature met on Saturday, he had to stay in Albany. After a discussion with a rabbi, he kept notes in pencil instead of pen. He explains, "The prohibition against writing on Saturday is against writing something that will be permanent. If the writing can be erased, it is not as permanent." Goldman also asked colleagues to make the necessary checking phone calls for him. He also elects to take his vacation at Passover, thereby avoiding a whole week of complications.

Along with the resurgence of Orthodoxy, an even more rigid interpretation of Jewish law has become fashionable. In 1917, the Jewish Center on New York's West Side was built as a synagogue and private club for "influential people." For many years there was an operating swimming pool, but for cost reasons it was discontinued during World War II. A few years ago the pool was reactivated for mixed swimming. A tremendous furor ensued with the opposition stemming not so much from Jewish Center members but from neotraditional rabbis in Brooklyn who wished to keep the sexes separate. The Jewish Center found a solution. The pool was licensed to the Aerobics West Fitness Club that now runs it as a private club. At certain times there is coed swimming, but the club keeps the Sabbath. It does not open on Saturdays.

In many instances the children of the Orthodox are more Orthodox than their parents. Says Professor Liebman, "Talking about how religious their children have become is a favorite topic of discussion among couples between their thirties and fifties. Half admire it. Half do not."

Rabbi Rackman admits, "My grandchildren are more Orthodox than I am."

Orthodoxy's current popularity stems from a variety of causes. According to Professor Liebman, the most important is the feeling of many Jews that Orthodoxy is the voice of Jewish authenticity. They reason that Orthodox Jews have made the greatest sacrifices on behalf of their Jewishness. The life-style of the Orthodox Jew is an indication of sacrifice and commitment that many non-Orthodox feel admirable because they lack the willpower to adhere to these same restrictions.

Finally, many non-Orthodox believe that the Orthodox are the real Jewish survivors. They are the ones least likely to assimilate. Says Professor Liebman, "As spiritual survival of American Jewry increasingly emerges as the latent if not the manifest goal of Jewish organizations in the United States, it stands to reason that Orthodox status and hence Orthodox influence has expanded."

How does one account for the fact that Americanized, well-educated, upwardly mobile men and women engage in behavior that tends to appear strange from the perspective of everything else they do? How does one account for the fact that otherwise intelligent men and women will not turn their electricity on or off on the Sabbath, won't carry handkerchiefs or tear toilet paper on the Sabbath, and abstain from many kinds of food?

Jerry Rindner, a young New York businessman, puts it simply: "I like the original. Why take watered-down stuff?" If he is going to be Jewish, he wants to be the real thing.

AN ORTHODOX SYNAGOGUE PHENOMENON

Although others call him Orthodox, the extraordinarily popular Rabbi Shlomo Riskin of Lincoln Square Synagogue, New York, says "I do not like the term *Orthodox.* I am a Jewish Universalist. I believe in Jewish law. It is all-encompassing—a system of life which can speak profoundly to every Jew and contains the key to the establishment of a just and passionate society."

Rabbi Riskin has pioneered in the Orthodox Jewish community. Last year he conducted a series of Wednesday night lectures on sex for an audience of mostly single men and women, a first for the Orthodox Jewish community. Riskin's decision to even discuss the sexual dilemmas of unmarried Jews is seen by some as a tacit acceptance of sex among Orthodox singles. Said one attendee, "If you would ask any other Orthodox rabbi about sex, at best he would change the subject."

The synagogue has become the semiofficial meeting place for Orthodox singles in Manhattan. As one young lawyer says, "It is one of the few places an Orthodox professional can come, knowing he will meet others who are similar." In blunter terms, a young Barnard sophomore says she comes to "hear and meet." The Wednesday-night lecture is the synagogue's major singles occasion, and the Sabbath is the next most important. Well-dressed (no blue jeans here) young men and women sit (the women together at the rear of the round) in the synagogue's main Sanctuary, saving their introductions for the weekly social scene over paper cups filled with wine in the synagogue's lobby after services.

Riskin openly encourages the mating game when its ultimate purpose is marriage. He feels marriage is a cure for the ills of modern Orthodoxy—low birth rates and high assimilation rates (The only Jews with high birth rates are the neotraditionalists).

Riskin stresses the relevance of Jewish law to modern life. He was in the forefront of the movement to aid Soviet Jewry and, more recently, Riskin battled the local community board to erect a menorah as well as Christmas decorations at Seventy-second Street and Broadway during the Christmas season—and succeeded. He even chained himself to the White House gates to protest an arms sale to Saudi Arabia. He has awakened other rabbis to the educational needs of women and offers advice on everything from business ethics to homosexuality.

Riskin has a team that will make any home kosher (he does this twenty or thirty times a month). He also offers a crash course in Hebrew, a Saturday service for "beginners." He explains "We are trying to reach out."

Lincoln Square Synagogue "reaches out" in many ways. Cards on a bulletin board in a hall outside Riskin's office run the gamut: "Orthodox male seeks to rent apartment in area" . . . "Torah Head Start—looking for teacher in early childhood" . . . "Need female roommate. Must be kosher." A mailing from Ephraim Buchwald, Lincoln Square's educational director, offers hospitality on the Sabbath. To help a visitor avoid traveling on Saturday morning, the Lincoln Square Synagogue Hospitality Committee will make every effort to place him/her for meals (Friday evening and/or Saturday lunch) and/or sleeping.

Shlomo Riskin, often called "Stevie Wonder" because his first name used to be Steven, came from a family of Brooklyn Jews who attended synagogue only three times a year. He wanted more, and entered Manhattan's Orthodox Yeshiva University High School. There he first came under the influence of Rabbi Joseph B. Soloveitchek, a prominent U.S. Orthodox authority and Kantian scholar who emphasizes Orthodoxy's basic compatibility with secular learning. Riskin was awarded a full scholarship to Harvard but instead went on to Yeshiva University, where he was valedictorian.

In 1963, only twenty-three, Riskin was ordained and began teaching at a special branch of Yeshiva University for Jews with little religious education. Soon Yeshiva had an auxiliary job for him, as minister to a tiny Conservative congregation whose dozen or so members met only for the High Holy days in an Upper West Side hotel room. Riskin accepted for a six-month trial period after setting three conditions: (1) he would hold weekly services and weekly classes on Jewish law; (2) he would accept no salary; (3) the congregation's *Conservative* title must be replaced by *Orthodox.* (Conservative Jews are generally close to the Orthodox Jew in ritual but have dropped many Orthodox observances, such as separate seating for men and women in the congregation). Before the year was out the young scholar became the congregation's permanent rabbi and his Orthodox teachings their guide.

For Lincoln Square's chief rabbi, called by *New York* magazine "one of the most powerful rabbis in New York," the synagogue is only a temporary vehicle. Because of high rates of intermarriage and low birth rates among Jews, Riskin is pessimistic about the future of Judaism in the United States, believing that the destiny of the Jewish people lies in Israel. He says, "I have come to the conclusion that in America the only Judaism that will make it is very right wing." To that end, he is establishing a sister community in Israel for Lincoln Square Synagogue called Efrat.

Lincoln Square's success is so great that it serves as a model for other Orthodox synagogues around the United States. *Time* magazine called it the most exciting synagogue in New York. Every Saturday Lincoln Square features four Sabbath services to accommodate the varying needs of the crowds who wish to pray. The main five-hundred-seat Sanctuary has a great deal of community singing and discussion each week. There is a minyan at 8:00 A.M. each Sabbath morning followed by two classes, one in Talmud and one in Bible, for those who wish a more intense, intellectual experience each week. There is a 9:15-A.M. service for beginners, especially geared to those who have not frequently attended synagogue services previously. And there is a service which begins at 9:45 A.M. and features a thirty-minute Bible class each Sabbath morning and is concluded with a Kugel-Cholent lunch, replete with *zemirot* (hymns sung at the Sabbath table).

For Riskin, "Orthodox Judaism is the means for providing a spiritual dimension to those who lack it, providing it is taught right—by leaders who are teachers, teachers who care. This is a teaching synagogue."

THE ORTHODOX ELITE

Often the members of the new Orthodox elite are of Eastern European background, but the three current best-known names in Orthodoxy—Charles Bendheim, Ludwig Jesselson and Max Stern—are of German origin although they or their ancestors came to America much later than the Our Crowd German Jews. The Feuersteins, whom the Orthodox in the Boston area revere in much the same way that the Brahmins look up to the Cabots and the Lodges, came from Hungary five generations ago.

One can qualify as a member of the Orthodox elite in many ways, but always one must have "substance," "accomplishment," and, in most cases, "education." Serving as president of Yeshiva University makes Rabbi Norman Lamm very much a member of the elite. Everyone respects silver-haired, eighty-four-year-old Leo Jung, rabbi emeritus at the Jewish Center, whose father was the chief rabbi of London and who himself possesses a Cambridge degree.

Recalls Rabbi Jung, "When I first came to America, I went to Cleveland. I was the first Orthodox man the people there had ever seen who was Cambridge. I was like a messiah. Within two weeks the president of the City Club called. The speaker had gotten sick. He asked me to lecture on the philosophy of the Middle Ages. I did. I also built the first elegant *mikveh* in Cleveland. I got the money from the local Reform Jews!"

Herbert Tenzer, a lawyer, made the elite through politics. Herman Wouk got there by writing best sellers.

Other JEPs in the Orthodox world include Belfer (oil), Etra (paper boxes and law), Beron (oil), Goldman (industry), Freeman (silver), Hirsch (stoves), Klein (real estate), Merkin (finance), Rousso (clothing manufacture), Schottenstein (retailing), Jerome and Jane Stern (she is from the moneyed British Wolfson family and serves as president of the American Board of Overseers, Bar-Ilan University).

Education and accomplishment are important but money is clearly necessary. Says one member of the Orthodox elite who asked not to be named, "Years ago Charles Bendheim and Max Stern would not have spoken to Hirsch. What makes the Orthodox world today is money."

Recently a number of Canadian Orthodox Jews have become influential. The Belzbergs who tried to take over Bache (Prudential won out) are very observant. So are the Reichmann brothers —Paul, Albert and Ralph—who head Olympia and York Developments Ltd., the family real estate firm. According to the *Wall Street Journal,* Olympia's properties are estimated between $3 billion and $4 billion. The company owns 50 million square feet of office space in Canada (their home base is Toronto), the United States and Europe and has a further 20 million feet valued at about $2 billion on the drawing boards, including the big Battery Park City development in downtown New York.

Originally Vienna-based distributors of produce in Europe, the Reichmann family fled the Nazis in the late 1930s and settled in Spain, then Morocco, where they established a merchant bank. Political unrest in Morocco in the mid-1950s forced the family to move again, this time to Canada, where Samuel Reichmann, the father, founded Olympia as a floor- and wall-tile importer. The company entered the development market in the early 1960s.

As Moses Feuerstein, a dignified, white-haired man who is treasurer of Malden Mills Inc, a private family corporation based in Lawrence, Massachusetts, says, "The inner circle is made up of Orthodox who have succeeded." Some succeed financially and socially (they are "American," have gone to the right high schools and colleges; Feuerstein himself went to Boston Latin Yeshiva College and got his M.B.A. at and Harvard). But he stresses, "That is for one part of the Orthodox elite. The other part consists of those who have positions of leadership in philanthropy, mainly for Orthodox causes related to synagogues, yeshivas, day schools, Jewish religious schools of higher learning like Bar-Ilan and Yeshiva University, religious hospitals like Shaare Zedek Hospital in Jerusalem or hospitals with religious departments."

These people are a far cry from the stereotyped portrait of the Orthodox Jew removed from the world in mind and spirit. Yet they are Orthodox.

George Klein

Some JEPs star in the non-Orthodox community. Consider forty-two-year-old George Klein, who serves as a liaison between the White House and the Jewish community. He feels, "Orthodoxy has not impeded me." Klein serves on a steering committee which interprets the needs of the Jewish community to the White House.

He says, "I meet with major senators and congressmen. I do not know anti-Semitism. I am American the same as they are. We are all in the same boat, working for the same causes. We are all Americans. They are there to espouse the Republican Party. I have one additional aspiration: to see what we can do for the Jewish community and to bring home to these people that there is no condition. We can be Jews and be Americans."

(Klein is one of the few major Republican Jews. Maxwell

Rabb, ambassador to Italy, and Max Fisher, the noted Detroit philanthropist, are among others. According to Klein, 90 percent of Jews are "registered Democrats. This has been true since the Roosevelt era.")

Klein was born in Austria in 1938. Father Stephen Klein was Polish, went to Austria in the early 1930s, came here as a refugee and founded Barton's Candy. Specializing in the Jewish market, he was the first major retailer to keep his chain of stores closed on Saturdays and Jewish holidays. He was one of the founders of the National Society of Hebrew Day Schools, Central Yeshiva High School fors Girls, a founder and chairman of Torah Schools for Israel.

George Klein went to Crown Heights Yeshiva, then got his B.S. and M.B.A. from New York University, went to work for his father and eventually became president of Barton's. (Barton's was sold in March, 1981; at the time it had three thousand outlets.) Meanwhile Klein had switched to the real estate market, building 535 Madison Avenue and 499 Park Avenue, among others. Today Klein has no connection with the candy business.

He has his own explanation for the emergence of the Orthodox Jew: "Prior to the fifties they were not involved in communal activities. Now they have money, acceptance and involvement. The Orthodox community is educated today like everyone else. That is the great contribution of the educational system, secular and parochial."

He adds that "The weakness of the Jewish community is lack of involvement. The average person can get involved. You can just walk in the door. The government cannot service without people. More and more Jews are getting involved in the political scene."

Klein belongs to three synagogues, is a vice-president for the Federation of Jewish Philanthropies of New York and one of the first Orthodox Jews on its distribution committee.

He feels "A good Jew is a person who takes his tradition seriously, who thinks about his fellow Jew and community, lives an honest and decent life, believes in contributing—either monetarily or physically—and who knows he is a Jew.

"The young are turning to tradition because we live in a

society today that is void of purpose. People are searching. We lived through gurus and drugs. We want a purpose. There is the concept of roots.

"The greatest thing for the American Jew is that we are a democracy. This is a precious commitment that must be maintained."

Moses Feuerstein

Even though Orthodox Jews compete in modern industry, in their homes they still lead the traditional way of life. Says Moses Feuerstein, "I try to make Sabbath different from the rest of the week—to make it a day representing what life will be like in the world to come, a day that is free from the weekly interests and pressures. I attempt not to think about business, politics, sports, TV.

"Shabbos is a challenge to the Orthodox Jew—a real creative effort. I try to find interest in religious texts like the Torah, the Talmud. I do not read a best-seller. I do read the newspaper. If I really succeeded in my aim, I would not read the newspaper. We have a family dinner on Friday night and Saturday lunch time with singing at the table. The conversation follows the line of the search; we talk about how to make the world a finer one, and our conversation touches on social, political, economic ideas, a deeper understanding of religious objectives."

He adds, "Now on a Saturday I visit my father, who is in his eighties, my aunt, who is in her nineties.

Malden Mills, Inc was founded by Moses' grandfather Henry, who came from Hungary in the 1880s with $10 in his pocket. He started as a vestmaker, decided that was not for him, bought a basket of notions and walked up the Hudson River to Albany on one side and then returned on the other. Eventually Henry went into cloth and window shade business, and eventually into knitting mills. His son Samuel took over from him.

Today Moses' half-brother Aaron Feuerstein heads the family business, which makes pile fabrics and synthetic furs and upholstery fabrics.

Herbert Tenzer

In public life, observing the Orthodox laws is often problematic.

Herbert Tenzer, senior partner of Tenzer Greenblatt Fallon & Kaplan law firm, New York, served as congressman from the State of New York to the House of Representatives from 1965 to 1969. He was the first elected Democrat from the Fifth Congressional District since the founding of the United States. During the campaign prior to his election, Tenzer had to find creative solutions to the problems caused by the duties of Orthodoxy and the demands of political life.

He had told the chairman of the Nassau County Democratic Club that he would not campaign on Friday nights, Saturdays and thirteen other days of the year. The leaders accepted this, but then announced that President Lyndon Johnson would be coming to campaign in the third, fourth and fifth districts the following Saturday. Custom dictated that the incumbent ride and lunch with him. Said Tenzer, "You will have to tell President Johnson that he will have to ride without me." However, seeing the distress of the county leaders, he found a way out of the luncheon crisis. The luncheon was to be held at the Cloud Casino at Roosevelt Raceway. Tenzer stayed overnight at the Island Inn, walked the mile and a quarter to the luncheon. As he went through the receiving line, the president gripped his hands and said, "I want to commend you for observing in the traditional way you do."

Once in Washington, Tenzer was able to attend the Friday-night session of the House, sit there and listen to the debate. This did not require writing. However, he often missed his flight home and, on many occasions, spent a lonely weekend.

Although he will eat fish in a restaurant, Tenzer eats only kosher food. At one buffet given by Nicholas Katzenbach, then attorney general, Tenzer skipped the roast beef, took only a roll, salad and cheese and sat down. When Katzenbach asked "Why no beef?" Tenzer explained. "I cannot eat it unless it is ritually slaughtered." At the next event given for members of the House

Judiciary Committee, pot roast was served and, again, Tenzer did not eat the meat. When the attorney general asked, "How did you like the pot roast?" Tenzer repeated his explanation. However, it turned out that the pot roast was kosher after all, especially brought in for Tenzer from Baltimore. All the members of the Judiciary Committee had eaten kosher food—all except Tenzer!

In 1965 Rosh Hashanah fell on the same Monday that was District of Columbia Day, the day the vote was scheduled to give the district a representative in the House. Speaker John W. McCormack learned that because of the Jewish holiday, Tenzer would not be there. He put pressure on Tenzer to remain in town, saying, "I'll do anything. We have a prayer room. Use it." Tenzer checked with his hometown Long Island rabbi, who, in turn, contacted Rabbi Samuel Belkin of Yeshiva University. Belkin gave the go ahead. Speaker McCormack and Tenzer organized the prayer room, taking out the stuffed chairs, adding twenty straight chairs and a row of plant dividers to separate the women from the men. At the actual service there were about twenty-two people in attendance, including Tenzer's wife, Speaker McCormack, wearing a prayer shawl and skullcap, and Senator Abraham Ribicoff, who had heard about the special service and flown down for it from Connecticut.

Tenzer notes, "If one has the will, the desire, the motivation, it is not difficult to observe one's faith. In public life people will respect you if you observe and do not compromise. I respect people who are observant whether Orthodox, Conservative, Reform, Protestant or Roman Catholic."

His list of activities include service to both Jewish and non-Jewish organizations. He serves as President of the America-Israel Friendship League and participated in the organization of National Christian Leadership Conference for Israel. He has been president of the United Jewish Appeal of Greater New York, now serves as chairman of the board of trustees of Yeshiva University. For thirty-two years he has been president of Fight for Sight. This son of Polish immigrants (his father started as a peddler and to acquire a basket full of notions left his fur-lined coat as a deposit), is a graduate of NYU law school. Tenzer's proud possession is a genealogical book that dates his family tree back to 1690.

Ludwig Jesselson

The traditional Jews give freely to charity. Says Ludwig Jesselson, director, Philipp Brothers Inc., "I want to do something for my people while I am alive—not so much charity but serious undertakings for the survival of Judaism. That is what motivates and propels me. By supporting institutions, I am doing something for the survival of Judaism.

"If Jews were even more forthcoming in charity, it would do wonders for the future of Judiasm."

Jesselson was born in 1910 in Neckarbischofsheim, a province of Baden in southern Germany. In Germany he joined a large international metals firm, had his visa to emigrate in 1929, but "I did not come because the consul told me times were bad in the United States." He left Germany in 1934, spent three years in Holland and arrived in Manhattan in 1937, and joined Philipp Brothers. Jesselson started out at $60 a week; a couple of months later "went to Europe to drum up business." Before taking over his present post as director, he was president of Philipp Brothers "for a long time."

Despite his wealth, Jesselson keeps a very low profile. Little exists in the way of newspaper clippings or a *Who's Who* listing. Research shows only a brief listing in the 1971 *Encyclopedia Judaica.* Jesselson, father of three sons, says "Nothing is named after us. But there is a school in Jerusalem named after my mother—the Amalia School."

Jesselson, who was the first observant Jew to be elected chairman of the UJA-Federation campaign, says "I spend my time and my money on Jewish education. Some people talk about it the way they talk about motherhood, but they don't do a thing. There should be Jewish day schools under the Reform, Conservative, Orthodox all over the country so that Jews will stay Jews. Otherwise they will assimilate. Today young people feel uncertain. They miss a framework. The uncertainty has been created by World War II, Vietnam, the unsettled world condition. If they find a haven in religion, they will find fulfillment."

He comments about S.A.R. Academy in Riverdale, a coed elementary day school, "We have probably 50 percent of kids from non-Orthodox homes and we make Jews out of them."

In the elite Orthodox world many familial relationships exist. During his years in Holland, Ludwig Jesselson ate very often on Friday night with the Ivan Salomon family (Salomon was a deeply religious man who after World War II "saved Orthodoxy in Europe"). Later, daughter Els Salomon married Charles Bendheim. Bendheim's father Siegfried was a first cousin of Jesselson's mother.

Jesselson concludes, "Every industry is open for good people. The Jews who are no good do not get ahead. They attribute this to anti-Semitism."

Charles Bendheim

Charles Bendheim is a highly articulate, motivated man, a third-generation American on his mother's side. Father Siegfried left Germany in 1908, went to England, where he and Oscar Philipp were partners in Philipp Brothers, a metals concern. World War II started and his father had a choice: to be interned in England or go to America. In 1914 he arrived in New York.

The first week he was in America, on Saturday, Siegfried Bendheim went to synagogue at Ninety-fifth Street and Lexington Avenue. Because he was a visitor, the twenty-four-year-old youth with a thick German accent was called to read to the Torah. A man invited the stranger home for lunch and Bendheim met daughter Nanette Felsenstein ("Nettie"), who thought "This is just the kind of boy I have been looking for." Six months later they were married. After America entered World War I, Nettie Bendheim could take her children to the beach, but Bendheim had to stay four blocks away because he was an enemy alien. (Later Bendheim was invited to join the elite Harmonie Club; he refused because he felt the Harmonie objected to admitting Eastern European Jews.)

The very Orthodox Bendheims are modern big business and

relatively old money. During World War I Siegfried Bendheim started Philipp Brothers in the United States. The English company changed its name to Derby & Company. In the 1950s, Philipp Brothers, a leading metals and chemical company, bought Derby.

Siegfried's son Charles, born in 1917, spent his early years in the Bensonhurst section of Brooklyn. Then his mother, yearning for the country, moved the family to Sea Cliff on Long Island's North Shore. But "there were no Jews there," so they moved back to Brooklyn, this time to the Flatbush section. Eventually Nettie Bendheim decided that Brooklyn was becoming so "citified" that they might as well live in Manhattan and in 1928 the Bendheims moved to Manhattan. Charles Bendheim has been there ever since. In his teen years he commuted from Manhattan to a day school in Boro Park.

Again, Bendheim's collegiate history shows some of the manipulations necessary in order for Orthodox students to get an education. Originally, Bendheim was scheduled to attend NYU uptown. Registration was on a Saturday, so Bendheim spent Friday night at a Yeshiva University dormitory and the next day walked across the Heights. An Italian boy filled out the application forms for him. However, he learned that lab would be on Saturday. Bendheim went to see Dean Distler, who would not excuse him from the Saturday class. "I told him where he could go," he recalls with a smile.

Bendheim took a course at NYU downtown, decided he wanted to study mining engineering and enrolled at Lafayette College in Easton, Pennsylvania ("I did not have the grades for Columbia and the Colorado School of Mines was too far away. That left Lafayette").

At Lafayette he had a scheduling problem and went to discuss it with the dean, who turned out to be Dean Distler again, who had transferred there. Distler told Bendheim, "Look, we are both new here. Make your own arrangements. I won't interfere."

Like many others, Bendheim feels his Orthodoxy has never presented insurmountable problems. Obviously always a leader, he says "I try to educate my people. At Lafayette I was the only

Orthodox boy in school. I went to Saturday classes, but I did not write. I got a friend to turn off the lights on Friday night. One teacher always sent boys to the blackboard. I told him, 'I just cannot go. It is my Sabbath.' The professor then decided to give quizzes every Saturday and these would constitute 90 percent of the grade. I got one hundred on everything else but flunked the course because I got zero every Saturday.

"I was president of the dormitory. Without telling anyone, I would just go home for the Jewish holidays. One year I went home for Sukkoth. When I came back, there were notes all over my door saying 'The dean wants to see you.' Dean Distler wanted to know where I had gone. I told him, 'Look, we have a deal.' "

Bendheim graduated from Lafayette with a B.S. in metallurgical engineering ("I graduated second in the class—there were only two of us"). The school placement bureau wanted him to go to South America, where he could have had a job for $45 a week. Instead he took a job for $18 weekly in Philadelphia at Pennsylvania Smelting and Refining. Dean Distler sent a letter to Siegfried Bendheim urging him to put some sense in his son's head. Feeling he "could learn more" in the $18-a-week job, Bendheim started as a receiving clerk; nine months later he had risen to assistant night-plant supervisor. When his mother telephoned him one day, she was told he was sleeping because he worked nights. She reported this to Siegfried Bendheim, who said "Enough." On March 6, 1940, Charles Bendheim started work at Philipp Brothers.

Siegfried Ullmann—a first cousin of Siegfried Bendheim—had come to Phillip Brothers in 1923 (Ludwig Jesselson did not come until the late thirties) and became Siegfried Bendheim's partner.

It was very much a family business. In 1945 Siegfried Bendheim decided to retire and spend the rest of his life on "charitable endeavors." Charles was slated to take over his father's share of the business. He recalls, "That meant I would be on the same level as Ullmann. It was hard for him. I would be able to say no to him. There were altercations. We had a chemical department. Ullmann said I could take over his shares and he would take over the chemical department or he would take over my father's shares and I could take over the chemical department. It was a small chemical department. I would have needed a partner to take over the metal division.

"I borrowed the money to buy the chemical department of Philipp. In the first month I lost what I was supposed to earn in the first year. In the second month I lost half of that. In the third I broke even. At the end of that year I paid back everything I had borrowed.

"Philipp Brothers Chemical is a private corporation. I refuse to go public or to merge. It is a sizable business but not as big as Philipp Brothers. We have plants in Israel, seven plants here, warehouses, etc. My whole purpose is to be small. I give to charity—that is the only way people know about my money. I was never impressed by money. It is not the end-all. It is what you do for others that is important. My wife says we are a messenger to transmit to others."

Both in a financial and familial sense, the Bendheims are known as "the most successful" Orthodox family. Charles and Els Bendheim have seven children, twenty-six grandchildren. Asked how he met his wife, Bendheim replies "I won her in a golf game." One day Bendheim, Ludwig Jesselson and Robert Salomon golfed. Bendheim won. At the time he was selling tickets to a synagogue affair, so he told Salomon, "Instead of paying me, take two tickets. I will take two. I have a cousin for you. I will take your sister."

Els wanted to know what Bendheim looked like, so Jesselson took him over to perform the introduction. "She was very busy and had no time for me," says Bendheim, "so I told her 'I will see you next Saturday.' That was forty years ago. Today the Bendheims live in the apartment where her parents used to live. Two of their sons and a son-in-law work in the family business. Three of the children live within fifteen blocks. A daughter-in-law teaches at Rabbi Riskin's day school.

Els Bendheim has said, "All my children are Orthodox. That is my only measure of success—for myself and others."

How come the Bendheim children remained in the Orthodox fold while other offspring have become Conservative, Reform or completely unreligious? Bendheim explains "My wife came to the conclusion that we should marry the children off young. We would have six or seven young people sleeping over every weekend. All my kids went to day schools and they married the kids they went to school with. Philip was the only one who found his own—she was here from Israel visiting a cousin. Yeshiva University played a big part in their social life."

He says, "Young people today are old for their years at a very young age. They are not interested in Cinderella stories anymore. They see what their parents do with relationships. They search. They end up in Israel. They find authenticity in Israel. They go on digs. They see it really existed three thousand years ago."

He counsels, "Be an Orthodox Jew. Keep the Sabbath. If you work hard, people do not care if you are Orthodox. People used to talk about accents. You can speak the King's English and talk nonsense and you can speak with a heavy accent and say things that have meaning. When Kissinger speaks, you do not hear his accent."

Max Stern

Max Stern did not wait for Hitler to come to power. Watching inflation sweep Germany in the 1920s, the textile manufacturer from Fulda, near Frankfurt, decided the time had come to get out. "I saw trouble in Germany early on . . . saw the Nazi party taking charge. I did not want to be captain of the ship, the last one leaving," says the silver-haired, eighty-three-year-old philanthropist and former head of Hartz Mountain Corporation. "I did not know English. I did know Latin, Greek and French. I told only my parents and three friends that I was leaving. That was 1926."

Stern headed for the new world with a friend who dealt in the famous Hartz Mountain canaries and 2,100 birds. At first Stern sold to small pet stores, but, although he was successful, he found the pace too slow. So Stern set about selling the birds to mass retailers while his friend returned to Germany to buy more birds.

"I did not know any English," Stern recalls. "I used sign language. Hands. Feet. Anything." He remembers passing a store that was drawing high traffic. The sign read: W. T. Grant. "I did not know it was a chain store," Stern says. "The manager sent me to the main office." Stern clinched a major account for his birds—before he could speak English. And he learned the big money was in mass merchandising—a lesson he never forgot.

He quickly caught on to what such master merchandisers as the Gillette Company and George Eastman of Kodak had learned earlier: there is more money in selling the razor blade than in selling the razor. So in 1930 Max Stern moved into bird food.

According to *Forbes* (February 15, 1974), by 1959, after more than thirty years in business, the Hartz Mountain Corporation was doing $18 million a year in birds, bird food and bird accessories, a huge fish in a tiny pool. But the pool was getting stagnant. The parakeet boom, on which Hartz Mountain was riding, had already peaked. Max Stern was well off but the company was drifting. The growth of the family company was being "throttled by Stern's brother, who would not let him broaden the line to other pet supplies." But Max had an energetic and dynamic son Leonard who is no typical rich man's son. He graduated from New York University's School of Commerce and first turned to selling imported steel. Finally, when Max Stern bought out his brother in 1959, Leonard Stern came home to the family business and set out work broadening the line to dog and cat accessories, dog toys, cat litter and shampoos, tropical fish, hamsters and white mice. In *The Very Rich Book,* author Jacqueline Thompson estimates that Leonard Stern, forty-four, has a fortune between $500 million and $700 million. Stern owns huge amounts of real estate as well, including a piece of the New Jersey Meadowlands.

But while Leonard Stern made Hartz Mountain a pet-supplies power, it was father Max who started it and made the Stern name famous in philanthropy. Max Stern created Stern College for Women, a part of Yeshiva University. He is a very generous contributor to charity. He started Manhattan High School and built it, recently relinquished the presidency of the Jewish Center but is still active, serves as president of the Laymen's Advisory Council of the New York Board of Rabbis.

In his personal life Max Stern has been married twice. After a divorce from his first wife (now deceased) he married Russian-born Ghity Lindenbaum, whose father had been chief rabbi in Tel Aviv and Antwerp. Because of Hitler, she came to the United States. Her first husband died in an air crash. Max Stern served as executor of his will. They had known each other at the Jewish Center. She has four children (three boys, one girl); he has three (Leonard, Stanley, Gloria).

He reminisces, "I have been successful all my life. I am a hard worker. I have been interested in Judaism all my life. When I came to the United States in 1926, I was upset. I disliked the way they advertised synagogues for the High Holy days. There were big signs and verses for prayers. I felt this was not ethical, not the way one should get coreligionists into synagogues.

"When I had been longer in the United States, I learned that most of these people came from East Europe and had been in a straitjacket. They feared anti-Semitism. Instead they came to a free country and saw a different atmosphere.

"People then became very successful by making money, money, money. Then they saw something was missing. This only came through when they lost their children to mixed marriages.

"There was a time when East Europeans and West Europeans did not mix. At the Jewish Center all were Russians. They did accept me. I was a hard worker. These Russian Jews are capable hard workers. From nothing they had created many new industries. They did not give up their Jewishness. They built homes for the aged, invalids, social centers. They did not lose their Jewishness."

Tall, spare, dressed in printed smoking jacket with gray pants, Max Stern looks the sort one sees at Wimbledon or Ascot. Yet he wears a *yarmulke,* is a contributor to Shaare Zedek in Israel and many yeshivas. His apartment, filled with antiques and art, is as elegant as he. The story goes that one day an artist visited Stern and saw a Picasso in the vestibule. He said, "That is a nice

Picasso lithograph." Answered Stern, "There are no lithographs in this apartment."

In advising young people today, the courtly Stern says, "They should find out about their own ability and do what they like to do and be willing to work hard. Getting satisfaction out of life is the important thing. If I retired, I could not sleep."

Bur always the subject comes back to his Orthodox faith. He notes, "My father and grandfather were always active in religious life. So are all my children." Asked if his children remained Orthodox, he notes, with just a trace of wistfulness, "They are Orthodox in spirit."

THE FAMILIAL ASPECT OF ORTHODOXY

Family matters occupy much time in the life of an Orthodox Jew. Some make a complete social life out of attending weddings, births and funerals of relatives—many of whom they have not seen or talked with for years. Just as she did when her children were unmarried, Els Bendheim runs a constant open house for young people and, according to friends, seems determined to marry off every Jewish Orthodox single. Orthodox people always seem to know other Orthodox in other cities. They have connections. Mrs. Bendheim calls this "Jewishography."

Consider the glamorous Charlotte Feuerstein, wife of Dr. Sidney Feuerstein and a dedicated volunteer. From 1975 to 1980 she served on the Presidium of the women's club of the Fifth Avenue Synagogue. She has also been chairman, Manhattan Organizations, UJA. On the surface the family seems secular. Sidney and Charlotte Feuerstein are members of the Harmonie Club, certainly among the few Orthodox to be admitted. Their daughter Ronnie went to Radcliffe and Yale Law School and married lawyer Sam Heyman. Son Henry, a graduate of the Fieldston School, the Massachusetts Institute of Technology and the Columbia University School of Law, recently wed Elise Ann Meyer, owner and director of a New York art gallery. Even with the secular schooling, the family is firmly observant. All keep kosher. Elise's uncle is the chief rabbi of the Conservative movement in Argentina. When he married Ronnie, Sam Heyman was a Conservative Jew. Now he sits on the board of the Orthodox synagogue in Stamford, Connecticut. Ronnie's and Sam's children attend Hebrew day schools. All are close and see each other every weekend. Parents Charlotte and Sidney visit his parents in California four times a year.

Charlotte Feuerstein says, "Our closeness is taken for granted. I would not have it any other way. We enjoy our Orthodoxy. It has been a pleasurable experience. I like the boundaries, the discipline. Years ago Jews were not accepted socially, politically or academically. Today there are no boundaries for Jews. My kids can do anything; they have no boundaries except the rules of Orthodoxy. Holidays with us are a family thing. We are together. I knew that when my son sat down and ate a kosher meal that it would be difficult for him to intermarry."

She makes the point that a baby-naming ceremony has become a new custom for new-born Orthodox girls. She says, "It used to be that bar mitzvahs were important, then bas mitzvahs. We wanted to make the girl important also, so now we have the baby-naming ceremonies because girls have no *bris* (circumcision ceremony).

THE SEPHARDIC COMMUNITY

In the United States there are an estimated one hundred fifty thousand Sephardim and 70 known synagogues. These are congregations which do not follow the Ashkenazi form of worship and where members are not of Ashkenazi descent (German or Eastern European). The word *Ashkenazi* comes from Genesis, which names Ashkenaz as one of the great-grandsons of Noah. It was first used by Jews with a Spanish background to describe German Jews, for to them Germany was the East. Later, German Jews used it in referring to Jews of Hungary, Rumania, Poland and Russia. Sephardic Jews are largely of Spanish, Portuguese,

Syrian, Greek, Egyptian, North African and Yugoslav origin.

The Spanish and Portuguese, whose origins in the United States predate that of all other American Jews, are considered the most prestigious by many fellow Jews. As noted, the leading Sephardic congregation is Shearith Israel, New York. A few of the descendants of the old families are members—Edgar Nathan III, Emily Nathan, Ruth Shulson—but the senior rabbi is Ashkenazic (an aristocratic member comments with hauteur, "At Shearith Israel, we prefer to wear hats, not *yarmulkes*").

Most other congregations are predominantly first- or second-generation American with a strong home culture. Says Gary Schaer, director of the American Sephardi Federation, "For example, they are Moroccan Jews first and Sephardic Jews second. The cultures in which Jews lived affected them more than they admit. The Sephardim did not view others as enemies the way the Jews did the Christians. The Sephardim freely took elements of the Arab culture."

At the time of the Inquisition the Sephardic Jews left Spain. Some went to the Ottoman Empire: Turkey, Greece, Bulgaria, Syria. Later others found a refuge in Amsterdam and London. Some went to Recife, Brazil, and then came to America. The ones who went to North Africa joined an already existent Oriental-Jewish population and helped cause a rebirth of that Jewish culture.

Says Rabbi Emanuel Rackman, "In the United States the Sephardic community is not homogeneous. It depends on the community from which the people came. There is the Iberian, where you have people like the Nathans. Then one has communities that are detached from the mainstream like the Georgians [USSR], who are detached culturally and linguistically. The Syrians have retained their identity. But they all fall within the Orthodox community."

The Syrians have their own schools which teach children in the tradition of the parents. Deal, New Jersey, formerly the "Jewish Newport" of the old-time German Jews, has become a year-round residence for some Syrian Jews, but the vast majority live on Ocean Parkway in Brooklyn.

Adds Schaer, "Among Syrians it is common to marry young.

This is true among most immigrant groups. Few Syrian boys attend or complete their B.A.'s at the university. They must go into their father's business. Many rabbis campaign against their going to the university or going out into the world at night. They can be out in the world from nine to six, make money and go home."

In Queens, New York, there is a community from Salonika; in Cedarhurst, New York, from Turkey, Greece and the Balkans. New York itself includes all the Sephardic groups. In Los Angeles there is a large Sephardic group from Greece and Turkey, two synagogues of Moroccan Jews, an Indian-Iraqi synagogue, a Persian synagogue. Out of three Orthodox synagogues in Seattle, two are Sephardic. Miami has five Sephardic synagogues.

There is a difference between the Orthodox and Sephardic prayer book. The late David de Sola Pool, who served for many years as rabbi of Shearith Israel, wrote both.

Schaer comments, "Most people will say in conversation that the Sephardim are Orthodox. I refuse to use the term. I include Sephardic Judaism as another movement. We are kosher. We do have the laws of Shabbat."

The Sephardim have always numbered many famous people among their ranks. Old-timers included the late Supreme Court Justice Benjamin Nathan Cardozo, Emma Lazarus, who penned the ode to the Statue of Liberty, Haym Salomon, Judah P. Benjamin, secretary of state in Jefferson Davis's cabinet. Current Sephardim include soprano Victoria de los Angeles, hairdresser Vidal Sassoon, Mrs. Abba Eban, flamenco dancer Teodora Morca.

Many of the Sephardim have become very rich. In 1913 Louis Rousso came to the United States from Turkey. His sons Eli and Irving Rousso formed the Russ Togs Corporation in 1946, and the history of Russ Togs has become one of the Horatio Alger stories of American industry.

Yet, admits Schaer sadly, even with their success and famous names, as a minority within the American Jewish community, the Sephardic congregations face the problem of cultural dilution, even the danger of extinction.

DAY SCHOOLS

The rising interest in Orthodoxy is reflected in the increasing number of Hebrew day schools since World War II. In 1944 there were only thirty schools in the three states. There are now some five hundred schools in thirty-seven states. Most are located on the Eastern seaboard of the United States; there are some two hundred in the New York City area. However, they also exist in such communities as South Bend, Indiana; Albuquerque, New Mexico; Santa Barbara, California; Bangor, Maine; Annapolis, Maryland. Most come under the aegis of Torah Umesorah, the National Society of Hebrew Day Schools. Moses Feuerstein has been a member of the board of directors since 1951.

Perhaps the most elite is Ramaz in New York City, founded in 1936 by the late Joseph Lookstein (people called him "Holy Joe"), rabbi of Congregation Kehilath Jeshurun, New York. Kehilath Jeshurun is 110 years old. Rabbi Joseph Lookstein served there for 56 years. After Saturday service he would walk the mile to Mount Sinai Hospital, walk up the stairs and visit not only sick people from his congregation but other Jewish patients as well who did not have company. Today his son Haskel Lookstein serves both as rabbi at Kehilath Jeshurun, a formal congregation with two thousand congregants where ushers wear morning attire, and as principal of Ramaz.

The Ramaz School has a total population of some 875 students in both its upper and lower schools, which are housed in separate buildings, and fifty teachers. All high school students pursue a full program of religious studies that includes Hebrew language and literature, four years of Bible, three years of Talmud, Jewish history and philosophy.

Says Rabbi Haskel Lookstein, "The purpose is to give a solid Jewish education along with a complete education in Western civilization—the best we can offer." Writer Elie Wiesel's son goes to Ramaz. So does the child of Robert Abrams, New York State's attorney general. Leonard Stern's children went there. Harrison Goldin, comptroller of the city of New York, is a graduate. So is feminist Aviva Cantor.

Notes Rabbi Lookstein, "We do not have only Orthodox Jews as students. Some 50 percent are Orthodox. I would like it to be 60 percent. Ramaz is a real cross section. Every year one or two students receive Westinghouse awards. Of a graduating class of eighty, three may be National Merit finalists. Our graduates go to Harvard, Yale and Princeton. It is virtually a prep school for Columbia.

"We give the same education to girls as we give to boys right through twelfth grade. My daughter got early decision to go to Barnard, but she wanted to study Torah for a year in Israel. She went there to a right-wing school. At a bus stop near the school, for example, she cannot talk to a boy. When she gets married, she will probably keep her hair covered."

In accordance with the current move to the right, policy at Ramaz is also getting stricter. Says Rabbi Lookstein, "Last year we cut out dances. It is not the way we want to train our students. We like people to feel comfortable in our school. Dancing is just not in keeping with the spirit we want now. We have a young faculty. Some opposed it. I was torn. My father would have battled it. He would have said, 'If you do not like it, get out.' But in today's world, he would have lost faculty and students and also the kind of spirit he wanted in his school."

Says Abby Belkin, "The day schools are doing a tremendous job. The students get the plus of a dual education—secular and religious. But the popularity of day schools has brought about problems. Because the students receive a more religious education, they don't want milk and meat served together when they come home. They want a kosher house."

TALES OF ORTHODOXY

Just as in the Reform and Conservative groups, there is often disagreement about policy.

Shaare Zedek is a hospital in Israel whose board is headed by wealthy American Orthodox Jews like Ludwig Jesselson and Max Stern. There is a prohibition among the *Cohanim* (the Cohens—descendants of Aaron, brother of Moses, who was the first high priest) that they should not come into contact with dead bodies. When a pathologist, who was of the Cohen tribe, was named head at Shaare Zedek, not only was there a protest at the hospital, but, in New York, picketers lined up in front of Ludwig Jesselson's home in Riverdale and Max Stern's apartment building on Central Park West.

The Reconstructionist movement started because of the Jewish Center. Rabbi Jung's predecessor there was Mordecai Kaplan, now in his 101st year, who served as the JC's first rabbi. Kaplan then "took a walk," taking half the congregation's membership with him, and, in 1922, founded the Society for the Advancement of Judaism, based on the idea that "Judaism is a civilization." History repeats itself. Recently a group did not care for the current rabbi at the S.A.J., so about one hundred members left, formed their own *havurah* and now meet Saturdays at Central Synagogue, across town and Reform.

Despite the intensity of its religious commitment, the Orthodox community can also be rocked by scandal. One prominent member lost her husband to another woman. She quickly broke up another marriage, married the man and made him turn Orthodox. Now has become just as Orthodox as she.

The Orthodox Jew can influence a business associate—even a non-Jew. Seymour Propp heads Quincy Mining Company. After Harvard Law School, Propp served in the armed forces. Later, with money inherited from his father, he became stockholder in various copper companies, eventually in Quincy. W. Parsons Todd, an elegant Episcopalian, served as president of Quincy from 1924 until his death, at ninty-eight, in 1976 (he had joined the company in 1900). Propp was like a son to Todd, who, at the time of his death according to the *New York Times,* was "perhaps the oldest active executive of a publicly held American company." He had, in turn, an influence on Todd. Because of Propp, today a Todd Free Loan Fund operates out of Jerusalem. Todd also donated land for a Reform temple in Morristown, New Jersey.

But perhaps the greatest influence of the Orthodox is its effect on youth. Says Rabbi Bernard Goldenberg of Torah Umesorah, "The greatest commitment within the Orthodox movement today is from young people looking for values. Orthodox Judaism—its demands, its commitments and its consistency—makes sense to young people."

Says Professor David Roskies of Jewish Theological Seminary, "Many of the Orthodox Jews are *Baalei Teshuvas*—'those who return.' These are the born-again Jews. Their parents could have been Reform, Conservative, assimilated. The parents do not have impact except on the psychiatrist's couch. Young people have to find a place to channel their energy. They find it in ethnicity."

Some of the new Orthodox, the BT's, come from old German-Jewish families. Some are converts. Thirty-three-year-old blond, bearded John Kelley, a market researcher, was born a Protestant. John went to Northeastern, studied psychology at Yeshiva University and seven years ago formally converted to Judaism. In 1979 he joined Kehilath Jeshurun and became an Orthodox Jew. He says, "I always had Orthodox friends and informally converted when I was twenty-three. I had had the idea of being Jewish since high school. It seemed warmer to me than Christianity. In Christianity you get saved. Since I got into Judaism the whole black thing made more sense. You have your own roots. You don't have to ape the Protestants."

The way the Orthodox are retaining young people and attracting others shows something. It may be ethnic revival or authenticity. But as Professor Roskies says, "The key phrase is feeling—that Orthodoxy is the real merchandise."

11

THE JEP IN ACADEME

In the March, 1979, issue of *Commentary,* Diana Trilling reminisced about the difficulties her husband Lionel had experienced with anti-Semitism in the English department at Columbia University under the regime of President Nicholas Murray Butler. She recalled how in the days of the prejudicial 1930s Trilling's immigrant father had been unable to understand or reconcile the bigotry of the times with his unrealistic picture of American freedom. "We had been talking about Jews in college teaching, the failure they almost surely faced," she wrote. "His father, as always unperturbed in his reading of this world we presumably inhabited with him, had fixed his most unbearably pitying look on Lionel. 'Why son, this is America. A Jew could be President of Columbia University.' "

Today a Jew, Michael Sovern, *is* president of Columbia. The heads of Barnard (Ellen Futter), Brooklyn College (Robert Hess), City University's Graduate School and University Center (Harold Proshansky) are also Jewish. Other Jewish presidents in academe include Edward Bloustein of Rutgers, Leon Botstein of Bard, Irving Shain of the University of Wisconsin at Madison, Evelyn Handler of the University of New Hampshire, Henry R. Winkler of the University of Cincinnati, Marvin Wachman of Temple, Nobel-Prize winner Joshua Lederberg of Rockefeller, Marvin Goldberger of California Institute of Technology and David Saxon of the University of California.

Jews in academe have come a long way since the days after World War II when Albert Sprague Coolidge of Harvard told a

Massachusetts legislative committee, "We know perfectly well that names ending in *berg* or *stein* have to be skipped by the board of selection of students for scholarships in chemistry," because it was the department's understanding that there were no jobs for Jews in chemistry.

The Jew who has perhaps created the most stir in the academic world does not possess the title "president." He did not want it. Henry Rosovsky turned down both the presidencies of Chicago and Yale to remain in his post as dean of the Faculty of Arts and Sciences at Harvard. Had Dr. Rosovsky accepted Yale, his presidency would have represented a break in Yale's almost three centuries of tradition, not only by being the first Jew to hold the position but also by being the first to have no previous ties to Yale. It was quite a gesture for a refugee who arrived in the United States at thirteen without knowing a single word of English.

SOME ACADEMIC FACTS

The first Jewish-born president of an American university was Dr. Ephraim M. Epstein, a convert to Christianity in the late 1850s. Epstein founded the University of South Dakota in 1882 after a number of years as a practicing physician in Kansas and Ohio. The late Dr. Paul Klapper, a world-renowned educator who helped lay the foundation for the mammoth State University of New York, was the first professing Jew to become president of a publicly supported college. When Queens College became independent of City College in 1937, Dr. Klapper, then dean of the C.C.N.Y. School of Education, was designated as the first president of the institution.

Even in the United States, within the university system, Jews were held back from educational and job opportunities. Until the end of World War II important private universities had quotas limiting the number of Jewish undergraduates. Relatively few Jews were able to secure employment on the faculty of these schools. According to a report in the 1971 *American Jewish Yearbook,* "The change in favor of Jewish participation at the summit of American higher education in the past 25 years has been so extensive and totally accepted that some indication of how different the situation was at the beginning of the careers of the current generation of senior professors would seem to be in order."

Overt anti-Jewish prejudice within academe seemingly was at a high point in the 1920s and 1930s when large numbers of the children of immigrants began to enter college. This pressure led many schools to impose quotas on the admission of Jews to both undergraduate and professional schools. A. Lawrence Lowell, as president of Harvard, and Nicholas Murray Butler, then president of Columbia, openly defended Jewish quotas. And, as late as 1945, Ernest M. Hopkins, then president of Dartmouth, justified the use of a quota at his institution on the ground that "Dartmouth is a Christian college founded for the Christianization of its students." These restrictions carried over even more intensely to faculty appointments.

In his memoirs Ludwig Lewisohn reported how he was prevented from teaching English. Edward Sapir was told by his graduate-school professors that as a Jew he could not expect an appointment and had to go to Canada. In an article in *Commentary* Lionel Trilling recalled that he was the first Jew appointed to Columbia's English department. After Felix Frankfurter, the Harvard Law School did not appoint another Jew until 1939 when Paul Freund and Milton Katz were named assistant professors.

Since that time the situation has changed startlingly on both student and faculty levels. Schools which were notorious among Jews for their restrictionist policies suddenly opened their doors. In 1976, Dr. John G. Kemeny, a Hungarian immigrant, was chosen as the president of Dartmouth (he is now on sabbatical leave and will return to full-time teaching in the mathematics department). He was believed to be the first person of Jewish family background to head an Ivy League university.

Dr. Martin Meyerson, one of the nation's leading authorities on urban development, whose name was in headlines in 1965 while he was acting chancellor of the University of California during the student riots there, has been president of the Buffalo

Campus of the University of New York, president of the University of Pennsylvania, and is now president emeritus. From 1971 to 1980 Dr. Jerome B. Wiesner, onetime science advisor to Presidents Kennedy and Johnson, served as president of Massachusetts Institute of Technology. Edward Levi, whose maternal grandfather was the noted Reform rabbi Emil Hirsch, served as president of the University of Chicago from 1968 to 1975 and then became America's first Jewish attorney general.

Asked about the abundance of Jewish college presidents today, Dean Rosovsky offers the candid comment, "There are very few desirable candidates, and there are lots of Jews in the pool."

JEP PORTRAIT: DEAN HENRY ROSOVSKY

As custodian of the Faculty of Arts and Sciences, Dean Rosovsky oversees some sixty-five hundred undergraduates at Harvard and Radcliffe, twenty-four hundred graduate students, eight hundred and fifty faculty members, including five hundred full professors. He heads a "large bureaucracy" including the dean of the college, the dean of the graduate school, the dean of applied sciences. He is also responsible for a score of research laboratories, the Harvard College library, six museums. When he took the job in 1973, he had an annual budget of $70 million and a deficit of $2.5 million. He overcame the deficit and now has a budget of $150 million.

Rosovsky is chairman of the board of trustees and senior vice-president of the American Jewish Congress, occasionally attends services at the Harvard Hillel ("That is our temple"), where his son was bar mitzvahed. He and his wife Nitza, a seventh-generation Israeli, have a yearly *seder* and "always have *goyim* as guests."

Rosovsky is no absentminded professor with his mind on metaphysics. Highly personable and likable, he speaks in a clear-cut, precise, occasionally slangy manner. A neat, rather natty dresser, he wears a dark blue suit, button-down white shirt and a necktie with tiny yellow circles. However, the academic trappings are there: dark-rimmed glasses, pipe, unpretentious book-filled office on the second floor of University Hall in the middle of Harvard Yard, the fire blazing in early fall.

Rosovsky has definite opinions on a variety of subjects.

ON ELITISM: "Elitism means first class. The elites I am in contact with are elite in terms of academic excellence. Harvard and comparable institutions are elite. We bring the best people here and we produce first-class people. Some people—like the British aristocracy—view elites in terms of blood. Others see elites in terms of status. I am involved with the meritocratic elites and they are more mixed in terms of ethnic origin.

ON THE EDUCATED PERSON: "An educated person," he says, "should be able to communicate with precision, cogency and force. He or she should have an informed acquaintance with the mathematical and experimental methods of the physical and biological sciences; with the historical and quantitative techniques needed for investigating the workings and the development of modern society; with some of the important scholarly, literary and artistic achievements of the past; and with the major religious and philosophical conceptions of what man is. An educated American should not be provincial. He should have some understanding of and experience in thinking about moral and religious problems. Above all, he should reject shoddiness in all forms."

When Rosovsky took on his present post in 1973, President Derek Bok gave him the specific mandate of reappraising undergraduate education. Rosovsky first focused his attention on balancing the budget. Then in 1974 he set out to tackle the even more complicated issue of curricular reform. He wrote a letter to the faculty in which he discussed the problem of what he called a "laissez-faire curricular policy" and voiced his fear that a Harvard degree was uncomfortably close to becoming nothing more than "a certificate of attendance." The Harvard General Education program had proliferated into a cornucopia of courses—or "Chinese menu." Rosovsky called for a "more structured approach to general education."

Faculty task forces were set up to work on the problem, and this led to the introduction of the much publicized "core curriculum" in the 1979–80 academic year for the class of 1983. This means that regardless of a student's field of concentration, to graduate he/she must take the equivalent of one year or seven to eight courses in five academic areas. The areas are literature and art; mathematics and science; history; social analysis and moral reasoning; and foreign culture.

To satisfy the literature and the arts requirement, a student can elect everything from "The Literary Mind of the Middle Ages" and "Chinese Painting" to "Concepts of Musical Style" and "Opera: Perspectives on Music and Drama." History features such courses as "International Conflicts in the Modern World" and "The Rise of American Power." For science the undergraduate might opt for "Dynamics of the Earth" or "The Human Organism."

"These are not just odd courses," says Rosovsky. "They stress a common methodology and are put together in such a way that they are educationally equivalent. This is a network year of liberal education that should be a foundation of learning. The old categories of humanities had become too vague. Learning had progressed. It is a case of the issue, not the facts—of giving students a sense of the modes of thought, of ways of thinking. For example, nonscientists study science, not only to learn some of the important principles but also to understand what it means to be a scientist, what issues scientists are passionate about. So also for the scientists who will learn about art, literature and history. The willingness to talk to other people and see their point of view is what creates an intellectual community."

Under Rosovsky's direction, Harvard has developed some sixty to sixty-five courses to fit into the core-curriculum program, introduced music and art as part of it and a novel way of teaching history. He comments, "Because of the core curriculum we have gotten the best of the Harvard faculty into the classroom on the undergraduate level."

Not everyone is a fan. The Harvard *Crimson* ran a cartoon whose caption said that only after you study a subject in which you have absolutely no interest can you claim to be educated. "Students say they are locked in," notes Rosovsky. "Other people say the core curriculum is too loose. Educators are fixated on their own way of doing things. Everyone has different criticisms—which convinces me we are on the right track.

"The core won't turn out scientists or humanists; they will still have to specialize. But it will attempt to make sure all our students have covered five academic areas in terms of informed acquaintance and critical appreciation. A liberal education should provide a common core of intellectual experience for all students. No college can remedy the damage of poor secondary education, but we are determined to give those eighteen-year-olds who need it a second chance."

Rosovsky was born on September 1, 1927, in the Free City of Danzig. He is a Rosovsky on both the maternal and paternal side of his family, all of whom originally came from a small village called Rosovo, near Minsk, in White Russia. After the Russian Revolution, his father had to flee and settled in Danzig, now Gdansk, in 1920. A lawyer, he went into the timber business which had been his father's business. Running from Hitler, in 1937 the Rosovskys moved to Brussels and in May, 1940, when the Germans invaded Belgium, they made the classic refugee trek to France, Spain, Portugal and then to the United States. "My poor father was a refugee three times in his life," says Rosovsky.

In Portugal the Rosovskys managed to get passage on the S.S. *Nyassa,* which the Germans had given to the Portuguese as reparations for World War I. They landed in Hoboken on December 4, 1940, and before that Christmas vacation Henry Rosovsky was enrolled at Joan of Arc Junior High School at Amsterdam Avenue and Ninety-third Street in New York. He spoke not one word of English. While waiting for the ship in Pôrto, his mother had some clothes made for him, so on his first day at school he wore European-style short pants and long woolen stockings. He felt terribly embarrassed. He recalls, "I did not own a pair of long pants." However, he was rescued by a new-found old friend from Danzig days who came up to him, saying, "Get long pants and a lumber jacket. Make your mother take you to Klein's (a budget department store then on Fourteenth Street) tomorrow!"

Six months later Rosovsky took the examination for admission to Stuyvesant High School (a New York public high school for very bright students) and won admission. Asked how he could be admitted with limited English, Rosovsky says, "The Stuyvesant exam had two parts: quantitative—math, where I had no problems—and verbal. I learn languages easily. Some refugees have accents. Some do not. I have a good ear." Rosovsky speaks English, German, Japanese, French and Russian. He still talks to his mother in Russian. And he has no trace of an accent.

When the Rosovskys arrived here, they were penniless, but his father was a "good businessman" and began to manage sawmills for a Belgian baron of Jewish origin in Kinston, North Carolina, and elsewhere in the South. Rosovsky recalls that in those days at Stuyvesant, "The juniors and seniors went in the morning, freshmen and sophomores in the afternoon. My parents were away a lot and my mother did not want me just hanging around the house. Also, because we did not speak English at home, she felt I would never learn English properly. Even though middle-class Jews for the most part did not send sons to boarding school, they decided to send me to a progressive private school. They picked the Cherry Lawn School in Darien, Connecticut. It was run by a Swedish noblewoman who was married to a Russian immigrant. It was no Exeter or Andover but I had a wonderful education there. I also learned touch football. Alison Lurie was a classmate. It was 50 percent Jewish and there were lots of refugee kids. We had a graduating class of sixteen."

After Cherry Lawn, Rosovsky attended William and Mary for a year, then was drafted into the army, where he served in Europe in the Counter Intelligence Corps (he met Henry Kissinger, a fellow refugee, for the first time at Oberammergau when he took Kissinger's course in German paramilitary organizations at the European Command Intelligence School). After the army, Rosovsky took a reserve commission and returned to William and Mary, majoring in economics and history. He graduated in 1949. Under the G.I. Bill of Rights, he enrolled in graduate school at Harvard, studying economics, but in 1950, after the outbreak of the Korean War, was called back into the army and shipped to Korea. At this point he started developing an interest in Asia. In 1952 he went back to Harvard, where he became a junior fellow, elected to the Society of Fellows. He got his A.M. in 1953 and his Ph.D. in 1959.

"Being a Harvard junior fellow means you spend three years in which you do what you want to do," comments Rosovsky. "I started out studying Russian economic development in the last half of the eighteenth century. Then I became interested in Japan and decided to study Japanese."

It was during this period that Rosovsky met Nitza Brown (then working for the Israeli consulate and studying at Hunter at night), who has been his wife for twenty-six years. He recalls fondly, "I was twenty-eight, unmarried and marrying me off was a challenge to all my relatives. I wanted them to leave me alone. I was a junior fellow, studying what I wanted to study, and had a wonderful suite of rooms in Kirkland House. It was September 1—my birthday. My parents were away and I was alone in New York. My aunt invited me for dinner and there she was. We had a fight about Arab refugees. By June we were married and left for Tokyo on the day of the wedding. In Tokyo I worked on my Ph.D. thesis on 'Japanese Capital Formation, 1868–1940.' "

Today the Rosovskys have three children: Leah, twenty-four, who works for Paine Webber, the brokerage firm; Judy, twenty-two, who hopes to become a herpetologist; and Michael, sixteen, a high-school student.

After Japan, in 1958 Rosovsky became an acting assistant professor of economics and history at the University of California at Berkeley. By 1965 he was a full professor. "It was the beginning of the student problems," he later told the *New Yorker,* "and I was unhappy about what was going on. I strongly believed in high-quality public education. I had gone to Berkeley in the first place for ideological reasons. But I began to feel that many students and faculty did not believe, as I did, in this great institution. They were pecking away at the administration. They were abandoning important academic principles."

So without having another job, Rosovsky resigned, received a number of attractive offers, including one from Harvard, and went there as professor of economics in 1965. In 1969 he became chairman of the Department of Economics.

Rosovsky has received honorary doctorates from Yeshiva University, Hebrew Union College and Colgate University. In 1963 he received the Schumpeter Prize in Economics from Harvard. In 1969 he became a fellow of the American Academy of Arts and Sciences. He has served as visiting professor at Stamford, Hitotsubashi and Tokyo universities, and the Hebrew University of Jerusalem. He has been a consultant to the President's Commission on International Trade and Foreign Investment (1971), and to the Asian Development Bank (1977 and 1978). Active as a fundraiser for Harvard, he has also helped Robert Brustein bring his repertory theater from Yale to Harvard.

In his book *Making Scenes,* which tells of the move and the events behind it, Brustein compares Rosovsky with Harvard President Bok. He writes, "Bok is an extremely courteous man and so is Rosovsky, but they form a fascinating contrast. The dean is outgoing, expansive, emphatic; the president is deliberate, reserved, understated. While the relationship between the two men is warm and mutually respectful, their backgrounds are totally divergent. It is amusing to hear Rosovsky studding his speech with middle European anecedotes and Yiddish phrases which Bok has difficulty understanding ('Don't be so ethnic, Henry')."

Asked about the new emergence of Jews as both students and major heads in the academic world, Rosovsky offers Miami as an analogy. "When I went to Miami when I was about fourteen, I saw signs that said 'restricted,' " he recalls. "I was told that meant no Jews. But look at Miami today!"

He states firmly, "There is no quota. It has disappeared. Instead there is social engineering. People want regional, geographic and ethnic distribution. Obviously Andover or Exeter would not be comfortable with a 90-percent-Jewish student body. The question is not quotas but what has happened to American society.

"From World War II to the present, society changed. We had the civil-rights movement, the whole thrust of society to eliminate injustice, the creation of the State of Israel.

"And after World War II—from both faculty and students—came the meritocratic system. Once the gates were open—via

SATs or the promise of creativity—a large group of Jews were willing to take advantage of the opportunity. I believe 25 percent of the Harvard student body is Jewish and a smaller percentage of faculty. There have been more Jews in the last fifteen years than in previous years."

This is quite different from President Lowell's era (1909 to 1933) during which time the so-called quota controversy occurred. Narrow, ancestor-worshiping A. Lawrence Lowell had watched the proportion of Jews in the college rise rapidly. In 1900 7 percent of Harvard was Jewish; by 1918 it had risen to 10 percent, and, by 1921, it had reached 21.5 percent. In 1922 Lowell made a public statement saying that the proportion of Jews in the college was under consideration. Jewish leaders like Harvard Overseer Judge Julian Mack became upset. For an American institution as prestigious as Harvard to adopt a policy which seemed to imply that Jews as a class were "undesirable" could have been interpreted as an authoritative sanction of anti-Semitism in the United States.

Lowell's views were tested by the "Committee of Thirteen," appointed by the overseers in 1922. The committee, which had three Jews on it, repudiated the notion of quotas and the faculty adopted its report with the following statement: "That in the administration of the rules for admission Harvard College maintains its traditional policy of freedom from discrimination on the grounds of race or religion."

At the dedication of the Harvard-Radcliffe Hillel Society's new home in 1979, Dean Rosovsky told the audience, "Although the proportion of Jewish students at Harvard declined during Lowell's presidency, it started rising again during and after World War II, and has never been higher than at present. And, of course, many other ethnic and social groups have become more numerous. The door was half open fifty years ago. Today it is fully open."

Rosovsky voices concern about current aspects of American society: "I sometimes feel America is in danger of turning into an Ottoman Empire where every subgroup has its own laws, its own share of the pie. I worry because instead of one people there seems to be a coalition of different groups. This can lead to proportionate representation. At schools like Harvard we have a sizable Jewish student body that is much more than proportionate. If colleges only admitted Jews according to the Jewish population, there would be only 3 percent. This would not be good for the Jews. It would cut us back. It would be unmeritocratic. It would be a substitution of national origin for talent."

Asked about today's students in contrast to the activists of the sixties and preprofessionals of the seventies, Rosovsky answers, "It is so diverse at Harvard that it is mind-boggling. The dean of Harvard College commented to me recently about how today's students worry about their future. If I look at my own life, I had a lot of luck. I lived in an era that was extremely forgiving. Until I went into the army for the first time, I was lazy and a poor student. By going into the army, the slate was marked clean. I knew what I wanted to do. I had a straight-A record from then on. I took it into my head to study Japanese. Society was prosperous at the time. I got all those appointments.

"It is tough now when kids get poor grades. Recently I reprimanded my son about his marks and Michael answered back, 'But everyone knows you were a poor student.' I told him, 'Times have changed.' "

As did his sisters, Michael goes to a public school in Newton, where the Rosovskys make their home. Nitza Rosovsky, who from 1968 to 1976 had run the Cambridge Gallery Art Asia and who now is exhibit coordinator of Harvard's Semitic Museum, explains, "Most Harvard professors cannot afford to live in Cambridge. Also, we were and are great believers in public education and thought it good for the children to go to public schools. In Cambridge the children go to private schools."

Rosovsky feels he has never had any trouble with anti-Semitism. "I was in the army for three years—both as an enlisted man and as an officer—and I traveled all over the United States and never personally had a serious incident of anti-Semitism. I have never felt hampered by open Jewish identification. About 1950 my brother Alex changed his name. He is in the advertising business. It was a problem. Perhaps he would not do it today.

"In my case, my life has been positive. I was offered the presidencies of Yale and Chicago. No one is in doubt about what

I am. Rosovsky is as good a name as any other name at Harvard. Clearly, some Jews have problems I do not."

Rosovsky tells the story of the Yale man who told Mrs. Rosovsky he was not going to take no for an answer. "My wife told him, 'I know Henry. There is no use pursuing it.' The man said, 'I think he owes it to his humble origins to do this.' But I don't view my origins as humble at all."

Rosovsky has never been sorry about turning down the two presidencies. Shortly afterward he told the *New Yorker,* "I love Harvard. It would be a privilege to be connected with Yale, or with Chicago, but they are not mine. Harvard is *mine.*"

Nitza Rosovsky, author of the recently published *Jerusalemwalks,* adds, "I thought he should have taken Yale. Yale was then going through a difficult period. The job would be a challenge. Maybe he could do something at Yale based on his experiences here at Harvard. And, my God, there was the Jewish thing—it was so imaginative of Yale to offer him the job. And going to New Haven would help me make up my mind about leaving Art Asia. I could just say we were leaving the area. But every time I have made a strong objection, Henry does it the other way around. I loved Berkeley and wanted to stay there."

Ironically, according to the *Crimson* many people at Harvard thought it was Mrs. Rosovsky who kept her husband from switching to Yale because she wanted to stay with Art Asia.

Rosovsky stresses that both he and his brother are more Jewish than they were thirty years ago. He says, "My brother is more religious. I am not observant. My identification is more ethnic —with the people and the culture.

"My parents thought of themselves as Russians who were Jewish. My parents were refugees in Danzig, where I was born. I feel odd when I write *Poland* in my passport. We were always strangers in Europe—never part of society. That is why the United States presented such a great contrast."

Dean Rosovsky emphasizes that as a sabra his wife has a strong identification with Israel. He notes, "My kids think of themselves as Americans who are part Israeli. When my wife and I were married, deciding we would not live in Israel was a major decision. She regrets it. I told her very clearly that I wanted no false premises. Israel would not give me the same opportunities as America—for example, the university had no library on Asia. But that is a cop-out. I could have changed fields.

"If you take the ideal of America and the ideal of Israeli society, I am drawn to the American ideal—a multicultural society, the premises on which America was founded. Both my brother and I are unabashed American patriots. I am strongly drawn to the ideals of American society. That is why I did not want to move to Israel."

What draws Rosovsky is the "American restlessness." He says, "As long as the American restlessness is alive, it is good." He expanded this tenet in a commencement address to the graduating class of Deerfield Academy in May, 1981, when he told the student body, "There is a perpetual restlessness in the American spirit, a desire for greater perfection and a sense of discomfort with the status quo. These feelings have undoubtedly led to great progress in areas that many nations fear to touch, and indeed in areas where our problems are often greater than those of other countries. Our future, I think, depends on maintaining this restlessness—this dissatisfaction—provided that it remains creative and constructive."

Rosovsky feels America is going through "a period of great criticism and self-criticism on all levels. We are all trying to find our equilibrium."

He stresses that there will be "new opportunities for women academics. All institutions are recruiting women. Being a woman may have pluses." However, he cautions, "If you are a woman and want to lead a normal life, it is hard. You cannot have a maid on an assistant professor's salary."

In the future he foresees a series of changes in the academic world. He predicts:

"In higher education you will see far more rigor than in the last twenty years. There will be changes in curriculum appearing in the professional schools like law and medicine. Medical schools are due for an overhaul.

"There will be changes in the high schools which started imitating colleges instead of preparing the students for college. High school is a place where students should be taught the basics. People are beginning to see this. Leaders in higher education are not worried enough about what happens in primary and secondary schools. No one has taken Conant's place [James Bryant Conant, president of Harvard from 1933 to 1953, was extremely concerned about secondary education].

"A lot of Jewish students will not choose academia as a profession. From the fifties to the seventies a lot of Jews—the first generation of upward mobility who wanted the good life—elected academia. But now the academic life has lost its luster. For the next twenty years it will not be expanding. Will these same Jews choose law? And will law allow the same freedom as academia? Will you find a large percentage of Jewish partners in fifteen years? That is the question. I do not know."

Dean Rosovsky is quick to make the point that his knowledge stems only from experience at two major universities. "In the United States there are some thirty-five hundred colleges," he points out. "I have only been at two as a professor, and these are within the top five. You have to filter it. I know the large research university world and that is not the average. I do not know the world of small provincial colleges."

What does Rosovsky plan for his own future? His cherubic face turns serious as he says, "I yearn to go back to books and teaching. There is a beauty to professorial life. You wake up and say 'This morning I am going to read a book.' I did not enter this life to run big budgets and see fourteen people a day, and deal with politics and student operations. My life now is like a dentist—every half hour you say next, pain, next. I am fifty-four. I would like to stay here. When you are an administrator, you live on intellectual capital. I have been an administrator for thirteen years. While you are in this kind of job, you cannot build capital. You expend it. I feel a need to rebuild my intellectual capital. I believe in the John Quincy Adams principle. First he became president and then he became a representative in Congress."

12

THE JEP SUPERWOMAN: SYLVIA PORTER

SYLVIA PORTER sits in an elegant restaurant near her lower Fifth Avenue apartment and recalls, "My mother told me, 'You are going to have a career.' I think she started saying it to me in my cradle. She had a burning desire to be Somebody. But instead of becoming a nurse, she married my father at eighteen."

Suddenly, in the middle of a room filled with people, Porter's hazel brown eyes fill with tears. For several minutes she cannot stop crying. And then: "Anything I am is due to my mother. I am living her life!"

Porter is the Somebody her mother wanted her to be. Among the many Jewish columnists—Max Lerner, William Safire, Art Buchwald, to name just a few—she stands out as a press phenomenon. Her five-times-weekly column, covering everything from consumer protection to taxes and investments, appears in 450 newspapers and reaches 45 million readers. Avoiding "bafflegab" (her word for confusing jargon), she translates Wall Street happenings, government finance and economic trends into extremely readable and comprehensible prose. "They should all be able to understand what I write. I'm insulted when somebody doesn't."

At sixty-eight, a mother and veteran of three marriages (one early divorce, one thirty-three-year union which ended with her husband's death, and a current marriage), she is one of the few self-made women to have reached the top of a man's field in direct competition with men. She reached it—not by influence, inheritance or tokenism—but by sheer talent and a willingness to work day in and day out for years.

She has been required reading for the secretary of the Treasury in every U.S. administration since Franklin Roosevelt. Henry Morgenthau, Jr., survived her sharp criticism and later sent her roses on her birthday. Harry Truman's secretary John W. Snyder asked for her autograph. Eisenhower's first secretary, George M. Humphrey, mailed praise: "It is a treat to have good old Sylvia straighten people out."

Lyndon Johnson offered her a choice of jobs, starting with the presidency of the Export-Import Bank and extending to secretary of the Treasury. She turned them all down and told President Johnson she could not take a leave from her column ("If I did, I might not have one to come back to"). During the Kennedy administration she served on the Consumer Advisory Council and later played a key role in President Ford's consumer volunteer program to fight inflation. She was the only journalist invited to Ford's 1974 economic summit conference.

The second child and only daughter of Russian-Jewish immigrants, Sylvia Porter was born in Patchogue, Long Island, New York, to Louis Feldman, a physician and Rose (Maisel) Feldman. Her family life in Brooklyn, where the Feldmans later moved, was both middle-class and strongly intellectual. A classical violinist, Dr. Feldman regularly serenaded Sylvia and her older brother John, now a physician and ear, nose and throat specialist in Los Angeles, and escorted them to concerts. While her grade-school friends were reading books in the Bobbsey Twins series, Porter was reading Greek and Roman history.

Unlike her liberated mother, her father was a "chauvinist deluxe." Remembers Porter, "The sun rose and set on my brother John. He was programed to be a doctor. He could crawl around my father's office and read his medical books—but not little Sylvia. I was just a girl." Early in life she realized that competition is inbred and that "to get there in those years a woman had to be two to three times as good as a man. She still does."

When Porter was twelve, her father died of a heart attack. This only cemented her resolution to be Somebody. She dreamed of going to Vassar, of writing the Great American Novel. But the laws of economics closed in upon Dr. Feldman's survivors. Left alone to raise her children on not quite enough money, his widow made successive excursions into business: as the proprietor of a dry-cleaning emporium, as a real estate saleswoman and finally as a successful milliner.

In 1929 the Crash came and Mrs. Field (she had changed the family name) lost the $30,000 she had saved, most of it in Cities Service stock. The Depression left Porter, then in her freshman year at tuition-free Hunter College, just a five-cent subway ride from Brooklyn, very curious about what made the economic system tick. "As a member of a middle-income family, I just watched it all disappearing. I needed to figure out what was happening to the United States."

The next year she changed her major from literature and history to economics. She pursued the subject with such zeal that she earned a Phi Beta Kappa key as a junior, won every cash prize open to economic students ("I went out for them because we needed the money," she told *Ms.*), and graduated magna cum laude in three and a half years.

At the graduation ceremony her mother stood in for her. Porter had already gone off on a shoestring motor tour of the United States with seven young men. One of them was her husband Reed Porter, a tall, blond, budding financier whom she had met on a subway during her junior year at Hunter. She was eighteen. "Instead of having an affair, we got married."

After graduation, Porter took evening courses at the Graduate School of Business Administration at New York University toward a master's degree. She tried selling magazines for a while, even signed up as an Arthur Murray instructor, but these were only stopgaps. She wanted Wall Street. One day, while reading the business section of the *New York Times* in a midtown Automat, she found an ad announcing the opening of a new investment counseling firm, Glass & Krey, just up the street. She walked quickly there. Arthur William Glass spotted that Phi Beta Kappa key and murmured, "I've always wanted to hire someone with one of those. What can you do?"

Hired at $15 a week, Porter found herself in a cram course in the gold market, bonds, stocks, the whole range of finance.

For the next few years Porter apprenticed herself to a number of Wall Street firms to accumulate experience. At H. M. Gartley & Company she learned how to plot and predict business cycles. At the brokerage firm of Charles E. Quincy & Company she did early research in government bonds—a subject on which she is an acknowledged authority today.

While free-lancing for such journals as the *Magazine of Wall Street,* the *Commercial & Financial Chronicle,* she discovered she could write fluently about financial matters. In 1935, at twenty-two, she tried to get a job with the Associated Press. The AP refused: "We have never hired a woman in the financial department."

After free-lancing at space rates for the financial department of the *New York Post,* she finally was hired full-time. One day in August, 1938, in an economy drive, the *Post* fired the entire financial department. By 4:00 P.M. Porter was in the office of Editor in Chief Harry Saylor suggesting that she write a column to be called "Financial Post Marks." He agreed to give it a one-week trial, providing she would do *all the work of the men who had been fired.*

The column did so well that the *Post* later rewarded Porter with a by-line of sorts by changing its title to "S. F. Porter Says."

A woman had invaded the masculine domain of economics. Later in 1942 the *Post* decided to consider her gender an asset. Editor T. O. Thackrey wrote "The time has come for us to make capital of the fact that S. F. Porter is a woman." The unveiling of her sex with a very feminine picture tapped a new source of income for her: lecturing to audiences of male business leaders curious to see what kind of woman would write about money. As the only lady business columnist, she was in great demand. "After all, our second choice," wrote the executive secretary of the Massachusetts Bankers Association to Porter's lecture agency, "would not have the allure and woo-woo of Miss Porter."

The public unveiling brought an odd sort of celebrity. One longtime column correspondent moodily addressed his next letter to "Darling" instead of "Dear Mr. Porter."

At first, she had many ropes to learn. Early in her career, covering a bankers' convention, she froze at the dreadful prospect of phoning in her first deadline story, was gallantly rescued by a *New York Times* man who dictated her story for her.

But she learned quickly. "I can remember going to meetings of financiers in my Kitty Foyle dresses with the little white collars with little white cuffs and looking oh-so-innocent," she once told *50 Plus.* "These men inevitably said too much because they did not think I understood, but how wrong they were."

One time Porter attended a convention of investment bankers. It took place at a resort. Lying on the beach in a skimpy two-piece bathing suit, Porter heard two bankers talking openly about the upcoming first public sale of Ford Motor stock. "They simply assumed I was one of the wives and ignored me. Little did they know that S. F. Porter was listening in though later everyone wondered how the *Post* got the scoop that Ford stock was about to go public!"

Today, of course, Porter's name and face are known throughout the nation. She has appeared frequently on radio and television. Her column, syndicated nationally since 1947, is now titled simply "Sylvia Porter" and has made her one of the most influential women in America. Professionally, Porter keeps a political neutrality (however, she was a fervent Kennedy fan). As a result her columns appear in newspapers ranging from the most conservative to openly liberal. In addition to the daily column, syndicated by Universal Press, she writes a monthly column for the *Ladies' Home Journal,* and has written twelve books, including the thousand-page *Sylvia Porter's Money Book* (1975) and *Sylvia Porter's New Money Book for the 80s* (1979).

In her official biography her awards take up a full page single-spaced. They range from the 1981 National Headliner, the highest honor given by Women in Communications, Inc., to "Woman of the Decade," (one of ten), as selected by readers of the *Ladies' Home Journal,* in 1979. She has fourteen honorary degrees.

To achieve her vigorous and simple journalistic style, she imagines a faceless, ageless person sitting on top of her typewriter. This person keeps reminding her, "Be sure you understand it first, Sylvia. Write it simple." Thus she addresses the reader as "you" . . . "you, the small businessman" . . . "you, the consumer." The "you" is also highly possessive. It is "your recession" . . . "your pocketbook." In her drive for professional perfection she has been known to have temper tantrums when assistants deliver research that is not new.

The private woman who gardens, reads mysteries with a passion, swims, is as interesting as the professional or the public personality. She is chic in a pale green Ultrasuede dress and gray hat ("I can't do my hair myself and there is no time to get it done"). Detractors (almost always journalists who have not made it) call her "tough." But most find her extraordinarily warm, approachable, even motherly ("Stop writing and eat your shrimp").

She reflects on her three marriages, the last to a bachelor when she was sixty-five years old. Asked whether her brains—in an era when women were supposed to be dumb and helpless—had not deterred certain men from coming after her, she answers with the same straight language she uses in her column: "Certain men may have run away, but I was not aware of it."

Recalling her marriage to Reed Porter at eighteen, she says, "He was fascinated by my mind. It was in the thirties. We were young. We did things together—tennis, swimming. It was the time of the Spanish Civil War. We used to sit in bars under the Brooklyn Bridge wondering, What are we going to do?" At the time Porter was active in the New York Newspaper Guild; she left later because of Communist infiltration.

Reed Porter and Sylvia were married for ten years ("He taught me a lot of what he learned at the bank"). Later she described it as a "nice but meaningless" marriage. When they divorced, he sent her roses. He also met the train when she arrived from Reno. She told him, "We are not married anymore. Let me go."

She met Hearst Corporation executive Sumner Collins, husband number two, in the "B-Deck" bar of a ship while on a cruise with her mother. Collins heard the two women arguing and joined them. They were married for over three decades. She comments, "He was very attracted to someone in the newspaper business—actually fascinated. We drank, played, fought but there was no competition. He was on the business side. I was creative. He put up a sign on the door where we lived then at One University Place: 'No matter what you believe, one of us agrees with you.' "

Porter and Collins had a daughter Cris. They also started a newsletter *Reporting on Governments.* It was his idea. A current Hearst executive describes the Porter-Collins marriage: "They were poles apart politically. Collins was a Republican. Sometimes they did not speak to each other during campaigns. He was an outdoor sportsman, a fisherman, raised golden retrievers. He was boss in his own home and content to let her be the star on the outside." (Note: After one of their arguments, Collins sent her a note in which he called her his "lovable, beautiful, hyped up, cantankerous, tempestuous little dear.")

When Collins died of cancer in 1977—a "sad, dragged-out, horrible end"—Porter went through a difficult time. She did not have the heart to continue the newsletter she and Collins had started together.

Some years before she had had a brief meeting with James Fox, now a public-relations executive, during a visit to the Chase Manhattan Bank. "He heard me clacking down the corridor. A vice-president introduced us. Jim waited until I had my mourning—only I had had it while Sumner was alive—and then he telephoned. We went out for lunch. After lunch I asked him to stop at '21.' I was taking Mickey Siebert (that is, Muriel Siebert, the superintendent of New York State's banking department) out to dinner for her birthday and I wanted to order a cake. He liked that."

In 1979 she married James Fox ("He was very insistent!"). Laughingly, she recalls how the event came about: "My daughter Cris told me I should live with him first. I told her that was a fine thing for a daughter to be telling her mother, who, incidentally thanks to her, was soon to be a grandmother. Anyway, I thought it over and decided to take her suggestion. Jim and I decided to take a trip to London. We took the Concorde and were one hour from London when the plane developed engine trouble, dipped down about three thousand feet and went back to New York. Our friends were left waiting for us in London with rooms filled with gifts.

"Back in Manhattan the refrigerator was empty. I had given everyone time off. Jim and I decided it was an omen and immediately got married. We were married at the Church of the Ascension, then got on a boat, made friends with a rabbi and asked him if he would marry us in the Jewish religion. He did. [Porter and Fox used the words of Ruth, "Whither thou goest I will go."] The rabbi broke the glass. We stamped."

Porter has had three non-Jewish husbands. Yet she herself is openly and frankly proud of her Jewish heritage. While she has had no formal training in Judaism or any other religion, she is not an atheist. Both she and Fox were attracted by the antiquity and the romance of the Jewish wedding ceremony beforehand, and afterwards, by its mysticism and beauty, she says. It was she who asked the rabbi to use the story of Ruth.

Her advice on intermarriage: "Cool it. How we act depends on habits, a way of living. I feel anything Jim would do in terms of church is the normal thing to do. If he wants me to go to church with him, I'll go. As for me, I feel God is all around me and I need not go to a building to find him. I cannot imagine the subject coming up as one of importance with Jim. Nor could I have imagined Sumner bringing it up."

She talks about encountering anti-Semitism, and, like men afraid of her brains, she quips, "If I have, I would not have known it." There is one notable exception. Sumner Collins was a trapshooter and applied to a neighboring club to continue the trapshooting he did on his own grounds (she would not reveal the club's name). Porter had to apply separately and did. She was turned down, quite obviously because she was Jewish. She says, "Sumner never went back to the club. He never again saw anyone who belonged. The shutter went down.

"The few times I have encountered anti-Semitism, I have run away. I have not stopped to argue; what are words but ammunition for the anti-Semites? But I know it is out there. Jim and I believe in a civilized society. And we'll fight without qualification for what we both believe in."

Porter has definite opinions on:

HER DAUGHTER: "Cris married and moved to Maine. She has a different way of life. She bakes her own bread, is helping her husband build a house, teaches piano, which she was trained to do. Everything I do not do well, she does well. It is more than a difference in generation. Like other children of the sixties, she has repudiated my way of life."

ON WIDOWS: "At first do absolutely nothing. Don't change anything. Take a trip if you have to get away, but don't move. Don't do a thing about investments. The first investment you have to make is in yourself." When Collins died, Cris and her stepson Sumner Campbell Collins were grown up and no longer home. She was alone with the choice of becoming a "professional widow" or absorbing her loss and going on. She told the publication *50 Plus,* "You have two alternatives: You can look backward and keep remembering what you had and become an absolute bore or go make up your mind that you have a life of your own and say, 'Okay life, what do you have for me next?' Meet men. Meet another woman like yourself. Make new friends. Recreate a career."

ON HELP: "A working woman should look at household help in the same light that a man does his secretary." Porter does few domestic chores. She has a housekeeper in her Manhattan apartment and a couple ("He is Ukrainian and she is Scottish") in her Westchester country house. She adds, "I do nothing. I don't have a 'should' problem."

ON SUCCESS: "Success is fulfillment, something you feel within yourself. I see someone on the street. Is she successful? How do I know? She may be bleeding her heart out. I see another woman. She may look a mess, but she is gloriously happy because she has just finished a book." She remembers that she was alone the night she finished writing *Sylvia Porter's Money Book.* She had a drink of Scotch and cried for two hours. Later the book was on the best-seller list for forty weeks, number one for half a year. "That's success," she says, "but fulfillment is something else. I would feel happy if people around me were to have what they want."

Despite her success as supercareerwoman, supermother,

superwife, Porter has had her failures. "I have failed at poetry and fiction," she states frankly. "I cannot write dialogue. I was sure I would be a poet." She is the author of many poems, some published, some unpublished, and two unpublished novels. She wrote one at six dedicated to "My Public" and a second during the first year of her first marriage entitled *Those That Never Sing.*

She notes, "Years after I wrote books in the financial field my literary agent said, 'The luckiest thing that ever happened to you is that no publisher ever printed your novel, or you would still be apologizing for it.' I still have that novel."

ON WOMEN: "Oh, God, we have barely begun." When she accepted the 1979 Elizabeth Cutter Morrow Award, presented by the YWCA for her professional achievements in the field of finance, she challenged an audience of New York City female executives and their bosses: "Yes, we've come a long way, baby —and what a sexist slogan that is!—but we're still far from that ideal time. In working conditions, in pensions, in credit rights, in Social Security benefits . . . we must stand up for each other and fight with and not against each other." The failure of the ERA bill to pass has been a terrible disappointment to her. "That Phyliss Schlafly" she says with a hostile gleam in her eye. She speaks enthusiastically of the Women's Forum group of New York: "There is nothing I want from the network now but if there were, the women would be there. . . ."

ON TODAY'S ELITES: "The old elites were like the Schiffs. They were born into wealth. They wore little white gloves and went to boarding school. Today's elites are people who can hold up their heads no matter what their financial beginnings, who don't give a dman about money. It is a different world. It is more than doing. It is standing up for yourself and what you believe in."

On her personal investment strategy: "Take a dollar. I have about forty cents allotted to AAA tax exempt bonds, guaranteed by the U.S. Treasury unconditionally. Called P.H.A.'s. I have about fifteen to twenty cents allotted to real estate. And the rest is allotted to high-grade stocks and a few real speculative issues." (Note: If Porter had her way, today economics would be a required course for everyone in high school.)

For all her tremendous productivity, she has surprisingly little help. There is a secretary, who used to work for husband James Fox, and "stringers," free-lance help located all over. Many people think she has a large staff. In a way she does. She has all the experts at the U.S. Treasury, the Senate, the House, the New York Stock Exchange, the major investment firms, the people who know what is going on in their fields—automobiles, hospitals. Her links and friendships have gone on for years ("It does not matter who is in or out; I write on").

Whether in her country house or in her neat, unpretentious office (white formica desk, a bridge table for extra clutter) in her apartment, Sylvia Porter works seven days a week. She comments, "Some people can retire gracefully. Me, I only know how to work gracefully." She keeps three carbons of book manuscripts—one in a bank vault. She also keeps track of the family bills. She and her husband go out almost every night, entertain a lot. Every moment is accounted for; yet she is calm and unflurried.

This is a Thursday. In just four days Porter and her husband will leave on a brief vacation. There are columns to be written, appointments to be kept, dresses to be packed. She says, "Oh, what I have to do before Thursday. But I will get it done." That's Sylvia Porter.

Henry Rosovsky, dean of the faculty of arts and sciences at Harvard University, turned down the presidencies of Yale and Chicago. Rosovsky came to the U.S. at 13 without knowing a single word of English. *Credit: Harvard University News Office*

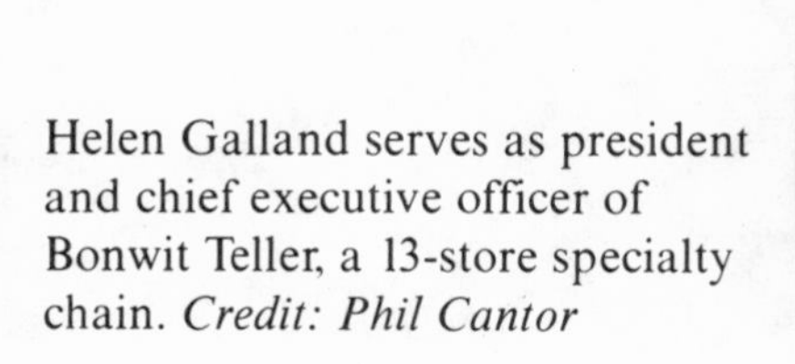

Helen Galland serves as president and chief executive officer of Bonwit Teller, a 13-store specialty chain. *Credit: Phil Cantor*

Adrien Arpel, founder of the cosmetics company that bears her name, launched her first cosmetics shop in Englewood, New Jersey, at 17, with $400 in babysitting money. Now she has 450 boutiques and skin care clinics in the U.S. and 11 foreign countries. *Credit: Tony Palmieri—Women's Wear Daily*

Soprano Roberta Peters (right) with the late Golda Meir, Prime Minister of Israel. *Credit: Wagner International Photos*

Frank R. Lautenberg, chairman and chief executive officer of Automatic Data Processing, with Rosalynn Carter at the 25th Jubilee Celebration of the Rabbinical College of America, June 16, 1980 at the New York Hilton Hotel. *Credit: New Jersey Newsphotos*

John L. Loeb, Jr., now ambassador to Denmark, with former President Gerald R. Ford at the 1980 exhibition "The Jewish Community in Early America: 1654–1830" at the D.A.R. Museum in Washington, D.C. Loeb and Ford are looking at a picture of his grandmother, Adeline Moses Loeb. *Credit: Ankers Capitol Photographers*

Maynard Wishner, president of the American Jewish Committee (left) presents the Mass Media Award to TV star Barbara Walters as former president Elmer Winter looks on. Wishner is president and chief executive officer of Walter E. Heller & Company, Chicago. Winter, a self-made businessman from Milwaukee, is the co-founder of Manpower, Inc. *Credit: American Jewish Committee*

Rabbi Shlomo Riskin delivers a Wednesday night lecture at the popular Lincoln Square Synagogue in New York. His goal is to give Jews the opportunity to become Orthodox. Lincoln Square Synagogue is known as a meeting place for singles.

Financial columnist Sylvia Porter with the late President Lyndon Johnson, who offered her a choice of jobs, from the presidency of the Export-Import Bank to secretary of the treasury. She turned them all down in favor of her newspaper column ("If I didn't, I might not have one to come back to").

President Jimmy Carter and Rosalynn Carter with soprano Roberta Peters and husband Bertram Fields before her trip to China in 1980. She was the first American singer invited to the People's Republic since diplomatic relations with the United States were resumed. Peters has sung for every U.S. President from Kennedy to Reagan. *Credit: White House Photo*

Warsaw, Poland–Henry Taub, president of the American Jewish Joint Distribution Committee (JDC) is shown placing a wreath at the Warsaw ghetto memorial in Poland during a July, 1981 visit. To the right of Taub is Ralph I. Goldman, JDC executive vice-president and Moses Finkelstein, chairman of the Union of Religious Jews of Poland. Behind Mr. Taub is Akiva Kohane, the JDC representative in Eastern Europe. *Credit: JDC Photo*

Founder of an important Jewish dynastic family, Colonel Henry Crown of Chicago, 85 (left), chairman of the board of Henry Crown & Company, son of a penniless Latvian immigrant who has parlayed his family's sand, gravel, lime and coal business into an immense range of interests, is shown here with his son Lester Crown, 57, president of Henry Crown & Company.

Ambassador Sol M. Linowitz (left) meets with Egyptian President Anwar Sadat at the Blair House, Washington, D.C. in August, 1981. *Credit: Wide World Photos*

Alan Greenberg, chief executive officer of Bear, Stearns & Company, a leading Wall Street investment banking firm. *Credit: Robert Phillips*

"Background does not matter any more. We care about talent," says Stephen Schwarzman, partner at Lehman Brothers Kuhn Loeb and a superstar in the Wall Street merger field. *Credit: Jamie Kalikow*

Ruth Hinerfeld, president of the League of Women Voters, meets with James Baker, chairman of the Reagan for President Committee (left) and Carter campaign chairman Robert Strauss (right) to work out the details for the Carter-Reagan debate in 1980.
Credit: UPI photo

Henry A. Lambert, a gourmet and amateur chef, opened the extremely successful Pasta & Cheese shops in New York City in 1976.

Moving in a world of men and women at the very top, Ambassador Sol M. Linowitz, formerly chairman of the executive committee, general counsel and chairman of the board of Xerox Corporation, shown here with Jacqueline Kennedy Onassis, openly avows his Jewishness. *Credit: Tony Palmieri—Women's Wear Daily*

Billie Tisch (left), the first woman to be elected president of the Federation of Jewish Philanthropies of New York, congratulates Elaine Winik on her appointment as the first woman to be elected president of the UJA of Greater New York. *Credit: Jerry Soalt*

Herbert Tenzer, senior partner, Tenzer, Greenblatt, Fallon & Kaplan law firm, shown here with Pope Paul VI in 1965. Tenzer, an Orthodox Jew, served as congressman from the State of New York to the House of Representatives from 1965 to 1969. He was the first elected Democrat from the Fifth Congressional District since the founding of the United States. *Credit: Vatican Photo*

13

THE SUPERCOUPLES

When Dr. Helen Singer Kaplan, the noted psychiatrist who runs one of the leading U.S. sex-therapy programs, works late, her husband, Charles Lazarus, chairman, Toys R Us, often termed a "merchandising genius," calls for her at her office. He claims, "I am her last patient." Together, they walk home to their Fifth Avenue apartment overlooking Central Park.

Shirley Goodman, the southern-born dynamo who has held every job at the Fashion Institute of Technology from acting president down, and her husband Himan Brown, the man who crusaded for fourteen years to revive network radio drama and succeeded, live across town in an apartment overlooking the park on Central Park West. She cooks, while he walks the fifty blocks home from his studio, stopping to pick up gourmet tidbits on the way.

The two couples do not know each other, but they share much in common. All four are self-made successes and at the top of their four different worlds. Both couples possess the trappings of success—antiques, art, a country home. More important, both symbolize two new trends in the American life-style. They represent the growing phenonomen of marriage between equals. They are remarrieds who have a second chance at a fresh start.

EQUAL OPPORTUNITY

Not long ago it was an accepted fact that behind every well-known male public figure was a housewife helpmate basking in his glory. The woman who opted for a career often stayed single or married a man weaker than she. In today's world, successful women have discovered that achievement is no longer synonomous with a lonely life. Many successful men want their wives to be just as successful as they are.

Says Dr. Herbert Fensterheim, clinical associate professor, Cornell University Medical College, New York, "Today many a man, particularly if he is strong and confident himself, no longer looks for a helpmate or satellite as a mate but wants a companion who is strong and competent in her own right, who can stand up to him and challenge him in all areas and so lead to a more respectful, deeper and more fulfilling relationship.

"When you get two strong people who come together in a strong relationship, the union takes on qualities of its own that are beyond the contributions of each of them. As a result, each gains more strength and is able to accomplish more and enjoy more than he/she could without the relationship. At the same time each is independent and part of a team."

For some this tenet is not new. Benjamin Buttenwieser, eighty-one, a banker with Lehman Brothers Kuhn Loeb Inc., New York, and his wife, Helen Buttenwieser, seventy-six, a lawyer known for her championship of liberal causes, have been married for fifty-two years. She claims, "I am women's lib." When asked how the marriage has lasted, he answers, "It's a cinch. When we married, we agreed Helen would handle all the little things and I the big. Life has since been full of little things." Asked how she has been able to do as much as she has, Mrs. Buttenwieser told the *New York Times,* "There are two reasons: good health and a good husband."

Mrs. Buttenwieser began her career as a social worker in New York in 1927. She decided to become a lawyer after working in the children's court, now the family court, which she decided was poorly organized and needed a woman on the bench. She enrolled at New York University law school while trying to raise a growing family. She has three sons. Asked about his lifelong working mother, oldest son Lawrence Buttenwieser, a lawyer who is chairman of the board of the Montefiore Hospital and Medical Center, says, "I never knew there were any other kinds of mothers."

For other superpairs the road has been rockier. In his memoirs *Javits, the Autobiography of a Public Man,* former Senator Javits talks about his thirty-five-year marriage to the former Marian Borris. He writes, "Marian feels I was so involved with my work that she was never able to catch hold of me emotionally . . . it was not Marian's fault that marriage could not overcome my devotion and commitment to public life." So Javits had his career as a legislator in Washington, D.C., and Marian Javits had hers as a public-relations executive in Manhattan. Javits notes "what she wanted of me was more than I could give."

Marriages between two achievers in the entertainment world have survived the special stress of separation. Violinist Isaac Stern, whose parents immigrated from Russia to San Francisco when he was ten months old, spends more than three-quarters of the year on the road. Vera Stern has won many awards for her extensive work with the America-Israel Cultural Foundation. They have been married for thirty-one years.

Israel-born Pinchas Zukerman is the superstar violinist and music director of the St. Paul Chamber Orchestra who is acclaimed all over the world. His wife Eugenia Zukerman is a well-known flute player with an independent career of her own. Mrs. Zukerman comes from an achieving family. Her father is a physicist and successful inventor. Her mother was a dancer who was also the first woman admitted to the engineering department of City College. Mrs. Zukerman once told *Newsday,* "I'll never forget what it was like seeing the world and hearing the world applaud Pinky, but I became more and more aware that I would have to do something with my own drives." She entered and won a competition which launched her on a musical career of her own. She has recently branched out into another area of the arts, by publishing a first novel *Deceptive Cadence.*

Eugenia Zukerman feels that being so separately busy keeps the partnership romantic. At one time, she was preparing for sleep in a motel after a performance in Sharon, Pennsylvania, when at midnight she heard a knock on her door. It was her husband. He had been playing in Cincinnati and chartered a plane to be with her.

Interfaith marriages have proven successful. Paul Cowan, staff writer for the *Village Voice* and author of, most recently, *Tribes of America,* is married to a fellow writer, Rachel Cowan. He was born into an assimilated family and has become increasingly involved in Jewish life. After fifteen years of marriage, Rachel Cowan, born into a New England Protestant family, recently chose to convert to Judaism. They have two children. Now they lecture together about the evolution of the Jewish content in their marriage.

The Cowan example is not always typical of interfaith marriages, but if the marriage works, religious differences do not seem to cause problems. Businessman and political aspirant Lewis Lehrman and his wife have five children. He says, "My wife is a Protestant, a practicing Christian. Her faith is one of the most important aspects of her life, as my faith is one of the most important aspects of my life. I respect it. Before we married she made clear her faith was central. I made the same clear to her.

"We decided she would be a member of church and I would go to temple. I go to B'nai Jeshurun and Temple Emanu-El and sometimes to Lincoln Square Synagogue. In the Jewish tradition, children of a Christian mother are Christian. However, my children get religious instruction from both me and Louise. They go to synagogue and bar mitzvahs of relatives. They know the seriousness with which I take my faith. Later we will let the children choose. It is no problem."

THE WORLD OF THE REMARRIED

These days remarriages make news. According to Suzanne Prescod, editor of the *Marriage and Divorce Today* newsletter for professionals, "For the first time in years, the U.S. marriage rate is up, and in any one given year, one-third of all marriages are remarriages. In fact, 75 percent of all women remarry. So do five-sixths of all men. We are fast becoming a nation practicing serial polygamy."

What happens in a remarriage between two stars?

Does material success mean they do not have problems?

"Two strong people with their own areas of successful achievement have probably gained strength from the breakup of the first marriage, painful and frustrating as it was," says Dr. Fensterheim. "Hence they go into remarriage with clearer ideas of what they are looking for, a better knowledge of how to achieve it and, strangely enough, a greater confidence in their ability to make it work."

Recently the *New York Times* carried a story about the wedding of two well-known people: Carl Spielvogel, chairman of Backer & Spielvogel advertising agency, which *New York* magazine termed "The Hottest Agency in Town"; and Barbaralee Diamonstein, a television writer, interviewer and producer specializing in cultural affairs. It is too soon to comment on the success of the marriage, a second for each, but it is interesting to note that the ceremony was performed in the Beth El Chapel of Temple Emanu-El, New York, by Rabbi Ronald Sobel. The bridegroom was attended by his two sons, the bride by her niece and two nephews.

Remarriage often means a more opulent life-style than is possible for first-time newlyweds. Leona Helmsley (Jewish) runs a chain of thirty-one hotels and that is only part of her husband Harry Helmsley's (non-Jewish) holdings. Beginning as a receptionist in the 1960s (when a divorce forced her to support her son), she became one of Manhattan's most successful real estate brokers, and, by 1968, when Helmsley hired her, he was willing to pay her $500,000 on her reputation alone. They married in 1972. In 1980 he named her president of Helmsley Hotels, a thirteen-state chain that includes New York's elegant Helmsley Palace. Mrs. Helmsley calls her husband "My Harry." She also insists, "My husband is my career." On Mrs. Helmsley's Fourth of July birthday, her husband lights up the Empire State Building in red, white and blue. He owns it.

PORTRAIT OF A REMARRIAGE

Helen Singer Kaplan and Charles Lazarus

Helen Singer Kaplan, the well known sex therapist, and her husband Charles Lazarus, founder and chief executive of Toys R Us, the largest retailer of playthings in the United States, are sometimes laughingly referred to by their children as the "Sex Queen" and the "Toy King."

She is dark, dynamic, surprisingly fragile. Her ideas have had a major impact on how sexual medicine is practiced throughout the world. He is animated, quick, affable. She has a Ph.D. and an M.D. He did not go to college, but according to *Fortune,* "he makes about $750,000 a year and has bought or optioned 7.5 percent of his company's shares, a stake recently worth $41 million."

Both were divorced. (When asked if he had ever failed at anything, Lazarus admitted with candor, "At marriage.") They married two years ago. Says Kaplan with intensity, "We are very much in love. It has worked out wonderfully. I prefer a self-made man."

Of his marriage to Kaplan, Lazarus comments, "I live in this. I am alive. I like going to work. I like coming home. For years I had excitement in my office. Now I have it in my personal life."

Kaplan and Lazarus reside in an East Side apartment filled with her paintings. They spend weekends and summers in a country house in the Hamptons on the water. This comfortable way of life did not just happen. They worked for it.

At the age of ten Kaplan came to the United States as a refugee from Vienna. Her family was unable to take any money out of Austria. Kaplan attended the Music and Art High School in Manhattan, attained her degree in fine arts at Syracuse University. "I was planning to be a painter, but after college I decided to become a psychologist instead," she recalls. "I think I was pretty good as a painter, but I did not have enough confidence in my creativity. Whereas to be a psychologist, all you needed—I thought then—was to be warm and caring."

She had no B.A., just the B.F.A. Columbia accepted her into

its psychology program "by error. After three months they were going to let me go," she explains. "I said 'What would you do if I were a student from Europe?' They let me take the Graduate Record Exam and I came out 99 percentile in everything but math."

Meanwhile, Kaplan had married, went on to get her M.D. at New York Medical College, where her husband, a psychiatrist, was an instructor.

At thirty-nine, she separated from her husband and was fired from her teaching post at New York Medical College ("In those days it was the female half of a pair both working at the same place who was let go when they split up"). She recalls, "I had been getting a token salary—my husband was the moneymaking person. I was getting no child support at the time. I had three children at private schools. I had to find a new position and establish a private practice. I had no thoughts about remarriage. I was interested in getting my act together."

Cornell University Medical College, New York, needed someone to organize a Human Sexuality Program. The timing was perfect. Kaplan took the position and turned it into a major research facility. Her sex therapy approach uses a combination of structured behavioral exercises and psychoanalytic techniques (such as dream interpretation) to help patients. She was the first sex therapist to integrate these two methods. Her program at The New York Hospital—Cornell Medical Center has become an internationally reknowned training facility for sex therapists.

She has written eight books, including *The New Sex Therapy, Illustrated Manual of Sex Therapy, Making Sense of Sex.* She writes, teaches, lectures and consults. Her private practice in New York attracts patients from all over the world, often referred by physicians who rely on her to diagnose and treat problems which have stymied others in the field.

In the ten years between her first and second marriage, she was one of the most socially sought after women in New York. Others complained, "There are no men." Not Kaplan.

She explains, "Many eligible women in their late thirties and forties are so eager to marry that they frighten men. I was a warm person but not out for marriage. I remember when I gave a Thanksgiving party for singles—four bachelors with kids. We played backgammon. The men I dated were in no rush to marry. Neither was I. I was safe."

Lazarus comes from a far different background. His father, one of thirteen children, had been brought up in the Jewish Orphanage in New York. "They trained the kids for a trade because they did not expect them to go to college," recalls Lazarus. The senior Lazarus learned printing and photo engraving, then went to Washington, D.C., where he eventually opened a bicycle-repair store.

At ten Lazarus had "street smarts." With his father, he would buy second-hand bikes, help strip them, rebuild, paint and then sell them as "new used bikes." At this time he started earning money—delivering newspapers. He showed what has been referred to as his "merchandising genius" early. At ten he realized that other young newspaper delivery boys did not like collecting payments. He made a series of "deals" and took on several collection routes. Soon he was making $25 to $35 a week. "That was a lot in those days for a ten-year-old," he comments.

"It is different when you start off poor," he analyzes. "You learn everything on the way up. You learn how to accumulate capital. Accumulating the first million in net worth is the hardest."

After a stint in the U.S. Army, in 1948 Lazarus took his savings and opened a juvenile-furniture store in his father's former bicycle shop. People came in asking for toys. "I learned the first lesson in the business," he emphasized. "Don't sell what *you* want. Sell what *they* want." Literally using a sledgehammer, Lazarus broke through the wall of the bicycle shop to the grocery store next door and created his first self-service, low price toy store.

The rest is legendary. From that simple beginning has come Toys R Us, the dominant seller in the United States of games, dolls, bikes and other products for children. In 1966 when Lazarus owned four Toys R Us supermarkets, selling $12 million worth of toys, he sold the whole operation to Interstate Stores and wound up with $7.5 million in cash. Lazarus kept expanding

Toys R Us, even after the parent company, Interstate, went bankrupt in 1974, a victim of ill-managed growth. Four years after the collapse, a reorganized corporation emerged, led, naturally, by Lazarus and called Toys R Us. *Fortune* termed it "a splendid resurrection." Comments Lazarus, "We did well enough in the toy business to pay back a $180 million debt with interest. No one lost a nickel. I am proud of that."

In the month of December, 1981, Toys R Us grossed more dollars than in its first fifteen years combined.

Lazarus, a mild-mannered, quick-speaking man who seems to speak in italics, credits his business acumen to an "encouraging" father. "He did not make much money himself, but he told me, 'There is nothing you cannot do,' " he says with love in his voice. "He was convinced, and he convinced me. I have never been a loser. I always think I will win. I am conflict free. I have no fear of success."

He won Helen Kaplan, who admits, "I was very frightened of remarriage. I had been on my own for so long. I was afraid of the commitments, of the demands marriage would place on me. I learned you become a couple—his needs become your needs."

Lazarus says, "I went in with more confidence than Helen. To be a retailer, one *must* be an optimist."

Between them they have five grown children (he has two daughters. One takes after her father. She is a merchandise manager for the May Company). Kaplan has two sons, twenty-one and twenty-five, who are medical students, and a college-age daughter, Jenny, eighteen. "Jenny is our baby," smiles Kaplan. Jenny admires Lazarus and teases, "If you ever get divorced, I want Charles to have custody of me."

Apportioning time represents a major problem in the life of this supercouple. They plan together for shared time. They love Manhattan. He commutes in reverse to the Toys R Us headquarters in Rochelle Park, New Jersey. He seldom attends business dinners. Since her marriage she rarely accepts speaking engagements ("I used to do ten to fifteen a year"). She does one out-of-the-country talk a year, and they try to schedule a vacation around it.

Known for her efficient use of time, Kaplan says, "You have

got to get over guilt about what you cannot do. There has to be a balance between your needs and others." Kaplan works hard but sets limits. She notes, "How can I tell people to have pleasure and balance their quality of life if I'm working myself to death. I have to practice what I preach."

She does not get flurried. Before her second marriage a beau called her at five o'clock and asked if he could bring a group of Japanese businessmen to dinner. On her way home, Kaplan bought pâté, then called Chicken Delight for several boxes of chicken, made a salad and served the fried chicken on an antique silver platter. Everyone raved about the dinner.

Her philosophy: "I concentrate on what I do at the time I do it." Sometimes, from years of habit, she gets up at 5:30 A.M. and writes. Most often she and Lazarus breakfast together at a table in the living room. Then she plans the menu for that night with housekeeper Suzie, who has been with her for years ("I give as much attention to fresh vegetables as a speech I am going to give"). Unless there is an emergencies she then goes to the hospital or office, coming home around 6:00 P.M. She does not answer the telephone at night ("I call people back"). "I won't let one activity impinge on another," she says. "I savor our time together. I am fascinated by his business. I love to talk to him about my newest concept. He was afraid he could not take part in my work, but creative minds have the common quality of thinking."

Intensely proud of his creative wife, Lazarus admits, "She is nothing like the other women I knew. She looks much like my mother, also my first girl friend at thirteen—dark and dynamic. I feel pride in her success and accomplishments. We go places where I am not known and I get a feeling of satisfaction. With a different crowd that knows me, she has the same feeling.

"When I met her, I was intensely attracted to Helen, and I am not easily attracted to women. She is so intensely alive. Shy, retiring women turn me off. She is never shy or retiring."

The Lazaruses' friends are "people like ourselves." Comments Kaplan, "They are from different fields, but they are all doers. They are people who make things happen, who are excited about what they are doing. Many are at least as successful.

Most important, they are all genuinely kind. They are engaged with life."

A strangely vulnerable man despite his meteoric success, Lazarus admits, "I am shy at big parties. I'm concerned about finding things to talk about."

They work to make this remarriage successful. She says, "We treasure our leisure time. We don't make dates without asking the other." He admits, "I had to learn to respect Helen's intense concentration. She picks up a book and she concentrates completely. I used to start talking. Now I no longer interrupt her, and she no longer interrupts me."

They argue, but less and less. Says Kaplan, "It takes a while to trust one's partner, to deal realistically with the other rather than childishly."

Says Lazarus, "Before this marriage, I was not open and above board. I would hide things if they were painful. I don't do that anymore. If I don't like something, I say so. It plays better."

She adds, "You have to make a fit. I got to know him. He got to know me."

They both chorus, "This marriage is wonderful."

IN SICKNESS AND IN HEALTH

Shirley Goodman and Himan Brown

"When I went to FIT, they converted a closet into an office for me. I went for one month. It has now been thirty-two years."

So says Shirley Goodman, one of the most respected, loved and honored women in the fashion industry. Currently executive director of the Educational Foundation for the Fashion Industries, Goodman is also executive vice-president emeritus of Fashion Institute of Technology, a community college that trains students for the fashion industry in areas that range from retail and wholesale merchandising to textile technology and communications to design and management.

She even has a building named after her: the Shirley Goodman Resource Center, which houses Library/Media Services and the Design Laboratory and Exhibit Galleries. The request was initiated by the membership of a union at FIT and unanimously supported by the faculty and board. Moved by the honor, Goodman was disturbed by the fact that it kept the college from accepting an endowment for the building from someone else who might wish to have his or her name emblazoned for posterity.

Brown, a warm, likable man, is a formidable character in his own right, having been the originator of many of radio's longest running serials and is presently famous for his incredible coup, in this age of TV, of returning people to their radio sets to listen avidly to the "CBS Radio Mystery Theater." Brown and Goodman have been married since 1970. Both have been divorced. She has two grown sons; he, a son and daughter.

The Browns live in a nine-room apartment, complete with butler's pantry, in the second oldest building on Central Park West. The bedroom is round on three sides. On the walls of one bathroom hang a collection of Brown's numerous awards for professional and philanthropic work. A grand piano stands in the living room. Goodman had once wanted to be a concert pianist. On weekends they go to their Connecticut country home. They use the forty-by-forty-five-foot studio and rent out the big house.

The phone rings constantly: the director of a school in Chicago . . . a noted designer who wants to know what time she is expected for dinner . . . the president of Phillips-Van Heusen, where Goodman has been reelected to the board three times.

They took different routes to this comfort, security and exciting life-style.

Goodman, sixty-six, grew up in Roxboro, North Carolina, then a town of two thousand inhabitants. "We were the second Jewish family, and we drove to Durham every Sunday so I could go to Sunday school," she recalls. "We had an Orthodox home. My mother's mother would send kosher meats from Norfolk, Virginia by train. A third Jewish family arrived and the man was a *shochet* ("ritual slaughterer"), so then we could buy chickens locally."

When Goodman was fourteen, her mother died. In the Depression her father, who ran the general store, lost everything. Goodman had won a scholarship to study music at the University of North Carolina. Because there was no money, she could not take it.

She attended a business school in Washington, D.C., where she lived with an aunt, then got a clerical job at the Public Works Administration. Subsequently she worked for three well-known men in New York City: as executive secretary to president Grover Whalen at the World's Fair Corporation, as confidential aide to Robert Moses at the New York State Constitutional Convention, and as assistant to Edward Weinfeld at New York State's first Housing Commission. Meanwhile, she had married Ben Fishman and had the first of two sons.

In 1948 she coordinated the mayor's committee for the city's golden anniversary. It was here she became involved with fashion, and then came her career at the Fashion Institute of Technology. She helped draft the legislation that would establish FIT as a community college under the program of the State University of New York. She served as liaison for the fashion industries presentation of the American National Exhibition in 1959 and again in 1967 when she represented the industry in Moscow at the International Trade Fair. Due in large measure to her efforts, the Fashion Institute of Technology has a newly expanded presence. With ten thousand students and seven buildings, it is an inescapable influence on Seventh Avenue.

Goodman has been a member of the board of directors of The Fashion Group, a past president of both Trends and Inner Circle (prestigious associations for professional women in the industry).

"I have no intention of ever retiring," declares Himan Brown, seventy-one, whose career spans five decades in radio and television. He grew up in Brooklyn, the son of poor immigrant parents (Goodman comments, "Hi did not have a childhood"). His father was a dress contractor. "It was not a religious home; it was a Yiddish home," says Brown. Gangster Bugsy Siegel was a childhood friend. Brown went to Brooklyn College with Irwin Shaw.

In 1929, still in his teens and apparently headed toward

becoming a lawyer, Brown became fascinated with radio drama. He packaged and sold to NBC a continuing story about the Goldberg family, called "The Rise of the Goldbergs." He played Papa. "Some six months later I was told I was no longer a part of the Goldbergs," he recalls. "Since I was a minor, my contracts were worthless. I just had to walk away from it."

Brown packaged other radio shows: "Dick Tracy," "Terry and the Pirates" (classmate Shaw wrote the scripts for this), "Grand Central Station," "Bulldog Drummond," "The Thin Man," "Inner Sanctum," "Nero Wolfe" and for TV, "Inner Sanctum Mysteries" and the "Chevy Mystery Theater."

Then, one by one, dramatic radio shows were canceled. The last to go, in 1959, was "NBC Radio Theater."

Brown believed—and still does—that "the spoken word and the imagination of the radio listener are infinitely stronger and more dramatic than anything television has to offer." For fourteen years he pounded on desks of every broadcast executive he could reach, crusading for the return of radio drama. "They all said I was crazy," he remembers. "Television did not kill off radio in Britain, France, Canada, Germany. Why here?"

Finally, Sam Digges, president of CBS Radio, listened to the messiah of radio drama and in January, 1974, Brown achieved his dream. The "CBS Radio Mystery Theater" went on the air. After its first year on CBS radio, the program won the George Foster Peabody Award, the most prestigious in the industry for "excellence in dramatic presentation." It was the first Peabody Award to a radio-network commercial dramatic series since 1947. It was Brown's second—the first came in the 1940s for a documentary on public health. Today three hundred stations carry the program.

While Brown was fighting his own battle for radio drama, Goodman was fighting her own personal battle—to live! They had known each other for many years (they met when Brown called her at FIT to ask if the classes would like to visit his West Twenty-sixth Street studio and see a film in production). Many years later each divorced ("I did not do it for Hi; I needed space," says Goodman). They married right after Thanksgiving in 1970.

Goodman had a medical history of a hysterectomy and benign breast lumps. "I was fine," she recalls. "We were refurnishing the apartment. Then in December, 1971, a year after my marriage, I found a lump in my breast." Brown took her to a surgeon friend who told her, "If it is malignant, you may have to have a radical mastectomy." It was malignant.

Her face calm, she remembers, "I went through it and went back to work as soon as I could. I refuse to be ill. In 1971, I had had as much X-ray therapy as you can have. I thought, 'I will get through the next five years and then I won't worry.'

"In 1977 there I was with another growth—a tumor on the chest wall on the same side. Malignant. A few months later I found a growth on the right shoulder. Malignant. Then a growth on my arm. This was nonmalignant.

"Periodically I have bouts of fever. No one knows why. I have no lymph glands in my right arm. I refuse to let this stop me from doing anything. Illness should not stop you from doing anything."

Goodman has not let it stop her. At FIT she is currently planning a thirty-year retrospective of Givenchy. Once a week she entertains at a small candlelit dinner party ("Our dining-room chandelier is not electrified") where there is a chance to "talk and visit." She has a housekeeper ("I want to be served my dinner") but Goodman does the cooking. Often she does this on Fridays, cooking several things at once and freezing them.

In the past eight years Brown has produced 1,750 one-hour radio shows, claiming "I think nothing of doing 130 hour shows next year. I am organized." He gives classes in radio acting and directing, directs and produces TV and radio spots, documentary films, docudramas with live narrators and "real people" for many organizations such as Hadassah, Federation, UJA, Israel Bonds, Anti-Defamation League, Albert Einstein College of Medicine. For eighteen years he produced the Hanukkah Festival at Madison Square Garden.

For this, he accepts no money. He says, "Let's say an album I produce for a philanthropic organization sells for $7 to $8. I get companies to press some records for thirty-three cents. I'm a *schnorrer* (beggar). The actors do it for free. The unions permit it. But I cannot get concert stars for free." Some of the stars who contribute their talent to Brown's projects are Charlton Heston and E. G. Marshall (neither is Jewish), Jack Gilford, Shelley Winters, Theodore Bikel. Brown also produces non-Jewish events. When Whitney Young died, Brown staged a memorial at Avery Fisher Hall. He did a TV memorial for Eleanor Roosevelt.

Goodman and Brown compromise on many things. She says, "Each of us goes to the other's functions. Before we were married I went to twenty-two functions of Federation where Hi was the key speaker. That was love." In the country he walks five miles a day. She "sprawls and reads." The children are grown. There are no problems there. Goodman is an owl; she goes to sleep at 1:00 A.M. Brown is a lark. He leaves the house by 6:30 A.M. and goes to sleep at 9:30 P.M.

How do fashion and radio drama mix? "Fashion is entertainment," explains Goodman.

Comments Brown, "She is in show business and I am in show business. A merchant is nothing but a showman."

Goodman is articulate about the fashion world: "It is not all Jewish anymore—just the manufacture of dresses and coats and suits. Merchandising is not Jewish. Neither is textiles. It began as an immigrant industry with people who had been tailors. That is how FIT came into being. They had to search for talent. Today the fashion industry is not just clothing; it includes advertising, display, merchandising, marketing. Textiles and apparel represent the third largest industry in the United States. Only housing and food surpass it. It is the largest industry in New York City."

Asked her greatest professional triumph, Goodman replies, "The Shirley Goodman Resource Center is very rewarding. But I felt most successful when I got the city and state of New York to realize what FIT meant to New York and to invest in and build a campus."

Her greatest private triumph is obvious in the tenderness with which she and Brown treat each other, the happiness in the home. She has fought cancer three times and won. She reiterates, "Illness should not stop you from doing anything."

With pride in his voice, Brown says, "Shirley is remarkable. She lives with the sword of Damocles over her head, but it has had no effect on the pattern of her work or living. The threat of devastating illness can affect the physical and emotional relationship with a husband. It has not done that. She has had three operations for cancer. She lives in the presence of cancer and cancer's evil. Yet she has plans for the next ten years.

"I was lucky. I was able to remarry a woman who fulfilled my idea of a meaningful, productive and creative human being—someone who is my equal."

14
SWEET CHARITY

THERE IS a new elite on the American scene—the charitable elite.

The members consist of those who give the most and those who get the most from others. In some cases, such as William Rosenwald and Jack Weiler, the givers and the fundraisers are the same.

A Who's Who of philanthropic Jewry would include such names as Tisch, Boesky, Tishman, Jesselson, Mandel, Wolf, Sherman, Fisher, Rose, Taub, the Stern family, the Crown family, the Pritzker family—to name just a few.

Has Jewish charity changed from the days when the German Jews tried to teach "our coreligionists" the American way to eat and talk at such institutions as the Educational Alliance on New York's Lower East Side?

Does money serve as the only way to rise to philanthropic leadership?

How do the charitable elites themselves feel about their world?

Says lawyer Lawrence Buttenwieser, honorary chairman of the board of the New York Federation of Jewish Philanthropies and the third generation of his family to serve as the organization's president, "Twenty-five years ago some people felt like outsiders. Today the game is open to a larger number of players than it was. There are no outsiders."

Richard Maass, president of the American Jewish Committee from 1977 to 1980, puts it succinctly, "Federation was once 100 percent Reform. As the community changed, elitism changed. Jews of German descent are not the wealthiest group anymore. Today elitism is determined by the size of the gift."

And the gifts are large in comparison to former days. In December of 1915 at Carnegie Hall the American Jewish Relief Committee for Sufferers from the War launched the first major fundraising campaign in America's Jewish history. According to the *New York Times* report, more than $1 million was contributed in cash, jewels, checks and pledges with four $100,000 donations (unofficially said to be from Jacob Schiff, Nathan Straus, Julius Rosenwald of Sears, Roebuck & Company, and the Guggenheim Brothers).

Today reportedly one conglomerate head gives $750,000 a year to the UJA-Federation campaign. Reportedly, a financier gives $1 million for a special project of Jewish education in New York—and wants to give more. He has offered to give $2 million yearly—if Federation and UJA will match it.

In 1981 Americans contributed $540 million to UJA-Federation. In New York City 109 persons gave gifts of $100,000 or more. The size of the city does not bear a direct relation to the size of the gift. According to the 1980–81 *World Almanac,* Cleveland ranks as the nation's seventeenth largest city and has only eighty thousand Jews. Yet, it ranked fourth in terms of giving to UJA-Federation.

"The old terms of the elite have to be redefined," says Sanford Solender, who recently retired after eleven years as executive vice-president of the Federation of Jewish Philanthropies of New York and now serves as its executive consultant, "Today it is a cross section which combines wealth and generosity with a deep commitment to the Jewish people and their future and a willingness to assume active responsibility in leadership, not only financially but for the organization and activities of the community. And these activities include support for Israel. The jeopardization of Israel generated a renewal of concern about the Jewish community.

"The money comes from both old families and those who made it lately. The people who made fortunes in the last generation are well educated. Except for the accident of birth, they are indistinguishable from the old families. Those lines are fading."

Mel Bloom, associate executive vice-chairman, UJA, expresses much the same idea. "The elites today are different. We are now dealing with educated third- and fourth-generation Americans. Some people have not lived through the immigrant experience and some were not adult during the years of the Holocaust and foundation of the State of Israel. There is a new educated elite: the Jewish communal elite who realize that commitment means giving—giving of yourself as well as money. Jewish leadership today means understanding Jewish issues—not wealth alone."

After the 1973 Yom Kippur War, the Jews gave $664 million in the national UJA-Federation campaign. Even under ordinary circumstances, the rate of Jewish giving is spectacular. America's 6 million or so Jews make up less than 3 percent of the population and often are divided on cultural, political and religious fronts. Yet virtually all share one common ground—giving. Their contributions go to both Israeli and American causes and include care of the aged and handicapped, aid to Jewish schools, services for the Jewish poor, handicapped and emotionally disturbed children, special camps, vocational rehabilitation, even assistance to Russian-Jewish émigrés.

WHO GIVES AND WHY

The charitable donors come from diverse backgrounds and contribute generously for a variety of complex reasons:

The committed. Glamorous, blonde Peggy Tishman, lay chairman of the Advance Gifts Committee at New York Federation, who was born into the socially prominent Westheimer family and is married to realtor Alan Tishman, identifies the committed: "They give year in year out just in the same way they brush their teeth. They are the humanitarians who possess a deep concern for and identity with the Jewish community. Without them the agencies could not survive."

The people who give for appearances. Comments Mrs. Tishman, "They do not want anyone to say they did not give, but they do not have that deep sense of commitment." Many people need the charities for a variety of reasons—primarily to advance business contacts or to make new friends."

The frightened. "This group gives out of fear," says Mrs. Tishman. "We saw that in 1974. They felt a cold breath on their backs. But when the heat came off, they climbed back into their caves."

Crises can sometimes set off "sparks of Jewishness," according to Gunther Lawrence, a public-relations executive active in Jewish causes. "Unaffiliated Jews can be oblivious. The 1967 Arab-Israeli War sparked a Jewishness within the unaffiliated group."

The legatees. They give because this has always been a traditional familial way of life. Words like *service* and *responsibility* have always been part of their vocabulary. The late Felix Warburg was the first president of the New York chapter of the Federation of Jewish Philanthropies and a founder and chairman of the Joint Distribution Committee. His sole surviving son Edward has also been prominently identified with both organizations. William Rosenwald is considered the "dean" of today's philanthropists. He is said to have raised $250 million and given an equal amount himself.

However, while families like the Buttenwiesers, Klingensteins, Kohnstamms, Warburgs, Rosenwalds have continued the tradition of giving established by parents and grandparents, others have not. The late Sam Leidesdorf was a large donor to the Federation and an officer of the American Jewish Committee. While Sam Leidesdorf was alive, his son Arthur served as treasurer of the American Jewish Committee. However, when his father died, in the words of an AJC official, "Arthur stopped giving."

The non-Jew. Bob Hope, Merv Griffin, Frank Sinatra (who supposedly has never said no to a request) fall within this category. Sinatra opened his Palm Springs home for a UJA affair. At one Federation-UJA event a Gentile financier was said to have commented: "I am a Baptist and do not share your religion, but I do share your faith." He gave $1 million to the cause.

The silent Jews. For financial, personal and intellectual reasons, they give anonymously. One prominent Wall Streeter, who had spent his life proclaiming himself against a Jewish state even after Israel became a reality, contributed $250,000 after the 1973 Arab-Israeli War. However, he asked that his gift not be made public. Another man, a multimillionaire in the oil business, gives very generously to UJA but also requests anonymity for obvious reasons.

The people who have an edifice complex. Some have given big gifts to universities. There is the S. I. Newhouse School of Public Communications at Syracuse University, the Annenberg School of Communications at the University of Pennsylvania. Recently John L. Loeb of New York City, a 1924 graduate of Harvard College and a cofounder of the banking and brokerage house Loeb Rhoades, gave a $7.5 million gift to Harvard University to permanently endow fifteen chairs for its junior faculty. Incumbents of the new chairs will be known as the John Langeloth Loeb associate professors.

Builder Jack Weiler, active in fundraising for the Albert Einstein College of Medicine, recounts how Walter Annenberg, former ambassador to Great Britain and now one of President Reagan's inner circle, came to see him in New York. "I would like to do something for my mother," he said. At the time Einstein had a $120-million fundraising program. Weiler's answer: "Tell me how to raise the money." Some time later Annenberg returned with an idea: to put up a marble wall on the Bronx campus of the medical school with a bust of Einstein. Any donor who gave $1 million could have his name on that wall. "And, I will give the first million," said Annenberg, "I want my mother's name at the top."

Weiler thanked him, saying, "Soon, I will have five more names on the wall." Now there are about twenty-five, including Kennedy and the Ford Foundation.

Enid A. Haupt, formerly editor of *Seventeen* magazine, is the sister of Walter Annenberg, daughter of the late publisher Moses Annenberg and widow of Wall Streeter Ira Haupt. She exemplifies creative giving. In 1959, Mrs. Haupt established a glass-enclosed complex at the New York University Medical Center which promptly became dubbed "The Garden of Enid."

In 1978 she gave $5 million to the New York Botanical Garden for a complete restoration of the Italian-Renaissance-style glass-domed Conservatory. Known as the Crystal Palace, the building was officially named the Enid A. Haupt Conservatory of the New York Botanical Garden. Recently Mrs. Haupt gave another $5 million to endow the Conservatory; the income is used to maintain the physical facility and care for the Conservatory's plants. This gift was announced three days after she had given $1 million to the New York Public Library.

The charitable newcomers. Recently the New York UJA-Federation joint campaign sponsored a Rosenwald Mission which went to Israel and England. To qualify for the trip, the minimum donation was $25,000. Recalls Elaine Winik, who has held almost every leadership position at UJA, "There was a young couple on the trip who had just made money. They were so happy that they could give that $25,000."

In addition to the gratification that ensues from giving and/or working for charity, volunteers and contributors can receive a wide variety of rewards. These include: *a step up on the social ladder.* Philanthropy can open doors into a new and higher social world. One self-made millionaire finally attained a seat on the board of Hebrew University. At a private dinner one night, a guest asked him, "Why give all your money to Hebrew University?" His frank response: "I never had any education. I made a fortune all on my own. Now, because I am on the Hebrew University board, I go to a dinner and there is a Nobel-Prize winner on my left and a congressman on my right. How else would I have had the opportunity of meeting such people?"

Lyn Revson, who was once married to the late cosmetics king Charles Revson and wears a chain reading, "I am a Jewish princess," comments, "A lot of people will use charity to meet people. The women meet women and then they have little dinner parties. When I started in fundraising, they told me, 'You will meet people.' But that is not my motivation. I want to be told what to do and then go out and do it."

A sense of peer recognition. Says one successful solicitor, "It makes me feel good when I approach someone for a big donation and she says to me, 'Well, if *you* ask me to give, I will give."

A feeling of power. Comments Frederick P. Rose, chairman of Rose Associates, Inc., a major New York reality firm, "When you serve on a board, you are in the position of control. I enjoy applying the same talents that have been successful in my work to extracurricular life." Rose was the first head of the Yale Real Estate Investment Committee which manages millions of dollars of investment money.

Publicity. The local federations, which are listed under various names ranging from the Jewish Welfare Federation of San Francisco to the Jewish Community Federation of Cleveland, depend upon the local Jewish press as well as their own pamphlets, flyers, dinners to honor volunteer solicitors. Plaques, titles' certificates, all serve to gain media attention.

Self-satisfaction. For the paid worker, the challenge and pleasure of being part of the philanthropic world can be enormous. Says Addie Guttag, who heads New York Federation's special gifts department, and who last year got 1,600 gifts of $10,000 or more, "I never go away in December. I love opening my mail then. Sometimes I don't even know who the givers are. They do it then to get the tax break."

Certain people do not care about philanthropic publicity or power. Doctors are notoriously poor givers ("I give my time for nothing at the clinic and that is enough giving for me"). When a business person is solicited by a customer, a gift's size can affect his or her commercial career. For professionals—such as teachers, principals, editors, social workers, public employees—his or her livelihood does not depend on the goodwill of customers. Advancement is not contingent upon acceptable levels of charitable donations.

THE BASIC PHILANTHROPIC FACTS

Most groups—such as UJA-Federation—are philanthropic, raising money nationally and locally. In addition, there are programmatic groups which raise money for their own programs. These exist under a coordinating group, the National Jewish Community Relations Advisory Council (NJCRAC). Such groups as the American Jewish Committee, American Jewish Congress, Anti-Defamation League, National Council of Jewish Women, fall under this banner.

Charity is not as democratic as one would imagine. Says one philanthropic leader who asked not to be named, "If we got rid of all the small contributors, it would not make any difference. A few give the most. About 80 percent of money taken in comes from 10 percent of the people. Eighty-four percent of our givers provide 11 percent of the money. Sixteen percent provide 88 percent. We need the grass-roots umbrella to point out to people the democracy of fundraising. But we would go broke if we concentrated on democracy instead of autocracy."

Others take a different point of view. Says Richard Maass, "The grass-roots approach is worthwhile because giving to an agency expands the base of the agency beyond the financial end. Volunteers help for programs. And the seat of all wisdom is not New York, Los Angeles or Washington. The value to the national agency of a man in Rapid City, South Dakota, cannot be measured in terms of dollars."

In the Jewish philanthropic world certain organizations are "elite" in terms of quality and quantity of work, and prominent board members. According to Charles Liebman, professor of sociology at Bar-Ilan University, Israel, hospitals are considered "the most prestigious."

In 1852 a group of nine distinguished Sephardic Jewish New Yorkers secured a charter for the "benevolent, charitable and scientific Society . . . known as The Jews Hospital in New York." Several years later, as Mount Sinai Hospital, it would open its doors to patients from the entire community, regardless of race or religion. Today, according to archivist Dr. Albert M. Lyons, the board includes members who have been helping Mount Sinai for several generations: Alfred R. Stern of the Rosenwald family, Frederick Klingenstein, Edgar Cullman, Arthur Ochs Sulzberger and many others.

Montefiore Hospital in New York attracts its share of prominent board members too. Banker Jacob Schiff was the second chairman of the board at The Montefiore Home for Chronic Invalids. He used to approve all the admissions and came uptown to personally light the candles on holidays.

Today scions of the old families still serve on the board of the Montefiore Hospital and Medical Center: Robert Bernhard, Lawrence B. Buttenwieser, Sadie K. Klau, Lucy Moses, Edwin Stern III.

The City of Hope at Duarte, near Los Angeles, and The Hospital for Chronic Diseases in Denver also fall within the "elite" category of Jewish charitable organizations.

Other "elites" in the philanthropic world, according to twenty-five Jewish community leaders, include Hebrew Union College–Jewish Institute of Religion, the Jewish Museum, the Jewish Institute for the Blind (Peggy Westheimer met Alan Tishman, her husband-to-be, at the guild's former annual Thanksgiving Eve dance), UJA-Federation, Blythedale Children's Hospital in Valhalla, New York, the Ninety-second Street Y in New York City. Adds Professor Liebman, "If there were a Jewish Philharmonic, it would be prestigious."

Within the organizations themselves, a hierarchy of elitism exists. Comments Frederick Rose, "There are the important committees such as the Distribution Committee and communal planning committees for the central administration of Federation. They are elite."

Jews have pioneered in innovative fundraising techniques that have been extraordinarily fruitful. It was the Jews who, just before the turn of the century, first successfully solicited a single donation on behalf of a multiplicity of charities—an innovation that was the forerunner of the present United Way. It was Jacob Schiff who personalized Benjamin Franklin's concept of the "matching gift" when he agreed to put up half the money for a particular cause on the condition that the rest of the community contribute the remainder.

Jews also originated the technique of dividing a campaign into different sectors based on trade or business. The annual combined campaign of New York's UJA-Federation is organized into 118 district fundraising committees, each managed by members of a specific trade group or profession who are charged with getting as much money as they can out of their colleagues. Categories include Alcoholic Beverages, Brushes and Bristles,

Carbonated Beverages, Corsets and Brassieres, etc. Insurance has two groups: Life and General. Other committees include the Women's Division, Business and Professional Women and Special Gifts ($10,000 and over).

Country clubs play their part in fundraising. It is said that Palm Beach Country Club would not accept a certain man as a member unless he donated $25,000 to a specific charity. At Hillcrest Country Club in Los Angeles, there is a graduated scale for giving. Says accountant Harold Berlfein, chairman of the Admissions Committee, "There is a waiting list. We judge by community activity and donations."

In addition there are plate dinners costing $200 to $250 a head where a particular member of an industry is honored; face-to-face solicitation, "parlor meetings" and card calling.

In an article on "Parlor Meetings" in *Understanding American Jewish Philanthropy,* Los Angeles banker Bram Goldsmith recounts how one man interrupted the round-table solicitation's chairman by saying, "Look, would you mind calling on me next. I've got to go to the bathroom." Responded the chairman, "Well, it depends on what kind of commitment you are going to give us."

The man answered, "Last year I gave $3,000; this year I am going to give $15,000." He was allowed to go to the bathroom. A few minutes later, he returned and said, "You know, I feel so much better; put me down for another $2,000."

Another technique that has been highly successful is in-house solicitation. Certain successful businessmen like securities arbitrageur Ivan Boesky like to sponsor dinners at home for their own employees. It is hard to refuse the boss. Last year Alan Greenberg, chief executive officer of Bear, Stearns & Company, an investment banking firm, held two separate meetings at his Manhattan home—one for partners, the other for salesmen. Each gathering resulted in increased contributions to the UJA-Federation campaign.

Much of the success of Jewish philanthropy stems from a combination of factors: intensive research, creative programing and peer pressure.

At the New York UJA-Federation-Campaign offices, possible

givers are researched with care. Volunteers and paid professionals use private sources, the *Wall Street Journal, Forbes* and *Fortune* magazines, to "sniff out" what people are worth. Then they find someone who knows the particular person targeted—who perhaps belongs to the same business or social club—to make the initial contact.

For the actual fundraising, assignment sheets are made out for the solicitor with the prospect's name and columns headed "giving history" (the amount is listed for the last three years); "remarks" (here one finds club memberships, amount desired); and where the solicitation will take place (Wall Street dinner, December 9).

Aryeh Nesher, an Israeli who is a "Hitler survivor," heads Operation Breakthrough for the UJA. This project is an attempt "to get to Jews who do not fall within the framework"—in other words, undergivers, token givers, and nongivers. Nesher breaks down his project into "four instruments": finding the prospects, researching them, setting up appointments, and seeing them, always remembering that "People give to people, not causes. I've lost lots of money by being the wrong man."

Dr. Nesher, who teaches fundraising at the New School for Social Research, New York, and sociology at Haifa University, Israel, says "Our salesmanship in fundraising is a process in which you sell a product which isn't to people who don't want it for the highest amount possible." Nesher's reputation for getting erstwhile reluctant contributors to give is such that major manufacturer Abe Plough turned off his hearing aid when he saw Nesher—but gave anyway.

Nesher's operation teaches people to research prospects, trains over $25,000 contributors to fundraise other large contributors and instructs young people on the methodology of educating other young people. He says, "It is an educational and selling process. You are selling Jewish survival."

At times a special prize is used as incentive for prospective donors. For a $10,000 gift to the 1981 New York UJA-Federation Campaign, one could attend a Picasso exhibition at the Pace Gallery followed by a reception at the home of artist Louise

Nevelson. Each donor received a Nevelson work.

Peer pressure plays an enormous part in raising the amount of the donations. Addie Guttag explains: "Let us say there's a dinner to be followed by card calling. We make it our business to know in advance just how much many of the people plan to give. So we know that one business competitor plans to give $100,000 and a second competitor plans to give $50,000. We call the first competitor and call the second right after him so that he will experience the feeling of peer pressure. After hearing the first man announce the $100,000 pledge, it might be difficult for him not to do the same. He will want the other guests to think he is at least as well off as his peers."

What actually happens at a card-calling dinner?

On December 9, 1981, some eight hundred members of New York's Wall Street community, including such powerful figures as Ivan Boesky, Alan Greenberg and Laurence Tisch, gathered for the Wall Street Investment Banking Division dinner that was held at the New York Hilton for the UJA-Federation campaign for 1982. After the hors d'oeuvres and before the filet of beef, the names of guests were read off from index cards and the guests announced their pledges. The pledges ranged from $100 to $1.5 million and in one night a total of over $6 million was pledged. Obviously the amounts pledged were known to UJA-Federation officials in advance. Big donors and small givers alternated and variations of the sentence "I give $210,000 from my firm and $5,000 from me personally" were heard repeatedly. Another type of pledge: "I give $100,000 and $25,000 in honor of ———." This sort of pressure in front of business competitors obviously works. In one evening this division raised almost half its goal for the year.

For all these reasons, the extent of Jewish charitable donations far exceeds any other group. Says Richard Maass, "Jewish giving is much stronger in life than Christian. Compare UJA with the Protestant Sectarian Fund. Jews give more than Catholics. Jewish fundraising has been institutionalized to a degree that others have not."

SOME CHARITABLE CHANGES

Like most of America, philanthropy has become "Judaized." Says Mel Bloom, "Along with being more democratic, the Jewish philanthropic world has become more Jewish. We see this respect for an involvement in Jewish tradition increasingly."

Agencies now serve kosher food, close on all Jewish holidays, put emphasis on "rehabilitation" of Jewish day schools. There has been a recognition of the Orthodox as wealthy members of the community. In fact, according to Charles Liebman in the *American Jewish Year Book 1979,* the two New York gifts of $5 million to the Israeli Emergency Fund in 1973 came from Orthodox Jews.

Formerly, in many communities, especially New York, Cincinnati, Baltimore, St. Louis and San Francisco, assimilated wealthy Jews of German background were the most active philanthropists. Their aim was to help the Eastern European immigrants, arriving in the U.S. in vast numbers, to become quickly acculturated and self supporting, thus avoiding any embarrassment to their more established brothers.

Writes Steven Martin Cohen in the *American Jewish Yearbook 1980,* "While East Europeans eventually replaced German Jews as federation stalwarts, Jewish philanthropy remained for many years largely the province of affluent and relatively assimilated Jews. As a result, informed observers held a somewhat accurate stereotype of the Jewish philanthropist: he or she was active in Jewish public affairs but uninvolved in private Jewish behaviors."

In recent years a new group of philanthropists has replaced —and in some cases joined—the old-line activists. This new group is motivated less by *noblesse oblige* than by ethnic and religious concerns.

In the *American Jewish Yearbook 1979,* Charles Liebman writes, "Federation's present leaders are different from those of ten years ago. They are still a wealthy educated group, but they are somewhat more likely to be of Eastern European descent, far more likely to be synagogue members and to have had at least a minimal Jewish education, and far more concerned with questions of Jewish identity and survival."

Adds Peggy Tishman, "No one knows the difference anymore between German and Russian."

But Frederick Rose observes, "Formerly the East Europeans were more interested in Israel philanthropies and the Germans were more interested in the local ones. Today this distinction has disappeared."

THE ELITE PHILANTHROPISTS

Who are some of the prominent philanthropists today and how did they become what they are?

Henry Taub

Henry Taub, founder of Automatic Data Processing and now president of the Joint Distribution Committee and a member of the board of trustees of UJA Inc., grew up in Paterson, New Jersey, the son of an immigrant textile weaver. A warm, gentle man, he says, "Charity is a way of life. I learned it from my parents and grandparents. I was taught the concept of sharing with friends and neighbors. I never felt poor. Paterson kids always shared with their neighbors. We had a Young Men's Hebrew Association there. Everyone gathered there regardless of their economic condition. Those who were more fortunate supported it and made it possible for youngsters like me to enjoy the indoor swimming pool and to go to camp."

Taub, fifty-four, serves as a good example of the change in philanthropic elitism. He says, "The Joint Distribution Committee was founded by Our Crowd. But the last two presidents have been Jack Weiler (the highly successful real estate man who, as noted earlier, immigrated to the United States from Russia at the age of five) and Henry Taub." Weiler did achieve the presidency of JDC, but one fundraising insider notes, "He had to wait six years longer than he should have because he was not German."

Taub was graduated from high school at sixteen. During his

junior and senior years he had worked at Associated Transport, which used high-school students to send out its bills. Through this job he got involved with office procedures and cash flow. From the ages of sixteen to nineteen, he attended New York University and after school hours worked for a CPA firm, doing write-ups, processing the payroll and experiencing the feel of a small company. By the time he started ADP at twenty-one, he had some four to five years of good experience, especially in the area of office management.

Until four years ago Taub served as chairman of ADP. He had been active in the firm for thirty years; each year the firm recorded a growth of between 15 and 20 percent. He notes, "I was searching for what in academia you would call a sabbatical. I had acquired more wealth than I knew what to do with. I decided to do things pleasing to me and my family."

Taub gives twenty hours a week to JDC, serves on the executive board of UJA, is president of the local Jewish Community Center and heads the Business Employment Foundation, which operates in New Jersey, training minority teens in office skills and then placing them in industry.

He opts strongly for the grass-roots approach to philanthropy. "There are academics who have ideas, members of the religious community who cannot give in dollars," he says. "They are our intellectual and ethical resources. You have got to work with grass roots because from there come tomorrow's leaders."

Other Taub causes include the American Technion Society, Hebrew University, the Hemophilia Foundation, Joseph Papp's Public Theater. He also founded a chair of urban studies at New York University.

Taub speaks frankly about certain philanthropic world truths: "A big part of the leadership is money. But it is hard to get to the top if you do not have time to meet its needs. Philanthropy is an unpaid volunteer job."

From grim poverty to riches and philanthropic leadership: Taub's story is typical of American Jews. The same holds true for his brother Joe, who is president of the New Jersey Nets and also has a stable of sixty horses.

Ambassador Marvin L. Warner

Ask the professionals at the national office of UJA for the names of outstanding fundraisers in the United States and the name of Marvin Warner echoes repeatedly.

Warner, a Cincinnati businessman, who served as ambassador to Switzerland from 1977 to 1979, is the son of Orthodox immigrant parents from Latvia. Born in Birmingham, Alabama, he received his B.S. in commerce and LL.B. at the University of Alabama, his LL.M. from George Washington University, Washington, D.C., and a Doctor of Laws from American College, Leysin, Switzerland.

Former Ambassador Warner has always been a doer. In his younger days he was involved with the Y.M.H.A., the Boy Scouts, won the state *Birmingham News* Oratorical Championship and a debate scholarship to the University of Alabama. At the university he earned money grading papers, worked for the National Youth Administration fifty hours a month at seventy-five cents per hour, sold chemicals and on Saturdays worked at a local dry goods store.

Always driven to succeed, the handsome sixty-two-year-old developer explains, "The first generation of Jewish boys and girls had catching up to do and the opportunity to do it. I wanted to be successful but I always knew money was not the equivalent of success. I wanted to be a contributor to the community, to earn my own self-respect. My mother had the old world Jewish concept of charity. She thought whatever I gave was not enough."

Like Taub and many of the other self-made JEPs, Warner embodies the American dream. He admits it feelingly: "Without the democratic system—the open system—which recognizes the person's ability, there would be no room for accomplishment. It is analogous to the thoroughbred race horse. He might be best, but without the track, how would you know it?"

After a stint in the army, Warner returned to Birmingham and found that as a lawyer he could command about $150 a month. Unable to afford this, he went into real estate and insurance for

$250. He built housing in Alabama financed by the F.H.A. and when housing needs slowed in Alabama he scouted around the country to find other areas needing housing. In 1950, he headquartered in Cincinnati, building there, Dayton, St. Louis, Indianapolis and Kansas City. "Cincinnati was central, relatively southern. I liked the town and its people and there was a cultural atmosphere."

Today Warner heads ComBank Corporation, Orlando, Florida; Great American Bank, Miami, Florida; and owns Warner National Corporation, Cincinnati, a financial holding company. In the past he has been a part owner of the New York Yankees and Tampa Bay Buccaneers. He has a working thoroughbred farm twenty miles east of Cincinnati, "Warnerton," set on six hundred acres which he calls his "favorite place." He serves on the board of Hebrew Union College–Jewish Institute of Religion and was chairman of the Ohio Board of Regents and was awarded the Governor's Award for service to the state. President Johnson appointed him to the U.S. delegation to the United Nations and President Jimmy Carter to be U.S. ambassador to Switzerland in 1977.

It is interesting that this highly motivated man succeeded in Cincinnati, long known as a home of German-Jewish snobbery and still the kind of town where one hears—in the words of a local doyenne, "There are some new people. They are very nice," when she means, "They are not German."

Explains Warner, "The first generation was a hard-charging group. When people work hard and assert leadership, their presence can bend the old strata. In Cincinnati, perhaps the old ideas do exist to a certain extent. However, there are magnanimous people from the old families who welcome new blood and strength."

For Warner "service to the community" has proven his most satisfying experience. He points out that when he came to Cincinnati over three decades ago, a division existed in the philanthropic world. The Reform Jews supported Associated Jewish Charities, and the Conservative and Orthodox Jews supported the Jewish Welfare Fund. Warner with others succeeded in bringing the two agencies together into what is now called the

Jewish Federation of Cincinnati and became the organization's first president.

From his first wife he has three children, none from his brief marriage to Susan Goldwater (who had been married to Barry Goldwater, Jr.). Warner's children are firmly Jewish. His older daughter Marlin (Mrs. Stephen Arky) resides in Florida. "Her two children, Lisa, 12 and Todd, 9, go to religious school and light the candles," he states fondly. "When I go to her home, I do it too."

His younger daughter Alyson (Mrs. Herbert Kuppin, Jr.) lives in Cincinnati with her two children, Trey, 4 and Warner, 3. Son Marvin L. Warner, Jr., 24, has his own thoroughbred farm in Lexington, Kentucky.'

Warner enjoys Talmudic studies taught by a rabbi who visits him during the intermittent times when he is in town. The two men discuss the Talmud.

Asked what constitutes today's elite, Warner responds without hesitation, "People who do things, make things happen, give to others, provide leadership. The Jewish elite consists of people like the ones in Cleveland and Chicago who give so much: Milton Wolf, Mort Mandel, Philip Klutznick [he is president emeritus of the World Jewish Congress]."

Says Warner, "I am not a ritualistic Jew, but I feel deeply about religion. Many pressures exist in present-day society. Our ideas are subject to the challenge of soap-opera portrayals and the Moral Majority. We cannot continue with the very inept stoic stands we have taken for centuries. As Jews we must put more imagination and marketing concepts into religion. As elders we have to understand Judaism's dynamic force and take it to our children for their appreciation. Our children trust us. We must utilize the relationship."

Despite the "Judaization of Federation," old attitudes die hard. When the orchestra played "Hatikvah" ("Hope"), the national anthem of Israel, at a function, Benjamin Buttenwieser, former president, Federation of Jewish Philanthropies of New York, who comes from a distinguished German-Jewish family was overheard to say, "Why are they playing that?" Sotto voce, another guest commented, "At least he knows what it is."

Along with the emergence of children of immigrants in positions of philanthropic power, philanthropy has recognized that it should not grant these leadership roles to Jews who are not acceptable to the Jewish community. One example would be a person who fails to identify with Israel.

A "scandal" rocked the New York Federation of Jewish Philanthropies in the mid-1960s (the Federation campaign did not merge with UJA until 1973). Henry Loeb, from an old and elegant Wall Street family, was being considered for the presidential spot at Federation. However, Loeb was an active member of the American Council for Judaism, a national group opposed to the State of Israel.

Jack Weiler felt that the president of Federation represented the leadership of new York Jewry and that it would be improper for someone unfriendly to Israel to hold this important office. The acrimony lasted for months. Henry Loeb was not made president of Federation.

The intermarriage factor has had an interesting effect on Jewish philanthropy. "Some get lost; some stay," says Aryeh Nesher. "A lot depends on the wife, and some wives who are converted became the most active in the community."

Businessman Lewis Lehrman (a millionaire from Rite Aid drug chain) is married to a Christian and sends his children to private non-Jewish schools, but he is active in Torah Umesorah, the national society for Hebrew day schools, serves as a UJA vice-president and trustee for American Jewish Forums. Andrew Goodman, chairman, Bergdorf Goodman, New York, married a Catholic but has remained active in Jewish affairs. Even though he is Catholic, son Edwin Andrew is active in the American Jewish Committee.

Today many Jews work on cross-cultural charitable activities. "It has become an egalitarian society," analyzes Frederick Rose. "Now everyone in the general philanthropic field avidly solicits participation of qualified Jews for boards. They do not give a damn about background. The best Jewish leadership is now on the board of the Metropolitan Museum of Art, Presbyterian Hospital, Lincoln Center."

In his own words Rose has "cut it down the middle." He serves both on the executive committee of the board of the Asia Society and as chairman of the board of *Commentary.*

Jews have penetrated the boards of universities. Rose is very active in Yale affairs. Peggy Tishman serves on the board of Wellesley College.

Along with the Gentile Laurance S. Rockefeller and Louis Auchincloss, a number of Jews serve on the President's Council of the Museum of the City of New York. They include Mrs. Jacob M. Kaplan, Mrs. Richard Kaye Korn, Mrs. Mollie Parnis Livingston, Mrs. Henry A. Loeb, Mrs. John L. Loeb, Roy R. Neuberger, Lewis Rudin, Mrs. Arthur Hays Sulzberger.

Is this giving to cross-cultural institutions a trend? "It is an addition," says Richard Maass. "Jews have always been interested in the arts." However, Maass makes two points: (1) The perpetual crisis in Israel has brought back to Jewish charities gifts that might have gone for other purposes. (2) For the most part, the first- and second-generation wealth gives primarily to Jewish causes rather than to cross-cultural ones.

JEWISH WOMEN IN PHILANTHROPY

Another significant change: following years of "discrimination" and confinement to women's activities, Jewish women are finally making it to the top in the philanthropic world.

Billie Tisch

Traditionally, the president of the Federation of Jewish Philanthropies of New York has been a man and, if possible, a very well-known man—preferably a captain of industry or a financial wizard. They have included such Wall Street figures as Felix Warburg, Arthur Lehman, Benjamin Buttenwieser, Gustave I. Levy and dignitaries like the late Judge Joseph M. Proskauer and Irving Mitchell Felt (chairman of the board, Madison Square Garden Inc.).

The current president is not a famous captain of industry or a financial wizard. She is Wilma Tisch, whom everyone calls Billie. She is the first woman to be elected president (in the 1930s Madeleine Borg was not elected to the post but served out an unexpired term of a man who died in office) of the sixty-five-year-old charity which raises and distributes money to 132 member agencies and is believed to be the largest local voluntary organization of its kind in the world.

"The day of Lady Bountiful is over," claims Mrs. Tisch, who has been married for thirty-three years to Laurence Tisch, definitely a captain of industry. He is chairman of Loews Corporation and honorary chairman of the UJA-Federation joint campaign.

Mrs. Tisch began working for the Federation in 1962 as a board member of the Blythedale Children's Hospital in Valhalla, New York, and quickly moved up through the ranks. She has been chairman of several Federation committees, including the important Distribution Committee, which decides how to apportion the Federation's share of UJA-Federation joint campaign dollars, currently about $32 million, plus income from other sources.

"We are a philanthropy, not a charity," claims Mrs. Tisch. "These words say something about the new kind of professionalism. In recent years four major committees have been chaired by women. I was the first to head distribution. There was a time when a sense of the silver spoon was necessary, but for the last ten to fifteen years it has been different. However, it is taking a long time to dispel that idea."

Unlike the past male presidents, who ran their companies while they served as Federation heads, Mrs. Tisch devotes full time to the presidency. She says. "My main problem is trying to do the job well and still maintain my family life. When I took it on, I worried lest it become the kind of job done properly only by a woman who had lots of time or a man who had retired."

A neat, decisive, small woman with curly, short-cropped gray hair, Mrs. Tisch wears a navy Adolfo suit with red blouse accessorized by a gold chain. She met her husband on a blind date in 1948 when she was four days out of college. They were married four months later. She does not feel she married young, noting, "It was the thing to do."

She is the product of a German father and Lithuanian mother. In their home (there are two: an upper Fifth Avenue apartment and a house in Rye), the Tisches light candles on Friday night, observe the Jewish holidays and take great interest in things Jewish. As noted, three of the four Tisch sons are married—two to the daughters of a rabbi.

Mrs. Tisch points out that there are groups of people working at Federation who have been brought up "Jewishly illiterate." Many of these have organized into classes to study what they missed in childhood.

She feels strongly about the new receptivity of Federation, formerly considered an elitist group ("Our doors are open; if I hear they are not, I will go to great pains to rectify the situation") and a return to volunteerism ("I believe what one does with one's free time is an expression of one's deepest conviction. Women make a great mistake when they deny themselves this form of expression").

Did Mrs. Tisch get her job because of her husband? An active UJA professional says, "She has proven herself. She worked her way up."

Sylvia Hassenfeld

Blonde, blue-eyed Sylvia Hassenfeld of Barrington, Rhode Island, became involved with philanthropy through her late husband Merrill. Born in Philadelphia, a graduate of Cedarcrest, she visited relatives in Providence and thus met her husband-to-be. "My husband's family was very involved in philanthropy; they got me to feel I had to help," she recalls.

Unusually frank for a philanthropic world member, she bluntly makes a series of points that few charitable elites will admit: "Great wealth matters and there is no denying it—certainly it is the basic few percent who give the most money. The paid professionals are impressed by people with money. But the world is opening up. We have realized that leadership capacity is rare. To get the finest people, we cannot take only people with top dollars. We must take people who give as well as their capacity allows. For instance, we now go after academics. We did not go after them before."

Mrs. Hassenfeld was national chairman of the Women's Division of UJA and now serves as national vice-chairman of the overall campaign and as a member of the executive committee. She is also on the executive committee of the Joint Distribution Committee and a member of the board of the Center for Strategic and International Studies and Executive Committee APEC.

About women in philanthropy, she comments, "I think it is difficult. It is like a man's club. A few women do manage to make it."

Elaine Winik

"When you are in Jewish leadership, it has a price tag," says tall, blonde Elaine Winik. "The first person you have to fundraise is yourself."

In the philanthropic world Winik represents something special. She is well-to-do with a sprawling house on Long Island Sound, but as her peers say, she does not have "real money."

One of four daughters of Sam and Minnie Kappel, Elaine Winik was born in Brooklyn. As her Russian-born father, a clothing manufacturer, became more successful, the family embarked on a Marjorie Morningstar progression: from Flatbush to Great Neck to a penthouse on Central Park West.

From her young years Elaine Kappel was exposed to charity. Her tenth-birthday party was held at the Brooklyn Hebrew Orphan Asylum, where her father served as a trustee. As a child, she wondered, "What would I do if I had a million dollars?" and decided, "Give half to charity."

One of the Kappel sisters married a Scottish Jew. When World War II was over, the Kappels rushed to see her and the newborn child. It was just three months after the end of the war, and a friend took the Kappels to see a DP camp. Sam Kappel exclaimed, "What did we let them do to us?" Young Elaine Kappel went to see for herself. She comments now, "Everyone was crying over the bones in Auschwitz, but nobody wanted the ones who were left."

She came back a committed Jew and for thirty-five years has been an active UJA member. Asked how she rose in the philanthropic world without an unlimited bankroll, she claims, "I made it through UJA. I fell in love with the cause."

She has served as chairman of Rye Division, Westchester Division, Women's Division; national vice-president of the Women's Division; chairman of Greater New York; national chairman of Women's Division, assistant chairman of the joint UJA-Federation campaign. Remarried to Norman Winik seven years ago, she smilingly tells how he gave her a bracelet that reads, IDTA—meaning "I Did That Already"—as a response made to UJA officials asking her to take on added responsibility.

She was recently elected the twelfth president of the UJA of Greater New York, the first woman to be elected to the post.

She recalls, "There are spots in families. I had three beautiful sisters. I was a fat monster. The only spot for me was the smart spot."

Are small gifts worth the effort? Her terse answer: "It is much cheaper to get a million-dollar figure. It keeps the overhead down. But young people are your future."

Elaine Winik exemplifies the give-till-it-hurts approach to philanthropy. "When I was married to my first husband, I gave away my total income—$30,000," she recalls. Then her marriage ended. Her accountant advised, "This year you can give $1,000." She went to the head of UJA and said, "I can give $5,000. Do you want me to step down as national chairman?" He said no, and then on a mission to Israel, she increased the contribution to $7,500, telling the audience, "This is a bigger gift then the $30,000, which meant nothing. This cause means everything to me."

Mrs. Winik emphasizes the necessity of recruiting young givers. When she was nineteen, she hostessed a UJA luncheon at her mother's home. Each guest had to give $10. Fifteen years later she had a luncheon where $1,000 was the minimum pledge. She recalls with pleasure, "Every woman on the dais had been at my first luncheon."

She echoes the difficulties of making it as a woman in the philanthropic world. "When I became chairman of the New

York UJA, I thought I had opened the doors for women," she claims. "Then they had a prime minister mission for the chairman of the largest communities. I was invited, but was told, 'You cannot go. You are a woman.' But I went. For three years I went on this mission, but I had to fight for it every time. Now it is open to people who give over a certain amount. People in the philanthropic world tend to forget that dollars have no sex."

She notes that there has been a change in the level of philanthropic professionals and the lay volunteers. "At one point the professionals had no prestige," she comments. "Now we are getting bright M.B.A.s."

Solicitation calls for skills. "Let us say I am going to solicit Tom Jones. I do some research and then I call up and say I want a half hour of his time. He says, 'Can't you do it over the phone?' I refuse. Soliciting is easy. Getting the appointment is hard. Once I have it, I go to his office and make my pitch.

"I tell him, 'We are going to lose $22 million in federal funds. I am so tired of playing God and wondering what halfway house we are going to close. We can be quiet like we were before World War II or refuse to play that game any more. This year we are supposed to raise 30 percent more. Any money you give this year not only does the job but does a political job." Usually Mrs. Winik, with her warm, communicative manner, gets what she wants. She notes, "It is the ripple effect. If I leave that man's office with 50 percent more, I can go to ten other people and get more from them too."

Mrs. Winik's fundraising success may be due to her precept: "You don't just want money. You want Jews."

She points out the limited manpower for the UJA-Federation campaign. A recent innovation is the committee of 100. Each has to do ten face-to-face solicitations.

Winik, veteran of forty-two trips to Israel, has passed on the legacy of philanthropic activity to her children. Her youngest daughter is chairman of the Harrison, New York, chapter of UJA.

She is also known for her doggerel, often penned on UJA fundraising missions. Here is a sample:

When you look up, it's not
One—It is Two
What the hell do they
Want out of you
Only your money, less
Than your life—
When they finish with you—
They'll talk to your wife
So relax and be happy
As you part with your gelt
For never was a cause
More deeply felt.
For what is a Jew
Who will not share
And how sad it would be
If we did not care.
Your pocket is lighter
But so is your heart
Let's drink a l'chayim
Before we all part.

PHILANTHROPIC DANGER AREAS

As Steven Martin Cohen points out in the article, "Trends in Jewish Philanthropy" in the 1980 *American Jewish Yearbook,* "Questions about the future of Jewish giving then are, in reality, questions about the future of organized Jewry."

According to surveys conducted in 1965 and 1975 in behalf of the Combined Jewish Philanthropies of Greater Boston, the three groups making up the alternative household—singles, childless married couples and divorced or separated people—scored low on a Jewish Activities Scale. Seemingly, the unmarried and couples without children find little need to become participants in the organized Jewish community until children are born.

Comments Robert Smith, public relations director for the New York Federation of Jewish Philanthropies and UJA–Federation Campaign, "If we have disorganization in family life, it has to affect philanthropy. A single-parent family is not a potential contributor to philanthropy. The more the disruption of family life, the more the effect on philanthropy. If the children do not learn to give from their families, chances are they will not be philanthropic either."

In addition, younger Jews have been entering the salaried professions rather than becoming independent entrepreneurs. This shift from self-employed to salaries means that younger Jews will less often enter the pool of potential multimillionaires, that group which has most generously supported philanthropic drives in the past. It also purports that less social and economic pressure can be brought to bear on potential contributors. The careers of social workers, teachers, editors, supervisors are not dependent on the goodwill of customers as is that of a business person. As a result, individuals in these fields may feel less need to link themselves to the Jewish community through charitable giving. Who will replace the current "superdoners" of the business community?

In summing up the traumas and triumphs of the Jewish philanthropic world, forty-three-year-old Jane Sherman, an active fundraiser for the Jewish Welfare Federation of Detroit, stresses that changes must be made.

She points out, "There is a locker-room syndrome. Sylvia Hassenfeld serves as a fine example of a woman who did not achieve the top rank. She should have been a chairman of national UJA. Many were for her. It was a blatant mistake by UJA. However, there was the feeling that a woman cannot solicit a man for a major gift. Someday there will be a woman chairman. The woman who does get the top spot will probably have to be a woman of independent means—from her own work or inheritance—so that she has clout. Hopefully, the woman who achieves a top leadership role will get it because of her fundraising ability—not because of where the money came from or what she gives."

She reiterates the statement of many: "As of today you cannot achieve a major role without giving a major gift. But the day will come when we have a chairman who gives $10,000 and the community will understand. Now, fundraising is becoming geared to the professions, and professionals just do not make big money."

Mrs. Sherman makes no mention of it, but everyone in the philanthropic world knows that she is the daughter of Max Fisher, the Detroit businessman, son of a White Russian immigrant peddler, who never had a bar mitzvah and went to Ohio State on a football scholarship. According to an article in *Monthly Detroit,* Max Fisher is a "triumph of the original revolutionary myth of equality: that any man with intelligence and energy can rise to wealth and power in the classless freedom of this new society. It hasn't worked for a lot of people, but it has certainly worked for Fisher."

A poor boy from an obscure Ohio village, Fisher parlayed a chance encounter with oil and a native genius for hard work into an immense personal fortune. Keeping a low profile, Fisher gives away millions each year to charity (he has estimated that he gives away half his income), raises millions for charity ("I believe in leadership giving"), has served as unofficial financial advisor to the Israeli government and has been called "probably the most prominent Republican in the country."

For twenty years daughter Jane Sherman has followed her father's example. She has worked for the Joint Distribution Committee, served on the board of the executive committee, national UJA Women's Division, is national co-chairman of UJA Project Renewal and co-chairman of the Women's Division of the Detroit UJA. "I came from a philanthropic household with no Jewish training," she recalls, "but my husband and I first went to Israel in 1962 on a Young Leadership mission. I was hooked. I have spent the last twenty years studying Jewish history."

In ninth grade Sherman went steady with a Gentile. Her father told her, "You should not marry a non-Jew. It makes for problems." Today she states, "This made an impression on me. I do not want my children (two boys and a girl) to marry outside their religion. I hope I do not have to cope with this problem."

The Sherman family is Reform with a deep commitment to things Jewish. On Friday nights they say kiddush. Mrs. Sherman makes *challah.* They always dine together on Fridays. She proudly states, "I am more religious than I was as a kid. Our home was Reform. But my husband's parents kept kosher."

Mrs. Sherman prefers to use the term *community pressure* rather than *peer pressure.* She says, "Community pressure exists much more here than in New York. Giving is the thing to do. Here, every Jew knows every other Jew and if you want to be part of the community, you give. Recently, I was reading the *Jewish News* and saw the name of a local man I did not know. This was unusual. New York is a separate country when it comes to fund-raising."

She adds, "There is no German-Russian thing in Detroit. I have never seen it or been aware of it. Today Jews are Jews and heritage does not make any difference."

Mrs. Sherman gives every weekday to philanthropic work and attends many night meetings. "Except for my family, this is the most important thing in my life," she says. "You need the support of your spouse, or the marriage would break up. My husband Larry is associate vice-chairman in the campaign but he is not as emotionally involved as I. You could not have two crazies in one family."

Mrs. Sherman wondered how her children would react to the tremendous time she gives to philanthropy. She need not have worried. All three make their own annual pledge to the UJA-Federation campaign. They earn the money they give. For example, younger son Scott pledged $65 last year with money earned from his paper route and has promised to increase the amount this year.

"They see it," she says proudly. "They understand the importance of their roots."

Just prior to his bar mitzvah at a local temple, older son David, now a student at the University of Rochester, had gone on a mission to Israel and was deeply impressed. At this temple, it is the custom to have the thirteen-year-old stand in front of the ark and pledge to continue his Jewish education. David insisted on writing his own "meaningful" pledge. He vowed that "Masada will never fall again. The future starts with my education."

Mrs. Sherman says simply, "I cried. This was the culmination of everything Larry and I had tried to do as parents."

Has philanthropic work changed her? "Yes, it has made me a better person," she answers. "I am more understanding of people around me. It has made me both tolerant and intolerant of people who do not feel the way I do. I cannot remain friends with people who are not concerned with others.

"I love what I am doing. I would not change one minute of it. I am having a little part in guaranteeing that wherever they want to live, my kids will live freely as Jews. I want them to be able to say 'I am a Jew' from the rooftop, just as I can do it now."

15

THE JEWISH ELITE WAY OF LIFE

IN MANHATTAN the members of the Jewish elite give catered dinner parties on Wednesdays and Thursdays because on Friday they desert the city for their country homes.

In Westport, Connecticut, at certain parties there is a special area allotted for-children-only. There the youngsters play and receive special food and service. Explains one mother, "Kids do not like filet. They want hot dogs." Whatever the food, it is served on gleaming silver.

Author F. Scott Fitzgerald once wrote, "Let me tell you about the very rich. They are different from you and me."

But are the Jewish rich different?

"Sometimes the behavior of elite WASPs and elite Jews is the same," analyzes Dr. Harry Sands, executive director, Postgraduate Center for Mental Health, New York. "After they have made money, they feel the need to preserve themselves, to pass the name on to posterity. And so you have the Harkness Pavilion, the Vanderbilt Clinic, just as you have the Annenberg Building at Mount Sinai Hospital.

"However, there is greater security on the part of the non-Jewish elite. Most Gentiles with status have had it for a long time. The late Barbara Paley had been a Cushing. Gentiles have had money longer and also experienced greater acceptance in society. WASP millionaires have always felt they belonged. The Gentiles feel wealth is natural, an integral part of themselves. To belong, Jews have had to fight. As a result, because Jews are defensive about and occasionally uncomfortable with their wealth, they make ostentatious gestures. They do not feel their wealth is natural."

Bar mitzvahs sometimes serve as occasion to show off wealth. At one such event, the host presented every guest with a gold watch. To mark the proud occasion, some parents redecorate their apartment or home. In the South the celebration has been known to start on Friday and end on Monday.

The children of elite Jews enjoy the wealthy style of life early. Some attend traditional summer camps such as Tripp Lake (where the children of Our Crowders went generations ago), Pinecliff, Fernwood and Laurel for girls in Maine. Tacomic is coed. Boys camps include Winnebago, Androscoggin, Wildwood, Takajo, Kohut, Woodmere, Brandt Lake, Racquet Lake.

However, it is currently more *de rigeur* for children to spend the summer at one of the educational programs sponsored by Choate Rosemary Hall, Andover, Phillips Exeter Academy, Putney. Some go off to a ranch. Other high school and college students take costly European tours. Still another popular summer alternative for elite teens is to live on a *kibbutz* or a Chinese tea commune.

On one occasion an excellent teen-tour group attempted to attract teenagers in upper Westchester and the Greenwich, Connecticut, area. Explains a Greenwich JEP homemaker, "Gentiles do not spend money in the same way. They got little response in Greenwich. But they got a big response ten miles down the road in Westchester. There a trip to Europe for a fourteen-year-old could be accepted. Jews have had exposure to Europe."

Today, however, even Greenwich is not exclusively Gentile. Years ago, when the late Bernard Gimbel had an estate called "Chieftains" in Greenwich, the area was called "The Polish Corridor" (Gimbel himself was of German descent; not Polish). Today Greenwich has many year-round Jewish residents as well as weekend people like financier Sanford Weill.

"New Canaan is an up and coming place for Jews," comments one JEP informant. "They are also moving up to the Madison-Lyme-Old Saybrook, Connecticut area." Recently, *New York* magazine ran an article portraying the northwestern Connecticut area as the new chic weekend place. One reason: Dr. Henry

Kissinger and his wife Nancy rented for the summer the New Milford house currently the property of Lady Slim Keith and formerly the property of the late Frederic March and Florence Eldridge March. New Milford, once the home of cashmere wearing Congregationalists and Polish farmers, had once been regarded as "extremely anti-Semitic." Today playwright Arthur Miller and Ted and Caroline Newhouse of the publishing family are among the many well-known Jews who live in the area.

Wealthy Jews have acquired estates as grand as Gentiles and Gentiles enjoy being entertained there. Sunnylands, the California residence of millionaire publisher Walter Annenberg, former ambassador to the Court of St. James, and his wife Leonore, until recently chief of protocol for the State Department, was the site of a 1981 New Year's Eve celebration which included President and Mrs. Reagan, Secretary of State Alexander Haig, Jr., Defense Secretary Caspar Weinberger, Supreme Court Justice Sandra Day O'Connor and her husband, Mr. and Mrs. Frank Sinatra and almost ninety other guests.

The two-hundred-acre estate, twenty minutes from Palm Springs (he also has homes in Wynnewood, Pennsylvania, and Sun Valley), is Annenberg's winter home and location of the famous Annenberg collection of Impressionist paintings; a framed document signifying that The Honorable Walter H. Annenberg was knighted by Queen Elizabeth II, the only American ambassador to have been so honored; a pool nestling beside one of the twelve lakes that feed the golf course. Almost as coveted as an invitation for dinner or the weekend is being asked to play the golf course. In the past, Annenberg has here entertained former Presidents Nixon and Ford, as well as Prince Charles.

THE CLUB WAY OF LIFE

Says a sixty-two-year-old grandmother, "My father was a member of the Harmonie Club. When my mother married my father, my grandfather said, "He is nice, but don't expect his *father* to become a member of the Harmonie."

Comments an eighty-year-old grande dame, "When my husband was on the admissions committee of Harmonie, they were not so quick to take people in."

But today everything has changed. "Nothing is elite anymore," claims an elderly Cincinnati resident. The elite country clubs and downtown clubs of America, founded by German Jews, will "take anyone if they have the money and are not common."

Such clubs include the Standard Club and Lake Shore Club of Chicago; Harmonie Club of New York; Hillcrest Country Club, Los Angeles; Century Country Club, Purchase, New York; Losantiville Country Club, Cincinnati; Westwood Country Club, St. Louis ("My mother still asks 'Who are their people?' " says one fifty-year-old member).

Octogenarian Rosalie Goldstein, a cousin of the prominent Pritzker clan of Chicago, recalls that in her youth, her sister Esther was going with a very successful young man. "He was the first man I knew of that age who had his own car," she muses. "He wanted to join the Standard Club of Chicago and had to go before the board of judges. He was blackballed. He was told, 'I like you very much as a person, but I refuse to sit down to dinner with you.' "

A successful lawyer's wife evaluates the country clubs of the Westchester County, New York, area today:

"Century—total snob appeal.

"Sunningdale is number two. When they get older and more moneyed, they move to Century.

"Quaker Ridge is number three.

"Fenway—totally new money from the cloak and suit and textile world, but there are more Rolls-Royces there than at any other club.

"Fairview in Greenwich, Connecticut—very expensive and new rich."

Like all the prominent country clubs, Hillcrest in Los Angeles used to be dominated by German Jews and the movie crowd. This has changed. Now businessmen of Eastern European origin form the majority. However, members include Danny Thomas (not Jewish), Dinah Shore, George Burns and ninety-one-year-old Rabbi Edgar F. Magnin who "is a fixture."

New York's Harmonie Club on East Sixtieth Street just off Fifth Avenue was founded in 1852 and is one of the oldest social clubs in New York. For forty-one years it was the Harmonie *Gesellschaft;* German was its official language and the kaiser's portrait hung in the hall. Before moving to its present site, it had been located on West Forty-second Street, a little more than a block away from the fourth location of Temple Emanu-El. The Harmonie building site later became Stern's Department Store and then the Graduate School and University Center of City University. A woman cannot join the Harmonie on her own ("She might marry someone unacceptable," comments a long-time member). At one country club with similar rules, a widow did marry someone "unacceptable" and had to resign.

Like other clubs, the Harmonie has become more Jewish. Bar mitzvahs are now held here. In the old days a group wanted to have Abba Eban as a speaker, but the board refused. Then came the Six-Day War in 1967 and members asked, "Could we get Eban as a speaker now?" It was arranged. The event was a sellout. Eban is now an honorary member of the Harmonie.

Says a board member of the Harmonie, "Origins and money do not matter. We try to avoid controversial people. The way to get in is to have at least six people who are members and who want you."

The Standard Club of Chicago reflects the history of Chicago and the men who helped build it. When it was founded in 1869, the club was known simply as the Standard. Early members included lawyer Philip Stein, architect Dankmar Adler, livestock broker Isaac Waixel, physician Michael Mannheumer, banker Gerhard Foreman, meat packer Nelson Morris, Elias, Michael and Henry Greenebaum, also bankers. According to its centennial history *The Standard Club of Chicago: 1869–1969,* "They typified the varied interests, backgrounds—social, religious, business and professional—that marked the entire group. Most were quite familiar with a memorable utterance made by George Washington in 1776, at the time of the founding of America itself. What Washington said was, 'Let us raise a *standard* to which honest men may repair.' "

Dankmar Adler died in April, 1900. He had left instructions

concerning his burial that were a moving tribute to the Standard Club. On his grave there was not to be an ordinary monument but a *standard* from one of his prized early creations, his Central Music Hall—a granite support he perhaps had saved for that purpose when the Music Hall was torn down as he was erecting the Standard Club's second clubhouse in 1889.

Today formal club life seems the province of the middle-aged and elderly. Lunching at the Harmonie on a recent Saturday were oil man Leon Hess, jeweler Henry Lambert and real estator Harold Uris—all old enough to receive Social Security if they needed it. America's younger JEPs seem to prefer tennis clubs. Says one woman, who just inherited a sizable estate from her father, "I play at people's private courts. That is where the socializing takes place."

Perhaps the newest change in club life is that Gentile clubs are taking in Jews—for example, Scarsdale Country Club now has Jewish members.

TEMPLE EMANU-EL

The eliteness of clubs has diminished. So has the importance of certain temples. Sinai Temple, located on the South Side of Chicago and once a major U.S. Reform congregation, has lost status because of its location. But Temple Emanu-El, the nation's premier Reform temple, for the last fifty-one years housed in the stately edifice at Sixty-fifth Street and Fifth Avenue, New York, retains its fame. Many of New York's most elite men and women belong to it. They include Maxwell M. Rabb, who served as its president until he became ambassador to Italy; Leonard Goldenson, head of the American Broadcasting Company; Mrs. Richard Rodgers, widow of the composer and known on her own as a taste arbiter; Iphigene Sulzberger of the *New York Times* family—to name just a few.

Temple Emanu-El came into being out of *Der Cultus Verein* (Cultural Association), a small group of men who, in 1845, wanting Judaism to speak to them effectively in the contemporary language of their day, banded together to "create such a service that shall arouse and quicken devotion and thus uplift the house of God." Thus, in a small rented room at Grand and Clinton streets, Emanu-El (meaning "God is with us") became the first Reform congregation in New York, the third in the United States.

Other cities also have glamorous temples: the prestigious Rodef Shalom Congregation in Pittsburgh, for example, and the Wilshire Boulevard Temple in Los Angeles, which has to its credit a number of conversions of show business personalities.

However, Emanu-El possesses such fame and clout that it has national and international influence. Little competition exists. It is the largest Jewish house of worship in the world—and some say the richest. A ten-story building could fit inside. It has the largest Reform membership—over three thousand families, close to nine thousand individuals. It consists of three buildings: the Sanctuary and Chapel on Fifth Avenue, the community house at One East Sixty-fifth Street and the Religious School and Lowenstein Auditorium on East Sixty-sixth Street. The list of donors reads like an honor list of American Jewry. The bronze entrance doors to the Temple were given by Mrs. Jacob H. Schiff, Mrs. Frieda S. Warburg, Mr. Mortimer J. Schiff in honor of Jacob Schiff. The bronze entrance doors to the Chapel were given by Hugh Grant Straus in honor of his parents, Nathan and Lina Straus. Herbert Lehman gave the Rose Window in memory of Mayer and Babette Lehman.

Many have termed Emanu-El "the best bargain in town." For a minimal amount members receive many bonuses—free lectures by celebrities, an eighteen-voice choir, Sunday school for children, free marriage or burial services in the Chapel. As of this writing, a family membership costs $290 and some of this can be applied to seats for the High Holy days of Rosh Hashanah and Yom Kippur. For these special days, front-row seats in the Fifth Avenue Sanctuary run high and many have been held by the same families for generations.

It also is open to all. Anyone—whether foreign visitor, U.S. tourist or Manhattan resident—is welcome to attend services or simply to walk in and worship. The day after President Kennedy was shot, one young woman felt "I had to go somewhere for solace." She went to Emanu-El and found the Sanctuary jammed with people who wanted to be silent together in their sorrow.

Many celebrities belong to the congregation. Walter Mack, who once headed the Pepsi-Cola Company, serves as treasurer of the congregation. Robert Morgenthau, New York's district attorney, serves on the board. He represents the third generation of his family to be an Emanu-El member. His grandfather, Henry Morgenthau, ambassador to Turkey under President Wilson, and father Henry Morgenthau, Jr., also belonged. (Henry Morgenthau had been president of the Free Synagogue, New York, until he had a fight with Rabbi Stephen Wise over Wise's Zionist stand. He left the Free Synagogue and joined Emanu-El.)

Other current members include two ex-ambassadors (Walter Annenberg and Warren D. Manshel), a cosmetics-company chairman (Estée Lauder), a best-selling author (Theodore White) and several politicians, including Andrew Stein, borough president of Manhattan, and Congressman William Green.

Like the rest of America, Emanu-El has become more Jewish. It is a misconception that only rich German-Jewish Wall Streeters belong. There is a whole new membership that includes Seventh Avenue manufacturers, media experts, small businessmen, middle-management executives. A few members of the Old Guard German families still serve on the temple's board—John L. Loeb, Robert Bernhard, whose mother was a Lehman, Robert M. Morgenthau, Oscar Straus II and John B. Oakes (*Ochs* became *Oakes* at the time of World War I). The rest are primarily of Eastern European descent. Comments one longtime member acidly, "It is hard to get on the board. The temple keeps your donations and puts you in the men's club."

In recent years the temple's rabbis have all been non-Germans (this is a break from tradition; in the early years services were conducted in German). Says Rabbi Ronald Sobel, senior rabbi of the congregation, whose grandparents were Orthodox Jewish, "Because of the passage of time, the place of origin becomes less important. We can no longer speak of the German-Jewish congregation. We have an egalitarian congregation. New

York City is a mirror of America and—in the United States—Emanu-El reflects the American Jewish experience."

There has been a modest introduction of some elements of traditionalism; use of a little more Hebrew. One spots an occasional *yarmulke* ("skullcap"). Says a veteran member bitterly, "Years ago you would have been asked to remove it."

And, in 1972, because of parental pressures and an increasing desire for ritual, Emanu-El came full circle. It reintroduced bar mitzvahs for boys and introduced bas mitzvahs for girls. The bar mitzvahs for boys had been dropped by the temple in the early 1870s. It is said that Rabbi Sobel wanted to have his two young sons bar-mitzvahed and told the board he would have the ceremony performed at another temple if it could not be done at Emanu-El.

To acquaint members with this new policy, Emanu-El sent out "A Guide for Bar Mitzvah and Bas Mitzvah Celebrations," detailing the meaning of the terms, moral obligations, requirements, preparations for the ceremony.

The "Guide" offers suggestions for decorum, pointing out to parents that they should not stand and look for their guests since this serves as a distraction "for all those seated behind you." It also points out that family and friends should not wave or signal to each other nor take walks with their children inside the Sanctuary.

The "Guide" is specific on the customs of Temple Emanu-El: "It is not the custom at Temple Emanu-El to wear a *kippah* (skull cap) or a *tallis* (prayer shawl). If any of your guests are devoutly orthodox, please remind them that Temple Emanu-El is a Reform Congregation." However, it also specifies that if any male worshipper should request a *kippah,* the ushers will happily provide one.

The "Guide" concludes by noting that no food is ever served in the Temple following worship. It asks that "the reception for your guests after Service be marked by the same atmosphere in which the celebration took place—with simplicity, good taste, and graciousness."

According to Rabbi Sobel, "There was not one resignation because of the reintroduction of bar mitzvahs."

Rabbi Sobel has spent his entire rabbinical career, since ordination, at Temple Emanu-El—first as assistant rabbi, then as associate. The congregation gave him the post of senior rabbi in 1974. He has now finished his dissertation on the history of Temple Emanu-El. Many members of the congregation call him "Ronnie." In turn, he calls them—male and female—"darling."

Rabbi Sobel lives at what is called "the parsonage" on upper Fifth Avenue. Mrs. Julius Mark, widow of the noted Emanu-El rabbi, still lives in the Park Avenue co-op owned by the temple. When Rabbi Mark retired in 1968, the temple provided him with an office on the ninth floor of One East Sixty-fifth Street.

The temple wants to be of service to the community. It lends space in its religious school building to Hunter College for use as classrooms at a minimal charge. Numerous volunteer groups exist at Emanu-El, including English in Action, Help for Veterans, a Center for Older People.

Temple Emanu-El tries to give—financially, spiritually, practically. The three rabbis will provide counseling; they are available 24 hours a day. They have a fund (said to be around $100,000 annually) with which they can aid individuals in need, provide loans to worthwhile organizations or even increase pensions of former employees.

Recently a young Iranian refugee walked into the temple's Gift Shop. She had made some silk flowers which the shop took on as salable items. Lonely and eager for new friends, she eventually joined the temple. When it appeared she needed legal help because her husband was not sending the required child support for their two children, the temple immediately provided her with a matrimonial lawyer.

Emanu-El satisfies the needs of Jews who want Reform Judaism, religion without stress on ritual. The members love Emanu-El. One cantor loved the temple so much he named his daughter Emanuella. The late Richard Rodgers is said to have stated he received the inspiration for the ballad "You'll Never Walk Alone" from *Carousel* while sitting in a pew at Emanu-El.

Despite its democratization (black ties are no longer worn at board meetings), the occasional Yiddish jokes told at meetings (one lecturer used the word *shtetl,* then paused and asked the audience "Am I allowed to use that word here?"), the new multitude of members whose names end in *witz* and *ski* (Eastern European) rather than *stein* and *berg* (usually German), Emanu-El still symbolizes eliteness. Sunday school is held on Wednesdays and Sundays. Like mid-week dinner parties, it is a necessity. Many members of the congregation have country homes and want their children with them on the weekends.

MAKING IT SOCIALLY

A town or street bearing the family name represents the height of elitism. About twenty-six miles west of Modesto is a small town, Newman, California, with a population of about three thousand. Simon Newman, who had come to California from Germany in the 1870s, founded it in about 1880. The town still exists and Walter and Ellen Newman (she is the daughter of Cyril Magnin of the department-store family) are considered one of San Francisco's most elite couples.

Both Alan Kempner and his son Thomas live on Kempner Lane in Purchase, New York. The Kempners are considered among the most elite of New York Jewry. Thomas Kempner's wife Nan regularly makes the "Eye" column of *Women's Wear Daily* and the fashion notes of the *New York Times.* A recent item commented, "It would be difficult to find a woman as tall, thin, or sensibly fashionable as Viscountess Jacqueline de Ribes . . . the only woman in the same league as the Viscountess was Nan Kempner in a furry, silver coupe de velour one-shouldered dress by Carolina Herrera."

Courtly, Atlanta-born Earl Blackwell, who publishes the *Celebrity Bulletin,* a daily rundown of celebrities arriving in New York, where they stay and how they can be reached, moves at the core of New York society and has been termed "An Ultimate Party Person."

Asked whether a Jew can make it in the current equivalent of "the 400," he asserts, "I don't think there is any anti-Semitism at all. I am on the board of The Nine O'Clocks (an organization which exists for the sole purpose of sponsoring an annual ball) and Doubles (a private club). Being Jewish does not enter into it. It is whether you are eligible or not eligible. Eligible means attractive, personable and sometimes achieving. I am not aware of any difference between Jewish elite and elite."

Blackwell offers advice for those JEPs who want to make it socially:

- Take an active interest in the arts or charity work. Always be willing to work and donate money to charity. That way you will be welcome. You can't just send a check and think that will do it.
- Dress in designer clothes but underplay.
- Entertain but in a low-key manner.
- If you are ambitious socially, never show it, and be prepared to take a dozen years to achieve it.
- If you have flair, you can live anywhere, but you have to be very sure of yourself. Personality can make anything chic.
- Do not hire a publicist. People don't do this anymore. That has been a change of the last twenty years. In the fifties there was a café society—people hired public-relations people. New York had six or seven newspapers and lots of space to fill. Now designers such as Halston do have publicity people but they work for the firm. Suzy gets her information from restaurants, theater and motion picture companies and friends.
- Send your children to good private schools.

Female JEPs echo the "good school and club" refrain. Says one Connecticut matron, "Children get their social life through the schools. On weekends your son may get invited to go with little Johnny to a family farm in upstate New York, Litchfield, the Hamptons. But you have to prime the child. The Skating Club of New York is hard to get into. If they ask 'Do you like to skate?' and he answers 'No,' that will be the end of that."

SOME PEOPLE WHO HAVE MADE IT SOCIALLY

Some JEPs are born with a gold spoon in their mouth. Nevertheless, they are serious about helping others less fortunate. They adopt a life-style that encompasses more work than play, accepts challenges and promotes change.

Valerie Diker

Valerie Diker comes from the well-known Tishman family, once thought of as *parvenu*, now in the words of the Century Country Club dowager, "practically old money." She is the daughter of Norman and Rita Tishman, the cousin of Robert and Alan Tishman (see chap. 9). She was raised in the world of the New York Jewish elite: Hunter Model School, Dalton, Smith College, Camp Tripp Lake, Temple Emanu-El.

"I think observing is part of being Jewish," claims Diker, who married a self-made man from a Conservative background. Her three children have all been bar-mitzvahed or bas-mitzvahed at Temple Emanu-El. Her older boy, Bruce, twenty, and at Harvard, was among the first to go through the reinstituted Temple Emanu-El bar-mitzvah ceremony. Her daughter Patty wrote her own service.

The large Diker apartment on Fifth Avenue is monotoned, carefully designed to display their collection of modern art. Works by Warhol, Dubuffet, Nevelson, Arp, Martin hang in the living room.

"We are very much into the art community," says Diker. "We started collecting modestly as soon as we were married. When Chuck's career got underway, we really started to buy. The art changes all the time. When you put it in a new place, a painting gets a new life. The Dubuffet used to be out in the foyer. We fit in. We weed out. When something which has been on loan to a museum comes back, it has lost its place."

Husband Charles Diker exemplifies the man who has made it on brains. When he was in his first year at Harvard Business School, the late Charles Revson, the curmudgeon head of Revlon, Inc., came to Cambridge to give a lecture. Diker asked a question which impressed Revson. After the talk Diker went up to Revson to continue the dialogue. Asked the king of the beauty industry, "What are you doing this summer?" Thus was Diker's career launched. That summer he served as assistant to Revson, returned to the firm after graduation from Harvard Business School and, at twenty-nine, became a Revlon vice-president. Now, president of Charles M. Diker Associates and a limited partner at Weiss, Peck & Greer, he serves on the boards of Neutragena Inc. and Dico Petroleum, is a managing partner in U.S. Licensing, and also consultant to five major companies.

The Dikers have an elegant life-style. "We are at benefits almost every night, but we try to be home two nights a week," says Valerie Diker. They entertain frequently, sometimes at sit-down dinners for forty. She is known for her creative table settings. They belong to Century Country Club, the Harmonie ("It is not as exclusive as it used to be and would like to be. There are not as many German Jews who keep themselves in isolation. Now it is wealth without a history"). They have a country house. The two younger children attend Spence and Collegiate.

Yet, with all the signs of wealth, Valerie Diker is no pretty dilettante. She works full-time without pay as vice-president of the Israeli Tennis Centers Association (ITCA). Designed to provide free public tennis for the children of Israel, the ITCA opened the first free public tennis facility in Israel at Ramat Hasharon five years ago. Today fifty thousand youngsters from eight to sixteen participate and ITCA facilities also exist in Haifa, Jena, Kiriot Shmona, Arad, Ashkelon, and Jaffa-South Tel Aviv.

"Many of the participants used to be juvenile delinquents," notes Diker. "In some areas the crime rate among young children has declined by as much as 50 percent. There have been other changes. Children with no purpose or respect for authority are now learning court etiquette, sportsmanship and the importance of physical fitness."

Last year she helped raise $3 million. As vice-president, Diker heads up the eastern half of the United States. She gives speeches, gets prospective donors together, hosts meetings, handles public relations and "motivates people."

She explains, "At Kiriot Shmona every Sunday our tennis pro goes across the border and brings fifty Lebanese kids back to play with the Israeli children. They even have a bomb shelter. While their parents are shooting, the children are playing tennis."

"If they do not need the paycheck, more people who have time should be doing what I am doing," she adds intensely. "When society has given you a good life, it is basic that you give back. Giving money is easy. It is service that distinguishes the men from the boys, women from the girls."

Robert Sakowitz

"The son of any successful man—especially in the fashion field—has certain preconceptions to overcome. One is the misconception of a playboy in the business. All my life I have tried not to appear as one but as a businessman. I have never been interested in being jet set."

So says merchant prince Robert Tobias Sakowitz, forty-three, president, chief executive officer and board chairman of Sakowitz, Inc., one of the nation's last privately held group of fashion specialty stores.

"I was taught to achieve," adds the handsome bachelor (he is divorced). "I was expected to perform. I operated the elevator. As a kid of nine I marked shirts. I sold men's clothing at Christmas and during the summers, but did not get involved in the women's fashion business until I was adult. We were comfortable, but I did not feel wealthy. There was no cash flow because everything was reinvested in the business. Dad had a nice life but not flush with liquidity."

Robert Sakowitz's great-grandfather Louis came to America from Russia in the 1880s. "At Ellis Island he wrote his name in Cyrillic; the officials looked at the strange characters and wrote it as 'Sakowitz,' " proudly relates great-grandson "Mr. Robert." Convinced by a member of the Galveston Chamber of Commerce that the port city had opportunities, Louis Sakowitz established a ship's chandlery primarily for merchant seamen. His sons Tobias (Sakowitz's grandfather) and Simon opened their own gentlemen's haberdashery store in Galveston in 1902, and then a second in Houston in 1910.

By the 1920s Sakowitz had become a big name in the Houston retailing business. In 1929 Bernard Sakowitz, Tobias's son, joined his father and helped to further expand the business. Robert Sakowitz joined the business in 1963 and, together with his father, in the forthcoming decade, negotiated to buy out all other family interests. Robert became president and chief executive officer in 1975. After his father's death in 1981, he became chairman of the board. Even if he was born with a gold spoon in his mouth, Robert Sakowitz had made good on his own.

He has innovated several marketing concepts: "The Ultimate Gift"—a witty annual series of themes, and lessons, ranging from the "Gifts of Knowledge" to "Your Dreams Come True." He launched the European boutique concept in America, introducing André Corrèges in 1965 and Yves Saint Laurent Rive Gauche in 1967 in his stores. In June, 1981, he gained entry into the world of fashion publishing with the debut of *The Magazine,* a large-size tabloid in color, which he calls "a preview of the future in fashion." And he has gained national attention with a series of international festivals.

Even as a young boy, Sakowitz showed merchandising creativity. His family kept chickens in the backyard. Sakowitz used to take the eggs, place them in a box and sell them. First, he would note the price at Weingarten's Grocery and then charge two cents more a dozen. Prospective customers would inquire, "Why are yours more?" Sakowitz's response: "They were laid this A.M." and "I'm delivering."

After attending Sutton Elementary School, St. John's preparatory school ("I played Ronald Colman's part in *Lost Horizons*") he went on to Harvard, from which he graduated cum laude in economics and history.

For a while, Robert Sakowitz worked at Galeries Lafayette in Paris, then returned to the United States. He joined the air force reserve, spent six months on active duty and then told his father he wanted to enter the retail business in America. "I want to prove myself with another store," he said at dinner one night.

"When and if we can get together sometime, I'd probably like to come back to Houston, but only on a sink-or-swim basis."

Sakowitz obtained a job with Macy's, New York, first as an executive trainee, then as assistant buyer, then associate. One day in 1963 he received a phone call from his father in Houston. The buyer's job had just opened up in the junior department. "Report in thirty days if you're interested," ordered his father. He added, "Sink or swim."

Robert Sakowitz swam. Within two years he was merchandising for other innovative Sakowitz departments. He introduced a series of cultural and commercial festivals at the store ranging from the "Britannic Festival" to "Hats Off to Houston," from a "Great American Southwest Celebration" to "The Celebration of Franco-American Friendship" (at which he received the French National Order of Merit from Giscard d'Estaing.

In January 1969 Robert Sakowitz left his bachelor life behind when he married Pamela Zauderer in a spectacular nuptial event. After seven years the marriage ended in divorce. However, there is an adopted son Robbie whom father Robert Sakowitz adores.

Sakowitz is firm in his Jewish faith. He states, "We were married by our family rabbi from Temple Beth Israel in Houston. I always attend services on Rosh Hashanah and Yom Kippur and part of my divorce agreement was that I get my son on one of the two major Jewish holidays and that at the right age he go to Jewish religious school." Sakowitz is not observant in the ritual sense ("Religion is an institutionalized activity. Faith is a personal belief.")

During school he experienced anti-Semitism. He recalls, "St. John's was an Episcopal school. Unfortunately, I was one of the first Jewish kids there and children can be cruel. That is why I took up boxing." He was one of the first Jewish members in the exclusive Fly Club at Harvard. Remembers Sakowitz, "A prospective member made anti-Semitic remarks. When the time came to consider his candidacy, I told the others I did not want to be the only one to keep him out. The policy was that one blackball would do it, and I said I would prefer to abstain. When the 'shoe', containing the white balls and black balls, came to me, there were no black balls left to throw." He has not encountered anti-Semitism in retailing. "There are too many Jewish people involved," he says with a smile.

For his work Sakowitz, travels frequently to Europe and the Far East (between 90 and 150 days a year). He skis and scuba dives, collects art and wine. He has been named to the International Ten Best-Dressed list so many times that the organization retired him into its hall of fame in 1974 (his syster Lynn, the wife of Coastal States Gas magnate Oscar Wyatt, Jr., has also been retired).

"Responsibility, challenges, the shock of divorce and my father's death have rearranged my priorities," he admits. "If people wanted to perceive me as glamorous, I used to feel it was good for the business. The best-dressed list and hall of fame would not hurt my personal life and might help the business. As general merchandise manager, I was looking at immediacy and living in the now of business. As chief executive officer, my definition of 'now' is three to four years away."

Robert Sakowitz has received many awards and served on numerous boards, including the American Institute for Public Service (he helped found it), American Council for the Arts, Foundation for the Joffrey Ballet, Inc., The Houston Festival, National Conference of Christians and Jews, Houston Symphony and many others.

He comments, "Elites are people who achieve. Certain American cities refuse to allow new people in society until they have become established, but if you lock new people out, the city will decay. Houston allows in new groups of achievers. Money can be part of achievement. However, here if you are a good professor, but without money, you are in. That holds true for people from NASA and Texas Medical Center. People who define achievement as money do not leave room for any other form of success. It is unfortunate for them and society."

He feels that a retail store has a community obligation: "I was taught by my grandfather, great-uncle and father to have a tremendous sense of obligation to the community. If you make a lot of money, you can plow it back into the community in the form of philanthropic work."

The dimpled, dark Sakowitz has to be one of the nation's most eligible bachelors. Says a Houston businesswoman, "He is very naive about how attractive he is. Women call him at the store with some line like 'I am thinking of starting a store.' They get to him through business rather than society."

Sakowitz admits that friends talk to him about remarrying. Will he marry again? His answer: "I would like to. This time I would hopefully listen more and communicate better."

THE JEWISH GESTURE

As noted in chapter 14, on December 9, 1981, some eight hundred members of New York's financial community pledged over $6 million to UJA-Federation. The last pledge at the fund-raising dinner, held at the New York Hilton, was made by a teenage boy who told the assembled group of big givers, "I'm Bill Boesky and I pledge $100."

At fifteen, Bill Boesky, son of securities arbitrageur Ivan Boesky, himself a major contributor to Jewish charity, had made a *beau geste.* The senior Boesky had brought his children to the adult dinner; he wanted them to learn early in life the blessedness of giving—in accord with the biblical injunction "Thou shall open thine hand wide unto they brother."

Translated from the French, *beau geste* means "generous gesture." It can be graceful, selfless and magnanimous. It can also be selfish, idiosyncratic and prideful.

Sometimes the gesture can stem from an aristocratic untouchability. Even though the world may be falling apart, the person goes his/her own way. In the unpublished genealogical history of the Cone family, Benjamin Cone relates an anecdote about his aunt, the famous art collector, Dr. Claribel Cone of Baltimore. In 1917, at the time the United States entered the war against Germany, Dr. Cone was doing "medical research and art collecting" in Munich. Her brother Ceasar [*sic*] Cone had contacted many of the top men in President Wilson's administration to "arrange for her return to the United States with the American diplomatic corps in their private train." Dr. Cone refused this courtesy because she was not permitted a private compartment on the train for her ample person nor space in the baggage car for her ten to fifteen trunks. "She would not change her habits just because of a World War," wrote her nephew, "and she sat out the war in her Munich hotel with her many trunks and did not return home until the war ended."

In other instances the *beau geste* can occur because of political persuasion. In her *Iphigene,* Iphigene Ochs Sulzberger reminisces about her grandparents. Julius Ochs abhorred slavery and fought for the Union. Bertha Ochs was a die-hard Confederate who would cross the Ohio River from Cincinnati to the Kentucky side, smuggling drugs like quinine to the Confederates in the baby carriage of son George. When, twenty-five years after the Civil War, Julius Ochs died, a unit of the Grand Army of the Republic officiated at the funeral and the Union flag was draped over his coffin in accord with his wishes. When Bertha Ochs died two decades later, seventy-five members of her chapter of the Daughters of the Confederacy attended her funeral, and, according to her wishes, a Confederate flag was placed in her coffin. But love and primacy of family transcended political disputes. Julius and Bertha Ochs are buried side by side in the Mizpah Cemetery in Chattanooga.

Current day JEPs also base attitudes and actions on strong personal belief. Lyn Revson (widow of Charles Revson, but they were divorced before he died), who moves with a mixed set of Jews and Gentiles, almost all moneyed, refused to have her daughter come out. "I felt Jews don't do that," she says.

Some JEPs make the *beau geste* because their money gives them the confidence to do what they want to do—even if it flaunts social practices.

One JEP matron recently embarked on a liaison with a married president of a major industrial company. Both became ill simultaneously—she with diabetes, he with liver problems—took adjoining rooms in Doctors Hospital, New York, where it is possible to order food and beverage service, and give a cocktail party for a group of friends. In the sophisticated atmosphere of the East Side hospital suite, the martinis flowed.

In another instance, a wealthy Chicago couple—let us call them Mr. and Mrs. Jones—have two large apartments in the same building on Lake Shore Drive. Paula Smith, as she was then, met Ben Jones (both assumed names) at an elegant Valentine's Day party. She was the widow of a noted doctor, and he was married with a sick wife. They fell in love. For convenience' sake, she moved into an apartment on the fifteenth floor of his building. When, after years of a debilitating illness, his wife finally died, Paula Smith became Mrs. Jones. They kept the two apartments. She explains, "We live in the one upstairs. I use the one downstairs as an office and for guests."

In the life of the well-to-do, certain practices seem practical. During her years as editor of *Seventeen* magazine, Enid A. Haupt would leave the office about five o'clock and then proceed to get her "exercise." Handing her purse and briefcase to the chauffeur of her Rolls-Royce, she would stroll up Park Avenue while he drove slowly beside her. When Mrs. Haupt felt she had walked enough, she would signal him to stop and climb in the back of the car.

Mrs. Haupt has always been known as a very chic woman. Once while in San Francisco, she purchased several long and very expensive silk robes at Gump's, a local landmark. She ordered the saleswoman, "Cut them off at the knee. I prefer them that way."

A *beau geste* can alter a life-style or even attract a spouse. According to Leon Harris in *The Merchant Princes,* William Rosenwald, youngest and only living son of Julius Rosenwald, had been in analysis in Philadelphia for many years with Dr. Herman Nunberg. When Dr. Nunberg moved to New York, Rosenwald, not wanting to lose him, moved there too. It is said that one of the seven Annenberg sisters met her husband as they both bid for a Picasso at a Parke-Bernet auction.

Real estate ventures provide opportunities for *beau gestes* that result in comfort and convenience.

As is common knowledge, for many years Aline Bernstein, the theatrical designer who was married to the well-to-do Theo Bernstein, had an affair with writer Thomas Wolfe (younger than she and anti-Semitic, he used to call her "My dear Jew").

The Bernsteins had a house built in Armonk, New York. A private outside staircase led from the terrace to the Dutch doors that opened onto Aline Bernstein's bedroom. According to Carole Klein in *Aline,* some referred to this as "Tom Wolfe's stairway."

According to his sister, Mrs. Bennett Epstein of Scarsdale, Lawrence Greenbaum, one of the founders of the law firm Greenbaum Wolff & Ernst helped organize Beachpoint Club at Orienta Point, Mamaroneck, so that he could store his boat near his house. (When he went off to Williams College, his first stop was the golf course. Carefully, he checked out the club hours and then elected his classes so that the time would not interfere with his golf.)

Because he was Jewish, Jesse Straus, president of Macy's and later ambassador to France, was barred from the best of the Park Avenue apartment houses. This did not discourage him. In 1927, he purchased a corner of Seventieth Street and Park Avenue and there built 730 Park Avenue, at least the equivalent of the Park Avenue buildings from which he had been excluded. According to *The Merchant Princes,* he later built 720 Park as well

Many people like to live near their work. The late Edwin Goodman, retail merchant, built a large and lavish penthouse above Bergdorf Goodman at Fifth Avenue and Fifty-eighth Street, New York. When he learned that city rules forbade anyone except a superintendent to live in a building where manufacturing took place (in this case, custom clothes and furs), Edwin immediately listed himself as "janitor." Son Andrew Goodman, chairman of Bergdorf Goodman, still lives above the store.

Sometimes Jewish gestures are simply idiosyncratic. Banker James Seligman, son of immigrant David, was hard of hearing and his children, as described by his granddaughter, the late Peggy Guggenheim in *Out of This Century*, were "peculiar, if not mad." One of James's nieces was an incurable soprano. If a friend or relative happened to meet her on the corner of Fifth Avenue while waiting for a bus, she would open her mouth wide and sing scales while trying to make the other person do the same.

James's son Washington lived on charcoal and cracked ice and ate almost no food. He drank whiskey before breakfast. He gambled heavily, and when he was without funds, he threatened suicide to get more money out of James. He had a mistress whom he concealed in his room. No one was allowed to visit him and he finally shot himself. At the funeral, James greatly shocked his children by walking up the aisle with his dead son's mistress on his arm.

An action may seem idiosyncratic because it is unexpected. When Mrs. Irma Bloomingdale, now a Scarsdale resident, still lived on her Westchester estate, Elm Ridge Farm, she used to be quite active in the Women's Guild of the Jewish Community Center, White Plains. She would leave the meetings early. When others exited, they would find her at the open back door of her station wagon, selling eggs from Elm Ridge Farm.

Love and marriage offers the chance for a wide range of gestures.

According to close family friends, when she was about seventy, a member of the Lewi family of Albany, New York, read that an old boyfriend, whom she had known half a century ago, had lost his wife. She sent him a condolence note. He wrote back suggesting she look him up when she next came to New York. She did, and the courtship began. After one of his visits to Albany an elderly friend asked Miss Lewi, "Did you play cards?" She reportedly answered, "He does not come to Albany to play cards." But finally deciding she was just too old for marriage, Miss Lewi, in a generous *beau geste,* introduced her boyfriend to her niece, who was in her fifties. They married soon after.

As with their bar mitzvahs, Old and New Crowd Jews have long been known for the lavishness of their weddings. In his memoirs *Call Me Cyril,* Cyril Magnin, who has been called "Mr. San Francisco," recalls that when he married Anna Smithline, his grandmother Mary Ann Magnin paid for the reception at the Hotel St. Francis and also gave the bridal couple $5,000. He writes, "I must have been very special to her because when the other grandchildren, around twelve of them in all, were married, her gift to them was a grand piano." At Cyril Magnin's spectacular wedding, grandmother Magnin had her florist cut holes in the tabletops in which a bouquet of flowers was set. He remembers, "They appeared to be growing right out of the table. The silver flatware was gold-plated and the crystal and china were the finest money could buy. It was so grand it was almost overwhelming. I've never forgotten it."

In another lavish affair, the family business provided some special decorations. During the wedding ceremony of Mrs. Max Stern's daughter Madie Lindenbaum at the Jewish Center many years ago, Hartz Mountain canaries (the Stern business) flew about the Sanctuary, trilling majestically. At the reception later, recalls one guest, the centerpiece at each table was a cage, filled with flowers and a stuffed canary.

Sometimes the display of enormous wealth can impress the wealthy themselves. Consider the time in the mid-fifties when Ann Loeb, of German and Sephardic ancestry and daughter of financier John L. Loeb, became engaged to Edgar Bronfman of Eastern European ancestry—a union which would unite two of the world's wealthiest Jewish families. At a prenuptial luncheon, a matron came up to grandfather Carl M. Loeb, patriarch of the Loeb Rhoades & Company banking house. She gushed about this wondrous union of the beautiful young couple. The elderly Loeb replied, "At my age I am not sure I can adjust to the idea of being a poor relation."

In another nuptial *beau geste* which reflects the stylish acknowledgement of divorce in contemporary times, Edgar Bronfman, now the chairman of the billion dollar Joseph E. Seagram & Sons Inc., married Englishwoman Georgiana Eileen Webb on the lawn behind his Yorktown Heights, New York, mansion on August 20, 1975. Guests included Mr. Bronfman's first wife, Ann Loeb, who, according to a *New York Times* article, had spent the past week at the mansion together with the bride-to-be.

Giving also serves as a basis for the Jewish *beau geste.* In personal life gifts show panache. The late Samuel Irving Newhouse, the newspaper magnate known as S. I., bought the Conde Nast chain of magazines. He did it, he said, so he could give his wife, Mitzi, *Vogue* for her birthday.

Benjamin Buttenwieser, eighty-one, of the Lehman Brothers Kuhn Loeb banking house, is married to the former Helen Lehman, seventy-six, a well-known lawyer. Says the urbane and charming Buttenwieser, "When Helen became sixty years old, I asked her what she would like for her birthday. She answered, 'A driver.' Buttenwieser walks the five miles from his home to the office. He also has his bicycle. "I never use the car," he claims twinkling. "What is good enough for a secretary is good enough for me. I'm a nut on athletics."

Georgiana Bronfman, daughter of a retired architect who operates the Ye Olde Nosebag Inn in England, learned the Jewish elite way of life quickly since her aforementioned marriage six years ago. In 1981 Mrs. Bronfman gave Mr. Bronfman an eleven-year-old quarterhorse named Jesse James. At the time she said, "Edgar will have to buy the hay." It should not be too much of a problem for the Seagram executive.

There are also gifts that serve the public interest—for instance, Paley Park in New York, where weary passersby can rest their feet and Gerstle Park in San Rafael, California. Art collections provide the public with pleasure as well as perpetuate the name of the donor. There is the Guggenheim Museum, the Robert Lehman Wing of the Metropolitan Museum of Art, the Joseph Hirshhorn Museum and Sculpture Garden in Washington, D.C.—to name just a few.

Nate Cummings, a founder of Consolidated Foods and now honorary chairman of the board of directors (he is known as "Mr. Sara Lee") has a collection of Vuillards, Monets and Picassos that has been exhibited everywhere from the Metropolitan to the National Gallery, Washington, D.C. In a splendid *beau geste* he gave his valued Pre-Columbian Collection to the Metropolitan a few years ago and also donated the Nathan Cummings Art Center to Stanford University for the purpose of providing a multifaceted student facility for study and exhibitions. He also established the Joanne and Nate Cummings Art Center at Connecticut College for Women.

A gift can also be a *beau geste* that shows support. In February, 1981, Georgetown University in Washington, D.C., returned to the government of Libya more than $600,000 plus interest of a gift it had received to endow a professorship in its Center for Contemporary Arab Studies. The Reverend Timothy S. Healy,

Georgetown's president, said Georgetown gave back the gift because it did not want to have "its name associated" with a government that supports terrorism.

When Alan Greenberg and his partners at Bear, Stearns & Company read about the university's moral stance, they decided upon a gesture of their own. They sent Georgetown $100,000 of Bear Stearns money to help offset the school's sacrifice. Surprised and grateful, the Reverend Healy commented, "This is the first time I've ever seen a gift before I saw the giver."

Recent *beau gestes* reflect the new concern with Jewish affairs. In 1974 the late Benjamin Harrison Swig of Swig, Weiler & Arnow, celebrated his eightieth birthday by getting bar-mitzvahed at the western wall in Jerusalem.

In many cases Jewish weddings have become simpler and more Jewish. In *Our City* Irena Narell writes of a young couple whose wedding took place in a grove on the Stanford University campus in the late summer of 1976. Both were graduate students and had met five years earlier in a Jewish literature course. The bride, whose ancestors include the distinguished Lewis Gerstles and the Louis Slosses of San Francisco, had just received a degree from the School of Religion. The groom had distinguished himself as a decathlon champion.

They were married by a rabbi beneath a cloth *chuppah* ("wedding canopy") held up fittingly by four javelins. Afterward the pair went inside to change and emerged in jogging clothes. They wore identical T-shirts marked "Just Married." "They went jogging around Stanford to the roaring applause of their amused and delighted relatives," writes Mrs. Narell. Their wedding trip was to Israel. A year later the groom captured the gold medal for the United States at the Israeli Maccabiah Games for the second time. From Germany to San Francisco to Jerusalem in five generations.

Certain *beau gestes* have helped pave the way to harmony between Christians and Jews. In 1975 Rabbi Ronald Sobel of Temple Emanu-El spoke at St. Patrick's Cathedral (the first rabbi to do so) and then more than twelve hundred Jews and Catholics walked the fifteen blocks up Fifth Avenue to hear Mgr. James F. Rigney speak at Emanu-El. Said Rabbi Sobel at the time, "We have begun to learn what many of our fathers never knew; namely, that theological differences and divergent views of history's meaning need not be impediments to understanding or barriers to love."

And there is the *beau geste* of Jewish compassion which surmounts barriers of distance and language. Recently Elaine Winik, now president of the UJA of Greater New York, and a member of the executive committee of the Joint Distribution Committee, and her husband Norman Winik went to China. They had been given the name and address (in Chinese characters) of Max Liebovich, one of the members of a Shanghai Jewish refugee Community, who had gone there from Bialystok, Russia. For five years Liebovich had not been able to speak. With the help of a Chinese woman, the Winiks found Liebowitz living in a slum and wearing a *yarmulke.* In Yiddish, Elaine Winik, who was wearing a big Star of David, said "I am a Jew from New York. This is my Mogen David." Replied Liebowitz, "Mogen David" ("Star of David"). He refused her offers of financial aid but when she asked, "Would you like other Jews to come and see you?" his eyes shone. Everyone cried.

Surely the *beau geste* possesses the most significance when it expresses deep feeling, conviction and remembrance. In New York there is a special temple which calls itself Congregation Habonim. The congregation was founded on November 9, 1939. That date marked the first anniversary of "Crystal Night," when Hitler's hordes put the torch to all synagogues in Germany, thereby signaling the beginning of the end of Jewish life in Europe. The founders of the congregation were a different kind of German Jew from those who had come to America a century before to make fortunes. These were refugees who had managed to escape the Holocaust, save themselves from extinction in a death camp and find a haven in America. Immediately, they determined to rebuild in a land of freedom a House of Worship which, in a new and different environment, would enshrine some of the values and memories they had brought with them. And so they called their House of Worship Congregation "Habonim," meaning "The Builders."

Following World War II, permission was obtained from the

remnants of Jewish communities in Germany to bring to this country some of the rubble of Germany's destroyed synagogues. The stones, which came from Berlin, Aachen, Cologne, Essen, Hanover, Dortmund, Würzburg, Nuremberg and Mannheim, were made into a high sculpture by artist Emanuel Milstein, and Congregation Habonim's *Memorial to the Six Million* was dedicated on Passover, 1974. Conceived as a memorial tribute to the memory of the 6 million martyrs and the destroyed religious, educational and cultural institutions which European Jewry had built, the memorial conveys the spirit of the inscription at the base of the altar: "I shall not die, but live and declare the works of the Lord."

16

WHO WILL BE THE JEPS OF TOMORROW?

"MY FAMILY believes that everyone is created equal," says twenty-eight-year-old Tom Tisch. "They also feel that certain things essentially Jewish are worth preserving." Tom is the son of Laurence Tisch, chairman of Loews Corporation, and Billie Tisch, president of the Federation of Jewish Philanthropies of New York. He is a young JEP.

Who are these young JEPs?

Toward what careers are they headed?

What are their attitudes toward intermarriage?

From interviews with a number of sons and daughters of the JEPs profiled in this book, ranging in age from nineteen to twenty-nine, two facts emerge:

- They reflect parental conditioning. In an unstable economy, they too are superachievers.
- In many cases they possess a strong Jewish identity.

Tom Tisch

Although Tisch does not attend synagogue regularly, he does keep a kosher home (he quips "It is easy to keep a kosher home when you don't cook") so that his brothers who are kosher will be "comfortable" when they visit. He dates only Jewish girls. As noted in the first chapter, father Laurence Tisch had told his four sons, "You'll never marry anyone you don't take out. Take out only Jewish girls and you'll never have a problem." Young Tisch emphasizes that his policy of dating only Jewish girls does not stem from parental injunction. He claims, "It's because of the historical standpoint. If someone intermarries, it is because the person was not raised in a context where it was important."

Tall, brown-haired Tisch grew up in Scarsdale, New York, and went to Suffield Academy, Connecticut ("I was the class Jew. It did not bother me for a second. It was the thing that made me different in the crowd. So you call a bald man 'Baldie.' I did not think anything I was called was anti-Semitic"). He later attended Brown and NYU law school ("that was like being at a yeshiva; many of the students were Orthodox"). For two years he worked at Goldman, Sachs & Company, an investment banking firm, and now invests and trades stocks for his three brothers and himself.

Like his parents, he does philanthropic work. He sits on Federation and UJA boards. He also "subscribes to every Jewish newspaper east of the Mississippi."

Commenting on generational differences, he points out, "Jewish kids today have luxuries their parents did not have. They come from secure households. The parental objective was to make money and upgrade their lives. Kids today want fulfillment in their work. They are doing different things. Some are becoming rabbis. There is a woman rabbi at Yale whose father was a builder in Florida. Jewish women are entering professional fields. The question is will they stay overtime.

"There are always going to be new fields. We live in an information and knowledge-based society. There is just one place the Jews probably have not penetrated at a top level—the military."

Tisch notes two problems: (1) "Studies show there are more single Jewish women than men; the men are more inclined to intermarry." (2) "When you are young, Jewish and rich, you have to learn to say no. There are so many *schnorrers* ("beggars") in the Jewish community."

Jeff Toobin

Toobin, twenty-two, a senior at Harvard and accepted at Harvard Law School, is the son of CBS News correspondent Marlene Sanders and Jerome Toobin, director of news and public affairs at WNET-TV, New York. Brought up in a sophisticated home with constant exposure to creative and newsmaking people, he is obviously a comer.

In the past five summers he has worked on the *Crimson* and at the Harvard School of Government as a researcher; served as advance man in John Anderson's presidential campaign; worked as an intern for Carol Bellamy, president of the City Council, New York. Prior to that he worked as a researcher for the CBS election and survey unit and at Arrowhead Day Camp. Mother Marlene Sanders got him the CBS job. The others he got for himself.

He says, "I feel Jewish. It is more social and cultural than religious. The ritual has not been part of my life."

He feels the Jewish elites of the future will be very similar to the Jewish elites now, and comments, "It seems as if every field is open to Jews—except maybe president of a Gentile country club. They will be at the forefront of the academic and intellectual world—into hi-tech, genetic engineering. I have never felt anything was off limits to me or other Jews."

About anti-Semitism, he says, "I assume some discrimination exists but I have not encountered it. I have lived in a meritocratic society."

For the past two years Toobin has been dating a WASP from Cincinnati. He comments, "Given the ideal situation, I would marry someone Jewish. But if she is not, that won't stop me. I feel the cultural importance of Judaism should continue, but I cannot change my life for it."

Toobin plans to enter politics. Told that a limited number of Jews make it to the very top, he replies, with likable confidence, "If there is an exception, it might as well be me."

Jonathan Rose

Jonathan F. P. Rose, twenty-nine, a graduate of Horace Mann, Yale (a major in psychology and philosophy), holds an M.A. in regional planning from the University of Pennsylvania. He works for Rose Associates, Inc., a realty concern headed by his father, two uncles and a great-uncle. Rose, who comes from a German-Jewish Reform background, says, "I feel culturally strong because I am Jewish. I find peace in the cultural literature.

"I am like many young Jews. I do yoga and meditate. I am attracted to the larger question 'Why are we here?' The sympathetic answers come from the East." He is involved with the Havurah movement and B'nai Or (Children of Light), a movement run by Rabbi Zalman Schachter, professor of religion at Temple University. For the High Holy days he goes to Fellowship Farm, near Philadelphia where B'nai Or holds services.

Rose's world is divided between real estate and music. He has little interest in the "larger structures like Federation" (his father is extremely active in the philanthropic world), but serves on the boards of the Educational Alliance (one of Federation's organizations) and Harvestworks (which administers Public Access Synthesizers Studio where for a few dollars someone can use electronic music synthesizers or create new sounds never heard before).

Rose does date non-Jewish girls. He says, "I would marry one, but my children have to be raised as Jews. That rule about inheriting your religion from your mother is not my rule. Before I marry, there would have to be clear agreement about this." He notes that a close friend married "a non-Jewish girl but their kid had a *bris.* If my wife is of another religion, I will expect her to be supportive of my kids' Judaism."

On Friday nights Rose tries to stay home. He lights candles and says prayers over the wine. Usually a friend is there who "ends up saying prayers or listening while I do. My Judaism is clearly articulated. This is part of me. This is who I am. If she loves me for only part of what I am, it is not love."

He objects to the label JAP, saying "Only Jewish people use it. It's derogatory. When people want to fix me up with a blind date they describe the girl as JAP or non-JAP. I define her as a girl with a small world view and a large appetite for material things."

A slim, bearded man, Rose speaks with pride of his family: "I was given a vision of greater things to do when younger." He feels the JEPs of the future will (1) have the vision to take what exists and meld it into new ideas; (2) be able to articulate and effect this vision in the world through persistence, hard work, skills; (3) be adventurous enough to take risks to live for this vision.

Betsy Schorr

Dark haired, dynamic Betsy Schorr, nineteen, a sophomore at Tufts, daughter of Thelma Schorr, president and publisher of the American Journal of Nursing Company, and Norman Schorr, head of a public relations agency, says "I prefer JEP to JAP. My friends come from achievement-bound families and that makes them achievement bound. They want to be at least as good as their parents. Starting at the level we have been lucky enough to start at, there is not much that can stop us. When you come from a family who dared, you may be willing to try whatever you want to try." In her case, she is majoring in English and American studies, plans to work for a few years after college and then go to law school.

Betsy frankly admits she dates non-Jewish boys. "I'm nineteen. I am not at a marriageable age. I know what I am ready to do, and I do not think I would intermarry. The Jewish religion gives me so much. I feel such a tie to the past. With intermarriage you lose the heritage. I have a bond I do not want to lose. At home I am active in Jewish things. I like to attend synagogue. I always try to be home Friday night when I'm in town. It means a lot to me."

She claims her generation is "pragmatic. Even if you don't care about money, it's scary to take an esoteric major. At Tufts many kids are going into international relations. There are lots of economics majors and female engineers. Lots of Jewish girls are studying to be engineers. The coat-check girl in a local museum has an M.A.—that's the closest she got to using her art history."

She feels it is vastly important to express Jewishness: "If you hide it, you are saying it's okay not to have it exist. You are taking on others' value judgment."

Like Tisch, Toobin and Rose, she feels she has rarely been hurt by anti-Semitism. At sixteen, she was with her mother at a business cocktail party in Texas. Three men were talking in Spanish. She said, "I cannot understand you." One of the trio responded, "What do you want us to speak—Yiddish?" Stunned, Betsy said nothing.

Now from the vantage point of nineteen, she says, "I would pour my drink over them . . . walk away or say 'English will be fine.' But I would do something."

She adds, "After the war it was easy to be a Jew. Now Gentiles are reverting back because of economic conditions, the need for oil. Old prejudices come out. You have to say, 'Remember we exist.' It is a vital time for Jews.

"The best thing about keeping up with Judaism is the closeness you feel to people. On a Saturday morning all over the world Jews are saying the same prayers. Recently I went to a bat mitzvah (the Sephardic spelling of *bas*) of a friend. All the people there felt her joy."

A spokesman for the adult Jewish community bears out the attitudes of these young JEPs. Asked about the JEPs of tomorrow, Bertram Gold, executive vice-president of the American Jewish Committee, says "They are an independent breed steeped in the spiritual aspect of Judaism and in their own sense of being both Jewish and American.

"They come out of middle-class and upper-middle-class backgrounds. Unlike the generation of the sixties, they have not rebelled. We live in a postindustrial society. The professionals will be leaders in the electronics area and service areas connected with it.

"Young people do not worry about anti-Semitism. They have

not experienced it in the way of their parents and grandparents. They have not met it in getting into college or the job market. Anti-Zionism is not the same thing. I feel most young JEPs will not intermarry. If they do, they will stay Jewish.

"They are surefooted in their Judaism and their Americanism. They are very committed to spiritual values. The future of Judaism in America is unlimited."

INDEX

Guggenheimer, Elinor, 10, 23, 40, 67
  portrait of, 113–115